DATE DUE		

TIDES OF DARKNESS

HISTORICAL NOVELS BY JUDITH TARR

JUDITH TARR

TIDES OF DARKNESS

TOR®

A TOM DOHERTY ASSOCIATES BOOK

NEW YORK

TIDES OF DARKNESS

Copyright © 2002 by Judith Tarr

This book is printed on acid-free paper.

Edited by Beth Meacham

A Tor Book
Published by Tom Doherty Associates, LLC
175 Fifth Avenue
New York, NY 10010

www.tor.com

Tor® is a registered trademark of Tom Doherty Associates, LLC.

ISBN 0-312-87615-7

First Edition: October 2002

Printed in the United States of America

0 9 8 7 6 5 4 3 2 1

TIDES OF DARKNESS

ONE

THE HEIR TO THE PRINCEDOM OF HAN-GILEN, HIGH LORD IN THE Hundred Realms, child and grandchild and great-grandchild of mages, noble and royal prince of a line of princes, was drunk. Royally, imperially, divinely drunk. But not, he was happy to observe, therefore incapable of pleasing the three delightful creatures who tumbled squealing with him into a vague blur of bedclothes and curtains. They were not his bedclothes or his curtains. He had better taste. But they were adequate, and the three ladies were considerably more than that.

The dark one could sing. The golden one could dance. The sweet brown one had hands of surpassing skill, and lips . . .

He drifted in a sea of wine. He sang with the dark woman; he watched the golden one dance. The brown woman stroked and teased him, holding him just short of release. He groaned aloud; she laughed.

He seized her and tumbled with her in a cloud of scented silk.

Oh, this was a very fine brothel indeed.

The wine was wearing off. Pleasure, even at the hands of so skilled an artisan, could not last forever. He had the mage's curse: he could not fall into oblivion after. His mind was bitterly, brilliantly clear; and there was no wine in the jar beside the bed. Not even a drop to lift him out of himself again.

But he was no simple man, to be discommoded by a want of wine. He could send one of the women to fetch a new jar, or he could call for a servant. Or he could reach into the heart of him, where the magic was, and open the door that was there, and leap joyously into a world in which wine bubbled in fountains.

His three companions shrieked as the Worldgate cast them from lamplight into the full glare of the sun. It was a somewhat softer sun than they could have known before, but bright enough, and warm. The garden about them was full of strange sweet scents. Wine poured into the bowl of a stone fountain, rich red wine of a purer vintage than their own world could offer.

The brown woman and the gold were creatures of the moment; they drank till their lips were stained as if with blood. But the dark woman said, "I hear it's death to open Gates, unless you are a Gate-mage and consecrated in the temple."

He laughed. He had not drunk the wine, but he was dizzy with magic and with the sweetness of doing a thing so sternly and strictly forbidden. "No one will know," he said with sublime confidence. "Nobody knows what I can do. I'm the scapegrace, the fool, the pretty boy who knows nothing but the simplest magics. But I have Gates in me. Look, can you see? See them in my eyes."

She would not look. She was afraid. She gulped wine, choking on it. He was still laughing, because he would not have any of them think he cared for a whore's timidity. He whirled on the greensward that was not quite grass, among the flowers that had no kin in the world in which he was born. The Gates inside him spun into a blur of light.

The light winked out. He gasped. He was still on the greensward, but within him, in his magic's eye, he saw another vision altogether. There was a world—he had visited it, maybe, when he wandered alone through the halls of his magic. It had been beautiful, a world of sea and spume and sky. Now it was all ashen. Gaunt black birds flapped over a barren land; bones tossed in the dead sea. The stench emptied his stomach; he retched into the grass.

None of his companions came to comfort him. They were light women, toys to be used and cast away. They cared nothing for him, only for the gold he brought and the wine he gave them, and maybe a little for such pleasure as their kind could take.

There was a sour taste in his mouth and a bitterness in his heart. He gathered the women and flung them back through the Gate—back to the world from which they had come.

The fountains bubbled mindlessly into their basins. Somewhere, something trilled, that was perhaps a bird, and perhaps not. Out of sheer contrariness, he turned the largest fountain to ice, and its wine to water.

He should not have done that. Opening Gates, that was direly forbidden. Changing the worlds beyond Gates, unless one were a Gate-mage or one consecrated by them, was so deeply banned that he did not even know the penalty for it. Death, he supposed. Or worse, if such a thing could be.

Gates never betrayed him. He was part of them. But guardians watching over Gates could find the tracks that he had so unwisely left and follow them to their end.

If the guards had been women, he might have charmed them into mercy. These were men, and not young, with a look about them of people who had never in their lives known a moment's levity. They seized him in a grip that he did not try to break, which was half of magic and half of human strength. They lifted him and carried him through Gates, not swiftly or easily as he could do, but by the long way, through the emptiness between worlds. He made no effort to tell them how they should do it. Mages never listened. They knew only what they knew, and that was all there was to know.

"Indaros."

The voice was much sweeter than its tone. It was a beautiful voice, and its owner more beautiful still, with an extravagance of hot-gold hair imperfectly contained in a fillet, and a face carved in ivory, and wide-set golden eyes. He raised himself in the windowless cell into which his captors had cast him, and stared frankly at her. "You don't look a day over seventeen," he said.

She had twice those years at least, and no more care for his frivolity than the guardians who had brought him here. "Indaros," she said again. "Get up."

He had intended to rise in any case. He unfolded himself, stretching till his bones creaked, and yawning vastly. "I feel vile," he said. "Is there a bath to be had? Or at least a change of clothes?"

She looked up at him; he was much taller than she. Nevertheless she managed to make it clear that he was far beneath her.

And so he was, being a mere prince-heir, albeit of a great princedom, and she heir to an empire—and, some said, to all the worlds beyond the Gates.

"No bath," he said regretfully. "Well then, you'll just have to stand the stink of me. Though I'd rather die clean, if you don't terribly mind."

"You won't die," she said. "You'll only wish you had."

He laughed. His mirth was honest, if a little wild. "Oh, do kill me. It's no trouble."

She frowned slightly, looked him up and down, and walked completely round him. He hoped that she was edified. He had, before sleep and pleasure and prison cell, been dressed in the perfect height of fashion. It was sadly wilted and stained now, but there still was no denying that his coat was distinctively cut and slashed, with dags and ribbons fluttering at carefully random intervals; or that it was a particularly striking shade of green. Or that the trousers had one leg green and one leg nearly as bright a coppery sheen as his hair; or that his shoes were thickly sewn with copper bells. They chimed gently as he shifted his feet.

"It would be a pleasure to kill you," she said as she came round to his front again, "but it will be an even greater pleasure to cure you of this . . . whatever afflicts you. Are you color-blind?"

He blinked at her. "You're sparing my life because you think I have bad taste? Oh, my wounded heart!"

"You have a heart to wound?" She dismissed him with the flick of a glance. "Enough. You've been judged. Be ready when your escort arrives."

"Escort?" he asked, arching a brow.

She was already gone. There was no lock on the door, he noticed. The seal she had laid on it was wrought of magic, and it was stronger than he could break.

That cracked his composure beyond retrieving. He was the most insouciant of princes; he had made it his life's work. But this quiet woman with her maiden's face and her Sun's fire of magery had got beneath his skin. "Judged?" he demanded of her absence. His voice rose. "*Judged?* Where is my trial? My defender? My noble judges? I'm a lord of rank. The law grants me a fair trial. I demand it. I insist on it!"

The echoes of his bellow died. There was no answer, only a lingering scent of her scorn.

He could not bear that, either. He flung himself against the door. He was not a small man, nor for all his infamous indolence was he weak, but the locks were made of magic. They never even shifted.

He was lying on his face when the escort came. He was not asleep. A mute and mind-shielded servant had brought clothing not long before, and a basin with it, and water enough for a bit of bath. He was fresher, cleaner, but notably less fashionable now; the paint was scrubbed from his face and hands, and his lovely soiled garments had left with the servant. The coat and trousers and boots he wore fit him well but were distressingly plain, without even a bit of embroidery to enliven their dullness. They were riding clothes, he could hardly have failed to notice. But he had not been given a weapon, even a knife for cutting meat. The belt was bare of anything but the grimly unornamented buckle.

He was cold inside, and empty. Transgressions had consequences, his father had taught him well enough. But one had to care for those consequences, which he never had. Still he had never broken two of the strictest laws of mages in swift succession—or worse, been caught at it.

He heard the door open and felt the mage-wards go down. If he had been inclined, he could have burst through the space where they had been, flung open a Gate, and vanished from the world. But he was not as far gone as that.

His fear was fading. The lady Merian had let him live. She was the guardian of all the Gates, upholder of the laws, judge and, he did not doubt, executioner. When he transgressed, he transgressed first against her.

He rose to face his jailers. They were not the mages he had expected, but his father's guardsmen in green and gold, regarding him with stony faces. He knew them all by name, had roistered in a tavern or three with most, but that mattered nothing now.

His cell, he discovered as he walked out of it in a wall of guards, was a priest's cell in the Temple of the Sun in Han-Gilen. He hoped he could be forgiven for not recognizing it; he had no call to that order, nor had he seen more of the temple than its outer reaches. With luck he would not see it again.

"It seems you have no call to anything," his father said.

This was both better and worse than facing the Lady of the Gates. She was a stranger, and accordingly distant from his faults and foibles. This was his father, and his mother coming into the smallest of the audience chambers with a thunder-reek of magic and a distracted look about her. She hardly seemed to see her son as she sat beside her husband, raking tangled black hair out of her face.

The prince paused for her coming, but spoke again all too soon. Daros watched the play of expression across the stern dark face, and the gleam of morning sunlight in the bright hair. He looked little enough like either of them. They said he threw back to some long-ago prince or—if they were ill enough inclined—to some princess of exceptional beauty and equally exceptional fecklessness.

"Feckless you certainly are," said his father, following his thought with the ease of a mage and the arrogance of a prince. "You have no useful skills; you serve no useful purpose. You refused the priesthood. You turned your back on the mages. If you have any calling at all, it appears to be that of tavern-crawler."

"And libertine, Father. Don't forget that."

The prince looked ready to erupt, but his princess spoke before he could burst out in rage. "Don't lecture him, Hal. He won't listen. He knows his sins as well as we, little though he pretends to care about them."

"I *don't* care about them," Daros said tightly.

She smiled. She was not beautiful; her face was too strong for that. But when she smiled, she warmed even his heedless heart. "Of course you care, child," she said. "You're afraid it will hurt. Can you tell us why you took three rather expensive whores through a Gate, and what you hoped to accomplish by changing what you found there?"

"It was only a game," he said—sulkily, and hating himself for it, but his mother always had been able to reduce him to a child.

"A game that you well knew was forbidden," his father said, though the princess tried to hush him.

"Yes, and why?" Daros demanded. "What harm did I do? Who was hurt or killed by what I did? It was just a Gate, and just a garden. Why are Gates banned? What are the mages afraid of? That anyone but they will discover secrets?"

"You know the answers to that," his mother said. "Your very failure to understand those answers is proof that the laws are necessary."

"How do you know I don't understand? What if I'm sure I did no harm?"

"Are you?" She rubbed her eyes and sighed. "Most of the mages wanted you put to death. It wasn't compassion for me that stopped them, or even the fact that you are the only living child of the Prince of Han-Gilen. You have cousins in plenty, after all; and I would mourn you, but never fault them for upholding the law. No; it was the Sunlady herself who revoked the sentence. Piddling useless thing you may be, she said, but you opened a Gate without spells, workings, or great raising of power. You did it, in fact, as casually as if the Gate had been an earthly door. She wanted to know why no one had ever enlisted you among the Gate-mages."

"No one ever asked," Daros said.

"Because you were never available to be asked." His mother looked him in the face for the first time since she had come into the room. He gasped in spite of himself. Her eyes were clear and hard and brimming with magic. But they could not pierce the barriers he had raised. "Why?" she asked him. "What do you fear? We've pampered you, indulged you, spoiled you shamelessly. What would cause you to keep such a secret?"

He shrugged uncomfortably. "It's not a secret. It's only . . . really, no one ever asked. They all weigh me light. Even you."

"Why—" But she stopped him before he could answer. "It doesn't matter. You've been tried and sentenced, and your sentence has been commuted from death to one less final."

"A fate worse than death?" he asked. "A state marriage?"

His father looked again as if he would erupt; again his lady forestalled him. "That was considered," she said. "Imprisonment, too, and excision of your magic."

He shuddered at that, for all that he could do; his stomach twisted until he gasped with the pain.

They saw, of course. He could not tell if they were gratified.

His mother said, "We considered many things, but she silenced us all, and spoke your sentence. You will be exiled, Indaros Kurelios. You will be given to a guardian who cannot be tricked or cozened or circumvented. Until he deems you ready to return, you will remain with him, under his rule, bound to serve him to the utmost of your capability. If you fail in your duty, or if you try to escape, you will be put to death."

Daros kept his face steady. He was growing afraid again. "Who—" His voice caught. "Who is my jailer? You, Father?"

Prince Halenan did not answer. The Lady Varani said, "We declined the honor, since we've done so badly for these past nineteen years. You'll be sent to another, who will, says the Lady of Gates, keep you in such order as you can ever be kept in."

"Who? One of my myriad uncles? One of the cousins? Suvayan is dour enough, and hungry enough, too. He'd keep me in chains. That would please you all, wouldn't it?"

She shook her head wearily. "Stop it, Daros."

If she had been cross, or even conspicuously patient, he would have defied her. But she was honestly and visibly exhausted. She had not slept, he realized, since his transgression was discovered. Maybe none of the Gate-mages had. More softly then, and somewhat less insouciantly, he asked, "Who, then? Where am I to go?"

"You will go to Han-Uveryen in the north of the world," his mother said. There was grief in it, but she did not yield for that. "You will be squire and servant to the lord of the holding. Your life will be in his hands. He will rule you absolutely and command your every breath, until your sentence shall be served."

Daros barely choked at the name of the holding, although he had heard of it, dimly. It was as remote as human habitation could be, far away in the land called Death's Fells. He focused his mind on another thing, a thing of rather greater importance. "How long a sentence will it be?"

"As long as your new lord sees fit to keep you," his father said.

"My new lord," said Daros, rolling the words on his tongue. "What great mage and lord of the world would make his home in that godsforsaken place?"

"Watch your tongue, boy," his father said through clenched teeth. "And above all watch it when you come to him. He was an easygoing man when I knew him, but that was years ago. He won't have kept that ease, I think, living in the Fells. He'd never have mercy on a transgressor of Gates. He made the laws for good and sufficient reason, and he set his granddaughter's daughter in command of them."

Daros' mouth was open. He shut it. "*He* made the— You're sending me to the emperor? I thought he was dead."

"He is very much alive," his father said.

"Gods," said Daros. "He must be ancient. When did he hand the empire over to his granddaughter? Was I even born yet?"

"Barely," his mother said. "He is still emperor, though he's surrendered his priesthood and given the regency to Daruya and her consort. He is also still the greatest of the mages, and a master of Gates. You'll walk soft in his presence, child, and accord him the respect he deserves, whether or not it suits your fancy. Am I understood?"

Daros bent his head. "I understand you," he said.

Her glance was distrustful, but she held her peace. So, perhaps by her will, did his father.

"You leave now," she said after a pause. "The guards will take you where you must go."

She had dismissed him. No embrace, no kiss, no farewell of mother to son; only the cold words and the cold stare. She was a mage of Gates; he had transgressed the laws by which she lived. What he had done was unforgivable. Only now did he begin to understand the meaning of the word.

His father's wrath he had expected; Prince Halenan was notoriously short of patience where his son was concerned. But the Lady Varani had never been so cold before, never kept so remote a distance. "But I did no harm!" he cried to her, hating the whine in his voice.

"You did more harm than you could possibly comprehend," she said. She turned her back on him: rejection so complete, and so mortally wounding, that he could only bare his teeth in a grin, salute them both, and bid his guards conduct him where they would.

TWO

DAROS' DEPARTURE HAD BEEN ARRANGED TO ATTRACT AS LITTLE notice as possible. The guards quick-marched him through the more obscure portions of his father's palace, down dusty corridors and through empty rooms, to a court in which he had played as a child, far from his nurse's quelling eye. He had thought to find a Gate there, or mages prepared to open one, but instead there were a company of men-at-arms and a string of packbeasts and a gathering of mounts and remounts.

They were profoundly ordinary animals, the lot of them. He did not see one of his own fine seneldi anywhere, nor any that might have been worthy of a prince. Not only, it seemed, was he to travel the whole of the long journey into the north as simple men did, on foot or on the cloven hooves of seneldi, but he was also to be forbidden any mark or privilege of rank.

At least he was not to go in chains—or not in chains that men could see. When he stretched out a tendril of magery to test the minds and mettle of his guards, he met a wall. It surrounded him completely, and confined his magic to the narrow borders of his unassisted self.

Ah well, he thought as he greeted the guards—none of whom returned the greeting—and mounted the nondescript senel that waited for him. It was a gelding, and one of its stunted horns was crooked; its brown coat was drab, its amber eyes profoundly disinterested in any- thing but its task of plodding along with its nose to the tasseled tail of the senel in front of it.

Indaros set himself to endure the ordeal. It was a long way to the Fells, and a senile old man at the end of it. If he could not escape before he came to Han-Uveryen, surely he would have no difficulty there. The Emperor Estarion was older than mountains, and had long since with- drawn from any semblance of imperial rule. Some even whispered that he was dead. Great mage and emperor he might have been, but that was long ago. He would be no match for the young and determined heir of a line of mageborn princes.

Daros had frequent cause to remember that as the journey stretched from days into Brightmoon-cycles. His guards were all mages, and all chosen for their strength of will; they sustained wards that prevented any rescue, or even recognition. He had nothing to do but ride and think and try to charm his guards—and charm them he did, at least into offering conversation. They would not loose the mage-bonds; even his best smile and his sweetest words failed to budge them. But it was not as grim an ordeal as it might have been; when they camped in the nights, they were rather convivial, and more so, as they left civilized places behind.

The world grew bleaker the farther they rode; although it was still

summer in the Hundred Realms, in the Fells it was well advanced in
autumn, with chill wind and cold rain and an occasional grudging glimmer of sun. The land was no more delightful than the weather: an endless expanse of grey-green moor, surging into ridges and dropping
suddenly into black tarns. Nothing stirred here but, once in a great
while, a hawk wheeling in the grey sky. What quarry it pursued, they
never saw; birds there were none, and creatures of earth were too small
and quick to catch. They ate what they had brought on the packbeasts,
and drank from rills and tarns. The land suffered them to cross it, but
gave them no part of itself.

Of human creature they saw nothing. There were people in this
country, Daros had been assured: dour tribesmen, kin to the lords of
Ianon. But his escort kept well away from their forts and walled villages.
If they had need of anything from the towns, a company rode to fetch it.
He was never let out of sight, nor suffered to walk among people who
might, gods forbid, have granted him relief from the relentless companionship of his guards.

On a day in which the rain was edged with sleet and touched with
spits of snow, the captain of guards drew rein at the summit of a hill.
"There," he said. "Han-Uveryen."

Daros peered through veils of rain. As if to oblige him, they lifted for
a moment, uncovering the long rolling slope and the track of a little
river. The river flowed into a lake; by the lake rose a crag. On the crag
squatted a hill-fort.

Its walls were of stone as grey as the sky. A low square tower rose
above them. No banner flew there; no light, either magewrought or
earthly fire, burned to welcome the travelers.

Maybe, thought Daros, its lord was dead and his servants long gone.
Then all this journey would be in vain; he would be forced to return
through Gates to warmth and light and the arms of his friends and kin.
Maybe even his mother. Maybe even she would speak to him again,
since he had served as much of his sentence as he could.

It was a lovely dream as they rode in the bite of sleet, with wind working edged fingers through coat and mantle and chilling him to the bone. He could warm himself with a fire of magery if he chose, but he did not. He wanted the whole of the misery, to remember; so that he would never have to endure it again.

Han-Uveryen rose above them at last, perched on its crag. Ice dripped down from its battlements; the road that ascended to it was steep and slippery. They dismounted and led the seneldi, heads bowed against the wind that swooped down off the crag and did its best to fling them into the lake.

The gate, for a wonder, was open. There were people within, northern tribesmen, tall and dark, with grim faces. They had been warned of his coming and told of his crime and its punishment. They surrounded him, neatly easing out the guards who had brought him to this place. Those he was not to see again; they would rest and restore themselves, then return to the blessed warmth of the southlands.

He had no such fortune. These new guardsmen towered head and shoulders above him: true northerners of pure line, with hair to the waist and beard to the breast, and skin as dark as Mother Night. They were not to be charmed by a sweet smile or a ready tongue, nor had he any part in their canons of beauty. He looked into those cold black eyes and saw a manikin cast in bronze and dipped in copper, worthy of nothing but their contempt.

He grinned at the image. These were not mages. They were common mortal tribesmen, schooled in war but not in magic. The bonds upon him had all but fallen away. He could raise lightnings, walk in minds—but not open a Gate. He knew; he tried, and ran headlong into a wall. It was some little while before the headache passed from blinding to merely excruciating. Its message was abundantly clear. The one power he wanted and needed most, he was not to have.

He had expected grim stone, soiled straw on cold floors, stark barracks full of smoke and unwashed men. He was startled to find himself in a haven of warmth and light. The walls were stone, yes, but hung with tapestries of remarkable quality. There were rugs on the floors of the smaller rooms, and woven mats in the hall, and furnishings that would not have looked out of place in the hunting lodge of a prince in the Hundred Realms. The fire was contained in a broad hearth that funneled most of its smoke up out of the keep and away; what little remained served only to impart a pleasant pungency to the air of the hall.

The high seat was empty. The man who sat nearest it was younger by far than the emperor; he was pure northerner as the rest were, clashing with gold and copper in the antique style, with no garment but a kilt to warm him in the winter chill. Beneath the beard and the braids, Daros saw as he drew closer, the man was hardly older than himself.

He must be royal kin: he had the look, and the arrogance, too. The guards bowed to him. Daros did not deign to.

The northerner's expression was impossible to read, obscured as it was in curling black hair, but his eyes had narrowed slightly. "The emperor is waiting," he said without greeting or preliminary. "Raban here will direct you."

Raban was the tallest and grimmest of the guards. Was that satisfaction on his face behind the beard?

Daros' shoulders hunched. He straightened them with an effort. Something that he had done—perhaps as petty as his failure to offer proper obeisance to the nobleman in the hall—had hastened the time of reckoning. He rebuked himself for the stab of fear. The emperor was only an old man, however lofty his legend.

The old man, Raban informed him with rather too much pleasure, no longer lived in Han-Uveryen. "He's gone up the mountain," he said. "You'll find him there."

The mountain rose on the far side of the lake. Clouds and rain had veiled it, but as Raban brought Daros to the battlements to see where he must go, the wall of cloud lifted.

He caught his breath. This was a land of plains and sudden mountains, but this high peak he had never expected. It reared up and up, cleaving to heaven. The jagged summit was white with snow.

"He's up there," Raban said. "You'd better leave soon, if you want to be on the mountain before dark."

Daros considered all the possible things that he might have said, and rejected them all. He only said, "Show me the road."

He had not won the northerner's respect, but maybe he had lessened the man's contempt by a fraction. He was allowed a cup of spiced wine, almost too hot to drink, and a fresh loaf and a wedge of cheese, before he was cast out into the cold.

There was no escort. He was alone. They had saddled a senel for him—a considerably better beast than he had ridden from Han-Gilen—and filled its saddlebags, but given him no packbeast. If he did not find the emperor before his ration was gone, he would be thrown upon his own resources.

The sleet had stopped, at least. But the road was treacherous, and the cold was closing in, promising to be bitter once the sun's feeble warmth was gone.

The senel had been blanketed with a thick mantle of the northern wool that was the softest and strongest in the world. Its price in the markets of Han-Gilen would have taxed even his princely purse. He was simply glad of its warmth now, wrapped about him and trailing over the mare's rump. The striped dun trod lightly on the icy track, wise and surefooted and impervious to the cold. She picked her way round the lake, rising to a smooth trot where the track allowed it. He let her do as she chose; she knew this country better than he.

He had never been alone before. Even at his most solitary, he had been surrounded by the appurtenances of a prince: servants, guards, hangers-on. Now he was the only human thing within his eyes' reach.

He was forbidden Gates, but there was nothing at all to prevent him from escaping as any mortal could do, well mounted for a run into the Fells. But he was less tempted than he might have been. He was curious. He wanted to see what was on the mountain. A tomb, he would wager, and old bones in it, and mocking laughter at the boy who had gone so trustingly into the jaws of the jest.

Let them have their pleasure. He was not quite as soft as they thought, nor as ignorant of the world beyond the walls of a tavern.

He had ample opportunity to regret his foolishness as the dun mare carried him up the mountain. The way was steep and the sun sinking fast, and the road was long still before him.

He lit a fire with his magic to warm himself and his mount and to light the way once the dark had fallen. He was beyond weariness. He would find the tomb or the house in which the ancient was kept, pay his respects, then run, and be damned to the consequences.

He climbed from sunset into starlight, on a track that grew ever steeper. Greatmoon rose in a tide of blood; Brightmoon ascended like a white jewel in its wake. In that doubled light he saw as easily as by day.

He paused at intervals to rest the senel and to let her drink from rills that ran headlong down the mountain. She grazed a little then on bits of green hiding among the rocks; he fed her handfuls of grain, but for himself he took nothing but a little water. He had left hunger down below in Han-Uveryen.

Exhaustion hovered on the edge of awareness. He refused to give way to it. He would sleep when he found the emperor. The sooner he did that, the sooner he could escape.

He came on the shepherd's hut at dawn. The storm had cleared in the night; the cold was bitter enough to crack bronze. The hut stood against an outcropping of cliff, overlooking a surprising expanse of green, a deep bowl of meadow in the mountain's side. A chain of springs and pools surrounded it, steaming in the frosty air; the reek of sulfur was strong, but that of green things came close to overwhelming it. Even from the track, the heat of the springs was unmistakable, a waft of warmth and scented breeze.

The shepherd's flock grazed in the meadow, long-fleeced grey creatures too dim of wit to notice a stranger above them. As Daros paused on the track, the shepherd came out of his hut: a tall man, broad of shoulder, wrapped in a cloak of the same rich wool as the one Daros wore. He was a northerner: Daros glimpsed his profile, like that of a black eagle. His hair was thick and long, black threaded lightly with grey; his beard was a little greyer but still more black than white. He had a pair of buckets on a yoke, with which he drew water from the spring nearest the hut; if he was aware at all of the one who watched him, he showed no sign of it.

Daros slipped from the mare's back and left her rein dangling, and stood in the man's path. He trudged up it with his head down, lost in his own thoughts.

Just before he would have collided with Daros, he halted. The buckets were large and must have been heavy, but his shoulders barely bowed with the weight of them. He had the look of a man who had never known a moment's sickness, though he was small as northerners went: no taller than Daros. There were no marks of age in his face; he was in his prime, and strong with it.

He raised his eyes. Daros fell back a step. The man's lips twitched. He must be well aware of the shock of first meeting: that face so purely of the north, but those eyes of another tribe and nation altogether— eyes of the Lion, startling yet unmistakable. The Lady Merian had them, softened somewhat, like golden amber. These were the true pure gold, bright as coins in the night-dark face, large-irised as an animal's, and full of wry amusement.

Ancient, Daros thought as he fell on his face. *Senile.* Oh, indeed.

The Emperor Estarion lifted him with easy strength and set him on his feet, and said in a voice like a lion's purr, "Sun and stars, boy, I can't be that appalling a prospect!"

"You can't *be,*" Daros said. The words tumbled out of him through no will of his own. "You can't be a day over thirty."

"Forty," said the emperor. "Don't be charitable."

"But you're at least—"

"Oh, I'm as old as this mountain." The emperor straightened as if to belie his own words, and stepped around Daros, toward the hut.

Daros followed him. The shock was wearing off. It would be a while before he recovered completely, but he could think again, after a fashion. Here was a jest indeed: a man not only strong enough to keep him in hand, but young enough, in body at least, to give him a fair fight. In magery . . .

He was strong. Daros staggered with the strength of him. Tales that called him the greatest of mages had not gone far off the mark, at all. He was so strong, and so sure in that strength, that he did not even trouble to conceal his thoughts.

For an instant Daros looked out of those eyes and saw himself as the emperor saw him: young and callow and altogether feckless, but with just enough spark of native wit in him to make him worth the uproar he had caused. The emperor was relieved at that. He had risked much, and gambled somewhat wildly, in suffering Daros to live.

"*You* decided my sentence?" Daros burst out.

"They all wanted you dead," said the emperor. "I reckoned it worth letting you live for a while longer, to discover what this gift of yours is, that eluded every mage who might have brought you into a temple."

"I have no calling to that life," Daros said. "My father says I have no calling to anything but trouble."

The emperor grinned. "I always did like your father's way with a word. Come in to breakfast. You must be famished."

Daros had felt no hunger at all until the emperor spoke of it; then his stomach clenched into a knot. The emperor grinned even more widely at his expression, and led him into the hut.

Breakfast was woolbeast stew, hot and savory with herbs and a tongue-searing hint of western spices. The emperor warmed it over a stone hearth while Daros tended his senel; they sat in the hut with the morning sun slanting through the open doorway, and ate in silence that was, to Daros' startlement, companionable. He was an easy man to keep company with, this lord of Sun and Lion.

Daros ate three bowls washed down with remarkably palatable ale, sat back and belched politely, and said, "I thought I'd find a tomb or a deathbed."

"Why, have they declared me dead in the southlands?"

"No one knows," Daros said. "You've not been seen for twenty years."

"Ah," said the emperor. "You're asking if I've been tending woolbeasts since before you were born. It's a good life. Peaceful. Useful, too. That cloak you're wearing came from these beasts."

"But you ruled the world," Daros said.

"So I did," said the emperor. "For years out of count I did it, from the time I was a child. When I left it, I was older than most men live to be; but it seems I have the family curse, to be unbearably long-lived. Either we die young, for foolish cause, or it seems we live forever."

"Truly? Forever?"

"Do I look like dying at any time soon?" the emperor asked.

"No," Daros said. "You look younger than my father."

"I looked like this fifty years ago," the emperor said. "I'm frozen in time, boy. Are you horrified yet? Are you about to open your Gate and run away?"

Daros' teeth clicked together. "You aren't supposed to—"

The golden eyes narrowed. For an instant Daros saw the man who had indeed ruled the world: a lord of power and terror. Then he was the shepherd of Han-Uveryen again, sitting back on his stool, sighing and shrugging and saying, "It seems we both do a number of things we aren't supposed to do. Don't try to run away, boy; the Lady of Gates has set guardians on all the worldroads, with orders to kill anything that passes there without her leave. They most certainly will kill you."

Daros needed no worldroads; his Gates were a different thing, and perhaps a thing that mages had not known before. But he had no inten-

tion of letting this man know that. As amiable as he was, he was still
Daros' jailer.

Daros bent his head and lowered his eyes and pretended to be suitably cowed. The emperor did not trust him: he could feel that. But he
was let be. That was enough, for a while.

THREE

MERIAN WAS INTOLERABLY WEARY OF GATES. SHE HAD LIVED and breathed them for as long as she could remember; they were in her, part of her. But of late she had begun to understand how an emperor could give all his glory and power to his granddaughter and her consort, turn his back on them, and walk away.

This was no time to dream of flight, or even of escaping for an hour or a day, finding a quiet place and simply being whatever she pleased to be. At best she could steal a moment to dream—and when she did, she was startled and somewhat dismayed to see who waited for her there.

The Gileni boy was disposed of—well, she reckoned, though the rest of the Gate-mages begged to disagree. Her great-grandfather would keep him in hand. He would also, she hoped, learn what the boy could do; useless idle thing that he was, it seemed he had a gift for Gates that was little less than Merian's own.

And there he was in her dream, this eve of Autumn Firstday, idling about in a garden of singing birds. He was as lovely as ever, with that face cast in bronze and those narrow uptilted dark eyes and that hair like new copper—mark of his lineage, and pride of his beauty, too. She had not troubled to notice the rest of him while she judged him, but her eyes had been marking every line. Under the soiled and ridiculous finery, he was not at all an ill figure of a man.

She had understood long ago, when she was younger than this boy, that there was no room in her for both Gates and lovers. It was her duty to produce an heir; she was royal born, she had no choice in the matter. But unlike her mother, who had bred her as if she had been a senel, Merian could not bring herself to do the necessary.

Maybe, she thought, she should let the dream lead her. The boy was as royally bred as she, and a famous beauty. He had magic in more than the usual measure—how much more, it might serve her well to discover. And he had a name for prowess in the bedchamber. The women of Han-Gilen, both noble and irretrievably common, had never an ill word to say of him, except that he could not choose just one of them. He had to have them all.

She fled the dream and the thought. All Gate-mages who could come to the city of Endros Avaryan had gathered for the rite of Autumn First-day: celebration in the temple and feasting after, and then, as night fell, a council.

There were a dozen of them in Merian's receiving room in the old palace, drinking wine or ale and nibbling festival cakes. Lamplight and magelight illumined faces of nearly every race that this world knew, from ivory-and-gold Asanian to night-dark northerner. But they were all mages of Gates, bound together by the same duty.

"I still say," said Urziad of Asanion, "that all worlds but ours are empty of human life."

"Something builds gardens and palaces," said Kalyi of the Isles. "Something sets rings of stones on headlands and leaves the wrecks of ships by alien seas."

"We know that there were people once," Urziad said. "But we've been standing guard over the worlds for close on fourscore years, and none of us has seen a living soul. The worlds are empty, all but ours."

"The worlds around Gates are empty," Ushallin said. "That doesn't mean the worlds themselves are. Maybe the Gates are shunned as evil; maybe people are afraid of them. Maybe—"

"Maybe all the people are gone," said Urziad.

"But where? What would have happened to them?" Ushallin asked. She came from the Nine Cities; she was a skilled opener of Gates. She asked difficult questions, too, that none of the others could answer.

Kalyi at least was willing to venture a guess. "They may be greater mages than we can ever dream of being. Or they decided long ago to dispense with Gates, and left them behind as useless remembrances."

"Hardly useless if they can still be opened," Ushallin said. "It seems that we've been left alone amid all the worlds of Gates. What if there is a reason for that? What if something comes to Gates sooner or later, and devours all thinking beings in the worlds beyond them?"

A shudder ran round the circle. Urziad made a sign against evil— catching himself just too late. "Surely we have more to occupy us," he said, "than fretting over children's nightmares."

"But are they?" Merian had been silent for so long that she startled them all. "Are they simple nightmares?" she asked them. "There are notes in the histories, commentaries on the people of Gates; there were meetings, conversations, suggestions that there might be embassies and alliances. But since my great-grandfather's time, there's been no mention of any such thing. It's all empty worlds and silent shores. There has to be a reason. What if this is it? They've withdrawn or been driven back from the Gates. Something is stirring there, something enormous. Haven't you felt it? It comes in the hour before dawn, or in the drowsy center of the afternoon, when we're least on guard. It feels like a storm coming."

They were silent. She looked from face to face. They were all respectful, but there was no spark of recognition in them. They had not sensed what she had sensed.

They were good men and women, and strong mages. But she would have given much just then to speak with one who understood the deeper matters.

The mages of Gates knew only what they had seen in living memory: empty worlds, open Gates, freedom to pass where they would—within the laws and the bindings, which none of them thought to question.

But there was one who remembered the times before, when the Guild of Mages ruled the Gates, and Gate-mages were unknown in the world. Merian excused herself as soon as she respectably could, and took refuge in her garden, sitting by the pool that was always still even when the wind blew strong. It reflected starlight at midday and the moons' light at night, whether the moons were in the sky or no.

He was sitting between the moons, wearing the face he wore in dreams: much the same as the one he wore awake, black eagle with lion-eyes. They were lambent gold, those eyes; they smiled at her.

"Great-grandfather," she said.

"Youngling," said the emperor. "You're troubled tonight."

He was always direct. It had served him ill in dealing with the more subtle of his subjects, but Merian found it restful, in its way. "Is he still with you?" she asked. She had not meant to say it, but it escaped before she could catch it.

"He's your trouble?" Estarion asked, though not quite as if he believed it.

She shook off folly—both his and hers. "He troubles me, but not in this."

"He should," said Estarion. "He's a living Gate."

"So I gather," she said.

"Did you also gather that he's not the idiot he pretends to be?"

"I did hope that there was more to him than he was letting us see," she said.

"There is a great deal more," said Estarion, "though he might not thank us for perceiving it. I was a considerable shock to him, but he's recovered since; he's decided that I must be at least a fraction senile, since I prefer a shepherd's cot to the delights of my own cities."

"I thought so once," she said, "but not of late. Were mages as blind when you were young, as they are now?"

"If anything, they were blinder." He raised himself up out of the pool, and stood dripping moonlight. "What are they not seeing now?"

"Gates," she answered him. "The worlds weren't always empty. Were they?"

"Ah," he said. "So you've noticed that, have you? I wondered if anyone would. No, when I was as young as this spoiled child you've saddled me with, we all knew that the worlds were populated, though there was considerable debate as to whether any of that populace were mages. None of them traveled as we traveled, that we ever knew. None came into this world. And none ever spoke to us or acknowledged us. But the oldest mages, who had the tales from long before, said that there was a time when the Gates saw a great deal of travel, and mages were aware of presences on the worldroads, going their incomprehensible ways."

"But none of them came into this world, or spoke to anyone from it."

"Not in those days," he said.

She frowned. "Tell me what you're not telling me."

"Not now, I think," he said. He smiled, but she knew how little hope she had of moving him. "This I can tell you. The boy knows something. He may not even be aware that he knows it."

"Would he divulge it to you?"

"I doubt it," he said.

She hissed at him. He only went on smiling. "You are always welcome in my house," he said.

He was gone before she could speak again. She considered flinging herself on the ground and indulging in a fit of pure useless fury. But she was too old for that, and maybe too much a coward.

Instead she walked through the Gate that was in her, and stood on a windy mountaintop, looking down into a starlit bowl of valley.

Estarion knew she had come. She felt the brush of his regard. What the other thought, she did not know him well enough to tell. If his reputation was to be trusted, he would not even be aware of her; but she placed little trust in rumor. Not about this one.

She waited out the night on the mountain, wrapped in a cloak of darkness and stars. The Gates lay quiet within her, save that, on the edge of awareness, she knew a glimmer of unease. Nothing troubled her, neither man nor beast nor bird of the air.

At sunrise she walked down to the shepherd's cot that was all the palace Estarion wanted in this age of the world. He had gone out before dawn, striding long-legged across the valley; he carried a staff and a bag, and had a bow slung behind him, as if he were going hunting. He had not taken the boy with him. The boy, she was well aware, had roused to see him going, then rolled onto his face and plunged back into sleep.

A creature of cities, that one, to sleep while the sun was in the sky. He had made a nest for himself in a corner of the hut, a heap of furs and blankets, but he had kicked them off as he slept. She had a fine view of his shoulders and back and buttocks, and his ruffled bright hair that was growing out of its dreadful close cut.

She sat on her heels and waited as she had on the mountain, with the patience of a mage. While she waited, she explored the Gates, searching out the strangeness. It kept eluding her, until she began to wonder if she had sensed it at all.

After quite some time, the sleeper began to twitch. His shoulders flexed; he wriggled, as if to burrow into his bed. He groped blindly for coverlets.

She was sitting on them. He opened a clouded eye and stared blankly at her. She stared coolly back. The eye went wide. He scrambled up, still half in a dream, and seemed torn between the prince's urge to bow and the fugitive's urge to escape.

She stood between him and the only door. He was still too aggravated with her to offer royal courtesy. He settled for standing in the tumble of his bed and glaring at her.

"I would think," she said, "that with your master gone out hunting, you would be expected to look after the flock."

He started as if struck. Shock of remembrance chased guilt across his face and hid behind outraged temper. "Are you my master, too?"

"I might be," she said, "if you prove to have a Gate-mage's gift."

"You don't want me," he said. He sounded just barely bitter.

"No? You imagine you're the only scapegrace who ever vexed his betters' peace?"

"I don't imagine I'm worth much at all."

She looked him up and down. It was a pleasant occupation, and one she was not inclined to finish overly soon; particularly when the slow flush crawled from his breastbone to his brow. "What is this play of worthlessness? Is it a fashion? A game? A way of tricking the dark gods into ignoring you?"

He shrugged, sullen. "Maybe it's the truth."

"You know it's not." She pulled a shirt from beneath her and tossed it at him. "Get dressed. I'll help you with the flock."

That startled him. "But you don't—"

"I did a year of my priestess-Journey here," she said. She tossed breeches in the wake of the shirt. He caught those, glowering, and pulled them on with rather more than necessary force. She caught herself regretting the breeches and the shirt, and the leather coat that went over them. They suited him better than his old finery, but his skin suited him best of all.

He was more adept at looking after woolbeasts than she might have expected. He was less sulky, too, once he had set to work. There were pens to mend and feet to trim and the ram to feed where he lived in his

solitary splendor; young ones to count and older ones to look over for
signs of trouble. There was a peaceful rhythm in it, that she remembered
well.

The sun was high when they were done. They had not exchanged a
word since they left the hut. When they went back to it, to dine raven-
ously on cheese and last night's bread and flagons of bitter ale, the
silence had set into crystal, too beautiful to shatter.

Yet shatter it she must. As pleasant as this idyll had been, she had
duties waiting, and mages calling down the worldroads, needing her for
this urgency or that. She drained the last of her flagon, sat back on the
bench in front of the hut, and turned her face and hands to the sun. Her
left hand was ordinary enough, but the right burned and flamed, bearing a sun of gold in its palm: the *Kasar*, brand and painful price of her
lineage. "Tell me what you sense in Gates," she said.

His silence changed abruptly, to the temper of heated bronze. Yet
when he spoke, he sounded as light and useless as he ever could pretend
to be. "What should I be sensing?"

"Tell me," she said.

"Nothing," he said. "Nothing at all."

She moved so swiftly that he could have had no warning. Her hand
clamped over his throat. She gave him the full flare of her royal temper,
fierce enough that even he had the wits to blanch. "Stop," she gritted.
"*Stop* lying to me. There is something out there. You have seen it. Tell
me what it is."

"You're not my master," he said.

She flung him down and set a knee on his chest. He made no effort
to resist. His eyes on her held no fear. She kissed him hard, until he
must have bruised, and flung herself away.

He lay where she had left him. His expression was blank, stunned.
Slowly, as if in a dream, he said, "Something sweeps across the worlds. It
feels like a storm coming, or like the sea rising. Moons shatter in its
wake. What rides ahead of it . . . it rapes and pillages, burns and slashes
and kills. People are dying, and worse than dying. You feel them, don't

you? I hear their cries when I sleep. I see the flames even awake."

Whatever she had hoped for, it was nothing as distinct as this. She groped for the rags of her voice. "How long?"

"Since I came to this place," he said. He sat up. His mask was gone. There was still not a man beneath, but the boy was less feckless; he had seen things that harrowed the heart. "When you caught me, I felt something—saw a broken world. I didn't want to think anything of it. But after I came here, where there is little to do but tend woolbeasts and sleep, I saw more and more." He peered at her. "You don't see it. None of you does. Even he doesn't know."

"I think," she said, "he does." She would give way to that fit of anger later. "I'm beginning to feel it. The rest sense nothing."

"That's the guard on the Gates," he said. "It protects you mages."

"And not you?"

"I'm not bound by rites or vows," he said.

"No?"

"I'm not going to swear to anything," he said, "or be bound to anything."

"Indeed?"

She was aggravating him in spite of his best efforts: his nostrils had thinned and his lips were tight. "Indeed, your royal highness."

Her lips twitched, which piqued him even further. She forbore to laugh aloud. These matters were not for mirth, however amusing it might be to test his temper. "I do think it best that you remain as you are: renegade, apart from orders and guilds. But I would ask a thing of you, for this world's sake if not for my own: that you will tell me of your dreams, and take me into them if you can."

"Not likely," he said, biting off the words.

"Tell your master, then," she said, "and let him choose whether to tell me."

"What if he won't?"

"That is between the two of us," she said levelly.

He glowered at the sky, which was growing a thin fleece of cloud.

Even without wishing to walk in his thoughts, she could feel the roil of confusion, the anger and defiance and childish resentment, mingled hopelessly with that same fear for the world which had brought her to this place and this aggravating person. He did care for what might come; his masks were a defense. Beneath them he was remarkably, almost shockingly passionate in his convictions.

She escaped before he caught her in the inner halls of his self. She was just in time: he focused abruptly, sat straight on the bench, and said, "I'll do what I can. I won't be your servant. Bad enough that I'm his—I don't need two of you ordering me about."

"No?" she asked silkily. "Is he not your emperor? Am I not the heir of his heir?"

"When you are empress on the throne of Sun and Lion," he said, "I will give you reverence as your rank deserves. But while you are mistress of Gate-mages, I am none of yours. You can kill me after all, if you like. You won't change my mind."

"Nor do I intend to," she said. "I am thinking . . . if I give you freedom of Gates, will you promise, for the world's safety, to do nothing that will endanger you or any of us?"

He sucked in a breath, shocked out of all sensible speech. She resisted the urge to shake him until he stopped gaping at her. In time he mastered himself; he found words to say. "You're—letting me—"

"With conditions," she said. "You go nowhere alone. Either my great-grandfather goes with you, or I, or another mage of suitable power and good sense. Observe that stricture, and the worlds are yours. Search among them; find what you can find. Bring back such knowledge as you gain. And guard yourself. It would be a pity to lose you."

"It would? What if I won't suffer a nursemaid? If I go out alone, what will you do? Kill me after all?"

"I doubt we'll need to," she said.

He eyed her suspiciously. "You can't be changing the laws this easily. Are you that afraid?"

"I am that uneasy," she said.

"You're afraid." That seemed to comfort him in some odd way. "Very well. I'll do it. Not for you, princess; don't delude yourself. I don't want to see this world burned to ash, and all its people taken away into darkness."

"Yourself among them?"

His eyes flashed at her under the lowered brows. "*I* could escape."

She had to incline her head at that; it was a just stroke.

He thrust out his hand. "Allies?"

"Certainly not enemies," she said as she completed the handclasp.

FOUR

ESTARION KNEW WHEN MERIAN LEFT HIS HOUSE, AND KNEW quite well what Daros did afterward. He was rather surprised that the boy did not leap at once into a Gate and vanish among the worlds. That had been his plan, and Estarion had watched while he refined it and elaborated on it. He was quite a subtle creature when he wanted to be, and astonishing in his gift for Gates. Did he know how strikingly unusual it was? Estarion would have said unique, but he shared not inconsiderable portions of it with Estarion himself, and with Merian—and with no one else that Estarion knew of, in their world at least.

Daros should have taken his freedom and run with it. But he was devotedly contrary, and he had no intention of gratifying anyone's expectations. Therefore he stayed about the hut, tending it and its garden as a good servant should, and waiting conspicuously for its master to return.

Its master would do that, but in his own good time. He had been hunting as the children believed, but his hunt was for nothing as simple as the mountain deer. He hunted among Gates, following the track of a shadow.

It was a subtle track, well hidden, and protected behind strong walls. The strength of the magic that sustained it made him catch his breath. He was strong; there was none stronger in his world. To this, he was but a feeble child.

He had not felt either young or weak in longer than he cared to remember. It was rather refreshing. He shielded himself as best he might, and hunted with all the stealth of which he was capable. That was considerable: even Merian could not find him unless he wished to be found.

The darkness ran in tides like a sea. It seemed to come from farther out, beyond the reach of his world's Gates, but with each ebb and surge it drew closer. It had buried worlds that he had walked on not so very long ago, distant worlds, far down the worldroads. It lapped the shores of several that he had passed by, or that he had not marked before. He prowled soft-footed round the edges, glimpsing bits of worlds: a flash of green, a spray of foam, a stretch of stark red sand.

It struck him without warning, falling on him from behind. Such substance as it had was like a great cat made of darkness visible, fanged and lethally clawed. He twisted, lashing out with a crack of power. The thing drank it as if it had been water, waxing with the force of it, rising up over him. He flung himself out and away.

The thing smote him so hard that his senses reeled. He was dimly aware of a Gate, and of falling. Then darkness was about him, black and deep.

The gods' curse had fallen on this land between the river and the desert. Their demon-servants stalked the night, rending any who ventured the darkness. The king was dead because of them, foraying out one long blue evening to avenge the slaughter of his people, and returning at dawn on the shoulders of his guards, so torn and broken that the priests despaired of mending his body for its journey into everlasting.

The king's wife had taken the scepter in her lap, close against her womb that had borne him six sons, but none of them had lived to see the men's house. She was all there was to rule the city, now that he was dead; his brothers had died of sickness and war, and his nobles were not of the true line. Kings and lords of other realms up and down the river were as sore beset by the unknown enemy as she, and as incapable of either war or invasion. And above all, in the end, the priests favored her. They fancied her a weak and pliant woman, a wife but not a queen.

She had played that part well while she lived as the king's wife. Now for this past year of her widowhood, she had smiled and listened and pretended to be awed, and ruled as her husband had done, with care to do nothing too untoward—not yet. In secret she brought out the weapons that had come with her from her mother's house, and began anew the exercises that she had practiced in her youth. She was not so young now, and not so supple, but she set her teeth and persevered; her servants, who were loyal, helped her as they could.

Even a queen might leave her city by daylight, if she professed a fondness for hunting on the river. However dread the night, the day was still safe; and a hunt was welcome—to bring in fresh meat for the pot and to restore spirits too long confined within walls of mudbrick and fear.

It was also opportunity to practice her archery, which was difficult within the palace. She could manage to be separated from the rest of the hunt, to wander among the reeds until there seemed no other boat in the world, and no other people but the boatmen and servants who accompanied her. They were all part of her secret, and glad of it, she reckoned as she ran her eyes over their faces. It was a warm day: they were gleaming with sweat, though even the rowers were resting, letting the current carry them along the reed-grown bank.

When they were well out of sight of the city and the hunt, she bade the boatmen steer the boat to the bank and moor it there. This was rich country for waterfowl, thick with flocks so numerous and so bold that they barely troubled to shift themselves out of range.

She would hunt them later. At the moment she had a desire in her heart to walk for a while between the green land and the red, between the nurturing earth and the stark hostility of the desert. It was a thing her husband had done, to remind himself of what his country was: rich yet precarious, and sharply divided from the world of gods and jackals.

The division was sharper than ever now, the desert more inimical. It was searingly bright in this hot and sunstruck morning: red sand and sharp stone and a clutter of scrub, and cliffs rising sheer beyond, a wall between the river and the deep desert. After the flocks that teemed on and above the river, and the fish and the crocodiles that fought their perpetual war in the water, this place seemed empty of life, save for a falcon that hovered against the sun.

She bowed to him, in homage to the god that he was. The air here was harsher, drier than it had been beside the river. Dust caught at her throat. Her maid offered her a skin of water, but she declined. She was thirsty, but not enough, yet, to act upon it.

She began to feel, deep in her heart, that she was called to this place. The gods were speaking, if she had ears to hear. Something waited for her, something wonderful. She went forward eagerly, with great lightness of spirit.

Only her maid and the captain of her guard went with her into the red land. She left the rest on the edge of the green, with orders to wait for her return. They were not unhappy to be left behind; the desert was a dread place, and more so since the night had become full of death.

There was a track out upon the sand, narrow and barely visible. She did not think that humans had made it. It led, she knew from long ago, up over the high hill and through a narrow cleft, to a valley with a spring and a shy hint of green. Gazelle came there to drink from the spring, and lions, too, and jackals questing for carrion.

Vultures were circling as she struggled up the steep slope. Lions' kill, she thought, but the lions must be gone: she caught no sound or scent of them. The call was strong in her. She could not have turned back even if she would.

She went on cautiously, with her bow strung and an arrow fitted to the string. Her guard would have gone ahead of her if he could, but the track was too narrow.

She reached the top with heart beating as much from excitement as from the exertion of the climb. She dropped there and crept forward like a snake over the stones, until she could see through the cleft into the valley.

It was almost devoid of green in this season, but the spring bubbled from its rock, ran into a pool hardly larger than a woman's hand, and sank back into the sand. A human figure lay by that bit of dampness, sprawled on its face. It was dressed in the kilt and broad belt of the people of the river, but the length and breadth of its body, and the night-darkness of the skin, spoke of a man from the south, where the sun had burned the earth's children black.

At first, with crushing certainty, she knew that he was dead. But as she watched, his hand stirred, long fingers closing into a fist, then opening again. Completely without thought, drawn irresistibly, she rose to go down into the valley.

The captain of guards caught her arm. "Lady! He could be one of the night's demons."

"In the full light of day?" She stared at his hand until it removed itself from her person. "Bring your spear, and be on guard. But don't harm him unless he threatens me."

He was not happy, but he was a good servant. He lowered his eyes, firmed his grip on his spear, and followed her down into the valley.

It was a large man indeed, and very dark. His hair was thick and plaited to the waist. Its blue-black waves were threaded lightly with grey, but his body was a young man's, taut and strong. With care, and very much against her captain's wishes, she turned him onto his back.

She had not seen a face like that before, not on the blunt-featured men of the south; this had the profile of the hawk that had come to circle overhead, driving off the vulture with its divine presence. The shadow of its wings seemed for a moment to enfold him.

She closed her eyes briefly. That face—that hawk's shadow. She knew it. How or where or when, she did not know. But to her heart he was no stranger, no more than one of her souls.

Her mind was very clear, not clouded at all. "Help me," she said to her captain, and to the maid who had trailed behind them both. Among the three of them, however unwilling two might be, they lifted him and carried him the long hot way to the river. When they came in sight of the rest of her guard, those strong young men came to relieve them of their burden; they carried him to the boat, and laid him in the shade of the canopy.

He had stirred now and then on the journey, but he had not roused. Once he was laid in the boat, he sighed and was still, except for the rise and fall of his breast as he breathed.

That was the gods' mercy. They could be kind to one of their own.

That this was a god or a son of gods, she had no doubt whatever. She would offer him honor, and not lock him in the granary as half her advisors bade her do; the rest would prefer that she have him killed before he could wake and doom them all.

None of them, not even the priests, could see what she saw. When she looked at him, she saw the sun's fire encased in the dark wood of the south. A night-demon, she was certain, would be dark to the heart of it.

She tended him herself. Tomorrow she would have duties that could not be escaped, but for this day she would do as she pleased, and as the gods willed. She saw him bathed in cool water and scented with oils, his hair combed and plaited and his beard smoothed into order. Only his right hand would not yield to their ministrations. It was clenched tight about a gleam of gold: some treasure, perhaps, that he guarded even in his dream.

When he was clean, the queen's servants laid him in the bed that had been the king's, in the colonnade that opened on the garden. Coolness washed him there, the breeze of fans wetted in water, and sweet scents, and relief from the glare of the sun.

The priests would not speak their spells over him to heal him, nor would they pray to the gods on his behalf. She said such prayers as a queen might say, sitting beside him, watching as the light shifted slowly from the blaze of noon to the softer glow of evening.

In that long light, at last, he stirred and gasped. He opened his eyes.

They were full of the sun. She fell before them, on her face as even a queen should do before a god. She heard the catch of his breath, the rustle of coverlets as he rose, and felt the warmth of his hands on her, raising her. She would let him lift her to her feet, but she would not look at him. One did not stare a god in the face.

She could stare at his hands clasping hers, and as he let her go, at the thing that he had guarded with such care. The sun again, but set in his hand, burning in it as fiercely as it ever did in the sky. It cast sparks of golden light across her face, and glinted on the walls and the floor.

He clenched his fist about it once more and said in a voice as warm as it was deep, "Don't be afraid." The words had a strange sound to them, as if they had begun in a language she had never heard, but had shifted and transmuted into words that she could understand.

"One should fear the gods," she said, still with her eyes turned resolutely down.

"God? I? You worship the sun here?"

"Is not the sun most greatly to be worshiped?"

"We do believe so," he said.

She was silent.

When the silence had grown almost awkward, he said, "Tell me if you will—where is this?"

"You are in my city," she said, "by the river that feeds the black land. We found you in the red land, where gods and demons walk. We cry your pardon if we acted in error."

"No," he said. "No, you did well. That's no friendly country, this red land of yours."

"It is not ours," she said, politely, but firm nonetheless. "This is ours: the green and the water, and the black earth. It was blessed once. Now . . . one thing we do fear, even more than gods. We fear the night."

He stiffened just visibly. "What do you fear in the night?"

He must know, as gods did. But it seemed he needed to hear it spoken. "We fear the things that walk in the dark; that rend flesh and devour souls. My people believe that you must be one such. But I see the sun blazing in the darkness."

"Ah," he said. "No wonder you won't look me in the face. I won't blind you, lady, or suck out your soul. I am a man, though one or two of my forebears were gods."

She did not believe him, but she nerved herself to look up.

If he was a man, he was like no man that she had ever seen. He was smiling at her. His golden eyes were warm. He did not frighten her, but neither did he put her at ease. "You came from the gods' country," she said, "from the land beyond the horizon. Don't deny it; I see it in you. You are not of mortal kin."

"Not of this world," he admitted. "The things you fear—I came hunting them. Your world is in great danger."

"You hunt them?" she said. She was not daring to hope, not yet. "You have weapons that will kill them? Powers? Magics?"

"I don't know," he said. Her face fell; he brushed it with a fingertip, a touch as light as a whisper of wind. "Lady, we've only now become aware of them; we don't know what they are, where they come from, or anything but that they are destroying worlds. If I can discover the truth, I will. But you shouldn't hope for too much. I'm only one man."

"But surely," she said, "there are others where you come from. They can come here, too, yes? They can join us in our war."

"There are others," he said, but his face for once was somber. "Whether they can come here . . . I barely managed it, and the darkness had had no warning of my coming. I don't know whether I can go back, or whether my people can find me. There are so many worlds. And none of my people knows—none of them believes—that any of them is occupied."

She did not understand him, except that he was troubled, and that he might not be able to summon reinforcements. The rest was a matter for gods.

This she understood: that he was still weak from his passage from the gods' world to that of men; and that she was sorely remiss in her hospitality. She summoned the servants, bidding them bring food, drink, cooling fans, and a basin of water in which had been scattered a handful of sweet-scented petals.

He partook of it all with regal courtesy, and gracious manners that began to win over the less suspicious of the servants. He even knew how to dismiss them so that they were not offended; they told one another in her hearing that he was tired, he had had a long journey, he must rest.

She was of the same mind, but when she made as if to go, he stayed her with a word. "What may I call you?" he asked. "Lady? Queen? Majesty?"

"Tanit," she said before she could catch her tongue.

He bowed to her. "Tanit," he said. "And I am Estarion."

"Seramon," she said.

"Estarion," he said.

Her tongue could not shape those sounds in that order. "Seramon," she said, struggling.

He shrugged and smiled and spread his hands, the one that was dark and the one that cast shards of light over the wall. "Seramon," he said.

FIVE

ESTARION WAS GONE.

Daros had indulged in a fit of pure pique, devoting himself after Merian's departure to all the tasks he had been given, and all of Estarion's, too. By sunset of that day, he was too exhausted to do more than eat a bite of bread and fall into his bed.

Morning brought a soft mist of rain and no relief from solitude. He might have reveled in it, seized it and escaped, but the thought persisted that this was a test. They wanted him to bolt. Therefore he would not.

By the sixth day he was deathly weary of his own company. Wool-beasts had no conversation. The senel had no interest in it. The stores of necessities—ale, salt, grain for grinding into flour—were running low. Every cycle of Brightmoon, either Estarion had gone down to Han-Uveryen to fetch provisions, or the fortress had sent a packtrain up the mountain. The moon had come to the full the day after Estarion went away, but no train of beasts had come winding up the trail. Obviously they expected the men on the mountain to come down.

On the seventh day, he ground the last of the grain, baked a day's worth of bread from it, and knew that either he went down the mountain to beg at the castle—and begging it would be, without Estarion to speak for him—or he went through Gates as they all seemed to wish him to do. Then of course, if he did that without a chaperon, he would be caught and killed, and they would be rid of him at last.

Unless . . .

She was in the midst of something that, from the taste that came to him through a tendril of magic, was both tedious and obligatory. It felt in fact like a court function.

He made so bold as to borrow her eyes. Yes—there was the great hall of audience in Starios of the kings, that Estarion had built between two great and warring empires. He glimpsed the regents on their twinned thrones below the golden blaze of the throne of Sun and Lion: Daruya like an elder and somewhat darker image of her daughter, and her consort not greatly unlike Daros' mother: tall and strongly built, with broad cheekbones and narrow black eyes. The court stood in ranks before them, glittering in regal finery.

Merian was enormously and unbecomingly bored. Courts of the law, imperial audiences, embassies, those she could bear; they were interesting. But High Court was dull beyond belief.

He was tempted to linger in this hidden corner of her awareness, where even she had no inkling of his presence. It was a surprisingly pleasant place to be. Her mind was not at all as he had expected; there was nothing either dour or repressive about it. It reminded him of the water garden in his father's summer palace: bright, melodious, full of sudden delights and fluid order. The wall she had built about it was thick and high, overgrown with thorns; but the heart of her was wonderful.

He hated to leave it. But she would be furious if she knew, and just then he did not want her anger. He slipped free, curved round, presented himself for her notice.

His wards were almost not enough to shield him against the full glare of her attention. She was Sun-blood, and that was pure blazing fire. She did not even give him time to speak. "Have you found him? Where is he?"

Daros could not make his mind shape words. She caught hold of him, opened one of the Gates in him, and stepped through it.

She did it to punish him; she could perfectly well have opened her own Gate. But that would not have proved that she was his master.

He allowed it because he was still so enthralled by what he had seen inside her. They stood in the shepherd's hut, with the rain dripping sadly from the eaves, and stared at one another.

She was as splendid as a firebird in her court dress, all gold from head to foot. He in plain worn leather, with no ornament but the copper of his hair, bowed as a prince should to an imperial heir.

Her lips narrowed at that. He had not meant it for mockery, but he was set too long in the habit of insolence; he could not perform an honest obeisance.

She seized him and shook him. He did not stiffen or resist, but let his head rock on his neck. *"Where is he?"*

It dawned on her eventually that if she wanted an answer, she had to stop rattling his teeth in his skull. She let him go. He dropped to his knees. "I don't know," he said through the ringing in his ears. "I came to ask you. This isn't a test? You aren't tempting me into running through Gates?"

"Why would I—" She bit off the rest. "You would think that, wouldn't you? You haven't seen him at all?"

"Not since the morning you came," he said.

"And you let this happen? You haven't gone looking?"

"You forbade me to go alone," he said.

He thought she would strike him, but she struck her hands together instead. "You could have summoned me!"

"Isn't that what I just did?"

She did not like it that he was being reasonable and she was not. He watched her gather herself together. After a while she said, not too unsteadily, "No one knows where he is. That's not terribly unusual—he vanished for the whole of a year once, before we found him on a ship on the eastern sea. But my dreams have been strange. This morning when I woke, I wanted to ask him something, and he was nowhere. He is not in this world."

Daros could not claim to be surprised. "He must have done it while we were engaged with one another," he said. "Otherwise one or both of us would have known. And if he did that . . ."

"There are worlds beyond worlds," she said. "And he can hide himself wherever, and whenever, he pleases."

"Why would he do that?" Daros asked. "Is he testing us both?"

She shook him off. "No. No, that's absurd. He wouldn't play that game now. Which means—"

Daros finished the thought for her. "He's trapped somewhere."

"Or dead," she said starkly.

"No," said Daros. "You would have known if he had died. So would I, if he'd died in a Gate. Power like that doesn't just vanish when the body dies."

"Unless the power itself had been consumed," she said.

But he was stubborn. "He's still alive, somewhere among the worlds. I'm going to find him."

"He might not thank you for that," she said. "If this is a hunt, and you come crashing through his coverts, you'll only make it worse for all of us."

"Lady," Daros said, and he thought he said it quite patiently, too, "either you want me to find him, or you don't. Either he's safe or he's not. You can't have both."

"I don't think he's safe," she said. "I'm going hunting. Will you come?"

"You think I can be of any use?"

"You can sense the thing that I suspect he was after."

"Ah," he said. "I'm to be your hunting hound."

"Call yourself what you will," she said. "We leave as soon as I can gather a few necessities."

"Gather a few for me," he said. "Unless you'd rather wait a day or two while I fetch them from the castle?"

"I'll fetch them," she said. "Be ready."

She melted into sunlight. He stood for a moment, simply breathing. The Gate inside him begged him to open it now, and vanish before she came back to plague him.

He was growing wise at last, or else he was turning into a coward. He gathered a change of clothes, a waterskin, one of the woolen cloaks; he rolled them together round an oddment or two, and the half-loaf that was left from his morning's baking. That bundle, with Estarion's second-best bow and a quiver of arrows, and a long knife, were all he could think to take.

She took her time in coming back. He began to wonder if she would; if she had thought better of it and gone alone. But the Gates were quiet. She had not passed through them.

He was napping when she came, propped against the house-wall in the sun. Her shadow, falling across his face, woke him abruptly and fully. He was on his feet, shouldering weapons and bundle, before his eyes were well open.

Her golden robes were gone. She was dressed much as he was, in coat and trousers, with a small bag slung over her shoulder. She had brought no weapon but a knife at her belt. Her hair was plaited tightly and wound about her head. She looked even younger than she had before, but strong, too, and a little wild.

She said no word. He had the briefest of warnings: a flicker in the Gates. She gathered him with her magic and swept him with her through the walls of the world.

* * *

They stepped from sunlight into firelight in a hall of stone. Now it seemed as vast as a cavern, now hardly larger than the shepherd's hut on the mountain. "This is the Heart of the World," he said. "I've heard of it. I've never been here."

"Never?"

He ignored the bite of Merian's disbelief. "You would have known about me if I had."

"So we would," she said grimly. "Now sit. This place belongs to us, to Gate-mages. It's as safe, and as shielded, as any place can be. You will remember it, where it is, how to come to it. This is where we will meet if either of us is separated."

He had always known where it was, but he held his tongue. He sat where she bade him, on a bench that he could have sworn had not been there a moment before. She stayed on her feet, frowning at the fire. It was hot; it danced as flames should. But it was no mortal fire. Power of Gates was contained in it, and worlds spun like sparks.

"We will find the trail here," she said. "You will be obedient; you will set aside whatever arts and fashions you may be enamored of, and be my servant until the emperor is found."

"And then?" he inquired. "Do I finally die?"

"Do you want to?"

He did not answer.

"If by fecklessness or folly you endanger the emperor, or prevent us from finding him at all, I will kill you with my own hand. Find him, help me bring him home safe, and I may see fit to free you from your bonds and your sentence. Then you may go back to your taverns and your women."

"For how long? Until our world flares into ash like all the rest?"

"That won't concern you, will it? Your service will be done. When the fire comes, if it comes, you can die with a flagon in your hand and a doxy on your knee, and never know a moment's grief."

Daros could hardly give way to anger. He had cultivated his reputation with great care; he had made certain that no one ever overestimated him. It made life simpler and much more pleasant.

But here, with this daughter of gods, he wearied of the game. He rose, quick enough to startle her, and stepped past her toward the hearth and the fire that was not fire. She spoke; he took no notice. He was sifting the sparks, searching among the worlds for a thread of gold, a memory of passage.

The blight on the worlds had spread. He saw it as black ash and blinding smoke, a darkness in the heart of the fire. The size of it, the breadth and sweep, caught his breath in his throat. No mage had such power; even if all the mages of this world banded together, they would not come near to the strength of this thing.

It was not a living will, though living will must drive it. He thought of walls and of shields—of a shieldwall, and an army behind it.

As if the thought had unlocked a door, he glimpsed . . . something. He was just about to grasp it when her voice shattered his focus. "Daros! You fool. Get back!"

Her hands were on him. He was leaning over the fire; his cheeks stung with the heat. She dragged him back.

He was glad of the bench under his rump, but not of the woman who bent over him. "Don't you know enough not to startle a mage out of a working?" he snapped at her.

That rocked her back on her heels. She could not have been reprimanded for such a thing since she was a tiny child.

He pressed such advantage as he had. "Lady, I don't think we can do this alone. We can hunt for the emperor, yes. But the other thing, the thing he was hunting—it's coming toward us. If you would have a world to bring him back to, you would do well to call on your mages and set them to work building such shields as they can. They can do that, yes? Even if they don't see or believe in the reason for it?"

"It has been done," she said.

He flushed.

She was not inclined to be merciful. "You will leave the searching of the shadow to the mages. Your task is to find your master. Do you understand?"

"Yes," he said tightly.

"Good," she said. "See that you remember."

He lowered the lids over his eyes before she saw the extent of his defiance. The shadow was the key, he was sure of it. If Estarion was not inside it, then he was very close to it. "Do I have your leave to hunt?" he asked. And added, after a pause, "Lady."

"Hunt," she said. "But watch yourself. Don't fall into the fire."

For answer he sat more sturdily on the bench and knotted his hands between his knees. He was well away from the fire, if not from the lure of its myriad worlds.

She set hands on his shoulders. So mages guarded one another in workings. And so, he thought, could she keep him chained to her will.

She did not know all there was to know of Gates, or of his magic, either. He sent a part of himself down the safe road, threading the loom of worlds. The part beneath, after a careful while, he sent back toward the shadow.

He had done such a thing before, more than once, to elude his father or his mother, or to escape the testing that would have bound him to Gates or temple. But he had not done it in such close quarters, under such a watchful guard. The lesser hunt must seem to be all the world, and the greater must leave no trace at all. To divide himself so, he needed every scrap of power he had, and every bit of discipline that he had taught himself. That was more than anyone knew. Whether it would be enough, only time would tell.

The lesser hunt skimmed the sparks of worlds, finding no trace of what it sought. The greater one skirted the edge of shadow. It was a shield, he was certain now, but how it was sustained, what had wrought it, he could not tell.

He sought the source, the life behind the wall. It was elusive; it warded itself well, shields within shields. He looked for a face, a mind, anything that he could grasp, to draw him behind the shield.

He was not strong enough. Merian wore at him with the weight of her watchfulness. If he could have focused on the shadow alone, he could have found its makers, but the fruitless hunt through worlds not yet touched by shadow kept him from discovering the truth.

He must find Estarion. The emperor had gone hunting the shadow; Daros was sure now that he had found it. He was strong enough to face it; nor need he bow to any will but his own.

Daros let go the greater hunt and focused himself on the lesser. He pressed it as close to the darkness as he dared under Merian's eye. There was a hint, a glimmer—

It dropped away. He pulled back in frustration, into the hall again, beside the fire that never shrank or went out. But if all the worlds were laid waste, would it not, itself, vanish into ash?

Merian set a cup in his hand. It was full of honeyed wine. She gave him bread to sop in it, to fill his belly with care, quenching a hunger as strong as it was sudden.

He ate and drank because he must, but his mind was not on it. "I have to go back," he said.

"Not now," said Merian. "You'll rest first."

"But I almost found him. He's there. I couldn't—quite—"

"I saw." She pulled him to his feet. "Come and rest."

He fought her, but his knees would barely hold him up. "Stop that," she said, "or I'll carry you over my shoulder."

He did not doubt that she would do it. Sullenly but without further objection, he let her lead him out of the hall.

This was a castle after all, with stairs and passages, and rooms that seemed mortal enough, if ascetically bare. One of them had a bed in it, and a hearth on which she lit a mortal fire. He lay because she compelled him, and suffered her pulling off his boots and covering him with a blanket as mortal as the fire, worn and somewhat musty, as if it had been long unused.

The starkness of it comforted him. It was real; there was no magic in it. He was deathly weary of magic, just then.

* * *

He lay on the hard narrow bed in the stone cell. Merian was gone. He was aware of her in the hall of the fire, holding council and audience from afar with the army of her mages. She had kept a part of herself, a thin thread of awareness, on guard over him, but that could not constrain his vision.

He stood on the shores of a wide and heaving sea. It was a sea not of water but of shadow, of darkness given substance. Things stirred beneath, great beasts rising from the depths and then sinking again with a sound like a vast sigh.

Because he was dreaming and knew it, he set foot on the surface of the darkness. It felt firm and yet yielding, like a carpet of moss on a forest floor. It was darkly transparent, showing the play of shadow within shadow in the depths beneath.

Slowly as he trod those swelling hills and sudden hollows, he began to distinguish among the shapes below. They were worlds, each floating in a bubble of darkness. Those that were nearest the surface came clearest to his vision. Some of them he knew, others were strange. He stooped to peer through the dark glass.

It was a war. He had never seen one; there had been no more than bandit raids in his world since before he was born. Yet he had heard of battles, and seen them through the memories of those who had fought in them.

Armies faced one another on a wide and windy plain. The beasts they rode, the armor they wore, were strange, but there was no mistaking what they were or what they did. One side was smaller by far, and had a desperate look. The other came on like a black wave.

There, he thought. He bent lower, peering as closely as he could. The dark warriors were all armored, their faces hidden, their shapes not quite human.

The sea surged, flinging him off his feet. A vast shape rolled over the world and its warriors. An eye opened, as wide as one of the worlds. It turned and bent, as if searching.

He was tiny, a mite, a speck of dust in the vastness of the worlds. He was nothing; no more than a breath of wind. The dark thing need take no notice of him. It was far too great a beast for such a speck as he was.

It rolled on beneath and left him gasping, tossed on the restless sea. He was lost; the land was gone. In concealing himself from the great guardian, he had concealed himself also from the Heart of the World.

SIX

ERIAN LEFT THE BOY TO SLEEP FOR PERHAPS TOO LONG. THERE
was a great deal to do, and her mages, while willing to be obedient,
lacked belief in the task. Even after she had let them see as much
as she had seen, she still sensed the current of doubt and heard the murmur among them: "She's a great mage, we all know that, but we also know
that she is a living Gate. What if the Gate in her has driven her mad?"

That murmur would grow if she loosed her grip on any of them.
There were always doubters and naysayers; nor was every mage her
friend, though she had ruled them since she was little more than a child.
If she was wise, she would give up this foolishness and return to her
palace, and let the emperor find his own way home. Had he not done so
before, and more than once?

But this was not the same. There was an urgency in her, a sense almost of desperation, as if there were no time left—as if each moment that she let pass, she wasted, without hope of replenishment. She must find the emperor; there was no hope otherwise.

This was nothing that she could say to any of her mages. They were blind to it, and worse than blind.

"It could be said," said Urziad from amid the Heartfire, "that you are deluded and we see the simple truth."

"My old friend and frequent adversary," she said, "so it could. Do you believe it?"

"I believe that what you see terrifies you," he said. "I dislike that you place your trust in a useless frippery of a boy."

"He believes in what I see," she said.

"Surely that should tell you how well to trust it, and him."

"The emperor also believes," she said. "And before you tell me that he's a senile old man who has been questionably sane from his youth, do recall that no mage now living can equal him."

"Except you," said Urziad.

She shook that off, however true it might be. "I think this boy may be stronger than any of us imagines. He's the hunting hound. I'm his huntsman. Will you see to it that there is a world for us to return to?"

"I would prefer that you never left at all," Urziad said.

"So would I," she said. "But needs must. Be watchful, my friend."

"For your sake," Urziad said, "and for no other reason."

"Gods grant it be enough."

He vanished from the Heartfire. She stretched and sighed. There was no measure of time here, but in the world of the sun her forefather, the day had come and gone. It was deep night, almost dawn.

The boy had had long enough to sleep. She went up to the room in which she had left him. He was sprawled on his face, perfectly still: the pose of one who had raised laziness to high art.

She laid a hand on his shoulder to wake him, and gasped. He was rigid. The skin of his neck was cold.

She heaved him onto his back. He was still breathing, shallowly. His face was grey-green, his eyes rolled up in his head.

She hissed at the folly of the child. He had fallen into a mage-dream; it had swallowed him whole. And she, worse fool yet, had left him alone. She should have known what he would do.

If there had been another mage to stand guard over her, she would have gone hunting him down the paths of his dream. But she was alone, and time was wasting. She flung him over her shoulder—grunting a little for he was not a light weight, but she was stronger than most men would have liked to know. She carried him out of the cell, down a passage and a stair, to a cavernous room in which glimmered a pool of ever-flowing water.

The water was cold—icy. A flicker of magic could have warmed it, but she had no interest in his comfort. Quite the contrary. She stripped him of his clothes and dropped him unceremoniously into the pool.

For a long moment she knew that she had erred; that he was too far gone. He sank down through the water, limbs sprawling, slack and lifeless.

Just as she was about to dive to his rescue, he jerked, twitched, thrashed. Eyes and mouth opened; he surged up out of the pool, gasping, choking, striking at air.

She moved back prudently out of the way and waited for him to find his sanity again, such as it was. He scrambled to the pool's edge and lay there, breathing in gasps, skin pebbled with cold.

When it seemed clear that he would refrain from attack, she wrapped him in a cloth and rubbed him dry. His eyes were clouded still; he submitted without resistance. Only slowly did he seem to see her or to know who she was; even then he only stared at her dully.

Her heart constricted. Not, she told herself, that she cared overmuch whether he lived or died, but she needed him alert and sane, to hunt for the emperor. Indaros with his mind gone was of no use to her.

Little by little the light came back into his eyes. He straightened; he shuddered so hard that she heard the clacking of teeth. When he spoke, his voice was raw. "How long—"

"Part of a day and most of a night," she said.

"Not so bad, then," he said with a small sigh. "Lady, what I saw—" He was shaking uncontrollably. "Armies, lady. Wars. And something . . . I don't know what it is, how they raise it, what sustains it, but it rolls ahead of them. We aren't strong enough, lady. Not even all of us together."

"We are going to have to be," she said grimly. "Show me."

He opened his eyes wide. They were as dark as the night between stars, and shimmering with bubbles that were worlds. Before she could speak, move, think, she was deep within his memory.

He was strong, she thought distantly. Stronger even than she had imagined. As strong as she. Untrained, yes, but far from undisciplined. He had taught himself—really, rather well.

She gathered everything that he had told her, found Urziad where he drifted on the tides of dream, and sent it all to him, whole, as it had been sent to her. His shock knotted her belly.

There would be no doubt among mages now. Not after this. She struggled free, raising every shield she had.

In the silence, alone within herself, she stood staring at the boy from Han-Gilen.

No—let him be the man and mage that he so evidently was. Let her give him his name, Indaros Kurelios, prince-heir of a small and yet powerful realm. "Why?" she asked him. "Why hide yourself so completely?"

"I never wanted temples," he said, "or orders of mages. It seemed they never wanted me."

"I am thinking," she said slowly, "that it's great good luck for us all that that was so."

"What, that I'm a coward and a layabout?"

"Stop that," she said. "This needed someone outside the walls. Someone who could see unimpeded; who could go where none of us was able to go."

"Does that mean my sentence is commuted?" he asked sweetly.

"You still broke the law," she said.

He sighed, shrugged. The color had come back to his face, the insouciance to his manner. She was growing used to it; it grated on her less now than it had. "And the emperor is still missing. I know he's somewhere on the shores of the shadow—but where, I can't tell."

"We will find him," she said, "if we have to walk on foot from world to world."

"I don't think there's time for that," he said.

"What else can we do?"

He bit his lip. It was odd and rather gratifying to see him so far removed from his easy insolence. "I can track him. I think. . . . if you ward me and protect me from the dark, I can find the trail he left. It's still there; I can almost see it. But it will fade soon."

She searched his face. He was speaking the truth, or as much of it as he could know. "Do it," she said. "Do it now."

He bent his head. She was prepared this time for the swiftness with which he acted. He had no deliberation; he knew no rituals. He simply gathered his magic and flung it forth. It was inelegant, but she had to admit that it was effective.

They flew on wings of bronze over a dark and tossing sea. What he followed was as subtle as a scent, as faint as a glimmer in the corner of an eye. She could find it only through him.

That piqued her. He was royal kin, but she was royal line.

He was her hunting hound. She let him draw her onward through the swirl of worlds. They clustered near the edge of the shadow, gleaming like foam on a dim and stony shore.

She who was a living Gate, had never seen nor imagined such a thing as this. There was no worldroad, no simple skein of worlds. It was a much greater, much more complex thing, too great for mortal comprehension.

He rode these shifting airs as if born to them. She, earthbound, could only cling to him and be drawn wherever he went.

He circled a cluster of worlds far down that grey shore. The tide lapped but did not quite overwhelm them. They gleamed like pearls, or like sea-glass.

He had begun to descend. Broad wings beat and hovered. His eyes were intent, fixed on the worlds below.

Without warning the sea rose up and clawed the sky. It seized the tiny thing circling in it, struck it, smote it down.

They whirled through darkness. Winds buffeted them. His wings were gone. He clung as tightly to her as she to him, rolling and tumbling through infinite space.

She flung out a lifeline, a thread of pure desperation. It caught something, pulling them up short, dangling in the maelstrom of wind and shadow. Hand over hand she climbed up the line, with his dead weight dragging at her until he gripped the line below her. She hesitated, dreading that he would let go and fall, but he was climbing steadily, if slowly.

Light glimmered above them. Wind buffeted them, striving to pluck them free. Her fingers cramped; her arms ached unbearably. She set her teeth and kept on.

The thread began to rise as if drawn from above. The wind howled, raking flesh from bone and body from spirit.

The Heart of the World hung below her. She reached for it with the tatters of her magic, seeking the power that had sustained her and every Gate-mage since the dawn of the world.

Just as she touched it, the darkness struck. It had been waiting like a great raptor poised above its prey. It roared down with power incalculable.

There were wards, walls, structures of magic so strong and so ancient that they had been reckoned impregnable. They melted as if they had been no more than a wish and a dream. All the woven elegance of spells and workings, remembrances of mages eons dead, great edifices of art and power, crumbled and fell into nothingness.

The Heart of the World was gone. It had whirled away below her, drowned in darkness. The place where it had been, woven in the core of her magery, was echoing, empty.

This could not be. The Heart of the World was not a place, nor a world. It was a living incarnation of magic.

The dark had devoured it, swallowed it, consumed it. It was rendered into nothingness, just as the worlds had been beyond the lost Gates.

Shocked, shattered, stunned almost out of her wits, she fell into light. A grunt and a gasp marked Daros' fall beside her. She was far too comfortable on real and living ground to move or speak. That was cool stone under her, or—tiles?

Tiles indeed. She knew them well. Painfully she lifted her head. The two of them lay in a heap in the innermost shrine of the Temple of the Sun in Starios. The light about them was pure clean sunlight flooding through the dome of the roof. For a long blissful moment she basked in it, sighing as pain and fear melted away. Her whole being was a hymn of thanks to the god who had freed her soul from the black wind.

Daros groaned and rolled onto his back. His eyes narrowed against the light, but he did not flinch or cover them.

Movement caught Merian's eye. A pair of priests stood staring at them. Both were young, in the robes of novices; their eyes were wide, their mouths open in astonishment. One of them held a basket of flowers, the other clutched an armful of clean linens. They had come to tend the altar.

She rose stiffly. The novice with the flowers dropped onto his face, hissing at his companion to do likewise. "Lady!" he bleated. "Lady, forgive, we didn't recognize you, we—"

"Please," she said, cutting across his babble. "Go on with what you were doing."

He took it as an order, and no doubt as a sacred trust. The young and eager ones invariably did. Daros, to her relief, said nothing; he creaked even more than she, and when he followed her from the shrine, he walked lame. He did not complain, which rather surprised her. She would have expected, at the very least, an acid commentary on the ailments of mages.

Her aches eased as she walked, though the void in the heart of her felt as if it would never heal. He said nothing of what he might be suffering, if indeed he felt anything at all. He was not bound to Gates as she had been; the Heart of the World was no great matter to him as it was to her—and as it would be to every mage of Gates in this world.

She had taken the inner ways of the temple, away from the eyes of priests and the faithful; there was not even a servant to stop and stare. They descended by narrow steps into a maze of tunnels, lit by a wisp of magelight that bobbed ahead of them.

Daros stumbled. She was almost too late to catch him. His weight dragged at her; his breath rasped in her ear. He had overtaxed himself—fool; child. But she was worse than that, for allowing him to do it.

There was nothing for it but to press on with what speed she could. The urgency in her had come close to panic. It took all the discipline of both mage and priest to keep walking, and not to drop the stumbling, gasping boy and run back into the light.

An eon later, though not so long by the turning of the sun, they came out at last in a forgotten corner of the palace. There was still some distance to go before they were truly safe; she paused in the dim and dusty cellar, plotting her path from a memory decades old.

She heard no footstep, sensed no presence, and yet her hackles rose. She could not whip about: Daros impeded her. She had to turn slowly, every sense alert, braced to drop him and leap if she must.

She nearly collapsed in relief. Her stepbrother lifted Daros in strong

arms, taking no notice of his feeble protests, and said, "The others are in
the autumn garden. Can you walk that far?"

"Easily," she said.

Hani's glance raked her mistrustfully, but he shrugged, sighed, turned
to lead her onward.

The autumn garden grew in a corner of the palace wall, where the sun
was warmest in that season, and there was shelter from the first blasts of
winter. Flowers grew there even into the dark of the year; the fountains
flowed later than in any other of the gardens, and birds sang long after
they had left that part of the world.

It was nearly summer-warm when Merian came there, the sun shining in cloudless heaven, the water singing into the tiers of stone basins.
This world knew nothing of darkness or loss—not yet. It was almost
painful in its beauty.

By the lowest of fountains, on the porch of the little house that ornamented the garden, her mother sat with Urziad and Kalyi and the high
priestess of the temple with her golden torque and her eyes that, though
blind, could pierce to the heart. Their faces mirrored the shock that
seemed set indelibly in hers. That they were alive and conscious spoke of
their strength and the strength of their power. Through their eyes she
could see the losses: mages dead or broken, Gates fallen, spells and magics in ruins.

The princess regent stirred, drawing Merian's eye. She shared the gift
or curse of her line: she seemed hardly older than Kalyi, who was but a
year past the Journey that had made her priestess as well as mage. People said that Merian was like her mother, though paler; she was gold and
ivory, but Daruya was honey and bronze. Merian bowed to her as the
chief of Gate-mages should to the regent of Sun and Lion. Even as she
straightened, her mother drew her into a bruisingly tight embrace. "We
thought we'd lost you, too," she said. "Whatever possessed you—"

"I did." Daros had startled them: he was conscious, struggling free of

Hani's grip, swaying on his own feet. "I found him. I found the emperor."

Daruya wasted no time in foolish questions. "Where?"

"On the edge of the shadow," he said, "almost inundated by the tide."

"And you left him there?"

He faced her with a perfect lack of fear. "Lady, he's trapped. I barely found him, and I knew where to look. Before I could come closer, the tide drove me away. I did try, lady. I'll try again, but first I have to rest." That was not a thing he admitted easily; he was young and male and proud. But he was brave enough to tell the truth.

"You will not try again," Daruya said. "No one can. Do you understand, boy? The great Gates are gone. The Heart of the World—the center of our magic—is lost."

"But that's not—" Daros shut his mouth just before Merian would have shut it for him. He bent his head, concealing the rebellion in his eyes.

It seemed the pretense deceived the rest of them, though Merian was in no way taken in by it. Daruya addressed him as if the rest of it had never been said. She was not belittling the great loss; she was making it bearable by focusing on what might possibly be salvaged out of the ruin. "The emperor is safe? Only trapped?"

"I couldn't tell," Daros said without too palpable a sense of relief. "I could only see that he was alive, tossed in the storm-wrack."

"That's the best we can hope for," Daruya said levelly, "and better than many of us can claim. We've lost too many mages—in body or in spirit—and all our greater Gates. Thank the gods and the foresight of those who built them, many of the lesser Gates are still standing—they were built and sustained through the power of this world, which is still intact. We'll keep them open, but closely guarded, for as long as we can. Every ward and shield that we can raise, we will raise. And we will pray that when the war is over, we can find our emperor again, and bring him back." She drew herself up and stiffened her back. "You will rest and restore yourselves, both of you. Tomorrow I will have need of you—as of every mage with strength or wits to fight. Until then, be as much at ease as you can."

Daros bowed as if in either weariness or submission, but Merian did not believe in either. She kept her own tongue between her teeth and undertook to seem more convincingly obedient than Daros. He was out on his feet; she was a little tired herself. Sleep would serve them both well, whatever came after.

SEVEN

OF ALL THE OUTCOMES DAROS HAD EXPECTED, TO FIND HIMSELF a guest in the palace in Starios was one of the more unlikely. He was given every comfort, even a pretty maid if he should be inclined; somewhat to his surprise, he was not. He was worn to the bone, and above all he needed sleep. His lack of interest had nothing to do with a certain haughty royal lady.

He slept like the dead, a sleep blessedly free of dreams. In that sleep, the raw edges of his mind began to knit, and powers taxed to the utmost began slowly to heal. When he woke, he felt as if he had been beaten with cudgels, inside and out.

He fully expected to find Merian sitting beside his bed, but the person there was almost a stranger. He knew the face, of course; Hani the prince, son of the regent's consort, was known even to layabouts in taverns. "Am I under guard?" Daros asked him.

The prince raised a brow. He looked remarkably like Daros' father, though his hair was black rather than copper; his voice too was very like, deep and soft, but the accent was of another country altogether. "Do you feel the need to be guarded?"

"That depends," said Daros. "Am I safe here? I seem to remember a sentence of exile."

"You're not in Han-Gilen, are you?" Hani yawned and stretched. "I'm to tell you that after you've rested sufficiently and bathed, and one presumes eaten, though that wasn't mentioned, the lady Merian will see you."

Daros' lips twitched. It was like Merian to remember a man's bath but not his breakfast. "I'd best get to it," he said. "By your leave, my lord."

"Ah," said Hani, shrugging. "I don't stand on ceremony." He snapped his fingers. Servants came at the run with bath and clothes and, yes, breakfast.

The bath was welcome. The clothes were good but plain—not court dress. Daros widened his eyes somewhat but offered no other commentary. Neither the servants nor the prince remarked on the myriad bruises that stained his skin, though their hands were gentle, to spare him such pain as they could.

Hot water and clean clothes restored him rather well. Breakfast set him truly among the living. He did his best not to fall on it like a starving wolf. Bread so fine, cakes so sweet, had not passed his lips since he left Han-Gilen.

He ate less than he wanted but somewhat more than he needed; then he was ready to be taken to the princess. Hani was his guide; the servants, dismissed, vanished wherever servants went when their lords did not need them.

He was sure, well before he came there, that he was a prisoner after all, and he was going into a cell deep in the bowels of the palace. But his guide brought him out of the tunnels and into a different place, which had the air and the proportions of a noble residence. He supposed that it was Merian's house, or perhaps her brother's.

It was a handsome house, well kept, and apparently deserted. But he sensed human presence elsewhere within the walls, and not only in the room to which Hani led him.

It was a library, and she was in the middle of it, half-buried in books, shuffling rapidly among a half-dozen scrolls and scribbling on a bit of parchment. She glanced up, preoccupied, and said, "Hani. Where did you put Vanyi's book?"

Hani slipped a scroll from the bottom of the heap, unbound it, and handed it to her without a word. She did not thank him, or acknowledge Daros at all.

He could sulk, or he could peer over her shoulder to see what she was reading. He recognized a history or two, a very old grimoire of which he had thought his father had the only copy, and what seemed to be a compendium of songs and gnomic verses.

"What are you looking for?" he asked her.

"Help," she said. "Wards alone won't be enough. But nowhere is there any word of such a threat as this."

"Don't you have priests and mages to do this hunting for you?" Daros asked.

"They are," she said: "all those that aren't flattened by the loss of their center."

He was not sure he understood. "The Heart of the World? But—"

"You really don't feel it, do you?" She sounded almost exasperated. "When it went down, weren't you rent to the core of you?"

"No," he said. "I can feel a gap in the fabric of magic—an emptiness where once was a nexus of Gates—but it doesn't touch me at all. The worlds are still full of Gates, and most of those are still open. Those that are shut, the shadow took, just as it took your nexus."

"To the mages of Gates," she said, "the Heart of the World is the very heart and center of what they are. The other mages, lightmages, darkmages—their power is born and nurtured here, in this earth, this sun. But the power of Gates was contained there, in the Heart of the World."

"Not for me," he said. "Nor for you, either, or you wouldn't be sitting here, being impatient with me. How badly are your mages hurt?"

She seemed surprised that he would care. "There are a dozen dead. Another hundred might as well be. The rest look as if they will recover. The lesser Gates are still alive; that sustains them. But how—"

"I'm not a Gate-mage," he said.

"That is obvious." She shook herself. "You're a great Gate—as I am; as, it seems, Estarion is. It's inside you. You can still leave the world."

"So can you."

"Yes," she said, but not as if it mattered. She turned back to the books in front of her. "I had been hoping to find something that would show us how to find the emperor."

"I know that," Daros said. "I remember where I found him. I could find it again."

"But should you? The danger is worse than ever. If the shadow can swallow the Heart of the World, it most certainly can swallow you."

"It can swallow him, too, and whatever world or place of magic in which he's found refuge," said Daros. "Lady, the sooner we get him out, the better. I don't know that anything can live, once the dark tide has rolled over it."

"We must know what it is," she said. "Else how can we fight it? But how can we do that, if even you can't go near it without being battered half to death?"

All his bruises twinged at once. He set his teeth against them and said, "I know where he is now. I don't need the worldroad, or the sea of night, either."

He thought she might seize him, maybe to strangle him, maybe to kiss him, but she did neither. "If you go, you may not be able to come back. You said he was trapped. What good would it do to join him in his prison?"

"Maybe none," he said. "Maybe a little, if we discover what the enemy is. Who knows? Maybe we can even destroy it."

"As well expect a gnat to destroy a mountain," she said. She rubbed her eyes as if they troubled her, and drew a long shuddering breath. "If we only knew what it was!"

"The Forbidden Secrets," Hani said abruptly.

They both rounded on him. He met their stares calmly. "There is on the far side of the world," he said, "an order of—priests is not the proper word. Devotees? Adepts? They call themselves the servants of the Great Oblivion; they worship the night without moons or stars. Their fastness stands on the summit of heaven. It's said that only those blessed of their gods can visit it, still less live there, because the air is too thin for simpler mortals to breathe."

"Would they know of Gates and dark tides?" Merian demanded. "Are they mages?"

"Some may be," he said. "I only heard of them as a story long ago, before we came to live in this empire. But I've heard since of the knowledge that they keep, that they say was passed down to them by their gods. What that knowledge is, only the initiate knows; it's not even known how it's conveyed, though most likely it's written in books. Still, there are rumors of what may be in it, whispers of strange things, dark things, things that feed on stars."

"Things that feed on stars." Merian stroked the scroll in front of her, absently, as if it had been an animal. "The books, scrolls, inscriptions, whatever they are, are forbidden, you say. I gather their guardians will be somewhat reluctant to present them for our inspection, even with an imperial decree. It's not their empire, after all, or their emperor who is lost."

"Even to save the world?" Daros asked.

"My own mages hardly believe that," she said. "Do you think devotees of a hidden order on the other side of the world will be any more willing to hear me?"

"You could ask," he said.

Innocent, her eyes said, and she did not mean it as a compliment. He shrugged.

"You *could* ask," her brother said.

"Find them," she said, "and ask them, if you have such hopes of them."

"I may do that," Hani said.

He wandered off. Daros would have liked to follow, but he was curious as to why she had summoned him. Surely it could not have been to watch her scowl at books that told her nothing.

At length she seemed to recall his existence. He had been reading the grimoire with widened eyes and guiltily beating heart, for he had never been allowed to touch its mate in his father's library. When he had tried, he had scorched his fingers, and been thrashed soundly into the bargain.

This had no wards on it, or none that could trouble him. Nor was there a great deal in the book to appall him. The magic was dark and the rites nearly all of blood, but he had seen worse elsewhere. Nothing in it spoke of shadows across the worlds.

Just as he came across a spell for opening Gates, which required the blood of a virgin boy and the soul of a saint, Merian said, "I set you free."

Daros blinked. "You— What?"

"You're free," she said. "You can go. Your sentence is commuted."

"But you just said—you need me!"

She raised her eyes to his face. They were tired, but there was something more, something that he could just begin to read. "I have no time for you," she said. "You lack training; your discipline is rudimentary. There's no leisure to train you, and none to protect you against the trouble you will inevitably get into if left to yourself. One of my mages will take from you your knowledge of the emperor's whereabouts, then bind your power within the circles of this world. You should suffer little inconvenience."

"You need me," he said stubbornly. "You said so yourself: I'm not bound by the limits of mages. I can go where they don't think to go, do what they can't imagine doing. I can find the emperor while they're still groping in the dark."

"But," she said with sweet reason, "you don't want or need to be involved in this war. Don't you miss your taverns? Your wine? Your women?"

"No," he said, and it was mostly the truth. "I want to finish what I started."

"Do you? Do you really?"

He paused. This was not a light thing that he was doing. Her eyes on him were bright gold. The tiredness was still in them, but she was stronger than he had thought. "I want to finish it," he said.

"If you would do that," she said, "I can't have you bumbling about like a weanling child. You will swear yourself to me by the laws of mages. I will not bind you with priest's vows, or with the lesser vows of my order. But you will be my sworn man. You will answer to me; whatever you do, you will do by my leave. If you cannot do this, then you will leave, and be bound, and never trouble my peace again."

Daros opened his mouth, then shut it. He could see the trap about him, the jaws open wide. She had plotted this with skill that bade him remember precisely who and what she was. She was royal born, bred to rule. She would use every weapon that she found to hand, however flawed, however ill-balanced it might be.

"I think," he said after a while, "that my decision was made some time since. You made sure of it, didn't you? You need me—but you don't want me free to do as I please."

"You are a spoiled and insolent child," she said, "without sense or discipline. You are also a gifted mage, a master of Gates, and the key to the emperor's return. I will use you, and if necessary destroy you."

"So you said," he said, "when you first sat in judgment over me." He knelt at her feet and held up his hands. "I swear myself to you, Lady of Gates, to serve you as I may."

"You will serve me," she said, "with your heart and your hand, with

your strength and your magic, to death or beyond, while the world
endures. Do you swear this, on pain of dissolution?"

"I swear," he said steadily.

She took his hands. Her fingers were cool and firm, but in the palm
of her right hand was a living sun. She laid that against his own palm,
and then against his heart. He gasped; it was as if she had pierced him
with a white-hot blade. "You are bound," she said, "and freed. No power
but mine may compel you. No oath can bind you, unless I choose to
allow. You are my servant. Serve me well; and may the gods defend you."

He knelt with the blade of the Sun in him and a weird high singing
in his ears. He had done many things that were irrevocable; trespassing
in Gates was not the least of them. Yet this was something more. For
once he did a thing for a purpose other than his own pleasure.

He wanted suddenly to run far and fast, and hide where no one could
ever find him. He had hidden for so long, pretended to be of so little
worth, that it was as if he had been stripped naked in front of the High
Court.

Well, he thought, as to that, he was not at all ill to look on. Might not
his mind and his magic be the same?

He let her raise him. She did not at once let go. Her eyes seemed
caught in his face, as if something there enthralled her.

Daros the libertine would have slain her with a smile. Daros the royal
servant lowered his eyes before she could see the smile in them. He was
sure now of several things, but he did not think that she wanted to know
any of them.

This was her house, that she shared with her stepbrother; he kept it up,
oversaw the servants, looked after her with quiet competence. He had a
wife and children, but they lived on the other side of the world, in the
country in which both he and his father had been born. Here he seemed
to have neither wife nor mistress; ladies of the court pursued him, but he
was adept at evading them.

Daros did not go to court. Merian went as seldom as she could; she much preferred the company of priests and mages. Of late, with the great loss among the Gates, the mages needed her more than ever. If she had no time to tame a reckless boy, she had even less to trouble with courtiers.

Of Daros she expected little, but he decided the first day that he would keep himself at her disposal. She rapidly grew accustomed to his presence in her shadow.

The shadow on the stars was growing stronger and coming closer. In his darker moments he was almost tempted to give way to it, but he was far still from despair. He wanted to live, for however long his world might have. He did not believe as too many of the mages did, that now the Heart of the World was gone, this world was safe; the darkness was sated, and would not come closer. It would come—later rather than sooner, maybe, but there was no escaping it.

He was remarkably light of heart. "Better dead than bored," he said to Hani a Brightmoon-cycle after he swore himself into Merian's service.

Hani was a man of middle years and impeccable reputation, but behind the stern mask of his face he was still a wild boy. They were sharing a jar of wine that evening, while wind and rain lashed the walls. A fire burned on the hearth; there were cakes and fruit and roast fowl to go with the wine; and Merian had gone to bed, freeing them to be frivolous. Hani knew even more scurrilous songs than Daros did; he had taught Daros the most reprehensible of them.

In the silence after the song, Daros sensed as he often had of late, that the tide was rising beyond the sphere of the moons. He said nothing of it, but Hani was a mage. "Will it be soon?" he asked.

Daros shrugged. "Who knows? Nothing's stopping it—but maybe there's a mage somewhere, or a Power, or a god, who can stand against it."

"You don't sound troubled," Hani said.

"Should I panic? We won't live any longer if I do."

Hani peered at him through the haze of the wine. "Ah. I keep forgetting. You're the living image of youth and ennui."

"I was," Daros said. "I set every fashion, and my whims were all the rage. I'm sadly fallen now. It seems I have a purpose apart from the cultivation of extreme taste. My old circle would be appalled."

"Are you?"

Daros laughed. "Terribly! But there's no help for it. I've become that most dreadful of creatures: a dutiful servant."

"May the gods avert," said Hani piously. He filled Daros' cup again, and then his own. They drank to duty—and to the horrors of courtiers. And with that, for a whim, to the tides of the dark, that came on inexorably, for all that anyone could do.

EIGHT

FATHER," SAID HANI, "WHAT DO YOU KNOW OF THE FORBIDDEN Secrets?"

The regent's consort was an older, somewhat smaller image of his son. He had never had Hani's lightness of spirit, or else years of ruling at his lady's side had cured him of it, yet Daros did not find him either dull or excessively stern. He had been visibly glad to receive Hani, that bright morning a handful of days after the first storm of the winter; he greeted his son's companion with grave politeness, as if Daros' reputation did not precede him wherever he happened to go.

When the courtesies had been observed, Hani came direct to the point. His father's brows drew sharply together; the air chilled perceptibly. "Why do you wish to know of this?"

"My lord," Daros said, "we've all been looking for something, anything, that might tell us of what we face. These books or whatever they may be—do you know where they are?"

"Only in legend and rumor," the prince consort said. "The secrets and their keepers have an ill name in my country."

"Are they in Shurakan?" asked Daros.

"No," the prince consort said. "Such things would not be allowed there, even after the ban was lifted on mages and their workings. Rumor places them in the mountains that claw the face of heaven, far to the north of Shurakan."

Daros had been a poor scholar, but he had a tenacious memory. His mind saw the globe of the world, with the empire of Sun and Lion gleaming golden on half of it, and to the east of it the blue ocean, and the other side of that, the land over sea, a broad plain rising up into mountains as lofty as stars. Deep in the midst of them, set like a jewel amid the snows, he saw the hidden kingdom of Shurakan beneath the mountain that was called the Spear of Heaven. North of Shurakan was a waste of ice and crag and stone. It was bleaker by far than Death's Fells, and even more remote.

He did not know precisely when he passed from memory to living vision. He was aware of the small audience chamber in the palace, and of the men in it; he knew when a servant brought food and wine, and when a messenger came from the regent with a matter that was of too little importance to call the prince consort away from his guests. All that, Daros was aware of, but in the same moment he was flying on wings of air above the jagged teeth of mountains.

The others had fallen silent, watching him. They did not, as Merian might have done, attempt to interfere. He felt Hani's presence like a warm handclasp, following him where he flew.

"Fascinating." That was the prince consort's voice, that deep burr with its accent of Shurakan. "She told us what he could do, but the reality is . . . fascinating."

"One can see why they bind mages with oaths and orders," Hani said.

"I don't think most of them are as strong as this."

"Not nearly," Hani conceded.

And all the while, Hani followed Daros over the mountains. Daros was hunting; he took little notice of the two who watched and judged. There was a nest of shadow among these peaks. It was not precisely the same as the dark thing that had swallowed so many worlds, and yet Daros would have reckoned that they were kin.

Hani's satisfaction warmed him. He did not give way to hope, not quite yet, but this was the closest to it that any of them had had.

His flight slowed. He hovered above a range of mountains. They were not as high as some about them, but still they rose halfway to heaven. On the side of a crag, built sheer into a cliff, he found what he had been seeking: a line of walls and the jut of a tower.

He might have descended to peer closer, but Hani held him back. "Not till we have reinforcements," he said.

He was only being wise. Daros sighed and withdrew, leaving the mountains behind, returning to the clear pale light of late autumn in Starios.

Father and son regarded him with expressions that struck him as altogether strange. Respect; a little awe. No one had ever been in awe of him before.

Mercifully, they did not speak of it. Hani said, "Merian has to know of this. Mother—"

"I'll see to that," his father said.

Hani clasped his father's hands and pressed them to his forehead. Daros bowed. The prince consort was already on his way out of the room.

Merian had been instructing young mages in the lesser arts. They, thank the gods, seemed barely shaken by the upheavals among their elders. As Daros paused by the door, he was nearly flattened by a swooping mageling, with a second in hot pursuit. He caught the first with his hands and the second with his magic, depositing the latter firmly on the nearest stool. He set the former beside her, smiled sunnily at both, and made his way through the swirl of airborne magelings.

Merian was in the midst of them, sitting at ease a man-height above the floor. She lifted a brow as Daros rose to join her, but did not pause in the flow of her instruction. He exercised himself to be patient, to listen; it was interesting, what she told them, and who knew? It might be useful.

It spoke well for the magelings that they barely blinked at the presence of a stranger. From the progression of whispers round the room, he would wager that any who had not known him when he came in would know him when the lesson ended.

Merian finished in leisurely fashion, admonished them to practice their lessons, and sent them out. Not all went willingly. Somewhat after the door had shut behind the last of them, Daros heard a squawk. One of the eavesdroppers had met the bite of Merian's wards.

"Tell me," she said.

"Surely you already know," said Daros.

"Only what Hani knows," she said. "He was with you, not in you. You think you've found some knowledge of the shadow?"

"Or something like it," Daros said. "I wasn't close enough to discover more."

"Can you go there?"

"Yes," he said with as much patience as he could muster.

She slanted a glance at him, but did not upbraid him for impudence. "Of course you can. Some of my masters of mages are tugging at the leash—they're clamoring to examine you, to discover everything that you can do. They'll wait till this is over, if there's a world left for any of us."

"I'm nothing remarkable," he said. "I'm an untrained, undisciplined mage; it's nothing more than that."

"We think it is," she said. "But there, we'll have that quarrel later. You'll lead an expedition of mages through your Gate. They will find what is to be found. You will guard the Gate."

He bit his tongue. He was sworn to her service; it was not his place to protest what orders she might give. But he had not surrendered his spirit. He spoke carefully, with, he hoped, a suitable degree of submission. "Will we leave soon?"

"Tonight," she said. "My mages are preparing themselves. If there is anything you would do—eat, rest—you should do it now. Your Gate will open at sunset."

"It will be dawn in those mountains," he said. "Do they want to invade the castle by day?"

"If the night's children are within," she said, "day is best."

He had to grant the wisdom of that. "May I have your leave to go?"

Her glance was suspicious, but she did not tax him with it. "Go," she said.

He ate; that was well thought of. He would rest when all was done. He found the mages in one of their halls, a room like the one in which Merian had instructed her pupils: wide, high, bright with light from its tall windows. There were six mages; they were all young, with the look of warriors rather than scholars. One, a woman of the Isles, was dancing in a shaft of sunlight, in a whirl of blades. No living hand wielded them; they hummed like a swarm of bees.

Daros walked carefully wide of those. The others prepared themselves in less dangerous ways, either sitting apart with eyes closed and mind focused inward, or conversing quietly by a window.

Those three looked up as he came toward them. No awe there, only a long, slow, measuring stare, and a slight curl of the lip from the yellow-haired Asanian with the well-worn weapons. He was not wearing either the robes or the veils, but his cheek bore the thin parallel scars of an Olenyas, a bred warrior. There were five scars: he ranked high, though not as high as the master of his order.

Daros had training in the arts of war; no one of royal or noble lineage could escape it. But he was not the prince of fighters that this man must be. He bowed slightly and smiled, a salute of sorts, and said, "Good day to you all."

They nodded or bowed in return, civil but no more. Even that was better than he had expected. "My name is Daros," he said. "If we're to fight and die together, should I know yours?"

They thought about it. At length the tall woman from the north named herself and each of her fellows. She was Irien; the Olenyas was Perel. The others were Kalyi of the Isles and Adin from the Hundred Realms and the twins Sharai and Lirai who had been born in Shurakan. They had the same face and accent as Hani and his father, or for that matter Daros' own mother.

"It is said," said Perel, "that you have no weight or substance whatsoever; that your spirit is a leaf blown on the wind."

Daros smiled. "It's also said that I've never left a woman unsatisfied or a tavernkeeper unpaid. Surely that counts for something?"

"We're trusting our lives to you," Kalyi said. "Tell us why we shouldn't be afraid."

"Of course you should," he said. "Fear will keep you honest. We know nothing of this place to which we go—only that dark powers built it and live in it still. I'll find what they keep, and learn what I may. May I trust you to protect me?"

"But you were not—" Irien began.

"Let him tell us," said Perel. "What is this plan of yours? Is it better than ours?"

"I have one use in the world," Daros said. "I'm a fine hunting hound. Whatever I seek, I find. Does any of you share that gift?"

They glanced at one another. All six were about him now, drawn together in a circle. It might be protection; it might be a threat. He chose not to be afraid.

"None of us is a hunter," Perel said. "We are all warrior-mages."

"Warriors to hunt a secret." Daros sighed, shrugged, smiled. "Ah well. I'll hunt, you'll guard. Who leads you?"

Their eyes slid toward Kalyi. He bowed to her. "Madam general. I will find the book or whatever it is that holds the knowledge we need. The rest is yours. Only be sure that when my hunt is over, all your troops are within reach. When we go, we'll go as fast as we can."

Again they exchanged glances. "Better," said Perel.

Irien lifted a shoulder in a shrug. "Certainly not worse. Though if he's our Gate, the last thing we want is to risk him in the fight."

"I'm not going to fight," Daros said. "I'm going to hunt. *You* will fight. Keep me safe, and bring us all out alive. That's all I ask of you."

"A simple thing," said Perel. "Indeed." Suddenly he grinned. "I like this plan."

"*She* won't," Kalyi said.

"She told us to trust the Gate," said Perel.

"So she did," Irien said. "Though I don't think she meant—"

"She meant that we should trust him," Perel said. "I'll risk it. After all, if he endangers us, it's a simple matter to kill him."

Daros laughed and applauded him. "A man after my own heart! Shall we two go, and leave the rest safe here?"

"You trust me as far as that?" Perel asked him with an arch of the brow.

Daros' flick of the hand took in the scars on Perel's cheek, and the number and quality of his weapons, both open and hidden. "I think I can trust you to keep me both safe and honest."

"We will all do that," Kalyi said grimly. "If you can rest, do it now. There's not much time left."

"Madam," said Daros with a bow and a flourish. Her glance was sour, but he thought there might be a hint, a merest glimmer, of softening about the mouth.

He would rest, for a while. They would not go without him: they could not. He was their Gate.

He went back to his room in Merian's house. It had been cleaned; the bed was fresh and scented with herbs. A bag waited by the door. He did not doubt that it was filled with whatever the servants had decided he would need.

He had been asleep on his feet, but once he lay down, he remained stubbornly awake. He was not afraid, not enough to trouble him. The Gate within had fixed on the place where he must go, but he was aware also, deep down, of the emperor's presence, nearly lost in shadow. Part of him wanted to go, to find Estarion, to bring him back. The rest knew that he could not do both at once.

He must have dozed: he opened his eyes, and Merian was sitting on the bed beside him. For a moment before she could have been aware that he had roused, he saw a face that she had not shown him before: soft, reflective, a little sad. He wanted to kiss her, to make the sadness go away.

She came to herself with all her armor intact, and the hard bright edge that forbade anything so familiar as a kiss. Because he was born contrary, he took her hand and kissed it, and held it to his heart. She let it rest there for the whole of a breath before she snatched it away. "Are you a general?" she demanded. "Or a lord of mages?"

He raised his brows. "Why, no. But I am a hunter."

"So I've been told." She knotted her fingers in her lap, glaring at them as if they had been as intractable as he. "You have no gift for obedience. I could bind you, and so compel it, but like an idiot, I prefer to trust your sworn word. Will you be obedient to Kalyi and do as she bids?"

"If her bidding isn't mad or suicidal, yes," he said.

She looked ready to slap him. She breathed deep, straightened her shoulders and face, and said, "She has convinced me to let you lead the expedition. But if she sees the need for a change, you will do exactly as she tells you. Do you understand?"

"Yes," he said. Then: "Is she in a great deal of trouble?"

"Not as much as you," she said. "Come back alive, with knowledge that we need, and I may—I may—forgive you both."

"Forgiveness is worth fighting for," he said. He kissed her hands again, quicker than she could elude him, and sprang to his feet. The shadows were growing long. He held out his hand. "Come with me," he said.

She was taken aback by his presumption, so much so that she had yielded before her wits recovered. He offered no insolence past that of taking her hand in his. Hand in hand they went to find the rest of the hunt.

NINE

THEY WERE ALL EXPECTING A RITE OR A GREAT WORKING. DAROS hated to disappoint them, but he needed his strength for what might come. The six of them gathered about him, linking arms in a circle, strong as a shieldwall. Merian reluctantly retreated. He was sorry to let go her hand, but this was a deadly thing they did. The imperial heir could not risk herself so recklessly.

He kept his eyes on her as he opened the Gate within. The last he saw of that place was her slender figure in the fading sunlight, the gold of hair and eyes washed over with the color of flame, or of blood.

He brought them to a sheltered place just below the crag, a hollow in the stone that was not quite deep enough to be a cave. Merian had warned them, but they were greatly disconcerted to travel so quickly, without resort to the worldroad.

There was a little time for them to recover while he ventured up the track that led from the hollow. It was not quite dawn; the air was thin and cold. He was glad of the cloak that he had brought from the Fells, and the small working that let him breathe here on the roof of the world.

He peered up the steep slope. The castle loomed above. No light shone from it; no banner flew from its turret. Yet there was life within, a flicker of living presence.

He looked for wards, but found nothing that spoke to him of any such thing. Did they trust in the remoteness of this place, and in the terror of its name?

"It could be a trap," Perel said, coming up beside him. He had recovered first of all the mages; he was still a little white about the lips, but his eyes were steady, staring upward. "They'll lure us in, then strip us of flesh and souls."

Daros shuddered in spite of himself. "You know something of them?"

"I've made a study of the dark arts," Perel said.

"Darkmagery?"

"Nothing so innocuous," said Perel. "Black sorcery, forbidden arts—we've banished them from the empire. But they're still alive in the world beyond our borders."

"So I see," Daros said.

The Olenyas looked him up and down. "You do, don't you? No wonder the mages are in such a taking. You're not supposed to exist. We want all our mages neatly bound up in packets and arranged on a shelf. Not racketing about the world, being much too strong for anyone's good."

"I hope to be worth something here," Daros said dryly. He cast his magic up like a line. Part of him was shuddering in instinctive horror; part was raising wards, forging armor of light. This was indeed kin to the thing beyond Gates. It drew its strength from the old dark powers, from blood and putrefying flesh, from sacrifice of the living soul, and from surrender of all light to the devouring dark.

One learned in the Hundred Realms to understand the dark as soul's twin to the light, bound together with it, inextricable and inevitable. Without dark there could be no light; without light, the dark could not endure. This was nothing so beautiful or so balanced. It was to the Dark Goddess, and darkmagery, as diseased and rotting flesh to the clean-picked bones of the vulture's prey. It was a perversion, a sickness.

He had never understood the old zeal of the priests of the Sun against the powers of the dark. When he heard tales of the Sunborn, Merian's firstfather, that told of his relentless hatred of all that was of the dark, he had been suitably censorious; for after all, as great a king and conqueror as the man had been, his beliefs had been sorely mis-guided. Now at last Daros saw what the Sunborn must have seen.

He swallowed bile, gagging on it, and forced himself to look at what crouched above. It was a fortress of age-worn stone, built into the crag. He counted a score of living beings within—men, he thought, though he could not be sure. They were bound with cords of darkness.

He was not hunting men, even men whose souls had been walled forever against the light. He needed knowledge—truth of what had overwhelmed the worlds. If not a book, then an image, a song, an inscription, anything at all.

The mages had recovered: he sensed them behind him. He did not turn to look at them. Wordlessly he began to climb.

Long before he came to the top, he knew that this place needed no pro-tection but itself. The track was narrow, and in places sheer. It needed the agility of a mountain cat, or of a mage, to ascend that path. The slightest slip or slackening would cast him down a thousand man-lengths, and shatter him among the crags.

The castle was aware of him. Its people, no; he would have sworn to that. But the stones themselves, and the darkness woven through them, knew that a stranger had come.

He made himself as small and as harmless as he could: innocuous, insignificant, no danger at all. He cloaked himself in that surety. He was a breath of wind gusting up the mountain, a glimmer of sunlight falling across the gate.

A firm hand of magic closed about him. "Let me," Kalyi said. He resisted; he had not learned to trust anyone else's power. But he was not altogether a fool. He relinquished the wards and the shield to her, however reluctantly, and turned again to his hunt.

The gate was wrought of iron, enormous and impossibly heavy. Yet it was balanced so lightly that if it happened to be unbarred, the thrust of a hand could shift it. Perel and Irien moved past the rest, laying hands on it, raising powers that made the small hairs prickle along Daros' arms and down his spine. The wall and tower above them seemed to stir in its sleep, half-rousing, opening a blurred eye and peering down.

They passed through the gate as if through a wall of mist. There was darkness within, thick and palpable, and a faint charnel stink. The mortar that bound these stones had been mixed with blood.

They paused in a shadowed court. At a glance from Kalyi, the twins slipped away along the colonnade. Adin and Irien went ahead. Kalyi, with Perel, stood still by the gate, enfolding Daros in the cloak of their magic.

Daros sighed faintly, trying not to breathe too deep of the tainted air. The walls, the tower above him, even the brightening sky, weighed heavy on his spirit.

He turned slowly. The heaviness was stronger—there. Ahead and to the left, toward a corner of the colonnade. His guardian hounds went with him, Perel ahead, Kalyi behind. His shoulderblades tightened. But her knives were not for him—not while he served her order's purposes.

It was a great effort to set one foot in front of the other, to go deeper into the maw of the castle, and not turn and run. He was aware in his skin of the twins in a dim hall, wrapped in shadows, watching as a skein of men with shaved heads and black robes wound, chanting, among the pillars. The shiver along his ribs was the presence of Irien and Adin, seeing to it that the way ahead was clear: dim passages, sudden turnings, ascents or descents that seemed set at random to catch the unwary.

They had begun to veer off the track, diverted without knowing it, shifted subtly aside by the power that waited in the castle's heart. He could warn them, or he could follow the straight way and let them be drawn to some semblance of safety.

His own guards slowed little by little, almost imperceptibly. He caught a hand of each, and set a spark in each mind: a binding to follow him wherever he led. Perel yielded to it with a twist of wry amusement. Kalyi resisted; but Daros was in no mood to be gentle. She, thank the gods, had wits enough to give way before she broke, though he would pay for his presumption.

Better to face her wrath later than to pay for her weakness now. His companions' rites and vows made them vulnerable. The power here knew mages and priests of the Sun, and turned on them as on an enemy. Daros it seemed not to perceive at all. He was small, he was harmless, he carried no taint of the Sun's priesthood. It took no more notice of him than of a rat in the wall.

Even ignored, he felt the power growing darker, deeper, eating away at his memory of light. He must come to the center of it, but whether he would be alive then, or sane, he did not know. He could only press forward.

These halls were deserted. The order must once have been numerous and strong: the castle was ample to house hundreds, even thousands. The score that were left huddled together in a tower near the outer wall.

There were guards ahead of him, but they were not human. They crouched like great beasts athwart the path that he must follow. Their eyes were shut, their bodies still; they might have been carved of stone. Yet they were alive, although they slept. Their dreams were all of the terrible light, how it burned, how it destroyed what they were bound to protect.

He was a shadow, a breath of wind, a skitter of leaf across the floor.

The sun did not stain him. The light did not rule him. He was utterly a part of this place and this darkness.

The guardians of the secret crouched on either side of its door. To the eye they were a pair of stone lions, each sitting upright, one paw uplifted, one resting on the globe of the world. Their eyes were living darkness.

Daros paused between them. They focused outward, not on him at all, and yet the force of their watchfulness buckled his knees. It was all he could do to shield himself and his companions, and walk forward, and keep both his fear and his purpose buried deep.

The door had no earthly substance. It melted before him. The heart of the darkness was almost painfully ordinary. It was a room, bare, with no beauty of carving or gilding. There was no inscription, no carving or painting, no book, nothing that might contain knowledge as his people understood it. Only a wooden table such as one might see in any poor man's house, and on the table a bowl no more beautiful than the room. It was made of unfired clay, the color of drab earth, and not well shaped, either; its rim was crooked, and it sat awry.

Kalyi moved away from Daros. He reached too late to pull her back. The shield stretched and snapped. She staggered and fell to her hands and knees in front of the table.

The thing that came down had neither shape nor substance. It seemed to grow out of the bowl, pouring over the table, hovering above Kalyi's bent head. It reared like a snake. Daros cried out, scrambling together his power. The dark thing struck.

He leaped, not at Kalyi, but at the table. The bowl writhed in his hands like a living thing. He could see—he could feel—know—understand—

He thrust the bowl at Perel and spun. The dark thing coiled about Kalyi. He struck it with an arrow of pure light.

It burst asunder. The floor rocked underfoot.

"The book!" Perel cried. "Where—"

Daros gathered all six of them together, wherever in the fortress they were. Something was surging up from below, some child of old Night, waking from a long sleep to a terrible wrath.

"Take the bowl," Daros said to Perel, quite calmly. "Bring it to her. The secret is in it. Tell her."

"But—"

Daros silenced him with a lift of the hand. The truth was as clear as daylight, as sharp as a sword. It was in the bowl, which contained all the world. He knew where he must go. What he must do . . . that would come to him in time.

The Gate in him was open. It must be shut before the child of Night came up out of the earth. He thrust Merian's mages through, and the bowl with them. The floor bucked under him; he struggled to keep his feet. The Gate had begun to fray.

His heart was hammering. He sucked in a breath and leaped. Even as the Gate swallowed him, the tower crumbled in ruin. A vast maw opened below, jagged with teeth. The castle whirled down into the oblivion to which it had been consecrated.

Daros too fell into dark, but it was no earthly night. The devourer of Gates had found him. Only one spark of light offered refuge. He spun toward it. Darkness clawed at him. It burned like hot iron, shredding flesh and spirit. He twisted wildly. The spark was close—so close—if he overshot it—if he fell short—

Hope was all he had, and knowledge that had flooded into him when he touched the bowl, knowledge more complete than could ever have been written in a book. He clung to it as he whirled down through the darkness.

TEN

THE TOWN WAS CALLED WASET. IT WAS A GREAT CITY IN THIS country, this narrow line of green between the river and the desert. To Estarion's eye it was little larger than a village, full of small brown people like none he had seen before. They were somewhat like the people of the Nine Cities, but browner, thinner, with long dark eyes in sharp-cut faces. They chattered like birds as he passed, staring, pointing, running after him. And yet the oddity of his breeding that had vexed him all his life, Asanian eyes in the northern face, did not frighten them at all.

They were calling him a god. Gods to them wore the bodies of men and the faces of beasts and birds; he, taller than any man they knew and darker by far, with his eagle's beak and his lion-eyes, was perfectly in keeping with their belief.

Tanit was the queen of these people. There was sorrow in her, for she had lost her husband to the things that ruled the night, but she was not consumed by grief. Estarion, searching in her eyes for the image of a memory, saw a man rather too much older than she for easy companionship, loved more like an uncle than a lover, but she had felt herself well served by the bargain.

Estarion understood royal marriages. He had had nine properly noble wives, and had loved a commoner whom he could not marry. Of all the things that made a man, love was the one he had thought of least since he left his empire behind. Now he could not help but think of it; he had thought of it since first he saw the queen bending over him, with her odd and striking beauty and the clear light of her spirit shining through.

This was a hot country. The women dressed sensibly for the heat: wrappings of thin white cloth about their bodies, baring the breasts more often than not, or if they were young or servants, they went naked but for a cord about the middle. They were easily, casually delighted to be women, and they loved to be admired. Those whose eyes he caught were more likely to smile than to turn away.

Tanit would not meet his glance, unless he startled her into looking up. Yet of them all, only she drew his eye, and she held it for much longer than was proper. She was not the most beautiful and she was far from the most alluring, but when she was there, he could see no other woman.

She saw him settled in her palace, which would have been a middling poor lord's house in his empire, but it was reckoned very great here. Her servants were as adept as he could ask for, and the house was clean—bright and airy, with painted pillars and a courtyard full of flowers. The food they served him was simple, harsh gritty bread and thin sour beer; they promised a feast later, but this was part of the rite of welcome.

He ate and drank for courtesy, and because he was hungry and thirsty. The servants kept changing. They were all making excuses to wait on him, to look on the god who had come from beyond the horizon.

It had been a long while since he was in a palace, but old habits died hard. The manner, the smile, the habit of charming servants, because servants could make a lord's life either effortlessly easy or unbearably difficult, wrapped about him like an old familiar mantle.

He was offered a bath and a clean kilt; the servants there were women, and young, and frank in their approval. They made him laugh, and be as glad as ever that his blushes never showed.

The queen found him so, clean and decorously kilted, with a pair of maids taking turns combing his new-washed hair. It was thick and it curled exuberantly, even wet; it gave them occasion for much merriment. On a whim he had let them shave his beard with their sharp flaked-stone razors; it had been long years since his cheeks were bare to the world, but in this heat he was glad of it, even as odd and naked as it felt.

He was rubbing his newly smooth chin when she came. Her stride checked; her eyes widened a fraction. That surprised him. He did not share the curse of excessive beauty that beset the boy from Han-Gilen, but it seemed that the canons were different here. She was frankly enthralled; and that made him blush.

She recovered more quickly than he. He was a god, after all, her shrug said. Her words were properly polite. "I trust my lord is well served?"

"Very well, my lady," he said.

She bowed slightly, regally. She had not the piquant prettiness so common here; her features were more distinctly carved, her face longer, more oval, her nose long and slightly arched. Her skin was like cream intermixed with honey. She was beautiful, and yet she did not know it at all. In her own mind she was gawky, gangling, too long of limb and plain of face to be anything but passable.

He would change that canon. It was fair recompense for her conviction that he was as beautiful as a god. He smiled and bowed slightly where he sat, and said, "Your pardon, lady, that I can't rise to do proper reverence. Your maids are lovely tyrants."

"I did command them to do their best for you," she said with her eyes lowered, but her voice had a smile in it.

"Sit, then, lady, and ease my captivity."

She sat on a stool near the bath, perched on its edge as if poised for flight. As she settled there, a small brown animal came stalking through the door.

It was a cat, or a creature like a cat; but unlike the palace cats of Starios, who had been large enough for a child to ride, this one was hardly longer than Estarion's forearm. Nonetheless it had the same keen intelligence and the same white-hot core of magic. It, unlike the humans here, would meet his eyes, gold to gold; it blinked slowly, deliberately, and said, *"Mao."*

"Mao," he replied gravely.

The cat blinked again and crossed the room in three long leaping strides. The third launched it into his lap. He hissed as it landed; its claws were needle-sharp. But he did not recoil, nor would he ever have flung the cat off.

It unhooked its claws from his stinging thigh and sat, and began to bathe itself with great concentration. It did not mind that he ran a finger down from its ears to its tail, finding its fur smooth and pleasingly soft. He found a spot that itched; it began to purr, as loud almost as one of his long-gone ul-cats.

As if that were a signal, a second cat, larger and somewhat darker, appeared from a corner that had been empty an instant before. It coiled about his feet, purring even more loudly than the first.

"The god and goddess welcome you," Tanit said. She sounded unsurprised and rather pleased.

The maids were less circumspect. "Now we know you're truly to be trusted," said the impudent one with the flower in her hair.

"I'm honored to be approved by such noble judges," Estarion said.

"So you should be," said Tanit. "These are the divine ones, the gods who walk in fur. They graciously accept our service, and bless us with their presence."

"Yes," Estarion said. "I see the fire of heaven in them. They're powers in your world."

"They are gods," she said.

He inclined his head and slanted a smile that caught her before she was aware. She smiled back. It was a wonderful smile, brightly wicked, though all too swiftly suppressed.

It was not time yet to touch her, but he could say, "Beautiful one, you should never hide your splendor. It well becomes a queen."

Her lips set in a thin line. "There is no need to flatter me, my lord."

"I tell you the truth," he said.

She rose abruptly. "Come, my lord. The feast is waiting."

His hair was combed but not plaited. He bound it out of his face with a bit of golden cord, and let the rest be. She was already at the door. He followed her with an escort of cats: both of the gods-in-fur of this place had elected to follow him.

It was good to be favored by cats again. He would like to be favored by the queen; but that, the gods willing, would come.

The court of Waset was waiting for him in a hall of painted pillars, seated at tables banked with flowers. The mingled scents of flowers and unguents and humanity were almost overpowering. He did his best to breathe shallowly as he walked down the length of the hall, beside and a little behind the queen.

The courtiers were not as open in their admiration as the children of the city, but they were wide-eyed enough. He saw the marks of grief on many of them, scars of loss and remnants of shadow. As fierce as the sun of this world was, it still had to give way to night; and in the night came the terror.

But it was daylight still, and they gathered in a guarded city. They dined on roast ox and fresh-baked bread and fruits of the earth, flavors both familiar and unfamiliar, and one great joy of sweetness. This world like his own had honey, and that was very well indeed.

They did not have wine; he regretted that. Their beer was a taste he had no great yearning to acquire. But he endured it. He had eaten and drunk worse in his day, and lived to tell of it.

He was not asked to entertain this court. That was for the musicians and the dancers, the singers with the voices like mating cats, and last of all, as the shadows lengthened, the small wizened man in the white kilt, whose voice was larger than all the rest of him put together.

He told the tale of the darkness. "It began to come upon us in the days of our late king, may he live for everlasting. There had always been walkers in the night, powers that had no love for the day, but this was a new thing, a terrible thing. It came out of the lands of the dead, from the horizons to the west, running with jackals in the night and vanishing with the coming of the day.

"For a long while no one knew it for what it was. The night was as dark as ever, and there are lions, crocodiles, nightwalkers and things that snatch children from their mothers' arms as they sleep. But this was stronger, darker, hungrier. It crept through villages and stole all the men and women who were young and strong, and slaughtered the weak and the children. Men would wake to find their gardens stripped bare or their herds gone, and the herdsmen gutted and cast before the doors of their houses.

"When our king had been on his throne for two hands of years, the night that had been perilous became truly terrible. Until then the dark things had never come close to the city; they skulked along the edges and raided the border villages, but round about our walls, men were safe. In that year, the dark things raided closer, and took more men and women, and in their wake left a hideous slaughter.

"Word came in from Gebtu, from Ta-senet, from Ombos—even from the chieftains of the south. They were all beset. It was everywhere, that horror. Traders were few on the river; they no longer came from far away. Every man was driven into his own town or city. Each kingdom had no choice but to protect its own. Trade, embassies, even wars and quarrels—all were ended. The world had closed in upon itself, and we were shut within our own boundaries like cattle within the fences of a field.

"Here in Waset, as everywhere, people had begun to take refuge in the city, and little by little the villages emptied of their weak and their fearful. The brave and the obstinate remained, and fools who swore that there was nothing walking the night. But none of them walked or sailed far, not any longer.

"In that tenth year of the king's reign, the river's flood that gives us the rich black earth for the tilling, was the lowest that it had been in the memory of the oldest of the river-god's priests. It barely rose above its banks, barely dampened the edges of the fields. The gods' curse was on us, and for all that we did to propitiate them, they only sent us a plague on the cattle and an army of walkers in the night.

"The enemy had no face. It was shadow incarnate, darkness visible. It had no name to give it substance; it was living nothingness. But in that void were claws, and teeth to rend both flesh and souls.

"A priest went out one night. He was a very holy man, consecrated to our lord the sun, and the light of the god was upon him. He thought to speak with this thing if he might, to discover what it was, and perhaps to bless it and invoke the grace of the god upon it, and either overcome or destroy it.

"They found him in the morning with no drop of blood in his body, and his head sundered from it and laid in his lap as he sat against the wall of the city. His eyes had been taken away, made as if they had never been. To this day, men who saw it wake screaming from their sleep."

There was a silence. Tears ran down the queen's face, tracking through the paint which she wore like a warrior's armor. Estarion did not mean to trespass, but her pain was so strong, her memory so distinct, that he saw what she saw: not the priest who had died before she came to be the king's bride, but the king himself, drained of blood as the priest had been, but not only his head was severed and his eyes unmade. Each separate limb was torn from the rest. They had found every part of him except one, and that seemed a brutal mockery: his manly organ was lost, nor was it ever found.

All of those who went out with him were gone, save the men who had been nearest him. They had heard nothing, seen nothing in the suffocating darkness, until it was gone and the dawn had come. They were alone, with their king strewn at their feet.

"No one knows what this is," the queen said at length, "or what it wants of us or of the world. The dark gods—they want blood and souls. Their needs are simple, their rites known, though spoken of in whispers. This seems to want what the dark gods want, but all efforts to propitiate it have only made the night more terrible. Sometimes it lets a fool or a wanderer live, or satisfies itself with the stripping of a field or the running of a herd. It has no pattern to it, no weaving of earthly sense."

"And yet," said a portly personage who sat not far from the queen, "it is not random or capricious, like the wind across the red land. It has will; it has malice, living and potent. None of us has power to stand against it."

That was manifestly true. The only magic here resided in the cats who deigned to share Estarion's lap. There were priests in the hall, but they were not mages; nor was there a mage anywhere among these people. They were defenseless against any power that chose to advance against them.

No, he thought; not altogether. The sun's light protected them, and it seemed that the walls of the city had some power, too, or else the enemy did not choose, yet, to pass through them.

They were all staring at him. His expression must be alarming. He smoothed it and said, "I don't know what power I have against this; but whatever I do have, I place at your disposal."

They glanced at one another. These were courtiers, nobles and priests, and like all their kind, they were born suspicious. "Suppose," said one of those nearest the queen—not the priest who had spoken before, but an elegant man in a heavy golden collar—"that you tell us who and what you are, and why you have come. With all due respect, of course," he said, bowing in his seat.

Estarion bowed in return. "I come from beyond your horizon. My name is difficult for your tongue to encompass. Your lady has named me

Seramon; that will do, if it pleases you. I am a priest of the Sun, and the Sun is my forefather. I was hunting shadow on the other side of your sky, and found it lapping the shores of this world. My own world is not yet threatened, but will be soon. If it can be stopped here—if it can be driven back—" He drew a breath. "What I am . . . have you workers of magic here?"

"Indeed," said the priest, "we work magic, who serve the gods."

Estarion raised a brow. He could hardly call the man a liar, but there was not one grain of honest magic in that well-fed body. "May I ask what you reckon among the magical arts?"

"He's a spy!" someone cried, back among the pillars. "He wants to know our powers, so that he can destroy us."

"I have no fear," said the priest, although his breath had quickened a fraction. "Am I to understand, lord, that you also are a worker of magic?"

"I am," said Estarion. "And you?"

"I am a master of the hidden arts," said the priest. "In the morning, perhaps we may meet in a less public place, and speak as master to master?"

"I would be honored," Estarion said.

"Show us now!" cried the man who had spoken before. He had come out from the pillars and stood in the light: a young man no older than Daros, with the passion of youth and the suspicion of a much older and wiser man. "Show us what you are. But promise us one thing: that you'll harm none of us here. Swear to it!"

Estarion bowed to that wisdom, however headlong the expression of it. "I will not harm you," he said. "You have my word."

"By the Sun your father?"

"By the Sun my forefather," Estarion said.

He rose. Some of those closest drew away, but Tanit sat still, watching in silence. He stepped down from the dais into the space where the dancers had been. It was empty now, lit by a shaft of sunlight through the open door. It was still some time until evening, but the shadows were growing long. All too soon, the night's terror would come.

He gathered the light in his hands and wove it as if it had been a garland of flowers. Breaths caught round the hall; he smiled. It was a simple magic, such as a child could perform, but it awed these courtiers. He bowed and presented his crown of light to the queen, offering it with a smile.

She stared at it. It shimmered, taking life from the Sun in his hand, the burning golden brand of his line. Slowly she stretched out her finger to touch the crown. It did not burn; that startled her. She lifted it with sudden decision, in hands that trembled just visibly. "It is beautiful," she said.

"Beauty for beauty," said Estarion. He flicked a finger. The crown lifted out of her hands and settled on her brows. Brave woman: she did not flinch.

He smiled sweetly at them all. "As for the great workings and displays of higher powers, I beg your indulgence; among my people they are not reckoned among the entertainments proper to a royal banquet."

"And why not?" the young man demanded. "Is there truly nothing else you can do?"

"Hardly," Estarion said.

"Then show us!"

Estarion sighed. He had been a fool to do as much as he had; it forced him to play out the game. He paused to gather the threads of his power. People were stirring, beginning to mutter. The boy with the loud voice curled his lip.

He never said what he had been going to say. Estarion brought down the lightning.

He broke nothing, burned nothing. When all of them could see again, they stared at the floor in front of him. In it was set the image of the Sun in his hand, as broad as his outstretched arms, gleaming like molten gold.

He raked his glare across the lot of them. "What more would you have, my lords? Shall I cleave the tiles under your feet? Lift the roof and leave you naked to the sky?"

"No," the boy stammered. "No, no, my lord. Please pardon—I didn't know—"

"Of course you didn't," Estarion said with edged gentleness.

That ended the banquet: even without the shock he had given it, the sun was sinking low. Those who did not live in the palace were eager to be home before the fall of dark. It could not be said that they fled, but they left quickly, without lingering over their farewells.

In a very little while, there was only Estarion in the hall, and the servants waiting to clear away the tables, and Tanit sitting like an ivory image. Her crown of sunlight had not faded with the day; it shone more brightly than lamps or torches.

He took her hands and lifted her unresisting to her feet. She looked up into his face—rather a long way, for although she was tall for a woman of her people, that was not even as high as his shoulder. But he never thought of her as small. She had a queen's spirit, high and proud.

"You are a king of your people," she said as if it had only just occurred to her.

"I was," he admitted, "somewhat more than a king."

"I see it," she said, "like a shining mantle. You left it, yes? To become a god."

He laughed in spite of himself. "I left to become a rootless wanderer, and then a shepherd. I'm no great lord of any world now."

"A god is somewhat more than a lord," she said. "You were sent to save us. The others don't understand. They're afraid. But you would never do us harm."

"I would hope not," he said.

The cats came padding down the table, among the plates and cups and empty bowls. The she-cat leaped to his shoulder; the he-cat sprang into her arms.

No magic? Maybe not as his own world would reckon it. But this queen of the people had power in no little measure. He paid it due reverence.

ELEVEN

WITH THE COMING OF NIGHT, SERVANTS DREW SHUTTERS across the windows of the palace and hung amulets and charms on the lintels of the doors. Priests walked the walls, chanting and sending up clouds of incense. Guards took station in strong-walled towers. The bright and airy city of the day became the fortress city of the night.

After so many years, there were few left who could not sleep even amid such fear. Estarion would sleep soon, but first he had to know what the night was in this world. He saw the queen to her rooms, but did not go at once to that which he had been given. He went up instead, to the roof.

The last light was fading from the sky. He saw the jagged line of cliffs across the river to the west, blacker than black, limned in deep blue and fading rose. Stars crowded the vault of heaven, not so bright as those he had known, but far more numerous, scattered like sand across a blue-black shore. This world had but one moon, smaller than Brightmoon, and wan; it rode high, but what light it cast was dim and pallid.

There was no other light in the world. The city was dark, walled against the night. Children here had grown to bear or beget children of their own, without ever seeing stars or moon.

Nothing yet stained the darkness. The night was clean, for a while. Not far away, a bird hooted softly, calling to its mate. Across the river he heard yipping and howling. Jackals, those would be: creatures like shrunken direwolves, scavengers and eaters of carrion.

Tonight he did not wait for the shadow. He was more weary than he had wanted anyone to know. He would rest, if he could, and in the morning, call on the priest who laid claim to magic.

He slept after all, as deeply as if drugged. If he dreamed, he did not remember. When he woke, the shutters were open; sunlight poured into the room. Servants were waiting to tend him, and there was breakfast: the perpetual bread and beer.

He felt sleepy and slow, but he roused as he ate. He must be as keen of wit as he could be before he faced the priests. They, even more than courtiers, drove straight to the heart of any weakness.

The servants saw to it that he was dressed in kilt and belt and broad pectoral of gold and colored stones. They plaited his hair with ropes of gold and red and blue, and painted his eyes in the fashion of their people. They declared him beautiful then, and fit to be seen, but insisted that he not go alone.

"That would not be proper," said the eldest of them, a man much wizened by years but still bright of eye. He crooked a finger at one of his subordinates, young and strong and as tall as men grew here. "You belong to him. Serve him well, or pay the price which I exact."

The young man blanched slightly, but bowed and acquiesced. He

carried a fan and a rod like a shepherd's staff, and walked ahead with an
air of granting his charge great consequence.

Estarion was glad of the guide, and somewhat amused by the swag-
ger the man put in his stride. He reminded Estarion a little of Daros, in
his youth and bravado and his conviction that if he must be anything, it
must be bold and bad.

The city had a temple for each of its nine greater gods, and a lesser
temple or shrine for a myriad more. The temple of the sun was the
largest and highest, a good three man-heights of hewn stone in this city
of mudbrick and reed thatch. Its walls were thickly and brilliantly
painted, inside and out; whole worlds of story were drawn there, tales of
gods and kings.

Estarion, priest of another sun in another sky, found this place
remarkably familiar. Its priests wore no torques like the one he had
given to the altar of the god when he left his throne, and they shaved
their heads and wore no beast's flesh or wool, only cream-pale linen and
reed sandals. Yet their chants and the scent of their incense recalled the
rites of his own god; their temple with its progression of courts was
rather like the Temple of the Sun in his own city.

He was at ease but not complacent when they came to what must be
the shrine. It was a long hall, its roof held up by heavy pillars; a stone
image stood at the far end, and before it the table of an altar.

Priests stood in ranks in front of that altar. They were all dressed in
simple linen, all shaven smooth: row on row of shining brown heads. The
priest whom he had met at the banquet was seated behind and somewhat
above them, surrounded by a circle of older and more august priests.

It seemed Estarion merited a full conclave. He decided to be flattered
rather than alarmed. There was no more magic here than there had been
in the queen's hall; what little there was, he could attribute to the cat
which, having followed him from the palace, now walked haughtily
ahead of him down that long march of pillars.

He halted at sufficient distance to keep all of them in sight. The cat
sat tidily at his feet. It was the he-cat; he had, between last night and

this morning, acquired a ring of gold in his ear. It gave him a princely and rather rakish look.

The priests regarded all of them, Estarion and the cat and the servant with the staff and the fan, as if they had been the children of Mother Night herself. They had heard the tale of the banquet from the one of their number who had seen it with his own eyes. They were afraid; and fear, in any mass of men, was dangerous.

Estarion smiled at them. "Good morning to you," he said.

The priest from the banquet bowed stiffly. The rest did not move or speak. They were a guard, Estarion began to understand; a shieldwall. Those whom they protected might have laid claim to a dim and barely perceptible glimmer of power. In Estarion's world it would not have sufficed to make its bearer even the least of mages, but here, maybe, it was remarkable.

Two of them boasted this ghost-flicker. One was an old man, toothless and milkily blind. The other was hardly more than a child. Estarion inclined his head to each. "My lords," he said.

The young one started visibly. The elder's clouded eyes turned toward Estarion and widened. Estarion saw himself reflected there: a pillar of light, towering in the darkness.

The old man came down from the dais. The younger one made as if to guide his steps, but he took no notice. He could see all that he needed to see. He stopped within reach, peering up, for he was very small and shriveled, and Estarion was very much taller than he. "You," he said in a thin old voice, "are nothing so simple as a god. I cry your pardon for the foolishness of my son; there are some with eyes to see, but he is not one of them. He does mean well, lord. Do believe that."

"I believe it," Estarion said. The plump priest, he noticed, was struggling to keep his temper at bay.

"We will not be mountebanks for you," the old man said, "nor strive to awe you with our poor powers. Some of us may be willing to learn what you can teach. Most will refuse, and I think rightly. Men cannot and should not pretend to the powers of gods."

Estarion bowed as low as to a brother king. "I see that there are wise men in this country," he said.

"Ah," said the old priest, shaking off the compliment. "I don't call wisdom what's only common sense. Any one of us can turn a staff into a snake, or water into blood—but you, lord, could overturn the river into the sky, and set the fish to dancing. We'd all be wasting ourselves on trifles. There's only one thing I would ask of you."

"Yes?" said Estarion.

"Promise," said the priest, "that whatever you do here, whatever you came for, you will do no harm to our people or our queen."

"I do promise," Estarion said.

"I believe," said the priest, "that you will try to keep that promise. Break it even once, however excellent your reasons, and even as weak as we are beside you, we will do our best to exact the price that such betrayal deserves."

"That is a fair judgment," said Estarion.

"Good," the priest said. "Good. This gathering was meant to cow you, of course, and overwhelm you with numbers and power; but I do hope that it helps you to understand: we serve the gods and the city, and the queen's majesty. As long as you do the same, we are allies."

The alternative was perfectly clear. "I see we understand one another," Estarion said. "That's well. I too am a priest of the Sun. It would be a great grief if we could find no common ground."

"You must tell us of your rites and your order," the priest said, "as far as you may, of course. But not this moment. My brothers have duties that they've been neglecting in order to put on this show of force, and I don't doubt that you have things that need doing. May we speak again under less nervous circumstances?"

"Certainly we may," said Estarion with honest warmth. "Good day, reverend sir, and may your god bless and keep you."

"And yours," said the old priest: "may he hold you in his hand."

* * *

Estarion had much to ponder after he left that place. Not least was the plump priest's expression as Estarion and the old man parted on the best of terms. There would be war in the temple after this, he had no doubt. He had been sorely tempted to stop it with a blast of cleansing fire, but it was neither the place nor the time for such excesses. He must trust that the old man could look after himself, and hope that the city and the queen were not forced to pay for the outcome.

He said as much to her that afternoon when she had taken a few moments' rest in the garden of her palace. She was dressed for the day in court, in fine linen and a great deal of gold; her face was a mask of artful paint. She still had the loose, free stride of a hunter or a warrior as she walked down the path from the pool to the little orchard that grew along the wall.

"Seti is neither as feeble nor as innocent as he seems," she said. "He was high priest for more years than I can count; when he handed the staff to his son—yes, that fat fool is the heir of his body—he surrendered no part of his actual power. If he approves you, the rest will follow. Some may snarl and snap, but none of them is strong enough to stand against Seti."

"Or so you can hope," Estarion said.

"So I know," she said, politely immovable.

Estarion bowed to her knowledge of the place and the people. "I'm a difficult guest, I know. I hope I've not created factions that will bring you grief."

"There are always factions," she said. "This may bring out one or two that we had been needing to know of."

"There is that," he granted her.

She passed under the shade of the trees, which was a little cooler than the fierce heat of the sun, and inspected the green fruit clustered on a branch. Her gown clung tightly to her body, so sheer and so delicately woven that it concealed nothing, only made it all the more beautiful. Her blue-black hair was plaited in a myriad small plaits, some strung with beads of gold or lapis or carnelian; they swung together as she moved, brushing her bare shoulders.

He would have loved to touch them, to run his fingers over the sweet curve of them, and know the softness of her skin. He was startled to discover just how keenly he wanted it.

She would not thank him for the liberty. He kept his hands to himself. She seemed to have forgotten him, but he sensed the spark of her awareness. She knew exactly where he was and what he did there.

He wandered back toward the pool, in part to test her, in part to cool his feet. The water was not particularly cool, but it was cooler than the air. He laved his face and arms, and stroked the bright fish that came crowding about him. They slid over his fingers with oiled smoothness, butting him with their heads but offering no insolence.

They seemed content in their captivity. He was not. This world was lovely, even with the heat; its people were well worth knowing. Yet he was not one of them. The shadow's strength had grown even in the scarce day's span since he fell out of it onto the harsh red earth. Whatever had held it back through a king's reign and into the reign of a queen was fading fast. His fault, maybe, for falling through the Gate. Maybe he had drawn the darkness' attention; maybe he had shown it a clearer way in.

There were no rents in the fabric of the world. The Gate through which he had come was gone, swallowed up in his deepest self. The tide of shadow darkened his sense of the stars, though it did not yet dim the sun.

He withdrew into himself and sighed. He was no nearer than before to knowing what the shadow was. What hope he had of defending this world, he did not know; he did hope that it was not too arrogant to think that he had been sent here, that the gods had given him this task. His own world, however great his fear for it, was as well defended as a world could be. It had hundreds, thousands of mages; it had its god-born rulers. It was a great fortress and deep well of magic. This world had, as far as he could tell, one lone Sunborn mage from beyond the sky, a tribe of small mageborn cats, and no more. Unless a warm heart and a strong spirit could be enough, the people here had no defense.

"If that scowl is for me," said the queen, "I'd best call my guards."

Estarion blinked and focused. Her face was stern, but her eyes were glinting. He found a smile for her and put away the scowl. "Do please forgive me," he said. "I was pondering imponderables."

"It looked as if they might be unthinkable."

"That, too," he said. He groaned, stretched, creaked. "Is there a place where a man may go to practice with weapons?"

"The court of the guards," she said. "I'll have you taken there. Is there a particular weapon that you prefer?"

"Something strenuous," he said. "I feel a need to wear myself out."

"You will certainly do that, at this time of day," she said. "Will you listen to a simple native, and hear another way? It's cool and pleasant on the river, and the cooks are always glad of fresh fowl for the pots. Will you come hunting with me?"

"Sitting at leisure in a boat? Lady, you're very kind, but—"

"You can take an oar if it suits your fancy."

It was a tempting prospect. Estarion loved boats and rivers and fishing; he was not averse to hunting waterfowl, either. But when he let loose the smile that tugged at his lips, it was for her, the beautiful one, that he said, "Very well. I yield to the royal command."

Estarion wielded an oar with skill that came back to him as he went on. At first he scandalized the boatmen, but when they saw that he knew what he was doing, they gave way grudgingly to his whim.

The boat was made of reeds, and floated high on the water. There was a high pointed prow and a high stern, and a canopy amidships, beneath which the queen and her escort could take their ease. Estarion chose not to indulge himself. He sweated in the sun with the rest of the oarsmen, pulling in unison to the beat of a drum.

It was good clean work, and it soothed him wonderfully. The tension poured out of him; the knot in his belly loosened. The thoughts and fears that had roiled in his head were quiet for once.

It was better than sleep, that day on the river. They brought back a boatload of waterfowl and the carcass of a young river-beast: a rich hunt and welcome. The river had been kind; they had lost no man or boat, nor even an oar, to crocodiles, and their quarry had been too numerous to count, all but flinging themselves on the hunters' arrows.

"He brings us luck," Estarion heard one of the boatmen say. They were all cordial now; he had proved himself to them, though he had done it with perfect selfishness. He had only wanted to lighten the burden that had fallen on him.

They all ate well that evening, but as before, with the coming of dark, everyone fled to the safety of his own walls. Estarion did not linger, either. His arms and shoulders ached; his hands stung with blisters. Yet he was wide awake, and he felt remarkably well refreshed, as if he had slept a whole night through.

He let himself be put to bed, to mollify the servants. Well after they had gone, he lay where they had left him. The sounds of the palace died one by one. Voices quieted, footsteps ceased. The strains of a flute, which had come and gone since he came in from the hall, slowly faded away.

He rose softly and put on a kilt, and took up the weapons he had brought from the other side of the sky: knife and short sword, bow and quiver, all made with metals that were not known here.

It was still light as he passed through deserted halls and empty streets. He walked without stealth, but with no desire to be seen. Only the cats could see. The two that were with him as often as not had elected to follow him; their cousins and kin flitted through the long shadows, calling softly to one another.

They were weaving wards about this city. It was subtle and rather marvelous, and quite elegant, like the creatures that wrought it. Their weaving tonight laid a path open for him to follow from palace to city gate, then out to the long stretch of fields along the river.

The gate melted before him. A large brindled cat perched atop it until it was gone; then the cat winked out, vanishing into the air with a sound like purring laughter.

The she-cat stopped just outside the gate, but her mate went on with Estarion. The cat had no fear. Estarion would not indulge in it until he had good and sufficient reason. He raised wards of his own about them both, a shield and a mantle wrought of magic.

He walked away from the walls, down the road to the river and then along the bank to a place that would do as well as any. It was far enough from the city to be out of reach of the wards upon it, but near enough that he did not have to walk far in the dusk. A line of boats was drawn up there, huddled together as if they too were afraid of the dark. He settled in one, sitting near the stern, gazing out over the river to the shadow on shadow that was the farther shore.

Every human creature might be shut away in safety, but night birds sang and jackals howled, and far away he heard the roar of a river-beast. The sunset faded to black; the stars came out in their myriads.

The cat curled purring in his lap. He stroked the sleek fur and leaned his head back, filling his eyes with stars.

The shadow came like a mist, a thin dank fog creeping across the river. The sounds of the night died one by one, save for the howling of jackals in the desert. Jackals, people believed here, were the guides and guardians of the dead. By morning, Estarion well might know whether that was so.

It made him almost happy. He would prefer to live, and this world might be the better for it, too, but he was not afraid to die. It was a passage through a gate, but only the soul could make the journey. The body was cast off, useless and forgotten.

The fog had a scent, a mingled effluvium of dust and damp and old stone. It was not itself deadly; plagues had not come with it in any tale that Estarion had heard. It flowed off the river, dimming the air about him, darkening the stars.

He had strong night-eyes; he needed no light to see. He sat still, save that he had, ever so softly, drawn the short sword from the sheath at his side. The cat sat up and yawned and began to wash its face.

The cat's calm deepened and strengthened his wards. He sat straighter, but did not rise to his feet. The cat finished its toilet and sat staring, still calmly, at the thing that came over the water.

The fog was nothing to be unduly afraid of. There was that about it which hinted of spells and powers embedded in it, enchantments that would feed madness and swell fear into blind panic. Because he had no fear, the spells did not touch him.

Could this alone be what had driven so many people mad, and rent their king limb from limb? Some of the darker spells had that power, but he could not believe that it was as simple as that.

He waited, as the stars wheeled slowly above the shadow. The fog lapped at the walls of Waset, curling tendrils round it but not venturing within. The river murmured to itself.

Something was coming. The cat sprang from Estarion's lap to the boat's prow. He rose then, sword in hand, power coiled within the circle of his wards.

They rode over the river as if it had been solid earth: half a hundred shadowy riders on strange beasts. Even to his eyes they were difficult to see, black on black as they were, but from a glint here and a gleam there, he was able to give them shape. They were human, or near enough: two arms, two legs, a head, encased in armor of strange fashion, and armed with weapons, some of which he recognized, some not. Their beasts were like the crocodiles of this river, but much larger, much longer in the leg, and much more agile and quick.

What army they came from, or by what Gate they had entered this world, he could not tell; but they had no scent or sense of this earth. They overran the shore, riding swiftly and with the air of those who knew their way. They struck for a village that had been safe before, as close to Waset as it was; it was nearly in the shadow of the northern wall.

Estarion slipped out of the boat, set his shoulder to the stern and sent it sliding toward the water. It slid smoothly in the rich black mud, but the splash of its launching stopped his heart in his throat.

The army did not pause or turn. He pulled himself into the boat before the current carried it away, found and softly shipped the steering oar, and let the river bear him down toward the embattled village, touching the oar only to keep the boat on its course.

They reached the village before him, riding like a storm in the night, yet eerily, supernaturally silent. They went for the storehouses and the fields. The former they stripped bare and loaded on beasts that they had brought with them, riderless, for that purpose. The latter they swept past, save one, which they raked with a strange dark fire. Then Estarion knew what those shadowy shapes were which the riders carried, which he had not recognized before: they belched forth flame, but flame transmuted into living, searing darkness.

There was nothing random about this raid. They left the villagers' houses alone, save, as with the fields, for one. That one they cracked open like an egg.

Estarion's fingers tightened on the steering-oar until surely it would snap in two. For now, he must only watch and learn. Gods, he hated to be wise; but for this world and for his own, he must not betray himself to these marauders until he knew surely what they were.

The villagers cowered in the ruins of their house. Their little bit of fire barely flickered in the gloom. One of the raiders stamped it out. As Estarion's eyes struggled to adjust to the deeper darkness, something stirred among the raiders. He could swear it had not been there before, but it was incontestably present now: a loom of shadow, with no shape that he could discern. It flowed rather than walked; it poured itself over the huddle of villagers.

The cold that came out of it, the sense of sheer inimical otherness, made Estarion—even Estarion, who feared little in any world—gasp and cower in the flimsy safety of the boat. The cat pressed trembling against his side.

The dark thing sucked the warmth out of them, and the blood, and

last of all the souls. It crunched them like bones, savoring every shrieking scrap. When they were gone, it shrank to a point of darkness,
sprouted wings, and flittered into the night.

The raiders dismembered the shriveled and bloodless bodies with the
skill and dispatch of butchers in a cattle-market, or priests in a sacrifice.
Their movements had an air of ritual; they arranged the limbs in a pattern that Estarion could not quite see. When they were satisfied, they
turned their beasts, both ridden and laden with spoils, and rode into the
deepest darkness.

The earth breathed a sigh. The stars recovered their splendor. The
moon shed its pale light again. The raiders were gone, departed from
this world—until night came once more, and once more they would rule
the darkness.

TWELVE

JUST AFTER SUNRISE, EARLY RISERS FOUND THE GOD FROM beyond the sky in a boat, asleep, with the lord of the palace cats draped purring over his middle. The boat was drawn up on the riverbank beneath the city's walls; it looked as if he had been there all night. And yet he was whole of limb, and as the boatmen stood over him, murmuring among themselves, he opened eyes that were as bright and sane as they ever were—although one sensitive soul avowed that they were sadder, and touched with a glimmer of godly wrath.

He greeted them with his white smile, and with words that were princely courteous. Those with amulets clutched them for protection, but his wits had not been devoured by the night. He was the same golden-eyed god that he had been the day before.

Tanit had learned that he was missing when a maid roused her at

dawn. Her guest's servant was standing in her antechamber, trembling
so hard that he could barely stand. It was a while before she could coax
any sense out of him. Even then it came out in gasps. "I was asleep," he
said, "across the door, as I should be. He had to walk over me. I woke up
and he was gone. He's nowhere here, lady. I looked and looked. All
night I looked. He's not in this house. Lady, I failed, I failed miserably. I
deserve to die."

"We shall see about that," Tanit said—coldly, to be sure, but her heart
was so constricted and her breath so shallow that it was the best she
could do. She bade the maids look after him, and took her door-guards
and braved the sunrise.

She came to the boat not long after the boatmen found him there. It
was the only crowd along the riverbank this early in the day, with the
sun barely risen and the dark barely put to flight; and he was standing in
the middle of it, head and shoulders above the rest, like a pillar of black
stone with eyes of hammered gold. She wanted, suddenly, to burst into
tears.

She had been queen too long to be a slave to her own foolishness.
The boatmen retreated before her; they recognized her even in a simple
gown, with no more than eye-paint, and no crown. Their relief was palpable. This god was more than they were prepared to contend with, particularly at this hour of the morning.

She held out her hand to him. "Come," she said.

He took her hand and let her lead him away from the wide-eyed
boatmen. She should have let him go once she was sure that he would
stay with her, but her fingers had a mind of their own. They liked to rest
within that big dark hand, with its warmth and its quiet strength.

They stayed there all the way to the palace, through the hall of audience and, with complete lack of conscious will, into her chambers. He
sat where she bade him, which was more for her comfort than for his:
she was not in the mood to crane her neck in order to see his expression.
He was glad to be fed bread and cakes and bits of roast fowl that he
shared with the cat, and to drink palm wine—the last a surprise, and a

pleasant one, from his expression. She had learned from the servants that he was not fond of beer.

When he had eaten and drunk, she sat across the small breakfast-table from him and said, "Tell me why you're alive and sane. Are you one of the walkers in the night?"

"You know I'm not," he said, but without apparent offense. "I did see them—or one manifestation of them."

"And yet you live to tell of it," she said with careful lack of expression. "A village almost under the walls was struck in the night. Were you part of that?"

His eyes closed; his face tightened. "I saw it," he said.

"You did nothing to stop it?"

"I could do nothing," he said through clenched teeth, "that would have made matters immeasurably worse. I watched; I don't know that I understood, but I will remember what I saw. Lady, may I summon certain of the priests, and such nobles as are familiar with your lore of magic?"

It was polite of him to ask. She considered refusing, because after all she was the queen. But he was a god. "Do as you will," she said. "I will give you the rod that permits a lord to wield power in my name."

"That is a great trust," he said.

"Yes," she said. Her maid Tisheri, ever wise, had found the rod that Tanit spoke of, a reed staff bound with bands of gold. Tanit gave it into his hand. "Guard it well," she said.

He bowed low. "My thanks, most gracious lady," he said. Then after a pause "May I gather them here? Your authority will give my words more weight."

"Do I want them gathered here?"

He knelt in front of her. She did not know where that snap of temper had come from, and his lack of anger only made her the more cross-grained. When he took her hands—again, gods help her—she lacked the will to pull free. "Lady," he said, "I am a guest, and here on your sufferance. I ask your pardon if I've overstepped."

"You haven't," she said. "I'm being foolish. It's been too long since I yielded my will to a man's. I've forgotten how to do it gracefully."

"And I," he said with a glint in his eye, "was a king too long. I give orders without thinking."

"They are wise orders," she said. She looked down at their joined hands. He began to draw away, but she held him fast. "My lord, we should agree before we go on, as to how we shall manage this matter of authority. I know I am only a woman, but—"

"Lady," he said deep in his throat. "I'll hear no more of that. In my country, the regent and ruling heir is a woman; and her heir, in turn, is a daughter and not a son. You are not 'only' a woman. You are a lady and a queen."

She had never been so soundly and yet so pleasantly rebuked. "If I am a queen," she said, "then I may command you and be obeyed. Yes?"

"Yes," he said gravely, but with a glint in it.

"Then I command you to go, and do what you must, and come back when you are done."

He bowed over her hands without too terribly much mockery, and kissed the palm of each, and let them go. Long after he was gone, she sat staring at those palms, as if the mark of his lips should be branded there in streaks of fire.

They were only her ordinary, long and thin, cream-brown hands. Whatever memory they held, it was not visible to the eye. Which was well—because if anyone knew what she was thinking, the scandal would keep the court buzzing for days.

She could not stop thinking it. That the command she had wanted to give was not the one she had given, at all. And that if she had bidden him do that other thing . . . might he perhaps have consented? There had been a look in his eye, that she had thought she could not mistake.

There was no time or place for that, not in this world. She gathered herself together and rose. There was a council to prepare for and a day to begin. It was some little while before she understood what was causing her heart to flutter so oddly. It was not only that beautiful and godlike man. It was—before the gods, it was hope. For the first time since she was a child, she began to think that the night would not always be cursed; that the walkers in the dark might, at last, be banished from the world.

The Lord Seramon had called eight priests and nobles to his council: nine, with the queen. The old priest from the temple of the Sun was there, and his son who could not in courtesy be left out, and the young one who was almost, in his dim way, a mage. There was a priest of their queen of goddesses, too, and the commander of the royal army, and two young lords who had been born at the same birth and were eerily, uncannily alike, and last and perhaps most baffled, the servant whom the chief of the queen's servants had given the Lord Seramon. He was no slave or menial; he was a free man of good family, who won honor for his house by serving in the palace.

Tanit had had them brought to her audience chamber with escort of honor and all due courtesy. They were barely courteous in return. Only Seti the old priest seemed at ease. The rest shifted uncomfortably, and either declined refreshment or hid behind it as if it had been a refuge.

The Lord Seramon was last to appear, accompanied as usual by cats. Their lord rode regally on his shoulder. He bowed to them all, and deepest to Tanit, and took the chair that had been left for him. "I thank you, my lords and lady," he said, "for coming at my call. I have a thing to ask of you. You may refuse; no shame will attach to it. But if you accept, the night may be a little less dark, and your people a little safer."

None of them brightened at his words. Seti spoke for them all, gently. "My lord, what can we do that you in your divine power cannot? Surely you can cause the sun to shine all night, and keep the darkness forever at bay."

"If I am a god," the Lord Seramon said, "then I am a minor one. The Sun is my forefather, not my servant. I could set a dome of light over this city, but I would have no strength left for any other working, or for defense against the attack that would come. The enemy that devours your children shuns the light. But the enemy's servants can endure it, even wield it if they must."

"You . . . saw the enemy's servants?" Seti-re made no effort to conceal his disbelief. "Yet you live; your body is whole. You seem sane. Are you certain that it was not a dream?"

"It was quite real," the Lord Seramon said. "I saw another thing, too, that interested me greatly. Because of it, I should like to ask that you yourselves, and such of your servants as are both brave and strong of will, may dispose yourselves like an army, and take turn and turn about in the villages."

"Indeed?" said the priest of the Mother. He seemed no more enamored of the Lord Seramon than Seti-re. "Are we to be a sacrifice? Or will we be given a weapon?"

"You will have a weapon," the Lord Seramon said, "and a comrade in arms." He bent his gaze toward the door. The others, as if caught by a spell, did the same.

A company of cats trotted purposefully into the hall. Being cats, they did not march in ranks, nor did they match pace to pace. Yet they were together, there was no mistaking it, and they had about them the air of an army. There were twice nine, and not all palace cats; some had the lean and rangy look of cats from the city.

They advanced two by two, and chose each a lord or a priest, and two gold-earringed beauties lofted lightly into Tanit's lap. She knew them; they were often to be seen about her chambers, and were much spoiled by the servants.

"These are the nobility of their kind," the Lord Seramon said. "Their cousins and kin will come to those whom you choose to fight in this army. Listen to them, my lords and lady. Let them guide you. They have power against this enemy that besets you."

The priest of the Mother laughed. "*This* is your great plan? These are your weapons? The gods do love them, lord, but what power can they raise against the walkers of the night?"

"Great power," the Lord Seramon said. "Did you never wonder why this city has not been attacked? It has walls, yes, but walls are nothing to this enemy. Your cats guard those walls. They take their strength from the sun, but the night is their mother. They rule on both sides of the sky."

Tanit shivered lightly. The cat in her lap seemed no more divine than ever, if no less; she was coiled, purring, blinking sleepily at her kin. Lightly Tanit laid a hand on her back. She arched it, bidding Tanit stroke it, yes, just so. Her purring rose to a soft roar. She reminded Tanit suddenly, vividly, of the Lord Seramon.

"I do believe you," Tanit said. "And yet, my lord, I ask you: If the cats have such power, why have they never defended the villages?"

"Because, lady," said the Lord Seramon, "they, like me, have limits to their power; and, being cats, they seldom think of gathering forces. It's their nature to hunt alone."

"Yet they guard our city together," she said.

"Each protects what is his," he said. "It happens that, in so doing, they protect all. They've agreed to ally themselves with your people; their power is yours to use. In return they ask for free rein among the mice and rats in the storehouses, and a tribute of milk and fish."

One of the twins snorted as if he could not help himself. "My lord! Pardon me, but that's absurd. You're a god; you may talk to a cat. What of us? We're only human."

"Listen," the Lord Seramon said. One of the cats at Kamut's feet rose on its hindlegs, stretching its long body, and flexed claws delicately, terribly close to his shrinking privates. The cat met his stare with one as golden and as steady, and quite as full of intelligence, as the Lord Seramon's own.

Kamut gasped and stiffened, but it seemed he could not look away. The cat yawned, splitting its face in two, curling its pink tongue, and raked its claws gently, ever so gently, down Kamut's thigh. Four thin lines of red stained the white linen of his kilt.

To his credit, he did not flinch or cry out. The cat sat once more, tail curled about feet.

"I . . . am only human," Kamut said after a long pause. "But *she* is a cat."

The Lord Seramon smiled that white smile of his. "Yes, young lord, you do understand. Will you be a captain in this army? I count a score of living villages within a day's walk of the city. All have been raided; but their houses still stand, and their people are holding on. Even one of you, with your allies, should be able to raise wards that keep the village safe, though the fields may be more than your strength can manage."

"It is a risk," Seti said. "If the dark ones fail to gain their sacrifice, they may strip the fields in revenge."

"The fields could be guarded," Tanit said.

"No man will leave the safety of walls at night," said the Mother's priest, with a slant of the eye at the Lord Seramon.

The Lord Seramon's mouth curved upward briefly. "No man will, but cats have no fear of the dark. The fields can be guarded. But you might wish to consider that wards of such size and extent may attract the very thing they're meant to repel. If I were to be asked, I would counsel that your people decide among them what they can spare—which fields, which houses—and withdraw from those."

"This is all very well," said the captain of the guard, "but defense only serves for so long. There comes a time when attack is the only wise course. Can this enemy be attacked? Can he be fought? Or will he wear us away until there is nothing left?"

"The raiders can be fought," the Lord Seramon said, "but how and with what numbers, I don't yet know."

"A *minor* god," Kamut muttered to his brother.

The Lord Seramon laughed. "Very minor! But strong enough, I hope, to be of some use. So, then, my lords. Will you join with us? A wall is the first defense. An army within the wall—that comes after. Will you be the wall?"

"As weak a stone as I may be," Seti said, "I will hold up my part of the wall."

"And I," said Kamut, rather surprisingly; his brother Senmut echoed him.

They all agreed, even Seti-re, and the Mother's priest, whom Tanit would have expected to refuse. It was a spirit of rivalry: they were not to be outdone.

The Lord Seramon left them to plot their strategies. She could admire the skill with which he did it. They were not even aware of his silence or, after a while, his absence. He withdrew so quietly that even she hardly knew when he was gone. One moment he was there, watching and listening. The next, he was not.

It took this new and strange guard a rather long while to settle on how it would begin. Tanit was very weary when at last they scattered to the duties they had agreed upon. Her head ached; there was a dull pain in her belly, where so many children had grown and died.

Her maids would have put her to bed with a cool cloth on her brow and a potion to make her sleep, but she was in no mood to rest. She went hunting a minor god.

He was on the palace roof, where the maids spread the linens to dry on washing-day. It was bare now but for the pots of herbs that rimmed it. He stood on the edge as if he would spread wings and take flight, gazing out over the city and the fields and the river.

In the bright light of day he seemed both more mortal and less. The sun caught the threads of silver in his hair. There were scars on his back and side, down his arm, cleaving his face from cheekbone to chin. Scars of battle, worn almost to invisibility. She tried to imagine battles among the gods. Were their weapons like the ones she knew, or did they wield bolts of fire?

He glanced at her. "We have swords and spears," he said, "and bolts of mages' fire."

A shiver ran down her spine. "Do you know every thought I think?"

"Only the ones aimed like an arrow," he said.

Not only her cheeks were hot; her whole body flushed. If she could
have sunk through the floor, she would have done it.

His hand was cool on her cheek, shocking her into a shiver. "Dear
lady," he said so tenderly that she could have wept, "you have nothing to
be ashamed of."

"No?" She looked him in the face. "Am I such a child to you?"

"Never," he said.

"I am no goddess, my lord."

"And I," he said, "in my own world, am no god."

"It has been so long a while," she said through a tightening throat,
"since—and I cannot—a queen may not—"

"May she not?"

"Will you corrupt me?"

"I might seduce you," he said.

She gasped. His effrontery was astonishing. And damnably charming, because he did not care, at all, for the ways of men in this world.

"The ladies of your court are free of their eyes and their favors," he
said. "Surely a queen may make what laws she pleases."

"What if she does not please?"

He tilted up her chin and kissed her softly on the lips.

She should have struck him. Not held him when he began to
straighten, and deepened the kiss until she was dizzy with it.

He tasted of strange spices. There was a quality to him, like leashed
lightning, or sparks that flew in the air when the hot winds blew out of
the red land. Magic, she thought; divine power. And yet he was as warm
as any mortal man, solid, real to the touch; he did not vanish like a
vision or a dream.

"You swore that you would never harm me," she said to him.

"I shall keep that oath, lady," he said.

"Then why—"

"Lady," he said, "there are gods above us all. Maybe it amuses them to
bring us together across the worlds; maybe they have a purpose for us,
which our wits are too feeble to understand."

"Maybe this was never meant," she said, but she did not believe it even as she said it. She did not want to believe it. She wanted—she yearned—

"Why are you afraid?" he asked her. "Am I so terrible a monster?"

"You are beautiful," she said.

"And you," he said, "were married to a man whom you admired and cherished, but for whom your body felt nothing."

"I am not young," she said as steadily as she could. "I have borne ten children. None lived long enough to walk the black earth. Now I have a thousand children, and they need my loyalty undivided."

"Would a king divide his loyalty by taking a wife?"

"A king is a man," she said.

"A queen is a woman."

He was seducing her. That soft rich voice, those luminous eyes—they cast a spell. She had known him two days, but every one of her several souls reckoned that a lifetime.

"Gods are quick to love," she said, "and just as quick to leave. Mortals, who have so much less time to waste, are slower with both."

"Many things have been said of me," he said, "and not all have been to my credit, though they may have been true. But one charge has never been laid against me: that I was light in love. A king must marry well and often. So I did. But when I left the throne, I left that behind me. My bed has been solitary since long before you were born."

Then it may remain so, she meant to say, but the words would not shape themselves on her tongue. "I may take a consort," she heard herself say. "I will not take a lover. That would dishonor my husband's memory, my family's reputation, and my own good name."

Once she had traveled with her husband to the cataract of the river, where it roared headlong through a wilderness of stones. She had seen how flotsam, caught in the torrent, whirled and dived and for long moments vanished, but then suddenly reappeared an improbable distance downstream. So her heart felt now, hammering in her breast. It had spoken, not she. Half of it wanted him to recoil in horror and go away and let her be. The other half wanted him to say what in fact he said.

"Are you telling me that I should marry you?"

"I am telling you that I will not take a lover," she said with what little breath was left in her.

Two days, she thought. Two lifetimes.

"Will your people be appalled if I say yes? Will you?"

"Why would you—"

"Life is short," he said, "and the night is long. And from the moment I saw you, I have loved you."

"I—" She could feel the water closing over her head, hear the rush and roar of the cataract. "Life is short," she said faintly.

"Will your people be horrified?"

"If their queen takes a god for a consort? They'll reckon it a great good omen. The nobles and the priests will be less than amused."

"Nobles and priests can be managed," he said.

She met his eyes as firmly as she could. "If this is a jest, my lord, or a mockery, then may the greater gods repay you as you deserve."

There was no mirth in his gaze, no mockery or contempt. "I never jest in matters of the heart," he said.

She laid her hand over it. It was not beating as hard as hers, but neither was it as strong and slow as she knew it could be. Once more she found that she could see beneath the veil of him. The light was as clear as ever. He was a pure spirit. The beauty of him, within even more than without, made her catch her breath.

"You will be consort and not king," she said. "Can you endure that?"

"I would expect nothing else," he said. And with a flicker of lightness: "It's still a fair step up from shepherd."

"And a long step down from king of kings."

"Ah," he said, shrugging. "I gave that up."

"You are a very odd man," she said, "but for a god, not so strange at all."

He laughed at that. He took her hands and pressed them to his lips and said, "I'll see that this goes easily."

"No spells," she said. "Promise."

"May I smile? Wheedle? Be charming?"

"No magic," she said. Then added: "Except the magic that is yourself."

"That will be enough," he said.

THIRTEEN

TANIT WENT TO SETI AS SOON AS SHE COULD, WHICH WAS NEAR
evening. The day had passed in a blur. She supposed that she had
held audience, met in council, overseen the servants, and performed the myriad other duties of her office. She also supposed that the
Lord Seramon disposed of himself in some useful fashion. He was seen
round about in the city and in one or two of the nearer villages, and
down by the river in the evening.

Her heart would have taken her there and begged him not to risk
himself again by night, but her colder spirit bade her let him be. He
could look after himself. This that she had determined to do was not at
all as simple as she had led him to think.

Seti was preoccupied with the evening rite and sacrifice. She waited
for him in a bare cell of a room outside the temple proper. A young

priest waited on her; she wanted nothing, but he seemed content to amuse himself in conversation with her maid. She half-drowsed, sitting upright, spinning in her mind the things that she meant to say to Seti.

When he came, it was as if it had all been said, and she could pay her respects and go away. But she was not quite as foolish as that. He greeted her gladly, and opened his arms for an embrace and the kiss of kin. His cheek was dry yet oddly soft under her lips, like age-worn leather. "Granddaughter," he said. "It warms my heart to see you."

"Grandfather," she said to her mother's father. She insisted that he sit in the one chair the room afforded. She could be at ease on the floor, curled at his feet, as she had done when she was small.

"Tell me," he said.

She laughed a little. "Am I so obvious?"

"Maybe," he said. "And maybe it will be night soon, and time's flying. What's in your heart, child?"

"Too much," she murmured. She lifted her eyes to him, though he could not see; she suspected that he knew, somehow, or felt in the air what movements she made. "I am going to do a thing that will shock every priest and noble in this city. Except, I think, you."

"Oh, I'm not past shock," he said. "What is it? Are you going to take the god to your bed?"

She started and flushed. Even knowing how perceptive Seti could be, she had not expected him to see direct to the truth.

"I knew the moment you met," Seti said. "There are stars that dance twinned in heaven, and souls that are matched, each to each. Even the walls of worlds and time, mortality and divinity, simple human and great magic, matter nothing to them."

"That is very beautiful," she said, "but we live in daylight, and the court and the temples will be outraged."

"So they will," Seti said. "Does it matter?"

"No," she said slowly. "But—"

"What do you think I can do? Command them all to accept what none of them can change?"

It sounded absurd when he said it, but she said, "Yes. Yes, I had rather thought that."

"I can command respect," he said. "Once I might have commanded more. You would do better to win over your uncle."

"Seti-re will never listen to me," she said. She was not excessively bitter. It was fact, that was all. "But he will still listen to you. If he says the words that unite us, no one else will dare object."

"You are set on this? It's not simple enough to take a lover?"

"A lover would give them a weapon against me," she said, "and weaken us when we need most to be strong. A consort proves before the gods that this is no decision taken lightly."

"You are stubborn," said Seti, "and determined to make matters as difficult as possible."

"If I don't do it," she said, "the court will—or my uncle, who has never been my dearest friend."

"Indeed," he sighed. "Tell me, child. What do you truly hope to gain? Is this your revenge on us all for expecting so much but giving so little in return?"

"That would be the taking of a lover," she said. "This begs the gods to be merciful to our city."

"By binding one of their own to it?"

She bent her head.

"He consents? Freely?"

"It seems so," she said.

Seti sighed. "Child," he said, "I will see what I can do."

She kissed him, less formally this time, and smiled. "Thank you, Grandfather," she said.

Estarion had found that day astonishing and disconcerting and in parts delightful, like the lady who had issued so remarkable an ultimatum. Of marriage he had no fear—he had done it nine times over. But that was long ago, and he had not lain with a woman in years out of count. It was the only thing that had made him think that he might, after all, be old.

Now it seemed he was not old but perhaps merely rebellious. He had had one great love in his life, and she had denied herself to him, because she was a commoner and a priestess and a mage of Gates, and he must marry where his empire required. When that duty was done, when those ladies had grown old and died, he had wanted nothing more to do with any of it.

He was a man for one woman. He had always known that. She was long dead—she had lived an ample span, but she was mortal after all, and aged and died as mortals did. He still mourned her, though her death had had no grief in it. She had gone not into darkness but into light, soaring up like a bird into the luminous heaven.

There was a doctrine in the Isles from which she had come, and in the lands beyond the sea: that souls did not live only once; that they came back again and again, striving to perfect this life which they had been given. He wondered, even as he passed through palace and city and to the nearer villages, whether this was she, after all, with her bright spirit and her strong will, and her solid common sense. Or maybe it was only that he was made for such a woman, and when he met her like again, his spirit called to her and wanted her for its own.

For he did want her. He had turned his mind away from the harder truth: that he was not of this world. If he could escape from it, he would do so. She could not bind him, not against that.

That would come when it came. As the day waned toward evening, he knew that she went to Seti; he could imagine what she said to him. For his own part, he went to the one who could make matters most difficult. It was reckless, perhaps, and she would not be pleased to hear of it, but he was in no mood for prudence. That was a lost virtue in this world under the shadow.

Seti-re was at dinner. He dined alone tonight, but he dined well. He had a roast fowl and a platter of fish and the inevitable bread and beer. The priests who guarded him never saw the shadow that passed among them. Nor, while he savored his dinner, did Seti-re. It was only as he picked at the last of the bones and sipped his third cup of beer, that Estarion let himself take shape out of shadows.

Seti-re started so violently that his cup flew out of his hand and shattered. Estarion made it new again, raising the shards and knitting them together, and set it gently on the table.

The priest stared at it. He seemed unable to take his eyes from it, or unwilling to look into Estarion's face. He was afraid; and fear filled him with rancor.

"My lord," Estarion said, "whatever our differences, may we not work together for the preservation of this city?"

"Is that truly what you are doing? You have the others well ensorcelled, but the gods protect me. I see you for what you are."

"Indeed?" said Estarion. "What am I?"

"Do I need to say it?"

Estarion raised a shoulder in a shrug. "Truly I mean you no harm. I was sent here to help; I will do everything I can, for the gods who sent me, but also for love of those to whom I was sent."

"Love?" said Seti-re. "How can you love what you barely know?"

"Some would say that love is easiest then—that only the best is apparent, until time dulls the sheen. As for me," said Estarion, "I have found much here to admire, and no little to love."

"Words are easy," Seti-re said. "Actions prove them."

"Indeed," said Estarion. "Will you say the words that join me to your queen as her consort?"

He had caught the priest utterly off guard. Seti-re stared, speechless. Just as Estarion began to wonder if he had any wits left, he said faintly, hardly more than a gasp, "If that is a jest, it is in extremely poor taste."

"No jest," Estarion said. "This too I was sent for; this I do in all joy."

"You want . . . me . . . to say the words." Seti-re looked as if he had bitten into bitter herbs. "You honestly imagine that I would consent?"

Estarion smiled. "Yes, sir priest. In fact I do. You are not a fool, and you have honest care for the city, whatever you may think of its queen. Or," he added, "of me. I frighten you. I am sorry for that. I would wish us, if not friends, at least to be allies; to make common cause against this enemy that threatens us all. My world, too, sir priest, and all worlds in its path."

"I believe that you are part of it," Seti-re said. "That you came not to save us but to destroy us."

"There is a thing that I can do," Estarion said, "which would place me utterly in your power if I break my word to the queen and the city. If I do that, will you lay aside your enmity?"

Seti-re eyed him narrowly. "What can you do? Offer your throat to my knife?"

"Better than that," Estarion said. "I will give you a part of myself to keep. If I betray my oath, that part will be snuffed out, and I will be gone."

"Dead?"

"And gone," said Estarion.

Seti-re drew a slow breath. Estarion resisted the temptation to discover what he was thinking. That was part of his good faith: to force no magic on this or any man.

At length the priest said, "I would have complete power over you. Or is this a trick? Will it be I who will suffer, and you who will laugh me into scorn?"

"By the god who begot my forefather," Estarion said, "and by the Sun he set in my hand, this is no trick. I offer it in good faith. Will you accept it?"

"You trust me as far as that?"

"One must give trust in order to receive it," Estarion said.

"What will you do?" Seti-re asked after a long pause.

Estarion realized that he had been forgetting to breathe. When there was air in his lungs again, he reached into the heart of his magic and drew forth a gem of fire. It was cool in his hand, hard and round like an earthly stone, but the center of it was living light. It pulsed with the beating of his heart.

Seti-re's eyes were wide. He trembled as he took the jewel that held the key to Estarion's life and soul. And yet he said mistrustfully, "*This* is your great weapon?"

"You know it is," Estarion said gently. "You can feel it thrumming to the center of you. That much power you have, turn your back on it though you will."

"But what am I to—"

Estarion wrought a chain of light, quickly, and strung the jewel from it, and presented it with a bow. It looked like a necklace of gold and fire-opal, luminous and beautiful but perfectly solid and earthly. "Guard it well," he said, "and beware. If you misuse it, it will repay you in kind."

Seti-re's lip curled, but he did not argue the point. He held the jewel gingerly, staring past it at Estarion. "Why does a god want a woman of her age, who is barren? Even though she is a queen?"

"Because she is herself," Estarion said. "Will you say the words?"

"Do you think you can compel me?"

Estarion smiled with awful sweetness. He held up his hand. In it lay a pebble. It was nothing like the fiery jewel he had given Seti-re, but within its grey dullness was a faint shimmer. "Trust for trust," he said, "and hostage for hostage. We bind one another, sir priest, and have each the power of life and death over the other."

Seti-re laughed suddenly. He was no more amiable than he had ever been, but in this laughter was genuine mirth. "Lord, you are devious! I almost begin to like you. What will you do with yonder stone? Swallow it? Fling it in the river?"

"Keep it," said Estarion, "against the time when our alliance is ended. Will you say the words?"

"I will say the words," Seti-re said. "On one condition."

Estarion raised a brow.

"That my enemies are your enemies. That if I call on you, you will answer, and aid me against them."

"If I may do so without harm to the queen or the city," said Estarion, "I will do it."

"Then I will say the words," said Seti-re.

FOURTEEN

THE NEW GUARDIANS OF THE KINGDOM WENT OUT THAT EVENING with their small furred allies, and disposed themselves among villagers who were more often baffled and suspicious than glad to be so protected. Tanit would have preferred to go with them, but the queen belonged in the city. She walked its streets at evening, unable quite to suppress the shiver of fear as the shadows lengthened, and saw how the cats built their walls of air. She could see those walls, how they rose and joined to shield the houses and people within.

"You have eyes to see," the Lord Seramon said. He came up on the city's walls, the walls of stone, not long after she had ascended there, and found her marveling at the intricacy of the wards.

"I'm not needed at all," she said. "This is entirely the cats' doing."

"Your people need to see you," said the Lord Seramon, "to know that you defend them."

"I think," she said, "that you gave me this title to keep me from demanding one less noble but more useful."

"You were queen of Waset long before I came here," he said with the flicker of a smile.

She hissed at him, but without rancor. Her hand had slid into his, entirely of its own accord. They stood together while the sun sank ever closer to the horizon.

Just when she was thinking that it would be wise to retreat to the palace, he said, "Seti-re will say the words that make me your consort."

"How in the gods' name—"

"We exchanged assurances," he said, "and agreed on an alliance. He has great love for this city, however poorly he may express it."

"He is my mother's brother," she said. "He arranged my marriage to the king. He was never altogether satisfied with the outcome."

"Because he couldn't control you?"

"And because there was no son and heir for him to raise and train in the temple."

The pain of that was old, and worn smooth. He did not shame her with pity, but he nearly broke her with the tenderness of a gesture: the soft stroke of a finger down her cheek. "You are what, and where, the gods will."

She spoke past the ache in her throat. "It will be dark soon. You may choose to spend the night under the sky, but I in my cowardice prefer the safety of a roof."

"Tonight we shall be cowards together," he said.

"Don't you want to see the wards go up across the kingdom?"

"I see them," he said in his deep purr of a voice.

She remembered then, as already she tended to forget, that he was not of her world. The awareness shivered in her skin, but somewhat oddly, it did not frighten her.

He followed her down from the walls, walking as a guard would, just behind her. They moved in a cloud of cats: his two, her two, a shifting circle of the city's defenders. At the palace gate, most of them faded into the twilight.

She had not been out so late since she was a reckless child. Even in the safety of the city, even knowing how well it was protected, she battled the urge to run through the gate and hide. She walked sedately as a queen should, pausing to greet the guards and to settle a matter brought to her by one of the servants, and to pray for a moment before the image of her husband's ancestor, the first king of Waset. His worn stone face grew dim as she prayed, veiling itself in dusk.

She looked up from that ancient face to the living one of the Lord Seramon. He was crowned with stars—the first that she had seen since, young and rebellious, she had gone up on the roof of her mother's house and looked full into the eyes of the night.

Darkness was terrible. Darkness was death. And yet in that face which was so dark, she found only comfort. He smiled at her. She wanted to melt into his arms, but she was not made for such softness. She turned from him, but without rejection, and led him into the royal house.

No human creature died that night, and no animal, either, nor was any villager stolen from his house. One field was stripped, but those near it were untouched. The wards had held.

There was festival in the villages. The people did not understand precisely what had saved them; only that priests and nobles had wielded magic, and that a god had shown them the way.

That their queen should take the god as a consort, they found perfectly right and fitting. The court reckoned it a scandal: three days he had been there, a shockingly brief time to come so far or to presume so much. But Tanit had expected that. She could see it, too: how sudden it was. Yet in her heart there was nothing sudden about it at all.

Seti-re brought them together in the temple before the gods and the people. He was a good and proper ally; he put on a face, if not of joy,

then at least of acceptance. He set her hand in the Lord Seramon's and
blessed them in the names of the gods, and performed the sacrifice of a
white heifer and a black bull-calf, pouring out their blood over the
altar-stone.

Tanit was in a world outside the world. She saw herself in royal state,
robed and crowned, with her face painted into the mask of a goddess,
and her hair hidden beneath an elaborate structure of plaits and beads
and gold. She saw him beside her, more simply dressed, but wearing
royalty as easily, as naturally as his skin. How strange that he the god
should keep no more state than any noble bridegroom, but she who was
inescapably mortal should wear the semblance of divinity.

His fingers laced in hers, his eyes warm upon her, brought her back
into her body. "From before time I have known you," she said.

She had spoken in silence, in a pause in the rite. Seti-re looked
affronted. But he mattered not at all. The Lord Seramon bent his head.
"From beyond the horizon I came to you," he said, "and when the
worlds have passed away, still I will belong to you."

Those were the vows that bound them, far more than blessings spoken by any priest. They were truth so simple, so pure and absolute, that
there could be no breaking them.

She did not, even then, feel constrained. For this she had been born.
Whatever came of it, she would never regret the choice that she had
made.

The wedding feast had been prepared in haste, but the cooks had outdone themselves. There was a roast ox and a flock of wild geese roasted
and stuffed with dates and barley, heaping platters of cakes made with
nuts and honey and sweet spices, plates and bowls of greens and roots
and fruit both fresh and dried, and an endless procession of lesser
delights. At evening the guests did not flee as they had so often before.
The bold would go home under protection of the wards, and the rest
would stay in the palace until the sun rose.

Estarion would not have been startled to discover that he was expected to play host to all of them through what should have been the wedding night. He had known stranger customs. He was seated apart from the queen, among the great men of the kingdom; she sat with a flock of ladies, as blankly unreadable as a painted image.

He set himself to be charming to these men who eyed him in wariness or hostility or, here and there, open speculation. He was somewhat out of practice in the art of seducing courtiers, but it was not a skill one could altogether forget. These courtiers were far less jaded than those of Asanion, if not quite as easy in their manners as those of his northern kingdoms. They were not warriors, but neither were they purely creatures of courts. They made him think of small landowners and gentlemen farmers of the Hundred Realms: bound to the earth, the river, the hunt; shaped in small compass, but not petty of either mind or spirit.

He liked them. They were as flawed as men of any other world, but there was honesty in them, and care for their people, even under the long weight of the shadow. He had learned the names of each, and would learn their lands, their cares, their kin—later. Tonight he learned their minds, how they thought, what they hoped for; what, apart from the darkness, they feared.

Not long after sunset, a servant bent toward his ear and murmured, "Lord. It's time."

He had been listening to a tale told by a lord from a holding upriver, of hunting terrible long-toothed beasts in the cataracts of the south. "They can bite a man in a half," the lord said, "and fling a calf out of his skin with a toss of the head. They have a taste for manflesh; they'll raid boats and steal the boatmen's children. Once I heard tell—"

The servant touched Estarion's shoulder, polite but urgent. "Lord!"

He excused himself as courteously as he could. No one took offense, even the teller of tales: a grin ran round the circle, and they vied in wishing him well. The warmth of their regard followed him out of the hall.

The servant led him not toward the queen's chambers as he had expected, nor to his own, but to a part of the palace which he had yet to explore. It was older than the rest, lower, darker, less airy and elegant. Its walls were plastered and painted, but the paint was fading. The air smelled of dust and age, overlaid with the scent of flowers.

They entered a chamber that might once have been a royal hall. Squat pillars held up the roof. The center was an island of light, banks of lamps arrayed in a broad circle, rising up toward the pillars and suspended from the ceiling. The extravagance of it, the soft clarity of the light, made all the richer the carpet of flowers that spread across the worn stone of the floor.

A bed was set there, strewn with fragrant petals, and beside it a table and a chest, the accoutrements of a royal bedchamber. She was not there. But for the servant, and the cat who coiled purring at the bed's foot, he was alone. In a moment, the servant effaced himself and was gone.

Estarion smiled. He had a fondness for the unexpected, if it was not too deadly. He took off his kilt and jewels and laid them in the chest, which was empty, and unbound the ropes of gold and strings of beads from his hair; then plaited it again in a single thick braid, bound off with a bit of cord. He sat cross-legged on the bed, and waited in the patience that priests and mages learned in youth.

Soft airs played across his skin. The scent of flowers was almost overpowering. Within himself he felt the wards upon city and kingdom. The darkness was late in coming; the night was quiet, the stars untainted. He knew a prickle of unease, of old and intractable suspicion: a deep mistrust of stillness in the heart of war.

Such quiet could be a gift, if a general had both wisdom and courage. Old habits were waking, fitting themselves to him like familiar garments. Yet he was calmer than he had been then, less impatient, less inclined to indulge his temper. He had learned to wait.

Almost he laughed. Patience indeed! Three days in this world, and he had bound himself to it with no honest thought for the consequences. And yet he could not find it in himself to regret it. What he had said to her in the temple was true. This had been ordained; this was where he was meant to be, and she, in this age of both their worlds.

He looked up in his island of light, into her face. She was standing on the edge of the darkness. Her mask of paint was gone, all but the jeweled elaboration of the eyes. Her hair was free, blue-black and shining, pouring down her back to the sweet curve of her buttocks. She was wrapped in a gown of sheer white linen, such as he had seen before. As before, it concealed nothing. The dark aureoles of her nipples, the triangle of her private hair, were but thinly veiled.

Her eyes were wide and dark, and blank, almost blind. Yet he knew that she saw every line of him. He frightened her a little with his size and darkness, the breadth of his shoulders and the strength of his arms and thighs. She was avoiding, with care, the thing that both frightened and fascinated her most.

He rose. He heard the faint catch of her breath, but she did not retreat. When he knelt, she eased a little. He was not so towering tall then, or so inclined to loom. He smiled at her. He might have thought that all those sharp white teeth would alarm her, but she warmed to his warmth, and smiled somewhat shakily in return.

She advanced into the light. Her feet bruised the blossoms strewn on the floor, sending up a gust of sweetness. She knelt in front of him, and lightly, almost trembling, brushed his lips with hers.

The leap of his body toward her took him aback with its strength. He mastered it before it flung him upon her. It seemed she sensed nothing. While he knelt rigidly still, she traced the lines of his face with her fingers. Her touch was like the brush of fire over his skin. She followed the track of a scar, the curve of his lip; she hesitated ever so slightly between smoothness of cheekbone and prick of close-shaved stubble. She coaxed his mouth open and stroked a salt-sweet fingertip across his tongue, and counted his teeth as if he had been a senel at a fair, catching her finger on the sharp curve of a canine. Her own were not so many; they were blunter, and her tongue, running over them, was pink.

Her scent was musk and spices. He breathed it in while she explored his body, downward from his face across neck and shoulders and breast, down his arms, along his sides. She turned his hands palm up, the dark

and the gold, and assured herself that indeed it was gold, born in the
flesh, rooted deep in bone and sinew. The fire in it, so much a part of
him that it had long ago ceased to be pain, flared suddenly, then just as
suddenly eased. He met her eyes and fell down and down, headlong
into joy.

The love of man and woman was an awkward and often ridiculous
thing. Tanit, in teaching herself the ways of his body, the things that
were subtly or not so subtly different, knew that she was putting off the
inevitable. With Kare the king, it had been a thing she did out of duty.
She lay as still as she could, and, did as he bade, and waited for it to be
over. Then in a few months, either the blood and the pain came, or the
child was born and drew a breath and died.

With this man who was not exactly a man, with his blue-black
tongue and his predator's teeth, she caught herself thinking thoughts
that she had never imagined she could think. Her maids did, and ladies
of the court, too—their gossip was full of it, how this man's face or that
man's eyes or another man's private parts made their bellies melt. She
had never melted for anyone—until, so brief a time ago, this stranger
from beyond the horizon lay unconscious at her feet.

He was fully conscious now, kneeling subject to her will, with a look
about him that made it clear how great an effort it was to remain so still.
He had mastered even *that* part of him. How she knew that it was force
of will and not lack of desire, she could not tell; she only knew that it
was so.

Her heart was beating hard. Her skin was now hot, now cold. Her
belly—yes, her belly was melting as she looked at him, his beauty and
strangeness. His eyes were as deep as the river. His lips tasted of honey,
drowning her in sweetness.

His breast, his legs and arms, were lightly pelted with curling hair.
She ran fingers through that on his breast. He quivered; then stilled. He
was waking below. His will was weakening, or he had loosed its bonds.

She should cast off her gown and lie on the bed and let him get it over. But the fear in her would not let her do that—fear, and something else. Something that was inextricably a part of the melting in her middle. She wanted—she needed—

He rose in one long fluid movement, sweeping her up with such effortless strength that she laughed, borne as on a wave of the river. Her arms linked about his neck. She had gone from fear to a dizzy delight, a singing brightness in which nothing mattered, no darkness, no terror, only those eyes meeting hers and that body warm against her. For long moments she was not even certain which body was his, and which hers. They were all one, all woven together, flesh and manifold souls.

It was not as awkward as she had feared. Her body knew, after all, how to dance the dance. When it was ridiculous, he laughed as hard as she, rolling together in the banks of flowers.

He ended on his back, she sprawled along the length of him. He shifted; she stirred. She gasped. He was inside her, filling her, just on the edge of pain; until with a sigh she let the pain go. He had sobered. His eyes were softer than she had ever thought they could be. She kissed the lid of each, and found the long slow rhythm, the ebb and surge of the world.

When the release came, she cried out in astonishment. She had never—she could never—

It broke like the crest of the river in flood. She sank down and forever down, cradled in his arms, in a sweetness of crushed flowers. He was breathing lightly, as if he had been running. Skin slid on skin, slicked with sweat. She lifted a head that felt impossibly heavy. His eyes were shut, his head tilted back, but she could feel his awareness like a brush of fingers down her spine. Was this what it was to have magic?

"This is what it is to love a mage," he said. He kissed the crown of her head. "Beautiful lady."

"Splendid man."

He laughed softly. Her heart was singing—and so, her bones knew, was his. They would raise the light, and break the darkness. She knew that, just then, in that night in which the shadows never came.

FIFTEEN

TELL ME OF YOUR WORLD," SHE SAID.

They lay together in the long stretch of night before dawn. She had slept; he had rested in the quiet. Deep quiet, empty of enemies.

She had awakened in his arms, rumpled and beautiful. Her thoughts murmured inside of his. The words grew out of them. "What is it like? Is it like this?"

"A little," he said. "The sky, the sun—they're very like. We have deserts and rivers and green country. Mountains; too, and seas, which are rivers that fill the world, and taste powerfully of salt."

"We know of seas," she said. "The river flows into one. They say it's green. Someday I mean to see it and know for myself." And after a pause: "Tell me more."

"There are two moons," he said. "One is red, like blood, and so vast that in some seasons it seems to fill half the sky. The other is white and small and very bright. Long ago people believed that the red moon was the darkness' child, and the white moon was born of the light. Now we believe that darkness and light are twinned; that one cannot exist without the other."

She sighed on his breast. "And you? You believe that?"

"I know that in my world it is true."

"That is rather wonderful," she said. "Fitting for a world full of gods."

"There are men, too. And women."

"But not you."

"I was born," he said, "of a line of divine madmen. The first of them was a renegade without a father, a priestess' son when priestesses were put to death for violating their vows of fidelity to the god. But she had lain with the god, or with a man who had been possessed by the god—no one ever truly doubted that, not once they knew him. He was . . . not as other men were. He won himself an empire, but saw his own heir turn against him, make alliance with the son of his great enemy and so cast him down. The two of them imprisoned him in a tower of magic and enchanted him into sleep, and so took him out of the world but not out of life. With that act they made a greater empire, and ruled it together. Their son inherited, and his son after him, and after him my father. Then I was born, and I was to be all that was most splendid in our world: mage, king, priest of Sun and Shadow.

"When I was twelve years old, a rebel killed my father. I destroyed the murderer, but nearly destroyed myself. It was long years before I was whole again. I was emperor for a mortal lifetime. I saw my son born, and I saw him die. I raised his daughter to be my heir, and she raised hers. When their time had come, I left the empire to them, and walked away."

"Such tales," she said. "Such brevity. I'll make you tell me the whole of every story."

"Only if you promise to tell me yours."

"Mine is nothing," she said. "I come from a lordly family near the border of Ta-senet. My mother is the old priest's daughter and the high priest's sister. I was married in youth to the king. The king died; there was no one else to rule the city. Now I am queen, and the rest you know."

"Such brevity," he said. "This is why there are singers and poets: because we who live the tales have no gift for telling them."

She laughed her rich bubbling laugh. "My singers will make a legend for you and spare you the trouble. May you be the son of a god and a goddess? Were they gloriously beautiful?"

"My mother was," he said. "She was a chieftain's daughter of a wild tribe, a priestess of the dark goddess. My father saw her dancing by the fire one night as he tarried with the tribe during a hunt. He loved her then and ever after. It was a scandal in its day: he had resisted every marriage that anyone tried to make for him, and when at long last he did marry, he married for love."

"Ah," she sighed. "You can tell a tale after all. Will I be a scandal among the gods? Will they be horrified to discover that you gave yourself in marriage to a mortal woman?"

Estarion's lips twitched. One corner of his mouth turned irresistibly upward. "My heir will be absolutely appalled. She was as rebellious a child as a king should ever hope not to have. She chose her daughter's father for his beauty and lineage, used him like a fine bull, and sent him home to his wives when she had what she wanted of him. It was years before even I learned who had fathered her child. But then she found a noble consort, a man of perfect probity, and married him and adopted his son and became everything that she had formerly professed to despise. She's a better ruler than I ever was, and more truly suited to it, but a more humorless creature I've seldom known."

"Humor is not a virtue in a ruler," Tanit said.

"Isn't it? I do love that child, but if she learned to laugh, she might be happier."

"Maybe someday you will teach her."

"I'm afraid it's far too late," he said wryly. "Her daughter, too—poor things, they're children of grim duty from the cradle. They honor me as an ancestor, but it's been a relief to them that I've retreated from the field. I'm much too light-minded for the cares of empires."

"Now you mock yourself," she said. She folded her hands on his breast and propped her chin on them, and contemplated his face. It seemed to give her no little pleasure. "The gods have no humor—all the priests assure us of that. It seems to me your heirs are very proper goddesses, and you are a properly fallen god. The priests will not be reassured."

"Should they be?"

"About this? Maybe not. They'll do well not to take you for granted."

"Such a delicate balance," he said, "between scandal and contempt."

"You are not only light-minded," she said, "you are wicked. What shall I do with you?"

"Love me," he said.

Her smile bloomed, slow and wonderful, transforming her face from loveliness into breathtaking beauty. Dear gods, he loved her. He had not known such fullness of the heart since he had loved a priestess who was a commoner, long ago in the turning of the worlds. With her too it had been the matter of a moment: a glimpse, a glance, a word spoken.

They had not been lovers long, though they had remained friends until the day she died. This one was sworn to him by vows that he meant to keep.

As if she had followed his thoughts, she said, "You'll leave me in the end."

"No," he said. "No, I will not."

"Of course you will." She sounded undismayed. "Your blood and kin will call you, and you'll go. Only give me what you can, and help our kingdom as you may, and we'll all be content."

"Even you?"

Her gaze was level under the strongly painted brows. "I never looked for this, never hoped or dreamed for it. Every moment that I have it is a gift of the gods. When it ends, I'll weep. I'm not made of stone; but neither am I a crumbling reed. I'll carry on, my lord, and remember that I loved you."

"I might surprise you," he said, "and stay."

"Don't make promises you can't keep," she said. "You've given me yourself while you can. That's enough. Now love me, my lord, and be glad of these hours together. Long after they're gone, they'll hold us in memory."

He shook his head, but he was not inclined to argue with her, not just then. The sun was coming. The shadow had let this world be for one blessed night. She was ready to be loved again, and he, he discovered, was ready to do the loving. He laughed for the simple of joy of that, and took her in his arms again, and kissed her as deep as either of them could bear.

She wrapped arms and legs about him and took him in her turn. She was no meek submissive woman; not she. He loved her for it, as for everything that she was or promised to be.

The shadow did not come back the next night, either, nor the next. People began to say that it was gone; that the god's coming, the walls of magic he had taught them to raise, the marriage he had made with their queen, had driven the enemy away. They would hardly lay aside years of fear and hiding, not in three days or four, but the young and reckless took it on themselves to go out at night, to see the stars; and there was festival in daylight, feasting and rejoicing, until between weariness and simple need to bake the bread and brew the beer, the festival ended and the people returned to their daily tasks.

When ten days had passed with no taint on the stars, even the most wary began to wonder if it were true—if the darkness had been driven away. It had become a game and a fashion to brave the night. At first it had been enough to ascend to the roofs, and the boldest slept there in the cool and the breezes. But youth was not to be outdone. Gatherings of young men walked beyond walls and wards, emboldened by an ample ration of beer and palm wine. Then some headlong soul took it into his head to embark on the river with lamps and torches and a troupe of musicians as mad as he was, for a carousal that echoed over the water and sounded faintly within the palace.

Tanit was ready to call out the guard, but the Lord Seramon stopped her. "They're safe enough tonight," he said.

"And tomorrow night? Will they be safe?"

"I don't know," he said.

"You think it will come back."

"I know it will," he said.

She did not know why her heart should sink. She had had no illusions; she had not imagined that this was more than a respite. But her heart had persisted in hoping against hope.

She rose from their bed and clapped her hands for her maid. He lay for a while, watching her, but when Tisheri had come, he disentangled himself from the coverlets and vanished in the direction of his own chambers. He would be back. There was less need for words between them, the longer they were bound together.

Tisheri did not approve of what she clearly was going to do, but it was not a maid's place to gainsay her queen. She dressed Tanit and arranged her hair, and adorned her in some of the lesser jewels. Then, with paling face but determined expression, she accompanied her lady out into the night.

The royal boat was waiting, the boatmen yawning but steadfast, and the Lord Seramon standing at the steering-oar, a shadow on shadow with a gleam of golden eyes. At first she thought with a small shock that he had come out as naked as he had left his bed, but when he moved, the torchlight caught the folds of a dark kilt. She rebuked herself for the quiver of regret.

It was very dark, even with torches. The stars were small and far away. The moon hung low. The world was a strange place, so full of hidden things, and yet while he was there, her fear could not consume her. She could see beauty in this darkness, as she saw in him.

The revelers on the water were not too far gone in wine and beer to be astonished that the queen and her consort had joined them. The tone of their carousing muted sharply; they were suddenly, painfully constrained. Tanit had herself lifted into their boat; they hastened to find a seat for her, to offer drink and what little food there was, and to cover their naked drunken women as best they might.

She kept her amusement carefully veiled. As she had expected, once they were burdened with the task of entertaining her, they grew much less enamored of their exploit—particularly the ringleaders, whose fathers were lords of her council. One tried to hide; the other covered his embarrassment with bravado, and might have offered impertinence if her consort had not appeared at her side.

The Lord Seramon was even more terrifying in the dark than in the light. His presence dampened the last of their enthusiasm. But when they would have ordered their boatmen to turn toward the bank, the Lord Seramon said, "Oh, no. It's not so very far to dawn. We'll see the sun rise on the river. Isn't that what you had in mind?"

Tanit doubted that they had thought so far ahead, but they would hardly say so to him. They were all too neatly trapped, and had no choice but to give way to his whim.

He folded himself at her feet, smiling at the young idiots from the city. The musicians, less far gone in beer and perhaps wiser, too, began to play a softer tune than they had been playing heretofore. Their singer had a remarkably sweet voice. The sound of it in starlight, trilling out over the water, was like nothing Tanit had known.

In a strange way it made her angry. The night should be hers, just as the day was. The shadow had robbed her of that.

She would take it back for always, not just for what brief time this respite gave her. She would have the stars and the moon, and the river flowing black but aflicker with starlight. The night was glorious. She would claim it for her own, as she had claimed this child of gods who lay at her feet.

SIXTEEN

DAROS FELL FROM DARKNESS INTO DARKNESS. THE SPARK OF light that had drawn him winked out just before the Gate took hold of him. He fell, rolling and tumbling, with his magery in tatters and his wits all scattered. He fetched up with bruising force against something that might, perhaps, be a wall.

He lay winded, throbbing with aches. He did not think his neck was broken. He could move his fingers, his toes. He could roll groaning onto his back.

Almost he might have thought he had fallen back into the chamber of the rite in the dark fortress, but he knew deep in his bruised bones that that was gone. This was a different room in a different world. Tall slits of windows surrounded it. Strangeness flickered in them, like flame, if flame could be dark.

A pale blue light welled slowly. In this darkness it seemed as bright as moonlight. He sat up with care. His hands were glowing with that sickly light; it seemed to come from within him, though he had done nothing, raised no magic, nor willed it at all.

Something stirred in the circle of light. It unfolded, straightened.

It had a man's shape: it stood on two legs, lifted two arms. But it was not quite a man. The face was too long, the chin too sharp, the mouth lipless. The nose was a sharp hooked curve. Its eyes were round and huge, like an owl's. They blinked at him.

His power was drained almost to nothing, but he had enough, just, to raise a shield about his mind. And none too soon, either. The blow that struck it swayed him to his knees.

He crouched on the cold stone floor. He had no weapon, no magery to wield. The creature stood above him. In some remote way he supposed that he should be afraid.

It lifted him to his feet. Its hands were four-fingered, like a bird's, and the fingers were very long, thin pale skin stretched over bones that flexed in too many ways, in too many places. It brushed them over his face, ruffling his hair. It spoke in a voice like a flute played far away.

He had the gift of tongues; it was common enough among mages. He understood the words, though there was a strange stretching, as if they did not mean quite what his sore-taxed magic tried to make them mean. "Recover quickly, please, and go. You are not safe here."

"You brought me here," he said, realizing it even as he said it. "Now you send me away?"

"You are not what I expected," the creature said.

"I disappoint you?"

The owl-eyes blinked slowly. "You are young," it said. "Your spirit is light. What I called . . . it was strong; a sun burned in it."

A bark of laughter escaped him. The creature recoiled as if an animal had snapped in its face. "I know what you called. I was hunting him. Shall I find him for you?"

"I called you," the creature said. "You, too. You both. He would come, you would come. One more would come. But not only you."

"Why?"

"I need you both," it said. "You are young, your spirit is light. He is a little less young, and strong—so very strong. Almost as strong as you."

"I am not—"

"You will be." The creature straightened. What had seemed a cowl, veiling its head, unfurled and shook itself free and rose, fanning like the crest of some great bird. It glowed in the blue light, shimmering in bands of white and blue and icy green.

He was gaping like an idiot. The creature loomed over him, beautiful and unspeakably strange. And yet, looking into those round pale-golden eyes, he saw a spirit that was not, after all, so very different from his own. "You are a mage," he said.

"Mage," it said. "You may call me that. Mage."

"Mage," he said. "What do you need of us?"

"I need you," it said. "This place—this prison—this thing I am compelled to do—"

Daros' head ached with making sense of alien words. He had little power left, barely enough to be certain that the walls of this place were more than stone, they were wards as well. What they guarded, what they forced upon the prisoner . . .

That was the knowledge he had brought from the citadel. The darkness was made, and magic had made it. There were oaths, covenants—

"But you are not a dark god," he said. "You're a mage, no more if no less. How could you have brought *that* into being?"

"Simply," it said. "You could do it. Be afraid of what might come from beyond the stars; ward your world. Build the wards to renew themselves. Bind them with darkness because it is stronger for this than light. Let the darkness grow too strong. Then—then—" It stopped, as if it had lost the courage to go on.

"Then see the darkness gain a will of its own?"

"Not its own will," the Mage said. "What I was afraid of—it came. My wards brought it, my darkness. It found me and took me prisoner. It compelled me to do its bidding."

"It? What is it?"

"Will to conquer," it said.

He did not understand.

The Mage furled its crest and lifted him without effort: though its limbs were stick-thin, they were strong. It cradled him as if he had been an infant. He struggled, but it ignored him. It flung him through one of the many narrow windows.

It was, as he had thought, a Gate. The Mage's awareness was about him, its power on him, though its body could not leave its prison. Enfolded in that half-alien, half-familiar magic, he slipped through mists and shadow onto a wide and barren plain. Wind blew across it, sighing with endless regret. Clouds veiled the stars, if stars there were.

A city rose on the plain. It was a city of night, lit by no moon or star. There were people in it—human people. He could have no doubt of that. Weak with exhaustion though his magery was, the Mage's power sustained him, and lent him a little of what he lacked.

It bore him on silent wings, soaring above the walls and towers, the dark windows and blank doorways. People moved through the streets, passed through the doors. They were blind: they had no eyes. There were no mages among them.

They labored with grim and endless persistence. What they did, he could not always understand. They ground grain, they forged metal. There were no fields to till; the grain must come from lands where the sun shone: lands that were raided, stripped and emptied of their riches. Just so were the people made captive, bound and enslaved, their eyes taken and their minds darkened and their souls held prisoner.

It was conquest, and absolute. "But why?" he cried to the power that cradled him. "Who would do this?"

It carried him onward, up through the levels of the city to a nest of towers at its summit. There was darkness visible, lightlessness so profound that he felt it on his face like the weight of heavy wool, clinging close, trapping his breath.

It tore away. He saw again with mage-sight, clear in the darkness. He looked down into a hall that, though alien in its lines and the shape of its pillars, was surely royal. Figures stood in ranks there. They were cloaked, cowled. He looked for faces, but saw none.

They were not like the Mage. They were men, he could have sworn to it—yet men who could not abide the light. They lived in darkness. Darkness was their element. They wielded it as a weapon. They clung to it as a haven.

They would blind the stars, and darken the sun of every world. They sang of it, a slow rolling chant, very like the chant of the priests in the citadel on his own world. The god or power to which they sang was the darkness itself. The Mage had opened its way into the worlds, fed it and nurtured it, and made it strong.

They had no magic, these men who lived in night. They were empty of it; and yet that emptiness lured the dark, and gave it substance.

He began to see as he hovered above them, why they had captured the Mage; what they needed of it, that they were so utterly lacking. The Mage was a weapon in their long and holy war. Light into darkness, darkness into silence, silence into oblivion.

He fled before it engulfed him. He twisted free of the Mage's grip, broke the wards, and with the last strength that was in him, flung himself through the Gate.

Death's wings beat close, so close that they brushed him with the wind of their passing. His bones cracked with the cold of it. He was stripped bare of will and wit. One thing was left, one memory, one presence. It drew him irresistibly from darkness into darkness.

He opened his eyes on the Mage's face. Its crest was upraised like a strange crown. "You are strong," it said, "but not yet wise. Do you see, young mage? Do you understand?"

"No," he said. His voice was a strangled gasp.

"The fabric of what is," it said. "I tore it. My world is gone, my people . . ." It made a strange whistling sound, like wind in a wasteland, eerie and unbearably sad. "They who came, they worship the void; they bind their souls to nothingness. They conquer in order to destroy. They would unmake the worlds."

"It seems they're succeeding," he said.

"You are too light of spirit," it said. "You do not know that you are mortal—even now, even believing what I tell you. You expect to live forever."

"I do believe that my soul will," he said. "Or are they going to destroy that, too? Will they even slay the gods?"

"Everything," said the Mage. "All that is."

He shivered. "There is no hope, is there?"

"Most likely not," the Mage said, "but I am alive, and I cannot keep myself from hoping. I called you to me, you and the other, with the strongest spell that was left to me. I set it to find the one thing that could stop this tide of nothingness."

"I? And my emperor?"

"He is an emperor?" The Mage seemed . . . disappointed?

Daros thought he could understand. "He's been a shepherd since before I was born."

"Ah," said the Mage in evident relief. "Kings and kings of kings, they are no use to us. It will not be pride or power that wins this war, if it can be won."

"I am a prince," Daros said. "Is that an impediment?"

"You are a well-bred animal," said the Mage. "It seems hardly to trouble you. You must go now—I have held us out of time, but now it turns in spite of me. I give you this. Keep it safe; when the time comes, you will know its use."

Daros found that his hand was clenched about something narrow and strangely supple. When he looked down, he saw that it was a feather,

glowing blue in mage-sight. He slipped it into the purse that hung from
his belt. Even as his hand withdrew, the Mage and the room and the
myriad windows whirled away. He spun like a leaf in a whirlwind.

He gave himself up to it. There was nothing else he could do. He let
his body go slack, his limbs sprawl where they would. His mind held its
center.

He burst through darkness into blinding light. It stabbed him with
blessed agony. It was so wonderful, so glorious, and so excruciating, that
he dropped to the splendid stabbing of stones, and laughed until he
wept.

Something jabbed his ribs. It was not a stone. Those were under him,
blissfully uncomfortable. This was alive: it thrust again, bruising several
of his myriad bruises. He caught it, still blind with light, and wrenched
it aside. The gasp at the other end, the grunt of a curse, told him what
he had known when he closed fingers about it: it was a spearhaft, and
there was a man gripping it.

Men. He could see now, a little, through the streaming of tears: shadows against the light. They were human. They were small; Asanian-
small, lightly built and wiry. Their hair and eyes were dark, their skin
reddish-bronze, rather like his own.

They all were dressed in kilts, and they all had spears. The man who
had brought him so rudely to his senses stood disarmed, staring at the
point of his own spear, angled toward his heart.

Daros lowered it slowly, grounded the butt of it, and used it as a
crutch to lever himself to his feet. The spearmen fell back before him.
The tallest came just to his shoulder.

He had never towered before. It was an odd sensation; he was not
sure that he liked it. Towering was for northerners. He was a plainsman;
he was accustomed to being a tall man but not a giant.

He resisted the urge to stoop. They were staring, but not, he realized,
at his height. He shook his hair out of his face.

The copper brightness of it made him pause, then smile wryly. Of course they would stare at that. Even plainsmen did, and they were born under the rule of red Gileni princes.

This was not his world, even a remote corner of it. He could feel the strangeness underfoot, the heartbeat of earth that was never his own. The sun was very hot, and he was dressed for the roof of the world. He stripped off his woolen mantle, his coat of leather and fur, his tunic, his shirt, his fur-lined boots, and—with the flick of a glance at the men who watched—his leather breeches. Even the light trews felt like a burden, but he kept those. He did not know how modest men were here, nor would it do to offend before he had even uttered a greeting.

He looked almost as battered as he felt. Bruises stained his skin along the ribs, down the shoulders and arms. One knee was a remarkable shade of purple, shading to livid as it ascended his thigh. He was not particularly lame on it, which was rather odd.

He gathered his garments into a bundle and bound it with his belt, fastened his purse with its precious burden about his middle, and said politely, "Good day, sirs. Would any of you have a sip of water to spare?"

The man he had disarmed had a half-full skin at his belt. He held it out, wordlessly. Daros bowed, smiled, sipped. He drank three swallows: far less than he wanted, but enough for courtesy, from the flicker of the man's eyes. He bowed again and returned the waterskin to its owner.

While Daros slaked his thirst, the man seemed to have reached a conclusion. "Tell me, lord, if you will," he said. "Do you come from beyond the horizon?"

Daros' gaze followed his. The horizon was a jagged black line beyond a wilderness of sand and stone. The sky above it was a vivid, almost unbearable blue. A winged thing hung there, in shape like a hawk. With no thought at all, Daros lifted his hand.

The hawk came down to it, plummeting out of the sky, braking with a snap of wings, settling lightly on his fist. Its claws pricked; he paid no heed to that small pain amid so many others. He looked into that wild golden eye, that pure feral mind. It had no fear of him. It was kin.

It leaped from his fist into the freedom of the air. He lowered his stinging hand. Beads of blood gleamed on it, scarlet on bronze.

The men about him sighed, all together. Their captain's suspicions had not eased, but it seemed he had had the answer he sought. "Come, lord," he said. "Come with us."

Daros sensed no danger in any of them, not unless he offered a threat. He tucked his bundle under his arm and offered his weaponless, nearly naked self for their inspection. "Lead, sir," he said. "I follow."

They led him away from the sand, over a sharp blade of hill and down to startling, glorious green: the valley of a broad river, bordered in desert. There were villages along the river, and towns, and one town larger than the rest, which here might pass for a city.

He would have given much for a senel to carry him, but he saw nothing of that kin or kind. They had cattle, not unlike the cattle of his world, but he saw no one on the backs of those. People traveled afoot or in boats, or once in a chair on the shoulders of brawny men, as men went in this place. They were still small and slight beside him.

He walked because he must, though he was going blind again, this time with exhaustion. When they paused for water, he drank three measured sips, and rather to his surprise, was offered three more. They had bread with it; he ate a little, but it was coarse and gritty and its taste was strange. He was hungry, but not hungry enough for that.

The sun was much lower when at last they came to the city. He walked because he had no choice. People stared; a murmur followed him. "A god. Another god."

He was too tired to wonder what they meant by that. The shade of walls was welcome, even redolent of crowded humanity.

They took him inside a house, large as houses went here, with a guarded gate and high thick walls. It was cool inside, and the stench of the city was less; he caught the sweetness of flowers. His companions left him there, and quiet kilted people took him in hand. They brought

him to a cool dim room, bathed him and dried him and laid him in a
bed, and cooled him with fans until he slid into sleep.

He slept long and deep. If he dreamed, he did not remember. He woke
with the awareness of where he was and how he had come there, complete in his mind, like the magic that had poured back into him like
wine into a cup. It was horribly weak still, and his head ached abominably, but he had known worse after a long night's carouse.

The servants were ready for him to rise. They had bread and thin
sour beer, fruit and cheese and a pot of honey. The bread was not so ill,
dipped in the honey. He was starving. He ate every scrap, to the servants' manifest approval.

He smiled at them. They smiled back. One offered to comb his
hair—an honor the man had won against the rest, from the look of him.
The color of it fascinated them. They had already satisfied themselves
that it was real, running curious fingers over his brows and lashes and
the light dusting of stubble on cheeks and chin. They presumed no further, which was well; he was not in a wanton mood this morning.

Fed and combed and shaven, and dressed in a kilt of lovely lightness
and coolness, he was judged fit to be brought before the lord of the
house. He was not moving so stiffly now; the raw edges of his magic
were healing. He kept it close within himself, letting slip only enough to
understand and be understood.

The servants led him through halls and courts, past people who
stared, some openly, some behind the screen of fans. Many were women;
some were lovely by any canon. They returned his glances with a clear
sense of welcome. He was a great beauty, they agreed in murmurs that
he was meant to hear. They wondered aloud if all of him was as beautiful as the parts that they could see.

Courts, it seemed, were the same in every world. He prepared his
most proper and princely face for the lord of this one, as well as his
patience, if he should be required to wait upon his highness' pleasure.

In that rather insouciant frame of mind, he entered a room of painted walls and heavy pillars, lit by shafts of sunlight. The lord was sitting just on the edge of one such blaze of brilliance, erect in a gilded chair. There was a creature in his lap, a very small but very magical cat. It eyes were the image of his, clear gold.

Daros laughed for pure delighted astonishment. "My lord!"

The emperor grinned at him, wide and white in a face that had lost half a score of years with the shaving of its thick graying beard. He shifted the cat to the floor at his feet and rose, sweeping Daros into a strong embrace.

Daros' eyes had spilled over. Foolishness; but he was tired still, and a little overwrought. The emperor held him at arm's length, looked him up and down, and said, "Avaryan and Uveryen, boy; something's been at you with cudgels."

"It was a long hunt," Daros said. He sighed. He was not particularly weak in the knees, but Estarion set him in the chair and stood over him, searching his face with eyes that saw everything Daros had to tell.

His hands came to rest on Daros' shoulders. Daros had no power to rise or to turn away. He had never been less inclined toward easy insolence.

"Show me," said Estarion.

Daros had brought the purse with its few oddments and its one great gift. He drew it out carefully. It weighed as light here as in that place between worlds, but in sunlight its appearance was transformed. It was pure and stainless white, and it shimmered like moonlight on water.

Estarion did not venture to touch it. A slow breath escaped him. He nodded slightly; Daros put the feather away, with a little regret and a little relief.

There was a silence. Daros broke it after some little while. "You really are the lord of this place?"

The emperor's brow arched. "That surprises you?"

"Knowing you, my lord," said Daros, "no. Are you working your way back up from shepherd?"

"I do hope not," Estarion said. "This is a little different from any occupation I've held before: royal consort."

"Royal—ah!" That did surprise Daros. "Does time move differently here? How many years is it since you came?"

"It's barely two Brightmoon-cycles," Estarion said, "and yes, that's mortal fast work. Come and meet her. Then you'll understand."

Daros set his lips together and settled for a nod. Nothing that he could say would be exactly wise. Estarion had a look that he could hardly mistake. Whatever this royal lady was, she must be beyond remarkable, to so enchant the Lord of Sun and Lion.

She was in a small court near the wall that surrounded the house, kilted like a man and armed with a spear, doing battle against three men. Daros recognized one: the captain who had found him in the desert yesterday.

She was fast and strong. She was as tall as the captain, slender without slightness, but he could have no doubt that she was a woman. Her breasts, in Han-Gilen, would have been reckoned perfect: neither large nor small, round and firm, with broad dark nipples. Her face was a narrow oval, her features carved clean, beauty without softness, as pure as a steel blade.

Oh, he understood: he would have been astonished, seeing her, to discover that Estarion had not taken her for his own. She was no callow child; she was younger than Merian, perhaps, but not by overmuch. If he had come there first, he might have had thoughts of claiming her for himself.

It was too late for that now. She finished her fight, and well, but he saw how she was aware of Estarion, how her face and body changed subtly in his presence. This was a woman in love, and with all that was in her. Nor was it unrequited. The force of the bond between them rocked Daros on his feet.

He had heard of such a thing, but never seen it. His mother, his father—they were reckoned a love-match, but not with the absolute purity of this. They were two who had joined for love and for policy. These were the halves of one creature.

She flattened one of her opponents with a sweeping blow, knocked one of the others onto his back with the butt of the spear, and froze the captain in midstroke with the tempered copper point of the spear against the vein of his throat. He bowed and surrendered. She smiled a swift vivid smile.

Daros was in love. It had nothing in it of lust; he would never touch what these two had, even if he could. As she turned toward him, he bowed to her as to the queen she was.

She raised him with a queen's dignity. Her smile lingered, illumining her face. "Welcome to my city, my lord," she said.

"You are most kind, lady," he said.

"It's only your due," she said, "as my guest and my lord's kinsman."

He bowed again, over her hands, and could find no more words to say.

Estarion was laughing at him. Let him laugh. Even the infamous libertine of the Hundred Realms could stand speechless before such a woman.

SEVENTEEN

THE MAGES CAME BACK TO THE TEMPLE IN STARIOS, BATTERED and half-stunned but safe. But Daros was gone from the world.

Merian had known from the moment he vanished. It was a tearing deep inside her, as if some hitherto unnoticed and yet essential part had been rent away. Even the Heart of the World had not wounded her so deeply—and it was far more to her and to her mages and this world than he could ever be.

She would kill him when she found him. With her own hands she would do it. He had broken every oath, every promise, every binding that anyone had laid on him. He was beyond incorrigible.

He was most likely dead, if not worse. The shadow had him. When she was not in a right rage, she might allow herself to mourn him. He had been a human creature, after all, and a lord of some worth in the empire.

"Lady?"

Perel's voice called her back to herself. Her mind was wandering; she could not remember when last she had slept. Her eyes fell on what he had brought back from the roof of the world.

It looked like a bowl, hollowed laboriously out of hard grey stone. The inside of it was stained, no doubt with blood. It was heavy and cold in the hands.

There was nothing in it. Nothing at all. It took magic and swallowed it; spells and workings cast upon it vanished as if they had never been.

It was a monstrously dangerous thing. "How like him to fling it in my face and disappear," she said.

Perel, for reasons best known to himself, had returned to the robes of his caste, black on black on black, and veiled to the eyes. Those eyes had a bruised look, but they kept their faintly sardonic expression. "It is a rather cryptic message to send before flinging oneself into the void. He did see something there, I think: something that he knew you would understand."

"I see nothing," she said.

His brows went up. "Might that not be the message?"

"You are as exasperating as he is."

"Not quite," he said. He bent toward the bowl. "We went in search of knowledge. We brought down a stronghold and brought back . . . this. I don't believe we failed, cousin. He said it was a key, although to what, he didn't say."

"To madness," she muttered. She propped her chin on her fists and glared at the thing. "Mages can make no sense of it. Priests bid me shun it. Servants of the Dark Mother swear that it's none of hers. Even my brother and his father know nothing of this. I need that maddening boy—and he, gods curse him, is nowhere among the living."

"I think," said Perel, "that he's not dead. Whether he's worse than that, I can't tell you—but if he were, you would know."

"How would I—"

His glance spoke all the volumes that he had failed to find on the roof of the world. She wanted to slap him. "I do not—"

"Don't lie to yourself," he said.

She flung herself away from the table and the bowl, round that shielded chamber in the temple of the Gates. The shields oppressed her, the riddle she could not solve, the one who was not there to tell her what it meant.

She needed to be elsewhere. A ride, a hunt, even an hour in a garden—

She was the general of this war. The defenses of this world were hers. She did not know what the enemy was or how to fight it. This should have aided her; should have told her what she needed to know.

She needed to be royal, to be a commander of the armies of mages. She wanted to be where he was. Even if that were the pits of the darkest hell.

She went in search of her mother. It had nothing to do with maternal comfort. She needed to remember why she could not abandon everything, as he had, and go hunting shadows.

The princess regent was closeted with her chancellor and his secretaries, engrossed in the minutiae of empire. Within moments of showing her face, Merian had a clean page in front of her, inks and pens to hand, and her mother pacing, dictating a letter to an imperial governor in Asanion.

Details of taxes and tribute raised a wall against her greater troubles. She was almost sorry to finish the letter and look up into her mother's eyes. They were piercingly keen. "Put that away," said Daruya, "and come with me."

The chancellor bowed. His secretaries paused in their work, rose and did reverence. Daruya acknowledged them with a nod. She swept Merian with her out of the workroom and through the maze of passages to a sunlit gallery overlooking the garden.

Even as late in the year as it was, flowers grew in this sheltered place, and bright birds darted among them. Daruya sat her daughter on the bench there and stood over her. "Tell me," she said.

Her directness was bracing. Merian had wanted it; she could hardly complain that it lacked a certain tenderness. Daruya was not tender. Honed steel never was.

"Have I been dutiful?" Merian asked her. "Have I been a proper royal heir?"

"In most things," Daruya said, "yes. There is the matter of an heir of your own."

Merian laughed. It was not mirth, exactly; more startlement, and a stab of guilt. "I may be proper in that respect, too, if the gods are kind."

Daruya straightened and breathed deep. "How unsuitable is he? Is he a commoner?"

"Not at all," said Merian.

"Is he old? Lame? Feebleminded?"

"None of those, Mother," Merian said. "He's a remarkably good match, as breeding goes."

"Then what is the impediment? There must be one, or you'd not be moping and glooming at me instead of rousing your mages to war."

"There is a small matter," Merian said, "of his having vanished into the shadow."

Daruya sat on the bench beside her daughter. She was not slow of wit, nor was she blind. "Ah," she said. "His lineage is impeccable, and a reputation, even one as . . . remarkable as his, can be outlived."

"A man has to live to do it," Merian said.

"Do you believe he's dead?"

"I don't know," said Merian.

"No? You are a mage."

"He's gone into the darkness," Merian said.

"So has our emperor," said Daruya. "We have to expect that they'll find one another, and hope that they come back."

"Are you comforting me, Mother?"

"No," said Daruya. "I'm comforting myself. That doesn't make it any less true. Are you waiting for me to give you leave to go hunting them? You won't get it. We need you here. You will be the Gate for them, if they can come back through the shadow."

"I hate you," Merian said mildly.

"Of course you do. I'm your mother."

Merian sighed. "Duty is a horrible thing."

"Yes," said Daruya.

"And I should go back to it." Merian stood. "Have I whined excessively?"

"No more than you ought." Daruya smiled, which was rare enough to catch Merian by surprise. "You've chosen well. He's had an unusually feckless youth, but then so did I. He'll be a strong man."

"I thought you despised him," said Merian.

"Only a fool would do that," Daruya said. "Go. Muster your mages. The tide is coming. You have reason now to survive it."

"Selfish reason?"

"Hardly selfish," her mother said. "You're taking thought for the continuance of the line."

"Am I? He doesn't even know. He thinks I despise him."

"Does he despise you?"

"I think he dislikes me intensely."

"That need be no impediment," said Daruya, "in a state marriage— and still less in such an arrangement as I had with your father. He's notoriously free of his favors. You are beautiful, and royal. I doubt there will be a difficulty."

Merian set her lips together. There was no profit in protesting to this of all women that she did not want to be bred like a prized mare, still less by a man who disliked her. She would have a lover or nothing.

She well might have nothing, when all was done. She left her mother still sitting in the sun, and returned to the temple and the shielded chamber and the enigma of the bowl.

It mocked her with its plainness and its perfect emptiness. Yet there was knowledge in it. He had found it. Both Perel and Kalyi had sworn to that. Truth was in this thing, if only she knew how to read it.

She had a council to sit in and young mages to teach. At evening she dined with her brother Hani. He was in a taciturn mood; they ate in silence and parted early.

She had been sleeping in the temple in the Brightmoon-cycle since the mages came back, taxing her mind and wits with the riddle that Daros had sent her. Tonight, partly for temper but partly for exhaustion, she stayed in this house. She was aware of Hani's presence nearby and the servants below, and the city all about them. There were no wards on the house but what any mage would set on the place where she was minded to sleep. After so long in the heavily walled and shielded precincts of the temple, she felt oddly naked, as if she had laid herself bare to the stars.

It could be dangerous to be a mage on the verge of war, and to sleep within such light wards. She courted that danger tonight. Sleep was a Gate, and dreams could bear one to the worlds beyond. Waking, she had found no answers. Perhaps in sleep, something would come.

She composed herself in all ways, buried her fears and anxieties deep. Her power gathered in her center. She opened the gate of sleep and passed within.

He was asleep on a low frame of a bed, in a room of shadows and dim lamplight. His skin was darker, his hair brighter than she remembered, shot with streaks of gold. His face was less girlish-pretty but no less beautiful. Something had stripped the silliness from him.

There was shadow on this world, but she sensed it dimly, beyond strong wards. The nature of them, how they sustained themselves, intrigued her, but before she could study them further, he sighed and opened his eyes.

They were dark, unclouded with sleep. The strength of power in them made her catch her breath. They came to rest on her as she stood over him. A slow smile bloomed.

If he disliked her, in this dream he showed no sign of it. "Lady," he said. "Oh, I am glad . . . lady, I thought never to see you again."

"In dreams we can see whatever we please," she said, as much to herself as to him.

"That depends on the dream," he said. He stretched, arching like a cat.

She had no power over herself at all. She lay beside him. She was as naked as he, gold to his copper, ivory to his bronze. His skin was warm under her hand, solid and strikingly real. When she raked nails lightly down his ribs, he shivered convulsively.

He tasted of salt, with an undertone of sweetness. He did not fling her off, nor did he shrink from the kiss. Not in the slightest. It was she who recoiled, poised above him, wide-eyed and wild. "That is not what I—"

"No?"

"Whose dream is this? Am I in your—"

His smile had come back. It made her dizzy, and drove the words out of her head. He closed his arms about her, but gently. She could have broken free if she had wished to. She did, truly she did, but when she tensed to pull away, she found herself stretched along the length of his body. Her breast on his breast. Her loins on—

He did not move to finish what she had begun. That was altogether unlike his reputation—but then he had never, in any tale that she had heard, been accused of taking a woman against her will. He was hot and hard between them, and his breath came somewhat quick, but he lay still.

She knew what one did. She was a mage, and no child. But she had never—

"Never?"

He was in her thoughts, soft as wind through grass. His surprise quivered between her shoulderblades.

"Never!" she snapped. But she did not wrench herself away.

"May I . . . ?"

No! her mind said. But her body, arching against him, cried, *Yes!*

He guided her softly, without haste. When she stiffened, he let be. After a while she eased a little; then he went on. The pain she had expected. The pleasure, so soon, she had not. She cried out in astonishment. He nearly let her go, but she held him fast. She knew this. She had been born knowing it.

It was so very, very real: the gusts of pleasure, the hot rush inside her, the gasp and muffled cry in her ear. Somehow they had shifted. It was his weight on hers, his body above her, his face gone suddenly, briefly slack.

He dropped beside her. She was thrumming like a plucked string. She barely had strength to lift her hand, and yet she had to do it, to stroke the sweat-dampened hair out of his face, to let her fingers drift across his lips.

He smiled with all the sweetness in any world. His eyes had been shut; he opened them, turning them toward her. The night was in them, and a glimmer of stars.

"I have to know," she said. "The message—what—"

"Nothing," he said. "Nothing at all."

She woke knotted in bedclothes. Her body was still throbbing. She fought to calm the beating of her heart. There was an ache in her secret places.

She stumbled to her feet. The water in the basin was chill—it made her gasp and shiver, but it cooled the heat in her. She washed herself with shaking hands, all over; and caught her breath.

There was blood on her thighs. The ache—the not-quite-pain—

Her courses. They were early. Had they bred this dream, then? She finished her bathing and did the necessary, then wrapped herself in a robe against the creeping cold. It was nearly dawn. She could try to sleep. Or she would take her aching self and seek out the library, and try to find something, anything, that might answer the riddle he had set.

Memory kept intruding. Lamplight on the high arch of his cheekbone, the proud curve of his nose. Salt taste of sweat. Fullness of him in her, fitting her perfectly, bringing her up and up to—

She shut that door and bolted it. The books told her nothing—just as he had. Nothing at all. She was left with memory that would not let her go, and a thoroughly improper desire to bring back the dream.

Of course she did not. She needed answers, not fruitless rutting born of impulses that should have been mastered long since. The books had none. The bowl offered nothing. The Gates were shut, the world walled off—yet she felt the shadow rolling toward it. There was no time for love, however real it had seemed, and however certain her body was that it wanted more.

EIGHTEEN

WIND HOWLED ACROSS THE PLAINS OF VOLSAVAAR, FAR IN THE west of Asanion. Snow had fallen in the night; the wind had whipped it away by morning, bringing bone-cracking cold. Even in a mantle of magery, Merian shivered.

She sat astride a slab-sided mare, with Perel beside her and the lord of Kuvaar a little ahead, looking down into the cleft of a valley. There had been a city there ten days ago, set on a crag at a meeting of roads. The traders' route from inner Asanion ran westward here, crossing that from the north into the south, and fording the river that flowed from the mountains of gold and copper. It had been a rich city, rough-edged on this border of empire, but fat and prosperous.

Now it was gone. The land was scorched bare, the walls battered down. Towers lay in ruins, in a cawing of carrion birds.

"Every man of fighting age," the Lord Zelis said. "Every woman able to bear a child—gone. All the dead are the old and the sick, and the children. Not one was left alive."

"It's the same in Varag Suvien," said Perel, "and in the Isles, and in Ianon—whole cities destroyed in a night, all across the empire."

"Across the sea, too," said Merian. "All shattered in the same way, and all in the night. This was the first, but a mountain fastness near Shurakan was next—on the other side of the world. Then Ianon and Varag Suvien, half a thousand leagues apart, both on the same night. There's no pattern, nothing that tells us what will be next, or where."

"They left traces here," Zelis said. "Tracks that make no sense, and vanish within a bowshot of the walls."

"Your mages? Did they find anything?" asked Perel.

"Nothing," Zelis said. "The city was not warded. People here put little trust in mages; they reckon that strong walls and a trained army will be enough."

"And in Ianon they reckon that there have been no such wars since the time of the Sunborn," Perel said, "and in the Isles, mages are still shunned as changelings and drowned in the sea."

"Whereas in the heart of the empire," said Merian, "we were so flattened by the loss of our great Gates, and so broken by the blow to our magic, that we never took steps to keep the enemy from coming in through Gates of its own. It slipped through the gaps in such wards as we had, and caught us unawares."

She sent the mare down from the top of the hill. The senel snorted and flattened ears and shied, but she was obedient enough. However reluctant she was, she did not spin and bolt.

Behind her, Perel said, "By your leave, my lord, your mages will meet in the morning in the holding. We'll see to it that there's no second attack here."

"Then . . . the Gates within the world are open for them? Not only for you?"

"We will bring them," Perel said in a silken purr, "from the places to which they've fled. You will be protected, whether they will or no."

"For that we thank you," said Zelis.

Merian sighed as she rode down to the ruined city. The empire had been at peace too long. Mages waged no wars, knew no adversity. They had become toothless scholars, working their magics for no greater stakes than curiosity. What threats had come upon them had barely taxed their powers. Those few that rebelled, or that seized too much, seeking their own gain, had been put down before they could grow strong enough to offer a threat.

Now this great enemy came, and none of them was ready. She rode the snorting, shying mare through the wilderness of devastation. There was a reek of smoke and burning, but not of decay. What the fire had not charred to ash, the carrion creatures had picked clean.

She felt no magic, no power. Nothing. No lost souls wandered the ruins. If this had been but one spate of destruction, she might have looked for an invasion, the beginning of a mortal war. But it had struck everywhere, all over the world. It came from the other side of the stars.

This city had fallen the night after she dreamed of Daros. She had been hunting him again through dream and shadow, but the shadow had been too deep. It had rolled like cloud across the stars, blinding her eyes and her magery. Lost in it, befuddled by it, she had wandered until dawn.

Word of the destruction had reached Starios on the third day, after Vadinyas fell in Ianon. The lord there was royal kin, and his daughter was an apprentice mage in Starios: one of the youngest, but very gifted, to her father's great pride. She woke screaming, and screamed until her voice was gone. Not even the chief of healers could bring her out of the darkness into which she had fallen.

In desperation they had called for Merian. She was not a healer, but she was Sun-blood; she could bring light where no other mage could. She went far down into the child's darkness, and brought her back, leading her by the hand. Merian washed her in light, gave her the sun to hold. Clutching it, speaking through tears, she told the tale of her kin and her people taken, the weak slaughtered, the land swept with lightless fire.

Then word came in from Volsavaar, from Varag Suvien, from the Isles. It was the same word, the same tale, without variation. The walls of the world were breached. The enemy had broken them down through Gates that owed nothing to any working of mortal mages.

Merian had come to Volsavaar first, because it was the first to be struck. She had come through the Gate within her, because it was swiftest and safest. No enemy had waited there, no darkness set to trap her. Yet she had felt the shadow, had known that if she tried to open a Gate from world to world, matters would have been otherwise.

She rode from end to end of that dead city, then back up the long road to the hill, where Perel and the lord of Kuvaar waited in silence. "You will do what needs to be done here," she said to Perel. "I think I know where they will strike next."

His eyes widened in the Olenyai veils. "Lady?"

He never called her by her title unless he was less than pleased with her. She chose to keep the title and ignore the displeasure. She turned to Zelis. "May I borrow this mare for yet a while?"

He bowed. He was baffled, but like all Asanians, he rested secure in one surety: she was the heir of the Lion, and was to be obeyed. She inclined her head to him, leveled a hard stare at Perel, and opened the Gate once more.

It was early afternoon in Volsavaar, but the sun hung much lower in the sky in Anshan-i-Ormal. Merian's Gate brought her to the marches of the sea, to a wild and stony coast dashed by winter waves. A storm had blown off to westward; the sun was descending in a tumble of cloud-wrack.

Merian rounded on Perel. He had slipped through the Gate behind her, as sly as a shadow. "Do you crave exile, too?" she flashed at him.

His golden eyes were bland. "I have no gift for calming children.

Ushallin will come in the morning and hold yon mages' hands. She will explain to them, with far more tact and diplomacy than I would ever be capable of, that unless they perform the office for which they were trained, they will be stripped of their power and whatever wealth it may have gained them, and sent home in disgrace."

"A penalty for which you may set the example."

"I don't think so," he said. "I was born a mage, cousin, but I was bred and raised an Olenyas. I'm of more use here, guarding your back, than herding mages in Volsavaar."

She hissed. "I am cursed with disobedient men. Stay at my back, then, and don't get in my way."

He bowed with correctness so punctilious that it skirted the edge of insolence. She turned her back on him, the better for him to guard it, and rode along the headland to the place that was calling her.

She was not a prophet; she had little prescience. But she had seen a pattern in the cities that fell, a shape in the web of lesser Gates that crossed this world. The shadow had struck in the gaps, in outlands, where mages were weak. But there was more to it than that.

"And that is?"

She did not turn to face Perel. Her thought had shaped itself where he could catch it if he wished. "Strength," she answered him.

She could feel his puzzlement, his brows raised under the headcloth. "Mages are weak here," he said. "Wards are feeble or nonexistent. Where is the strength?"

"In mortal hands," she said. "Strong backs, Perel. Fertile wombs. If you were taking slaves, what would you look for? Where would you go?"

"Where magic is weak," he said slowly, "and men and women are strong. To the outlands of empire. But how—"

"They have to strike here tonight," she said. "The tide of the lesser Gates, the turning of moons and stars—it's centered in this place. They'll break through just . . . here."

She paused on the edge of the headland. A sea-city crowned the promontory. There was a harbor below, a sheltered circle, full now with ships moored or drawn up against the aftermath of the storm. The walls were high and strong, topped with towers; she saw the gleam of metal, helmet and spearpoint. A chain protected the mouth of the harbor, breaking the storm-surge and, in gentler weather, keeping out invaders and pirates.

There were no wards on walls or harbor. She sensed a spark of magery here and there: a healer, a soothsayer, a seller of love-charms and pretty potions. Its temple of the Sun was tiny and deserted, its priest too ancient to perform the rites. The greater temples of the city were dedicated to the sea-gods, and those fostered no orders of mages.

This was a proud city; she might even have called it arrogant. As she rode through its gate, she took note of the strength of its guards, tall robust men with fair skin and sea-colored eyes. They raked those eyes over her, stripped her naked with them, and grinned approval, but they neither knew nor feared her. Perel in her shadow attracted more notice. They took count of his weapons, recalled a legend or two of black-veiled warriors from the distant east, noted that he was no taller than a boy of twelve summers, and dismissed him as they had her.

She would not waste either power or temper on hired brawn. She took the straightest way through the city, which was somewhat convoluted: there were three walls, with gates at different points along them, to slow the advance of invaders. The citadel rose high in the center, a tower of iron and grey granite, with a banner flying from its summit: gold sea-drake on scarlet.

There were a good number of people in the streets, and most seemed well-fed and well-muscled. Women did not go armed, but all the men did. She saw children everywhere—many naked in the winter's cold, but seeming impervious to it.

The gate of the citadel was open like the gate below. Its guards were just as arrogant and no more inclined to offer courtesy to a pair of yellow-eyed foreigners. They were, however, more wary. They barred Merian's way with spears. "No riding-beasts in the citadel," they said. "No weapons, either."

Merian shattered their spears with a flick of the hand. "I will speak with your lord," she said. "Bring me to him."

They were not fools. She was glad to see that. They knew a mage when they saw one. "You will wait," said their captain, and with somewhat of an effort: "Lady." As he spoke, one of his men departed at the run.

She did not have to wait overlong. During that time, Perel amused himself by honing each of his swords, then the daggers he carried about his person. He was on the third when the guardsman came back. The man's face was pale. "He says for you to go down to the city and wait, lady. He'll summon you when he can."

"Indeed?" said Merian. "How lordly of him."

She rode forward with Perel behind her. The guards, loyal to their lord, tried to bar her with their bodies. She flung the Sun in their faces. While they reeled, blinded, she rode through the gate and into the courts of the citadel.

The lord was in his hall, entertaining a goodly gathering. She recognized at least one notorious pirate, and would have wagered on a dozen more. The lord himself, she knew slightly: he had appeared in court some years since, to be confirmed in his demesne and to swear fealty to her mother as regent. He was a large and handsome man, a fact of which he was well aware. His black hair was thick and curled in ringlets, mingling with his great black beard. There were rings of gold in his ears and clasping his heavy white arms; a massive collar of gold lay on his wide shoulders. A jewel flamed on each finger; he was belted with plates of gold crusted with sea-pearls.

The roar of carousal died as she rode into the hall. She had brought the Sun with her, and a fire of magic that sent guards and servants reeling back. She halted in front of the high seat and looked into the lord's startled face. "My lord Batan," she said. "Your city is prosperous. I applaud you."

"You are bold, lady," he said. He grinned. "I like that. Here, come up. Sit with me. Adorn us with your beauty."

She held up her hand for him to kiss. He froze at sight of the Sun in it. She watched the race of thoughts across his face, and arrested it with a cool word. "I am not here for dalliance. This city will be dust and ash by morning. Would you save it? Then listen to me."

"Ah, great lady," said Batan. "Your fears are flattering, but you needn't fret for us. We're well defended here. Who's coming for us? Raiders? Pirates? Rebels and renegades? We're armed against them all."

"Against this you are not." She urged the mare forward, up the steps of the dais, until she stood over the lord in his tall chair. "Where are your mages? Why are your walls not warded?"

"Lady," he said, barely cowed by the sight of her looming above him, "with all due respect, mages and fighting men have little in common."

"Indeed?" said Perel. Merian had not seen him move, but he was off the back of his senel, leaning lightly on the arm of Batan's chair, with the point of a dagger resting against the great vein of the lord's throat. With his free hand he conjured a flock of bright birds that scattered, singing, through the hall. "Warrior and mountebank, I, and occasional imperial errand-runner. Do believe her, sea-lord. I've seen what this city is about to be, and it is not a pleasant sight."

"We are defended," Batan said.

"Not against this." Perel lowered the knife but kept it ready, angled to pierce either eye or throat if the man moved untimely. "You should not have let your mages die off or settle elsewhere. Strength of arms is all very well, but this requires strength of magic."

"Indeed? Then why isn't—whatever it is—choosing mages for targets? Is it hungry to taste good clean steel?"

"It shatters cities," Merian said, "and takes slaves. It comes from beyond the stars. I can defend you, but I ask a thing in return."

"Of course you do," said Batan. "What do you need of me, beautiful lady?"

"A hundred of your best fighting men, with mounts for them all. And leave for my guardsman here to do whatever he deems necessary for the defense of this city."

"Men and mounts," said Batan, nodding slowly. "And provisions? How long a campaign?"

"One night," she said. "From dark until dawn."

"Then you won't be going far."

"Just out of sight of the city," she said. "If there's a level of land within that distance, with room enough to build a city, that will do best. If not, we'll make do with what we can find."

"I know of a place," he said. "It was a city once. They say mages broke it in a war, ages ago, when mages still fought wars."

Her eyes widened slightly. She knew nothing of such a city, or of such wars as he spoke of. They must be ancient beyond imagining, forgotten in the mists of time.

Now they would live again. "Yes," she said to him. "That will do very well. Choose your men now. We mount and ride within the hour. It were best we be in place before nightfall."

"I do like a strong woman," Batan said. Perel's dagger had withdrawn; he rose. His armlets and collar clashed as he flung them on the floor. His people were staring, mute, comprehending only that there was a battle ahead of them. He singled out ten of them, swiftly. "Fetch your men. First court, now."

They flung off the fumes of wine and idleness and leaped to do his bidding. Merian nodded approval. Perel was not pleased with the task she had given him, but for once he did not object. This was battle—he would defer to his general, however little he liked his orders.

When she came to the courtyard, she found her hundred men already gathered. One more joined them: Batan on a seneldi stallion as massive and beautifully arrogant as he was himself. He was armored as they all were, cloaked against the cold, but grinning delightedly at the prospect of a fight.

She found that she was grinning back. Gods knew she was no pirate, but after so long in fretting and in waiting, she was more than glad to be taking some action, even if it should prove completely useless.

The sun was sinking, but there was time, Batan assured her, to reach the ruins and set up camp. They could ride at speed, with no need to spare the seneldi. The evening was clear, if cold; the wind had died to a brisk breeze.

As they rode at the gallop through the city gate, the wards rose into a high and singing fortress, a flame of golden light in the long rays of the sun. Merian sighed and let herself slump briefly on the dun mare's neck, before she straightened and urged the senel onward. The mare was desert-bred: that pause in the lord's hall had been as good as sleep and grazing to her. She would need water and forage soon, but with the gods' good favor, she would have it.

The ruined city lay somewhat over a league away, perched on a crag over a swirling maelstrom of waves. Its walls were broken, its towers tumbled in the winter grass. There was still a fragment of citadel, and enough wall to shelter this small an army. While they made camp, pitching tents and building fires and posting sentries, she walked the line of the old walls, gathering power as she went.

It had been some while since she made such a working, a great illusion and a subtle lure for the darkness. She could feel the stretching at the edges of her magic, the strain of arts and powers unused or little used, but she was not taxed unduly, not yet. If she had been less in haste, she would have brought with her a company of mages from Starios. It was only Perel's stubbornness that had given her such support as she had.

Too late now for regrets. If—when—she did this again, she would do it properly. Now she had to hope, first, that her workings would rise and hold, and then that she had guessed rightly; that the enemy would come here and not somewhere altogether unforeseen.

Batan followed her on her round of the walls. He did not vex her with chatter, but his eyes were a little too intent for comfort. She closed them out while she brought her magics together and raised the walls anew, stone by stone at first, then swifter, as the magic found its stride.

The earth woke to the working, and drew up power of its own, startling her, but she had wits enough to make use of the gift as it was offered.

She built a city of air and darkness. Each of the men who camped in it, she swelled to a dozen, then a hundred, populating the city with strong warriors. Herself she scattered through it, so that she was a myriad of women, young and strong, with babes at the breast and babes in the belly, and flocks of children.

When she was done, she encompassed multitudes; and this broken city seemed alive again, if any had looked on it from without. From within, without magic, there was little to see, save a flicker of shadows.

A few of the men were white-rimmed about the eyes. Those had enough power to sense a glimmer of what she had done. She mounted a heap of rubble that might once have been a stair, and waited for them all to take notice of her. The sun was nearly down; swift dusk was falling. She mantled herself in light, damping it lest she alarm the men, but letting it seem as if she had caught the last glow of the sun. "Men of Seahold," she said, "I thank you for this gift that you have given me. You are the shield and bulwark of your city, and its greatest defense. It may be that you will have to fight tonight. Don't be astonished if shadows seem to fight beside you. You may die; you may be taken captive. This will not be an easy battle, if battle there is. If any of you would withdraw, you should do so now. I can send you to safety while it is still possible."

"What will we be fighting, lady?" asked a whip-thin man with a terribly scarred face. "There's no threat from the land, and nothing will come at us by sea, not on this cliff."

"It will come from the far side of the night," Merian answered him, "and it will do its best to enslave you. You are bait, captain; if I've laid the snare properly, this invasion will pass by Seahold altogether and fall on us here."

"Ah!" said the captain. "Bait we understand. Deadly danger, risk of being boarded, captured, sold in the Isles—what! Are you shocked, lady? Do you think your laws can bind a pirate?"

"I think," said Merian, "that those laws might be enforced more strictly hereafter—but also that some sentences might be commuted for services rendered to the empire. If you survive. If this gamble succeeds."

"We are all gamblers here," another man said. Grins flashed white, spreading fast, for none was to be outdone by any other.

She had them. They were no cowards; they did not know enough to be afraid, nor maybe would they quail even if they had known. They took their ease as seasoned fighters could, alert but wasting no strength in fretting.

She settled on the broken stair, wrapped close in her mantle. Batan brought her a cup of wine, spiced and steaming hot, and a loaf of bread that must have been brought from the city. There was cheese baked in it, still warm, savory with herbs and bits of sausage. She ate every scrap, and sipped the wine slowly, until she was warm from her center outward.

Batan watched her, smiling slightly, as the twilight deepened and the stars bloomed overhead. In a little while both moons would rise together, but now there was only a gold-and-crimson glow along the eastern horizon.

His regard was deeply respectful, but offered more, if she would take it. If she had been another woman, she might have welcomed the warmth. But she was the cold daughter of the Sun, who carried the god's fire in her, but took none of it for herself.

She drew her cloak more tightly about her and shifted a little away from him. He shrugged, then smiled ruefully. He did not retreat to the greater conviviality of his comrades.

He was guarding her. She decided to allow it. When the fight came, if it came, she would need his strong arm and his skill in weaponry, until the trap was sprung.

They all settled to wait. The light in the east swelled so slowly that it was barely perceptible. Then the blood-red arc of Greatmoon's rim lifted above the horizon. Brightmoon blazed in its wake.

The silence was absolute. The phantom city grew stronger, more real, in that twinned light. No shadow came. Nothing stirred but the wind and the crashing of the waves.

Merian felt herself slipping into a doze. She shook herself awake. *He* was on the other side of dream, calling to her. But she could not answer. Not tonight. Not without betraying them all.

NINETEEN

A S THE MOONS CLIMBED THE SKY, SHADOW CREPT TO COVER
them. It seemed at first like mist or cloud, but it was too deep, its
edges too distinct. It was like a curtain drawn across the moons.

The dimmer their light grew, the more campfires seemed to burn
within the ruined walls. The city of shadows was stronger. It was feeding on old magic sunk deep in the earth, tapping roots that had grown
there in times before time. It was stronger than Merian now, and had
grown apart from her. It no longer drew from her strength.

There was danger in that, but no more, surely, than she had courted
in baiting this trap. The fabric of the world was tearing. Things were
pressing on it, seeking entry from without. Every instinct screamed at
her to raise wards against it, but she must not. She did not want to keep
it out. She wanted to draw it in, trap it, and if possible destroy it.

The tone of the waiting had sharpened. The darkness grew deeper, though the moons rose higher. The sea battered the cliff-wall. She could taste the salt of spray.

They came in the deepest night, when the only light was a struggling flicker of firelight. They rode through the tatters of the world's walls, an army of darkness mounted on beasts like nothing this world had seen.

The riders were human. Sworn and bound to darkness though they were, they were men. They were not mages. They were as mortal as men could be. The shadow was darkness absolute—but these riders had not wrought it. They wielded it, perhaps served it, but it was not theirs as the illusion of a city was hers.

They fell on it with a bombardment of weapons so strange that they caught Merian off guard. Siege-engines, even mage-bolts, she would have known how to face: feigned the proper response of mortal walls, and allowed them slowly to crumble and fall. This was like a blast of dark flame. It seared through the illusion. The western side of the camp caught the edge of it and puffed to ash.

There was no light, not even heat as she had known it. It simply destroyed whatever it touched.

Batan's men had no mage-sight. They could not know what had attacked them: their fires, dying too swiftly, revealed nothing but enveloping darkness. Those who had been in the western tents stumbled through the heaps of ash where they had been, naked and blind. The armor that they had worn, even to the garments beneath it, was gone, but the dark fire had harmed not a hair of their heads.

The raiders had stopped. One of them raised a weapon like a thick spearhaft and cast from it another bolt of lightless flame.

This time Merian was ready. The wall that met it had the strength of stone. It trembled before the assault, cracking and crumbling.

Batan barked orders to his men. Merian cast a magelight over them, shielded against the attackers, but clear enough that they could see as she saw. They spread across the field, weapons at the ready. As they moved, they doubled and trebled and doubled again. Her working had found its strength once more, rooted deep in this crag. Her armies of air were gathered. The living men took it for a dream, or understood and yet were not afraid.

Pirates, she thought with something very like admiration. They always landed on their feet, whatever deck they fell to.

The enemy broke down the walls, battering them relentlessly until not one stone lay atop another. If it astonished them to find an army arrayed against them, they betrayed nothing of it. The foremost rank raised their flame-spitting spears with a lack of haste that reeked of contempt. Swords and spears, even arrows, were no proof against them.

The earth quivered underfoot. Far below, beneath even the ancient magic, fire surged and swelled like the sea: fire of earth, born of the sun's fire.

Merian called it up. She grasped it with both hands, the hand that was mortal flesh and the hand that was immortal gold. She drew it into herself, filling her body with living flame.

Batan's men howled and sprang to the charge. The enemy lowered their spears. Merian loosed the fire.

They went up like torches. Their beasts, their armor, burned with a fierce white flame. The light ate them alive, devoured them whole. Nothing remained of them but a drift of ash, swirling in the wind.

Merian stood astonished. The wind blew the cloud of ash away. There was nothing left, not one thing. She had destroyed them utterly. Even the shadow was gone; the stars were clean, and the moons shining as bright almost as day.

"It can't be that easy."

Merian had called council as soon as the sun came up, gathering it in the fire in front of Batan's tent. She could see each one where he or she was: her kin in Starios, Ushallin in Kuvaar, Kalyi in the ruins of Yallin in the Isles, and Perel in Seahold, which had passed a peaceful night within the protection of his wards.

It was her brother Hani who had spoken, from the library that she missed with sudden intensity. "If a simple spell of fire could destroy them, they would never have come as far as this. Someone else would have lit them like torches long ago."

"I took them by surprise," Merian said. "They may come warded next."

"I'm sure they will," her mother said. "But do think. If they're so vulnerable to light—if they travel in a cloak of absolute darkness—we have a weapon against them. Light is our simplest magic, one that even the least of mages can raise. We can muster our mages with that knowledge."

"It is useful," Hani granted her, "but I can't help thinking, wouldn't it be better to track them to their lair and destroy them? If all we do is defend, they can keep coming and coming. We should attack."

"We need to know more," said Merian. "I saw men, not mages. Someone or something is behind them, and that has power enough to blind the stars, to break or ignore Gates, and to overrun worlds."

"Still an enigma," her mother said, "but a little less of one than before. If we can capture one of them, discover what he knows . . ."

"We'll try," Merian said. "They may come back here to find out what became of their raiding party. I'll be waiting for them."

"You'll have reinforcements," Daruya said, "but we can't spare many. We're spread dangerously thin as it is."

"We may be able to predict where they'll come," Merian said. "If we have mages ready to spring through lesser Gates at the first indication of the enemy's coming, we'll be able to do battle wherever he is."

Daruya nodded briskly. "Yes. That's well thought of. I'll see to it. Look for the newcomers before sunset."

"They'll find us here," Merian said. "I'll have men fortifying this place as much as they can—walls seem to be of some use, and better walls of stone than walls of air."

That ended the council. Merian lingered by the fire. She hardly needed its warmth: the magefire was still in her, burning with a steady flame.

Batan's shadow fell across her. Those of his men who had been touched by the dark fire were laid together in one of the larger tents; he had been with them until a moment ago. His face was grim. "They're blind," he said. "They flinch and scream when the sun touches them, but they can't see it. Their eyes are sealed shut."

Merian rose stiffly. She was weary; she had not slept since before she could remember. "Let me see," she said.

There were a dozen of them. The skin of those who were not already white-skinned seafolk was blanched to the color of bone. Their eyes were indeed sealed shut: the lids had melted into the faces. It might have seemed that they were eyeless, save that Merian could see the wild shifting of the eyes beneath the skin. When she came into the tent, bringing with her a shaft of sunlight, those nearest her writhed and moaned as if in pain.

Her lips tightened. Her anger was too deep for speech. She knelt beside the first man. He shrank from her; his skin shuddered convulsively. When she touched him, he shrieked.

She withdrew her hand, sat back on her heels, and drew a careful breath. The power she had was Sun's power, power of light. These men had been so poisoned that the touch of it was agony.

"Darkmages," she said. She spoke across the long leagues of the empire. "Mother. Send a darkmage. Quickly."

Daruya's mind touched hers, brushed it with assent, slipped away. She felt the press of power on the Gate within her. *Here,* she bade it. *Outside.*

She smiled in spite of herself at the one who came in, though she frowned immediately after. "Hani. You can't—"

"My father is taking his turn in the library," her brother said. He was dressed for travel in leather and fur, the common garb of Shurakan; his straight black hair was plaited behind him. He knelt beside her.

She had not even thought of him when she asked her mother for a darkmage. She never saw him so; he was her brother the scholar, the quiet and perpetual presence either in Starios or in Shurakan. He did not flaunt his power; even in councils of mages he spoke more often as a scholar than as a darkmage. Yet he was strong though he had come to it late; and he was skilled, as a scholar could be who had studied both the theory and the praxis of his art.

When he laid his hand on the wounded man's brow, the man twitched, then sighed. Hani echoed that sigh. "This is an ill working," he said, "well beyond my power to heal. Better all these men be taken where healers can look after them. There's too much broken, too much twisted. This horror of the light—it goes to the heart of them. Can you see?"

Through the mirror of Hani's power, she could. Without that, she was blinded by her own light. "We'll send them to the Temple of Uveryen in Kundri'j," she said. "You will stay here. If we manage to capture one of the enemy, he may be even more appalled by a lightmage than one of these men. We'll need you then."

"Very likely you will," he agreed. He fixed her with a hard stare. "And now, sister, you will rest while I see to what needs to be done."

"I can't rest," she said. "There's too much to—"

"I'll do it. You're out on your feet. Tonight we need you alive and conscious. Shall I throw you over my shoulder and carry you to bed?"

She glared. He was more than capable of doing just that, and rather too often had. "I can walk," she said tightly.

"Then walk."

There was a tent for her, pitched long since. Her belongings were in it—rather more than she remembered bringing with her. Someone had laid out bread, salt fish, strong cheese. She was not hungry, but she ate as much of the bread as she could choke down, and made herself swallow a bite or two of fish, and drank the sour wine that had come with it.

While she ate, she felt the rising of power, the opening of the Gate that took the wounded men away. She heard men talking: Hani and Batan, the latter at first brusque, then softening before her brother's unshakable good humor. The lord of Seahold was out of his depth, and not liking it; but she saw in him no taint of treachery. He would keep his oaths to the throne, however little it pleased him, and however poorly he understood the reasons.

The gods had been kind, to set this lord here, where such a man was most needed. She could rest. Hani would see that all was done that must be done.

She fell asleep to the sound of men arriving, masons and carpenters with the tools of their trade. They would build a wall to bolster her magic.

Her dream was drenched with sunlight. She caught a scent of flowers, and heard water lapping, waves of a lake or broad river on a green shore. The air was breathlessly hot, a great blessing after the damp and biting cold of winter by the sea.

He was standing on the bank, more deeply bronze than before, almost black against the dazzling white of his kilt. Sweat sheened his broad shoulders and ran in a runnel down his back. His hair had grown since last she dreamed him. It was cut in a way she had not seen before, straight across the brows and straight above the shoulders. A plaited band bound it above the brows. It was odd, but she rather liked it.

He had a bow in his hand and an arrow nocked to the string; he was watching a flock of birds that swam together on the water. They were large birds, grey and brown and white; their call was an odd and almost comical honking. In his mind was the thought that their flesh, when roasted, was very good to eat.

He was alone. She might have expected hunting companions, servants, a guard or two, but in this world of dream, there was only he.

He turned. The splendor of his joy weakened her knees. He caught her as she sank down, lifting her in a long delicious swoop. His laughter healed her of weariness and fear, cold and anger and the lingering touch of the shadow.

When he would have set her down, she drew him with her, body to his body, swept with a white heat of desire. He was ready for her after a moment's startlement: beautiful dream-lover, giving her her every wish.

They lay naked in a bed of reeds, breathing hard, grinning at one another. He stroked her hair out of her face, letting his hand linger, caught in curling golden strands. "It's been so long," he said. "I thought I'd lost you, driven you away with my wantonness. You are no light woman, and I—"

"I yearned for you," she said, "but our dreams never met."

"You don't hate me?"

He sounded so plaintive that she kissed him to console him. It might have led to other ends, but he was not as potent as that, even in dream. "I don't hate you," she said. "I'm rather sure I love you."

"You—"

"Yes, it is appalling, isn't it?" She meant to sound light; she hoped she did not seem too brittle. "Don't be afraid. I won't trouble you to love me in return. Give me what you have to give, and that will be enough."

"What I have to—" He broke off. "Lady, every day I remember that one night. Every night I sleep, hoping to see you again, but knowing— dreading—that my dreams will be empty. That you gave way to my importuning, but when it was over, you fled in horror, loathing every-thing that I was. I never meant to violate you so."

"Violate—" Now she was doing it: sputtering witlessly, too startled for sense. "I wanted every blessed moment of that. Every one. And every blessed inch of you."

She had struck him speechless.

She drove him back and down and sat on him, stooping over him, glaring. "Have you really been tormenting yourself ever since?"

He nodded.

She slapped him, not quite hard enough to bruise. "Idiot! Indaros of the thousand loves, they call you—didn't one of them teach you how to tell when a woman is desperately in love with you?"

"But," he said, "she usually is. But she's not you. She's not—*you*."

It made no sense, and yet she understood it. "You never loved anyone before."

"Not with my heart and soul," he said. "Not with the worship of my body. Not with the surety that if she truly hates me, truly I shall die of it. It's not . . . very pleasant."

"What? Loving me?"

"Being afraid that you hate me. If you merely dislike me, or find me a hideous nuisance, I can bear that. If you find me useful in the manner of a stud bull, as your mother did your father, that's endurable. But hate— that I can't endure."

"I do not hate you," she said, though from the sound of it, he might think she lied. "Damn you, we're quarrelling. We're worlds apart, there's a sea of darkness between, I fought a battle last night and face another one tonight, and you can bicker with me as if we were a farmer and his wife."

"You fought—" He had seized on that; of course he had. "It's come there?"

"Ten days ago," she said. "No—eleven now."

"We haven't seen it in five cycles of this world's moon," he said. "The world is closed in; it's globed in shadow. The only Gate away from it is the gate of dreams. But the attacks have stopped."

"It hasn't been that long since—" She stopped. Time ran differently on the other side of Gates. She of all people should know that. "Tell me what you know of this!"

"The bowl I sent you—didn't it reach you?"

"Yes!" she snapped. "And there is no answer in it. None. At all."

"But that is the answer," he said. "Nothingness. That's what the shadow is. You can't fight it. There's nothing to fight. It's absolute oblivion."

"Last night," she said, "we were attacked by men. Lightmagic destroyed them utterly."

"Those are its servants—they are mortal. The shadow is not. As long as it exists, its servants will keep coming, and worlds will be destroyed."

"How many of them are there? How many servants?"

"Legions," he said. "They make more with every world they conquer. They serve darkness absolute. They are sworn to utter destruction.

What you did to that raiding party—you should take care, lady; they'll come in ever greater numbers, craving the blessing of oblivion."

"What, they'll make me a saint of their cult?"

"A goddess," he said. "A queen of destruction."

She shuddered. He held her close to him, babbling apologies, but she silenced him with a hand over his mouth. "Stop that. I'm not fragile. I would rather not be what these madmen must think I am. But if it will serve this world or any other, I will exploit it to the utmost."

"Cold-hearted royal lady." But he said it tenderly, cradling her, covering her with kisses.

She caught his face in her hands and stopped him. It was not easy at all. She wanted to take him by storm. But this dream had given her all that she could have wished from the bowl of nothingness. She must take it back to the waking world. She could not tarry here, where her heart yearned to be.

"Beloved," she said, brushing his lips with hers. "You know I have to go again. As time runs between Gates, it could be an hour before I come back, or it could be a year. Do trust me—that I will come back. That I do love you."

"I do," he said, though he gasped as he spoke. "I do trust you. I love you with all my heart."

Such heart as he had, she might have thought once. But she knew him better now. With dragging reluctance she let go, relinquishing the dream, leaving behind the sun, the heat, the joy of his presence. She lay again in the winter cold, in the roaring of waves, in the midst of bitter war.

TWENTY

BATAN'S MEN HAD WROUGHT WONDERS WITH FALLEN STONE AND ships' timbers. It was not a large fort, but the wall was stout, and the tents within had been shifted out of range of the enemy's strange weapons. It happened that Merian's tent had become the center, where the general's tent was wont to be; it stood over the deep well of the city's magic. She woke in the embrace of it, and came out to find herself in the beginnings of a sturdy hill-fort.

The sun was still high, but had begun to sink toward the low swell of hills to the westward. The air was a little warmer than it had been, the wind a little less knife-edged. She kept the warmth of her dream inside her, wrapped about the fire in the earth. For a long moment as she stood in front of the tent, she remembered his arms about her and his voice in her ear, at once deep and clear: the kind of voice that could sing the full range from flute to drumbeat. She wondered if he sang. Surely he did. Princes were trained to dance, to fight, to sing.

She was losing her sense of what was real and what was not: forgetting that this was but a dream. Her body felt as if it truly had been locked in embrace with a man. She ached a little, was a little raw, but more pleasurably than not. Places in her that had been shut and barred were open, filling with magic.

There was a cult of priests in Asanion who worshipped the gods of love, and made of it a rite and a sacrament. They professed that the act of love was a great working in itself, and that mages who joined so could double and redouble their power.

She did not feel as strong as that, but certainly she was stronger than she had been before she slept. She sought out Hani where he stood with Batan, overseeing the raising of the seaward wall. It was the last to go up, because it was the least likely to meet with attack, but they were not making it any less strong for that. There was an army of men at work, stripped in the cold, laboring feverishly to be done before the sun sank too much lower.

Batan bowed to her. Hani smiled. He was more at ease, the closer to danger they came. When death threatened, he would be perfectly calm. Had she noticed before how much like the Gileni prince he looked? That line came from his part of the world, long and long ago. In this proud bronze face, she could see it.

"It pleases me to see you well, lady," Batan said, breaking in on her reflections. "It seems the rest did you good."

"It did that," Merian said, coolly as she thought, but Hani's glance sharpened. She ignored it. Batan's expression at least did not change. She was keenly aware just then of the weight of a man's eyes. This one wanted her, and would take her if he could, but not until the battle was over.

She was flattered. She was also inclined to geld him with a blunt knife. She regarded him without expression, until he flushed and looked away.

Be kind, Hani said in her mind. *He's a man—he dreams, as all men do.*

He could dream. She did not put it in words, not precisely, but Hani understood. He shrugged, half-smiled, sighed.

By nightfall the walls were raised, and the laborers rested under guard in the camp's heart. Most of them would rise to fight when the time came; weary they might be, but they had their pride. They would defend what they had built.

They had all eaten while the sun was still in the sky, even Merian, who surprised herself with hunger. She ate a solid ration and washed it down with well-watered wine. It stayed with her, feeding her strength, as the sun set and the darkness descended.

It was a long, cold night. Moons and stars shone undimmed; the sea quieted little by little. The men took turns to rest and share the fires. The guard on the walls changed again and yet again.

She had miscalculated. Wherever the shadow had gone tonight, if it had gone anywhere at all, it had not come here. She had driven it away.

Yet she did not put an end to the vigil. She was too stubborn; they had worked too hard. This hook was baited, and strongly.

It came well after midnight, yet swifter than before. Stars and moons winked out. A gust of icy air rocked the tents on their moorings. A hammer of darkness smote the raw new fort. In the same instant, wave on wave of warriors stormed the walls.

Merian lashed them with light. Her bolts struck shields. They cracked and buckled. She struck them again, again, as the forces behind them smote the walls. It was a battering of hammer on hammer, anvil on anvil.

Hani's magic poured like water beneath hers. It melted away the shields and lapped at the feet of the darkness. Light stabbed through the rents that it had made.

The enemy's slaves burned and died. But the darkness had swallowed the stars.

Hani raised wards about the walls. The remnant of the enemy

retreated. The defenders stood alone in darkness impenetrable, lit by their feeble sparks of fire.

Merian was almost startled to see the sun rise. It burned away the dark, and showed a ring of blasted heath round the walls. Seahold was still safe—Perel's wards had held—and nowhere else, as she cast her mind afar, had seen attack. She had succeeded: she had drawn the enemy's attention to this one place.

She could not keep it there forever. If it were possible to divide the enemy, to lure them to a number of guarded places, that might be a wiser course—"Now that we know they can be lured," she said to her brother.

Hani was looking bruised about the eyes. He had worn himself thin in a long day of building and a long night of magical battle. Still, he kept his feet reasonably well, and he seemed to have his wits about him. "Another council?"

"In a while," she said. "I need to think. Will you ride out with me?"

He had strength enough for that. Batan, gods be thanked, had let go his iron resolve at last, and dropped into the first tent he happened upon. The camp was under the command of one of his seconds, a man in utter awe of the mages. He would never have presumed to object to their desertion.

They rode past the circle of the enemy's attack to the place where their track began, and then a little beyond it. There was a hill of sere grass and a ring of ancient stones: another place of power, such as seemed unwontedly common in this harsh country.

"Maybe we should have studied the mages of Anshan," Merian said. "Were they as old as the dark brothers of the mountains?"

"Older, I would think," Hani said. "Even the stories are dim and all but forgotten; all that's left are ruins like these, spread in a wide circle within the borders of the country, and a name for them all: the Ring of Fire. I can't remember anything of any enemy they may have fought, or whether they knew Gates. Mostly they fought one another and subjugated lesser mortals. They might have been gods."

"They drew their power from the earth," Merian said, "and from the fires far below. It's still here, waiting to be tapped. What if—"

Merian broke off. Hani's eyelids were drooping shut. He kept his seat on the senel's back as an old campaigner could, with no need of conscious awareness.

She let him sleep. She was fiercely, almost painfully awake. The longer she was in this place, the more its power filled her. She was drawing it as a tree draws water from the earth, through every root and vein.

It was not lightmagic, but Hani seemed to have no awareness of it. The enemy must not, either, or they would never have come here. She was conceiving a plan, but she needed time and solitude—which through Hani's exhaustion she had won for herself.

She left her mare, and Hani slumped in the gelding's saddle, and sought the center of the stone circle. The sun was warm inside the ring. Buried in the grass she found another stone, flat and smooth, somewhat hollowed in the middle. It was like a shallow basin filled with clear water, though no spring bubbled through the rock, nor had it rained since Merian came to this country.

The water was full of light. Merian dipped her hand in it, found it icy but not unbearable. She laved her face and sipped a little. Its taste was cold and pure, but as it sank to her stomach, it warmed miraculously. She drew a long wondering breath. She felt as if she had slept the night through.

The warmth settled deep within her, below her heart. She sat beside the stone, basking in the sun, and let her thoughts drift free.

Visions stirred in the water. She bent toward them, drawn through no will of her own. She saw a ring of cities, and foregatherings of mages, and great battles against powers that came by sea and land and air. Some were dark, though she could not tell if any was darkness absolute. They forged weapons of light and shadow, and wielded them against their enemies, and sometimes won and sometimes lost, but always kept their pride and the pride of their cities.

They were all gone long ago, sunk into the grass. Powers faded, cities died; wars destroyed what weariness and neglect did not. Mages were seldom born now in Anshan.

The water shivered, though no wind had touched it. The ancient visions dissolved. A face stared up at her, a very strange face, somewhat like an owl's and somewhat like a man's. The round yellow eyes blinked once, slowly. "Help," it said clearly. "Help . . ."

Merian bent closer to the water, but not so close that her breath disturbed it. The vision moved likewise, until its face filled the basin. "You are the rest of him," it said. "You must meet. The worlds that float in void—they must touch. You must bring them together."

"Who are you?" Merian asked of the creature. "What are you?"

"Mage," it said. "He knows. Listen! Speak to him. He knows."

It was not human, this vision. It did not think as humans thought. Merian struggled to understand it. "He? Who is he?"

"The rest of you," the Mage said. Was it ever so slightly impatient? "You can end this. But you must listen."

"I am listening," she said as respectfully and patiently as she could.

"Listen," the Mage said.

Its eyes flashed aside. It gasped. Before Merian could speak again, the vision vanished. Darkness filled the basin, darkness absolute.

She recoiled from it. Something caught her. She whipped about.

Hani blocked the blow before it knocked him flat. He seemed much rested and blessedly strong. She rested for a moment in that strength, before the power in the earth and the heat of the sun began again to restore her.

"Shall I call council?" he said.

"No," she said. "After all, no. But I need more builders, and more mages. The Ring of Fire will rise again."

"Have we time for that?"

"I think we do. We're not the heart of their war yet. These are raiding parties. I'll wager that the army itself is still worlds away."

"I hope you win your wager," Hani said.

So did she; but she was not about to confess it. When she mounted the mare, Hani was close behind her, swinging onto the gelding's back.

By day mages and makers rebuilt the Ring of Fire, the chain of hill-forts and sea-holdings round the rim of Anshan. By night they stood guard against the dark.

Merian remained in the first of the ruined cities, which had a name again: Ki-Oran, Heart of Fire. That had been its name in older days, the men of Seahold assured her. A fort had risen within the walls, a small citadel and quarters for a garrison.

The enemy had begun to raid abroad in Anshan, in the smaller towns and the fishing villages. Those, unlike the forts and cities, had no mages to ward them. They fell in black ash, their strong people taken, the weak slaughtered. What had become of those who were stolen, mages feared they knew: Batan's twelve wounded men were still in Asanion, healing slowly and incompletely when they healed at all.

Yet there was no lack of men to offer themselves for defense. Men in Anshan were all either pirates or bandits at heart, and they knew no fear. Given a fight, even a fight they could not win, and faced with a fate that truly was worse than death, they laughed long and hard, and brought their brothers and cousins to join them in the villages. They were bait, the lure that kept the sea-dragons away from the fish, and it was their pride to be so.

Merian had not forgotten the strange vision in the water, but its meaning eluded her. There was too much else to think of: finding mages to ward every village without weakening the guard and the wards outside of Anshan; building forts and strongholds; raising a wall of light-magic that would, she hoped, keep the raids within its circle.

The gaps in the web of lesser Gates were closed, except here. It was a monstrous task, and strained the mages to the utmost. They were warding a world. Everywhere that human creatures were, they must be, and be strong.

Winter deepened. In the deepest of it, the raids grew less frequent. Then for a while they stopped. But only fools celebrated a victory. The world was still under shadow. The greater Gates were gone, the Heart of the World destroyed. A few brave souls had tried to raise the nexus again, or find some sign that it could be restored, but those that survived the attempt would never heal completely. Where the nexus had been was a maw of darkness, growing inexorably wider, deeper, stronger. It swallowed magic; it devoured mages. It was beyond any mortal strength to conquer.

With the first breath of spring, the shadow-warriors came back. Already in sheltered valleys, fighting men had turned farmer and were plowing the steep rocky fields. When Greatmoon waxed again, they would plant.

"Man's got to eat," one of them said to Merian. She had ridden out of Ki-Oran to the village where the enemy had struck anew. The raiders had taken five men but injured none; the village's young mage had driven them off.

He was in his house under a healer's care, with his magic half burned away. The enemy had new shields, stronger and more deadly. Merian would speak with him when—if—he came to his senses. Meanwhile she had left her escort to walk through the fields, past the men and oxen engaged in the plowing.

It was one of these who had paused to greet her. He was not as young as some; he had a stocky, sturdy look to him, and a roll to his stride, as if he had just come off a ship. Yet he seemed at ease with the oxen and the plow, and his furrows were straight and clean.

He was not in awe of her, and he was frankly admiring of her beauty. It gave him clear pleasure to stand with her, looking out across the rolling field. "Fighting's good," he said, "but a man's got to eat before he can fight. We can't stop farming just because there's a war over us."

"We could feed you from the rest of the empire, if it were necessary," Merian said. "You are our shield and bulwark. There's no need to trouble yourselves with lesser things."

"We're proud to be your defense, lady," he said, "but we take care of our own."

He was not to be shaken. Merian accorded him respect and let him be.

She strode on round the edge of the fields, alone for the first time in quite some while. She was a little tired, a little light-headed; it was not an ill sensation, but it was rather odd. If she stopped to think, the lightness was not in her head but in her center. She almost felt as if, if she spread her arms, she could lift and fly.

There was no more magic here than in any other tract of earth. The closest fortress in the Ring of Fire was a day's ride distant. Yet she was brimming with light, drinking the sun. The *Kasar* in her hand was burning so fiercely that she kept glancing at it, expecting to find a charred ruin. But her hand was its wonted self: slender, narrow, with long fingers; ivory skin, golden sun.

She was quite startled when her knees declined to hold her up, and even more so when her head decided that, for amusement, it would expand until it had encompassed the sun.

It was dim suddenly, and cool. There was a roof over her, low and thatched, and a light hand laving her face with something cool and scented with herbs. She struggled to sit up. The hands became suddenly iron-strong.

They belonged to a burly man in a leather tunic, one of the warrior-villagers. A woman appeared behind him, so like that she must be kin; she carried a wooden bowl, from which wafted the scent of herbs. She set it down beside the pallet on which Merian was lying, and looked hard into her face. "Good. You're awake." She flashed a glance at the man. "Let her go."

The man ducked his head and backed away. She nodded briskly and dipped a cup in the bowl. "Drink," she said.

It was a tisane of herbs. The taste was faintly pungent and faintly sweet; it cleared Merian's head remarkably. She saw then that her escort crowded outside the house, which must be one of the larger houses in the village. Two of them stood on either side of the door, glaring at the pair who nursed her.

"Out," the woman barked at them. "*Out!* When she wants you she'll call you back."

They growled but retreated. The woman returned to Merian's side as if nothing had happened, and went on pouring the tisane into her.

Merian endured three more sips, but the fourth gagged her. She pushed the cup away. "Tell me what you don't want my men to hear."

"What, did you want them breathing down our necks? This house is small enough without those great louts in armor."

"I am not dying," Merian said. "I'm not even ill. I'm a little tired, that's all. The sun made me dizzy."

"You certainly aren't dying," the woman said. "Do you really think it isn't obvious?"

Merian did not understand her. "What isn't—"

The woman's eyes widened. "You honestly don't know, do you?"

"What don't I know?"

The woman paused, breathed deep, lashed her with a question: "Do you remember when you last had your courses?"

"Yes! They were—" Merian broke off. It had been—cycles? Since the morning that she woke and—

"Oh, no," she said. "That's impossible."

"So they all say," the woman said dryly. "I've been stitching cuts and birthing babies in these parts since before my own courses came, and believe me, royal lady, it is possible."

"But I have never—"

"I took the liberty of examining you," said the woman, "and lady, you have. If you don't kill yourself running hither and yon, you'll bear the child in the summer."

Merian sat dumbfounded. Those had been dreams. She had not gone to him in body. She had had no slightest inkling—

Had she not? That great well-being, that sense of doubled strength: was that his child in her, doubly mageborn and conceived in magery?

Impossible.

Her hands spread across her belly. Was it a fraction less flat than it had been before? Was there a spark of life within? Was it floating, dancing, dreaming, waiting for her to become aware that it existed?

She truly had not known. She had dreamed of him again thrice—gone to him, loved him, lain in his arms. They had spoken of little beyond one another. It was not for knowledge that she had sought him.

The last dream had been but a handful of days ago; he had been nursing wounds, remembrance of a lion-hunt. He had killed the lion, and been lauded for it, too; its skin had been their bed. She had kissed each mark and scar, and healed him as much as he would allow, which was not much at all.

"I want to remember," he had said, "to remind myself why prudence is a virtue. And why I should try harder to practice it."

"There are those who would faint if they heard you now," she said.

He laughed. "Wouldn't they? It would almost be worth it, just to see their faces."

She had laughed with him, and made love to him gently, to spare his hurts.

It had not been a dream. None of it had been.

But how—

She escaped the village and the sharp-tongued healer with the too-keen eyes. Her men had heard none of it, gods be thanked. She assured them that her brief indisposition was only lack of sleep and magic taxed to its limit. They pampered her, fussed over her, and tried to slow their pace back to Ki-Oran, but that she refused to submit to.

Her mind was a roil of confusion. This she had never expected or planned for. Later, yes, if he lived, if he came back to this world, if what she had dreamed was true. But not now. Not in the middle of a war.

Yet now she was aware of it, there was no denying it. She was carry-

ing a most royal child: heir at one remove to the princedom of Han-
Gilen, and at two removes to the empire of Sun and Lion. She had done
her royal duty at last, done it well and most thoroughly—and her lover
had met with her mother's approval, too, which was as great a marvel as
any of the rest of it.

TWENTY-ONE

THE DARKNESS HAD BEEN GONE SO LONG FROM THE VALLEY OF the river that people began to believe that it was gone forever. The gods had done it, they said: the two who were in Waset, who had come from the far side of the horizon with the sun in their hands, to drive back the powers of the night.

They tried to build temples, to worship their saviors. Estarion put a stop to that with firmness that struck even Daros to awe. But he could not stop the steady stream of people who came to leave offerings on the palace steps in the mornings, or the crowds that followed both of them wherever they went, bowing and praising their names. Nothing that they could do would lessen it, least of all any display of magery.

It was rather wearing. Dreams were no refuge: *she* was seldom in them. Daros needed further distraction, but there was little allure in taverns or in the arms of women who were not she.

He approached the queen one morning, half a year of this world after he had come to it. Estarion was elsewhere; she was preparing for the morning audience, being painted and adorned like the image of a goddess. She smiled at him, somewhat to the distress of the maid who was trying to paint her lips, and said, "I hear that your recruits are doing well."

"They are," he said. He had been training young men in the arts of war, finding them apt pupils, as farmers and herdsmen went. Weapons were not particularly easy to come by; they had no steel, not even bronze, and copper was rare. But what they could do with stone and bone and hardened wood, they did well enough.

He said as much. The queen nodded. "These things that you have, it's a pity we can't get them. But we make do. You do expect the enemy to come back?"

"The shadow is still there," he said, "on the other side of the sky. But I didn't come to speak of that. There's another thing that's struck me strangely. Traders are coming back, plying the river. People are even traveling again. But there have been no embassies. Why is that?"

"Perhaps we're out of the habit," she said. "It's been years since king could speak to king. The enemy kept us all within our borders. Common people could travel, but embassies were always prevented in some way: slowed, stopped, killed."

"They were dividing you," he said, "the more easily to conquer."

"Yes," she said.

"Do you have spies, lady?" he asked her. "Have you talked to travelers? Do you know what's happening in your neighbors' kingdoms?"

She regarded him with those great dark eyes, as if she needed to study him. "I do have spies," she said. "I do listen. My neighbors are holding their realms together as I am mine. None of them is strong enough yet to think of war, if that's what you fear—though they may do so before much longer, and knowing that I've allowed you to raise and equip an army."

His stomach tightened. "Lady, that's for the shadow, not for them."

"One may hope they understand that," she said.

"Lady," he said after a pause, "I came here to ask your leave to mount an embassy, to visit the kings and talk to them. The enemy divided you out of fear—because an alliance was in some way a threat. While the enemy is gone, if you can unite in common cause, he'll come back to find you much stronger and far more ready to stand against him."

"That is so," she said. "I have considered it. But there's been no one I can trust to send, who has the skill to speak as an envoy. My lords are as closed in upon themselves as my brother kings. We all are—we've forgotten how to speak to one another."

"I haven't," he said. "I was raised and trained for this." As was Estarion, but he did not say that. Estarion did what he chose, as he chose. Daros did not pretend to understand him.

She was still studying him. "You think you can do this?"

"I know I can." He hoped he did not sound excessively cocky.

"I will give you a boat," she said, "and boatmen, and a retinue suitable to your rank and station. Waset's good name will be in your hands."

"I'll not harm it," he said.

"I think you will not," said the queen.

Later that day, as Daros instructed the latest band of recruits in the rudiments of archery, Estarion happened by with casualness that was just a fraction too studied. He distracted the recruits rather excessively. Their awe of Daros had begun to wear off; he was familiar, if terrifying. The queen's consort was an eminence so lofty that he stole away their wits.

Daros called a halt to the proceedings before someone put an arrow through his neighbor, and dismissed the recruits. They withdrew with dignity, but well before they were out of sight, they scattered like the boys they still were, whooping and dancing across the field to the city.

Daros would have liked to run with them, but he had an accounting to face. It was taking its time in coming. Estarion had wandered across the field to inspect the line of targets, taking note of the bolts that clustered in the center of one or two. "Good shots," he observed.

"They grew up hunting waterfowl," Daros said. He set about retrieving arrows, both those in the targets and those that had flown wide. Estarion lent him a hand.

When every bolt was found and put away in its quiver, they walked slowly back toward the city. Daros almost dared hope that there would be no reckoning after all; that Estarion had come simply for the pleasure of his company.

That was foolish, and he knew it even as he thought it. A moment later, Estarion said, "You're not a bad general of armies. Will you be trying your hand at diplomacy next?"

"You don't think I can do it?"

Estarion smiled thinly. "Why, lad. Don't you?"

"Isn't that what a prince does?"

"The general run of princes, yes. Is it a custom in your country to conduct the affairs of the realm in brothels and alehouses?"

Daros stiffened. "I haven't touched a woman of this world since I came to it, nor set foot in a tavern. I've been the very model of a prince."

"So you have," Estarion said blandly. "It's a remarkable transformation. I commend you."

"Yet you have doubts about this venture."

"No," said Estarion. "In fact I don't. I'm jealous. I can't go—I'm needed here."

"You want me to stay, so that you can go."

"No," Estarion said again. "It's only . . ."

Daros waited.

"We can ill afford to lose you. Promise me something. If one or more of the kings is hostile, promise that you won't try to force an alliance."

"I won't do anything dangerous," Daros said. "I'll swear to that."

Estarion's glance was less than trusting. "What you call merely dangerous, the rest of us would call lethal."

"I'll pretend I'm my father," Daros said. "Would that content you?"

"You're not capable of that much prudence."

"How do you know?"

Estarion cuffed him hard enough to make him reel. "Curb the insolence, puppy. If you can be wise and circumspect, and speak softly to these kings, then you'll do much good for this land. But if you grow bored or lose your temper, you may harm it irreparably. Do you understand?"

Daros set his teeth. He deserved this; he had earned it with his years of useless folly. And yet . . . "Surely I've at least begun to redeem myself since I came here. Have I been feckless? Have I been foolish? Have I been anything but dutiful?"

"You have not," said Estarion, "and that is a matter for great admiration. But one would wish to be certain."

"What? That I'll be resentful enough to prove you right?"

"Prove me wrong," Estarion said. "Because if you don't, I'll deal with you as painfully as I know how."

He was not jesting. Daros was torn between wanting to laugh and wanting to hit him. He settled for a baring of teeth. "I'll prove you wrong," he said. "My word on it."

"Good," said Estarion.

They were almost to the walls, but their pace had slowed. Daros had meant to be silent about another thing, but he was feeling spiteful. "I know you wish you could go. But your heart wouldn't be in it, would it? It's been a long while since you waited on the birth of an heir."

Estarion stopped short. He did not knock Daros flat, which rather surprised him. The emperor's voice was mild, almost alarmingly so. "I should have known you'd see that."

"Should it be a secret?"

"She's lost ten children, six of them sons, either miscarried or dead at birth. She's terrified of the omen if she dares celebrate this one."

"Yes," said Daros. "But she won't lose this child. Will she?"

"Not while I live," Estarion said.

"Nor I," Daros admitted. "I . . . laid a small wishing on her this morning, when I went to see her."

He braced himself, but Estarion only sighed. "Of course you did. So did I. She's wonderfully well protected."

"It's a son," Daros said. "Have you thought about what he will do to the line of succession in your empire?"

"He will do nothing," Estarion said. "Daruya will rule after me in Keruvarion and Asanion. This is the heir to Waset, son of the queen and her consort."

"Do you think Waset will ever understand what blood has come into its royal house?"

"Waset understands that its queen is mated to a god. And maybe," said Estarion, "this is proof that we will overcome the darkness. Sun-blood continues itself when it's most needed—always. Even here, it seems, on the other side of the horizon."

Daros bowed his head to that—not a thing he did often, at all, but he had a modicum of respect for the god who had begotten Estarion's line. "She is worthy of that blood," he said.

Estarion was not a jealous man. He smiled, by which Daros knew that he was in the royal good graces again. "Come in to dinner," he said. "Then don't you have an expedition to plan?"

"By your leave," Daros said.

"You'd do it regardless," said Estarion, "but I'll give it, for my vanity's sake." He flung an arm about Daros' shoulders and pulled him through the gate.

That was when the moon was halfway to the full. When it touched the full, the queen's own golden-prowed boat waited at the quay of Waset, with her picked men in it, and the best of Daros' recruits. There was also a deputation from the temples of the city, led by none other than the high priest Seti-re.

Daros would infinitely have preferred another companion, but it seemed that this was to be his first lesson in the art of being politic. Seti-re wore his accustomed slightly sour expression, although he lightened it considerably for Daros' benefit. For some unfathomable reason, though he did not like Estarion at all, he was in awe of Daros. Almost Daros would have said that he was infatuated, but it was not quite as fleshly a thing as that.

He was not the most comfortable companion for an embassy, but Daros had too much pride to object. He bade farewell to the queen and the queen's consort, not lingering over it; he hated endless good-byes. They had little to say to him that was not the empty form of royal show. All the things that mattered, they had said to one another in the days before this.

It was a strange sensation to ride the river away from Waset. It was all he knew in this world, and the one man of his own world was there, standing on the bank, unmoving for as long as he was in sight. The shadow of him remained in memory long after the river had curved, carrying the boat away from the city and the people in it.

The current was rapid in this season. The great flood of the river had passed, leaving its gift of rich black earth for the farmers to till, but the river was not yet settled fully into its banks again. Between the current and the oars, the boat seemed to leap down the river.

Daros should have sat under the canopy amidships with the rest of the embassy, but he had no great desire for Seti-re's company. He found a place near the high prow, leaning on it, watching as they skimmed through the black land. The fields were full of people and oxen, plowing, planting, tilling. Sometimes they paused to stare at the golden boat. Children and dogs ran along the banks, calling in high excited voices.

It was the same cry, as long as the boat sailed through this kingdom: "The god! The god is on the river!"

He thought of hiding, or at least effacing himself on the deck, but it was somewhat too late for that. He smiled instead, and called greetings to those who were close enough to hear. They answered, sometimes incredulous, sometimes delighted.

It was two days' swift passage to the border between Waset and Gebtu. The first night they stopped and moored near a town that offered them the best of its hospitality: a roasted ox, the inevitable bread and beer, and singing and dancing and a remarkable number of lovely women.

Time was when Daros would have taken his pick of the women. Certainly they were not shy in preferring him to other men. But he had no more desire for these than for the beauties of Waset.

He slept alone on the boat, with the boatmen and the stars, and the moon riding high overhead. He was becoming accustomed to a lone white moon, and no Greatmoon to turn the night to blood. Its cool light bathed him and flowed over the water. There seemed to be no shadow on the stars, but all Gates were still shut. This world was enclosed in a bubble of darkness.

There was still a gate, the gate of dream. He sought it, and her; and found her waiting, asleep in a narrow bed in a small bare room. Those walls needed no ornament but the gold of her hair, spread across the coverlet, and the beauty of her face and body as she woke slowly.

Long before her eyes were open, she was aware of him. Her smile bloomed, rare and wonderful. He bent over her and brushed her lips with his. Her arms enfolded him and drew him down.

Part of him knew that he was mad or worse, besotted with a dream. Yet another part, the part that touched on his magery, insisted that she was real. Dream had brought him to her, but when they joined body to body, they did so in living truth. Certainly after these dreams, he was sated as if he had indeed spent the night with a woman, but there was never any stain of spent seed on bed or body. Yet sometimes there were marks of teeth or nails on his skin.

Tonight they spoke of nothing but one another: her pleasure, his delight in her. They chose to forget the troubles that beset them, the war they both fought, the enemy that threatened both these worlds. There was nothing then but the two of them, and a joy so deep that he woke close to tears.

He was lost, conquered, besotted. He was in love with a dream and a vision, and no woman in the waking world could equal her.

TWENTY-TWO

THE KINGDOM OF GEBTU WAS NOT AS PROSPEROUS AS WASET. The shadow had been no more relentless there, but Gebtu had felt more keenly the loss of its young men and the stripping of its harvests. Beggars in Waset were few; the queen saw to it that the ill and the indigent were given a ration of barley from the royal stores, to bake their bread and brew their beer. Here it seemed the king did no such thing. Gaunt women and swollen-bellied children sat by the roadsides, begging from passersby, and swarmed on boats that ventured within reach of the bank.

And yet the city, when they came to it near the end of the third day out from Waset, was more splendid than that clean and well-fed but rather simple city. The walls were built of stone rather than brick; the gates were inlaid with gold, and the palace was notably more imposing than the palace of Waset.

A high and haughty prince of men received the embassy at the quay. His heavy collar of gold and his gold-sheathed staff proclaimed his rank; his belly was ample and his expression loftily noble. His retinue was large, rich with gold and colored stones, and arranged in meticulous ranks. Every one of them went down in prostration as Daros stepped from the boat to the shore. The nobleman bowed slightly more slowly than the rest, so that it was clear who was the lord and who were the commoners.

Daros kept his face carefully empty of expression. He would wait and watch and see what was to be seen; time enough later to act.

There was a chair waiting, and strong bearers to carry it. For an instant Daros had a fierce, almost painful longing for a senel. But there was no such beast in this world, that any of these people knew: nothing large enough to carry a man, only the tiny gazelle and the antelope of the desert, that were very like the senel in shape, but scarce a fraction the size.

With an inaudible sigh, he folded himself into the chair, which was not made for a man of his size, and suffered the bearers to carry him, rocking and swaying, from the river through the streets of the city.

The king of Gebtu might have kept a mere envoy waiting for days, but a god required more delicate handling. Daros was offered food, a bath, and rest, in that order; he accepted the first two but declined the third. The servants had been terribly cowed when they began, but he wheedled and smiled and coaxed until they could wait on him without collapsing in a fit of hysterics.

As they finished their ministrations, the door-guard announced a guest. Daros' smile of greeting was genuine. Seti-re was a familiar face, and welcome for that if for nothing else.

The priest was much more at ease here in this palace than he had been in the boat. He dismissed the servants with a flick of the hand, and put in a twist that made their eyes roll white.

"Clever," Daros said when they had gone. "Now only half of them will spy on us; the rest will hide to avoid the curse."

"Are you laughing at me?"

The man was quick to his own defense. Daros softened his smile and said, "Oh, no. Not at all. Is there news?"

"Nothing from Waset," said Seti-re, mollified. His eyes kept wandering to Daros' face and fixing there. It was beastly uncomfortable and rather distracting. "The king will summon us soon. I knew him long ago; he was a priest for a while in the temple in Waset, sent there by his father to learn the greater arts and the more famous magics. He proved to have some little talent for them."

"I had heard that," Daros said, "and that he was meant to be a priest, until his elder brothers were taken by the dark enemy. I've been trusting that you will help me with him, help me to talk to him in ways that he'll most willingly hear. I'm not a priest, you see, and I don't speak the language."

Seti-re stood a little taller for that. "My lord, a god can speak any language he chooses. A god such as you . . . he'll be captivated. Though he might ask to see some of your arts. Will that be a difficulty?"

"Only if he asks me to do something I can't or won't do."

"That would be true of any god," Seti-re said.

"Ah," said Daros. "I hoped I could trust a priest to understand such things."

Seti-re almost smiled. "My lord, if I may ask a great favor? You need not grant it, of course, in your power and divinity. But I would ask . . . may I speak as high priest of your cult?"

"You are high priest of the sun in Waset," Daros said. "Can you be both?"

"If you will allow, my lord."

Daros looked him in the face. He held steady, though he had gone grey, shaking with fear. "You want power," Daros said, "but that's not everything, is it? You think you love me, because I carry the curse of a pretty face."

"No!" Seti-re had gone from grey to crimson. "May not a man choose the god he wishes to worship?"

"Because he has what men call beauty?"

"You have great beauty," Seti-re said with dignity, "but that is only fitting for a god. You are a young god; your power is great, but it startles you somewhat still. Yet you carry yourself with grace, and you seldom mock even the great fools of the world. May not a mere mortal find that admirable?"

"How odd," Daros said half to himself. "I've been found admirable twice since I decided on this expedition—and that is twice in my life. Sir priest, if you would worship me, you should know the truth. Where I come from, I'm reckoned a fool and a wastrel. I am—I was—a frequenter of taverns, a lover of loose women. I was caught transgressing great laws, and sentenced to exile and hard servitude. I broke that sentence to come to this world, and for that my exile is now, it seems, irrevocable."

"Of course you are exiled, my lord," Seti-re said. "How else would a god suffer himself to live among mortals?"

"A wastrel god," Daros said. "A useless prince."

"Not in this world," Seti-re said.

Since that was true, and since Daros had made much of it to Estarion, he shut his mouth with a click.

For a man who had no humor, Seti-re had a surprising store of wry wit. "You see, my lord?" he said. "There is no escaping the truth: that you are a god, and worthy to be worshipped."

The king of Gebtu was a man of middle years, as Daros had expected. He still kept his head shaved in priestly fashion, but covered it with a wig of numerous plaits, and cultivated an odd small beard on the tip of his chin. His court was extravagant, numerous and visibly rich; Daros the setter of fashion easily recognized his like in these languid nobles.

They were not so languid now, for all their pretense. A god among them was a potent threat to their cult of ennui. They found Daros profoundly satisfying, a truly godlike god. He assisted them by drawing sunlight to him, wrapping it about him like a mantle. They blinked, dazzled, and the less bold dropped to their faces.

The king held his ground, only narrowing his eyes against the figure of living light that was his guest. When Daros halted, Seti-re advanced a few steps more and bowed before the king, and said, "My lord of Gebtu, I bring you the son of the Sun, the god Re-Horus."

Indaros, Daros thought, but he held his tongue. People did odd things here to plain Varyani names. Re-Horus he would be, then, as Estarion was Seramon.

He suffered the king's scrutiny as he did everyone else's, standing straight and offering no expression to be judged or found wanting. When he had had enough of it, he let fall his cloak of sunlight. He did not speak. That was for the king to do.

The king seemed inclined to sit still until Daros' image was graven on his brain—or, as they would have said in Waset, on his liver. Daros shifted slightly, easing his stance. At that, the king blinked and came to himself. "I welcome you to Gebtu, my lord Re-Horus," he said.

Daros inclined his head slightly. "Lord Kamos," he said. "I thank you for your hospitality."

"My lord," said the king, "if a temple would be more to your liking, or the service of priests—"

"No," said Daros. "No, my lord king. I'm well content."

That pleased the king: he lightened visibly. "That is well," he said. "And my sister queen in Waset—she is well?"

"Very well," Daros said.

"It is true, then? She has taken a consort?"

Kamos knew it was true, but he was not speaking for himself. For the ears of the court, Daros answered, "She has taken my lord to her heart, my master to whom I am sworn, a great lord and king beyond the horizon."

A long sigh ran down the hall. Fear sparked in it. The gods had come to Waset. Now one of them stood in their hall, looming over the tallest man in Gebtu, with face of bronze and hair as bright as fire.

Daros softened his voice almost to a croon, and set a little magery in it, too, to soothe their fears. "We came for all this world, not only for Waset—to lead your people against the darkness, and destroy it if we can. The enemy fears you, my lords; fears what you can do when joined in alliance. I have come to ask if you will turn that fear to living truth. Will you ally with us? Will you join against the enemy?"

"The enemy is gone," the king said.

"For a while," said Daros, "but he will come back."

"You are sure of this?"

"I am sure," Daros said. "This is a gift of greater gods than we, this breathing space. I don't doubt you've heard that I've gathered an army in Waset—or that you've wondered whether that army is meant to invade Waset's neighbors. I swear to you, it is not. I've gathered it against the common enemy of us all; and I come now to ask if you will join your army to it, and be willing to make alliance with others of your neighbor kings."

"There are no alliances," Kamos said. "There have not been since my father's day. Alliances break; kings fall apart from one another. Only one's own kin and kind may be trusted."

"So the enemy has taught you," Daros said. "He separated you, kingdom by kingdom, the more easily to conquer you. If you gather together, if you unite yourselves, you may have strength to oppose him."

"How can one oppose the dark itself?"

"With light," said Daros.

"Firelight? Torchlight?"

"Sunlight," Daros said, "and strength of will."

"The sun cannot shine at night," said Kamos.

"No," said Daros, "but the light of the gods can—the light of magic."

"We do not have that power," Kamos said.

"If I give it to you," said Daros, "will you swear alliance with Waset, and help me unite your neighbors to the north?"

"With Waset," Kamos said slowly, "we were friends and kin once, when that was possible. We might be so again. But to unite the rest . . . my lord, your power is great, but can you truly hope to bring together all the kingdoms of the river?"

"I can try," said Daros. "With your help, I might succeed."

"Will you make me a god?"

Daros found that his mouth was open. He shut it.

"Gods stand beside the throne of Waset," Kamos said. "How much stronger would Gebtu be if its king was a very god. Can you do that, my lord?"

"That is not within my power," said Daros. "I can give you the light. You have the capacity for that." And that was true. This man was as much a mage as any in this world. It was the feeblest of powers, but enough, just, for the simplest of all arts, the summoning of light.

A thought was waking in Daros' heart. He could not speak of it, not yet; it was not clear enough for words. But soon. He chose silence now, waiting on the king's response.

Kamos answered him after a long and reflective pause. "I will consider what you have said, my lord. Will you rest a while with us?"

"I will remain for three days," Daros said, "before my duty bids me go."

"That will have to be enough," said Kamos, not willingly; he was a king, and kings were not accustomed to observing any strictures but their own. But a god stood higher in rank than a king.

The king withdrew to ponder his choices. Daros, after three days on a boat, was restless; he refused to be kept mewed in his rooms, however richly ornamented they might be.

The guards at the gate tried to keep him in. They were terrified of their captain and in great fear of the king, but Daros' presumed divinity won him passage. He hardly even needed to fling the gate open with a gust of mage-wind.

He was not alone on his ramble through the city. A man had followed him from the palace: not a tall man but sturdy and strong for one of these light-boned people. He was young, younger than Daros; boys grew to manhood early here.

Daros did not confront him, not yet. He was a comfortable enough presence, silent and observant, as a guard should be. He left Daros free to think his own thoughts as he walked those streets, broad and clean close by the palace, but narrow and reeking as he moved outward toward the walls. It was as if, whatever the king could see, he kept in excellent order, but once it was out of sight, it vanished from his awareness.

Kamos was not a weak king. As kings went in this world, he ruled well. But Daros had hoped for better. His fault and his folly: he was his father's son in spite of everything, and had seen the rule of Sun and Lion in the great cities of another empire, on the other side of the sky.

Daros had not come here to teach a king how to rule. Nor was there time if he had intended such a thing. But the temptation to do something, say something, was overwhelming.

There was a thing he could do. He did not know that it had been done before, but the part of him that knew his magic was sure that it was possible. He would have preferred another place, and another king—or better yet a queen—but maybe, once the gift was given, this king would wake to the failings of his rule.

Or maybe he would close his eyes to them altogether and become a tyrant.

Daros must hope, and trust in his magic, which had led him here. He walked the circle of the walls, then back through squalor to wide avenues and noble houses. He was aware on the edge of his mind that people followed him, stared at him, tried to touch him—but his companion held them off with a hard eye and a raised spear.

He halted by a cistern, one of many in the city. Its lid was off, and jars abandoned by it: the women who had come to draw water had fled at the sight of him. He was sorry for that, but he did not think it would be wise to call them back.

He sat on the rim. The water was not far below; it shimmered darkly, reflecting the sky. It made him think of darkmages, how soft and deep their power could be.

He was not a darkmage. He was not sure that he was a lightmage, either. He seemed to partake of both. Or maybe he was something different.

The sun, even so close to the horizon, fed him its strength. The water, born of the river that was the lifeblood of this land, made him stronger. Even the stones and the beaten earth had become part of him, though this was never the world to which he was born.

He looked up from the water. The young man from the palace was watching him steadily, wary but not afraid. There was a brightness in him, a spark even stronger than that in the king. "You're the king's son," Daros said, for it was clear to see. "What is your name?"

"Menkare," the prince said, "my lord."

"Did your father bid you watch me?" Daros asked, though he could have had the answer for the looking.

"No, my lord," said Menkare. "You're full of light. Even after your spell ended in the hall, it stayed, under your skin. Is that because you are a god?"

"It's because I am a mage," Daros said. "Come here."

The boy came, light on his feet, alert, but obedient to the god's will. When Daros took his hand, he barely stiffened. He had a bright clean spirit, and a mind that thought in lines like shafts of sunlight in a dark hall. He was little like his father, except in the magnitude of his gift.

Daros was not devout, but he knew the gods existed—and not only mages who were thought to be gods. Looking at this son of the king, he knew why he had come here, and what he had been brought to do. He opened the gate of his magic and let it flow through their joined hands, into the brightness at the heart of this prince. It was headlong, eager; it took the full force of his will to keep it flowing slowly, lest it burn away the boy's mind.

Menkare's eyes were wide. "What—my lord—"

"The gods' gift," Daros said. "I give it to you."

"But—"

"There are greater gods than I," said Daros, "and this is their will. They ask that you not speak of it until they give you leave. Can you do that?"

"Yes, my lord," Menkare said. "But—"

"Come," said Daros.

Menkare followed slowly, stumbling a little. He was full of light, brimming with it. It streamed through his veins and flooded his brain, his heart, his lungs and liver.

He could not wield it yet. Daros had not given him that. He must grow into it, become accustomed to it. But when the shadow came back, if the gods were kind, there would be a new mage in this world.

Daros had been walking perfectly steadily and thinking perfectly clearly. He was astonished to find himself on his back and Menkare standing over him, and the gate-guards lifting him. He could not move at all.

His magery was intact. He had done it no harm. But every scrap of bodily strength that he had had was gone.

They carried him in and put him to bed. Menkare's glance swore the guards to silence. He stayed with Daros, as quietly watchful as ever.

Daros had a voice if he would use it, and words enough, too, but he elected to be silent. Sleep came swiftly, sweeping over him like a tide of night.

TWENTY-THREE

SLEEP RESTORED DAROS' STRENGTH AND BROUGHT HIM BACK TO himself. He woke to find Menkare asleep beside his bed, curled on the floor like a hound pup. The magic in him had settled more deeply: he looked to Daros' eye like a mage indeed, albeit young and unschooled.

Was this how Daros looked to the mages of Gates and temples?

Daros lay for a long while, feeling out the channels of his body, assuring himself that they were all as they should be. His power was fully itself. He had surrendered none of it. The price, then, was the body's strength—which could be inconvenient if he was to bring magery to this world without magic.

At length he rose carefully, relieved to discover that his knees would hold him up. His hair had not gone white; he had not poured away his youth. He was still his young and potent self.

Such vanity: his knees nearly gave way, but only with relief. He did love to be young and strong and beautiful.

He stooped over Menkare. The prince woke slowly, blinking, frowning up at Daros' face. "You changed me," he said. "My dreams—"

"You were a seed. I made you grow."

"What . . . am I a god?"

"If by that you mean a mage," Daros said, "yes. You are."

"That's not what I wanted," Menkare said. "You should have given it to my father."

"This gift was not for him," said Daros.

"*He* wants it."

"I'll give him what he can bear," Daros said, "and ask him for a thing in return. Will you come with me? Will you help me make these kingdoms one?"

Menkare sparked at that, very much in spite of himself. Yet he said, "I'm not sure I trust you."

"Or your brothers, once you're away and the field is clear for them to claim your place?"

Menkare laughed without mirth. "No, I don't trust them at all—but I'm not afraid of them, either. You, I think I fear."

"I am strong," said Daros, "and I am not of this world. It's wise to be wary of me. But I mean you no harm."

"You'll have to prove that."

"Then you will have to come with me, so that I can do it."

This time Menkare's laughter was genuine, if somewhat painful. "I'll go with you. How can I not?"

"How indeed?" said Daros.

Kamos took most of the three days to make the choice he could not help but make. In that time, Daros made himself familiar with the court, learned the names of the lords both greater and lesser, and became acquainted with each of Menkare's dozen brothers. Some were older, some younger. Two others were sons of the king's foremost wife.

She summoned him late on the second day, with her eldest son as her messenger. The summons was no great secret, but neither was it trumpeted aloud in court.

Women here did not live apart from men, nor were they kept in seclusion as they still were among the higher nobility of Asanion. But they kept to their own places, ruled their own realm of the house, the nursery, the ladies' court. He had met none of the queens, who had their own palace and their own court; he was sure that that was deliberate on the king's part. Kings, unless they were Estarion, had a certain predilection for keeping their women away from excessively attractive men.

That did not prevent the queen from sending her son to fetch the god from beyond the sky. She received him in a cool and airy room, seated on a throne much like her husband's, attended by a guard of women whom, for an instant, Daros took for northerners of his own world.

He had seen people from the south of this world: large, strong, very dark, though not the true blue-black as Estarion was. Their faces were broad and blunt, their lips full, their hair as tightly curled as a woolbeast's fleece.

These women were of like blood, but they were leaner, even taller, and their features were carved clean; and once his eyes had found their range, he saw that they were not so dark. They were deep brown with an almost reddish cast. He could not tell if their hair was straight or curled: it was shaved to the elegant skull. They wore kilts like guardsmen, and carried spears.

They were glorious. He smiled for the pure joy of seeing them, even as he bowed before the queen.

She was a woman of this country, as he would have expected. She looked a great deal like her son. He would not have called her beautiful, but she was pleasing to look at; her eyes were clear, with a keen intelligence. "You like my guards?" she asked. Her voice was warm and rich, much lovelier than her face.

"Your guards are splendid, lady," Daros said. "Where do they come from?"

"From a tribe far to the south," she answered him.

"There are tribes far to the north of my world," he said, "who are quite like these. Their women are warriors, too."

"Would those be my guards' gods, perhaps?"

"Anything is possible," said Daros.

The queen smiled. "And you? Do you belong to a tribe?"

"My people live in cities," he said. "My father is a ruling prince—I suppose you would reckon him a king, but my family takes a certain ancient pride in eschewing that name and rank."

"A prince among gods," said the queen. "We are honored."

Daros bowed to the compliment.

"You come bearing gifts," she said. "My husband is in great confusion of mind over that which you offer him. He hopes to be a god, but fears to be denied it."

"I can only give him what he is able to accept," Daros said.

"Is he as mortal as that?"

"All men are mortal," Daros said. "Some are . . . less so than others. He has a considerable gift, for a man of this world, but I can give him only a little more."

"Will that be of use against what comes?"

"I hope so," said Daros.

"You hope? You don't know?"

"Prophecy is not my gift," he said.

She sighed and rested her chin on her hand, narrowing her eyes, searching his face. "My eldest son says that when you go, you've asked him to go with you. As what? As a hostage?"

"As an ally," said Daros.

"Will you do that in every kingdom? Take the heir to serve your cause?"

"I will do what the greater gods bid me, lady," Daros said.

"It would be a wise thing," she said, "to take such royal hostages, both as threat and promise. But if you take my son, I would ask something in return."

"Yes, lady?"

"Give me what you would give my husband."

Daros had expected that. It was not easy for him to say, "Lady, to kindle a fire, I need a spark. Your lord has it. You, alas, do not. You are mortal. But," he said before she could speak, "this I can give you: I will keep your son safe. While I live, while I endure in this world, he will come to no harm because of me."

She read the truth in his face. It did not please her, but she was no fool. She bowed to it. "I will accept that," she said.

The king of Gebtu received his gift on the last day of Daros' sojourn in his city. It was given him in the court of the highest temple. Seti-re served as priest of a rite that Daros would have preferred to avoid; but Seti-re insisted.

"Gods live in ritual," he said. "A god without a rite is no god at all."

There was a great deal of chanting and incense, passes of hands and turns of a sacred dance. When Daros was close to eruption, Seti-re's glance gave him leave to do the small thing, the simple thing, that all this mummery was meant to conceal.

The king knelt in the center of the court. He had taken off his crown and his wig, and bowed his bare and gleaming head in submission before the god. Daros laid his hands on it. The spark within the king was no greater than ever, if no less.

Daros gave the king what he had to give. It was not the shining flood that had filled Menkare, but a glimmer of light, a gleam in darkness. It fed the spark, swelling it into a coal.

He withdrew then, before the coal burst into flame. Kamos was trembling violently. Daros soothed him with a cool brush of magery.

The rite rattled and droned and spun to a lengthy conclusion. The king remained kneeling through all of it. Only when it had ended, when silence had fallen, did he rise, staggering, but he shook off hands that would have supported him. He walked out of the temple, eyes blank, face exalted.

That exaltation carried him through the feast of parting. Daros managed to avoid speaking with him. Seti-re did what talking was to be done, chattering of anything and everything, and seeming oblivious to the silence on either side.

Only at the end did Kamos cut through the babble, reach across the priest's ample body, and grip Daros' wrist. "Tell me what I can do," he said.

"You can bring light in the darkness," Daros said, "and fill hearts with hope."

"Yes," the king said, rapt. "Yes." He raised his free hand. Light flickered in it, feeble enough but unmistakably there. He laughed with a child's pure delight.

"Remember also to bring hope," Daros said, "and to look after your people. That is the price I ask, lord king. Will you pay it?"

"Yes," said the king. "Oh, yes."

Daros did not believe him, but chose to let be. He had what he needed: an ally, and the king's son beside him when he set sail again on the river.

He left that day, though the sun was nearer the horizon than the zenith. The king did not try to keep him, nor seemed inclined to keep his heir. The lesser princes were more than glad to see their brother go.

Menkare did not look back once he had set foot on the boat. "My father is a happy man," he said as they sailed in the long light of evening. He, like Daros, had a fondness for the solitude of the prow rather than the close quarters of the deck.

"One may hope he will remain happy," said Daros.

Menkare smiled thinly. "His new toy will keep him occupied for a while. By the time he discovers that you gave him a single dart and me the whole quiver, we can hope that he's inclined to be forgiving."

"The alliance has been sworn in the temple, witnessed by all the lords and priests," Daros said. "I sealed it in other ways, which will become apparent if anyone tries to break it. It will hold at least until the enemy comes back again."

"I won't ask how you sealed it," Menkare said after a pause, "only be glad that you did—and hope it holds as long as you say."

"It will hold," said Daros, as much prayer as assurance.

"And meanwhile? Will you give godhood to every king's heir from here to the river's delta? Can you do that?"

"Only if there is a seed of magery to nurture and grow."

"I have a thought," said Menkare. "Men of this kind—they're drawn toward temples, yes? My father was. I was; I never went, because my mother didn't wish it, but the call was there. If you search in temples, you may find what you need."

"I have thought of that," Daros said. "I can't give this gift too often—its cost is too high. But if I can give it even a dozen times, that's a dozen more mages than this world had before. I can teach them as we go—then bring them back to Waset, where is a greater master than I. Then, if the gods give us time, each of you can return to your kingdom and raise walls against the enemy. Then—"

"I think," Menkare said dryly, "that it's enough for now to think of learning to use what I've been given. Let the rest come later—and other godlings with it."

Daros bowed to that. He had run ahead of himself; not wise, but sometimes he could not help it. There was a grandeur in it, a plan that was, without doubt, divine. But whether he could accomplish it before the shadow came back—who knew? Certainly not he. He was not prescient. He merely clung to hope, and left the rest to the gods.

TWENTY-FOUR

THE SEA OF THIS WORLD WAS GREEN, AS TANIT HAD SAID—WAS IT indeed a year since last Daros had seen her? He stood on the edge of the vast delta, in a land of marshes and reeds and breathless heat, and there before him the waves surged and sighed. They were salt; he had tasted them to be certain. Yet they tasted also of the river, the black mud and the myriad reeds, and the cities that ran in a skein from the cataracts to this wide green ocean.

He had a small fleet of boats now, and a retinue to rival a king's, of every nation from Waset to the shores of the sea. Twelve of them were mages, a dozen out of hundreds that he had seen in temples and palaces, cities and villages. Only Menkare was a prince. To Menkare's surprise, only Kaptah and Ramse were priests. The rest were lords of courts, royal or noble guardsmen, men of cities or villages. They had come in a dozen

ways, but this they had in common: they had been drawn to him, called
by the flame of magic in them.

Two of them were women, and both of those were villagers. Merit's
husband had been taken in the last raid before the enemy withdrew.
Nefret was to be married, but she left her young bridegroom and her kin
and her village in the delta, and came to Daros with as much a gift of
magic as he had ever seen in this world. She was almost a mage in his
reckoning, a healer—even as young as she was, she had been the herb-
healer and midwife for her village—and, as the gods would have it, a
seer.

She stood beside him on the shores of that grey-green sea, and said in
her light child's voice, "We should go back tomorrow."

"I had intended to," he said.

She shook her head slightly. Her eyes looked far out over the water,
but she was not seeing waves or spume or sky. "All the way back. Back
where you came from in this world. Back to Waset."

Daros' heart constricted. "What do you see? What—"

"It's coming," she said. "Not tomorrow. Not in a few days. But soon.
It's coming back."

He did not need or want to ask what she meant. He knew. Even
without prescience, he could feel it.

The others had drawn in close. The rest of the following, the guards,
the priests, the crews of the boats, were scattered across the sand. All
those nearest Daros were mages, and all sensed what he sensed. How
not? Their gift had come through him; he had taught them what they
knew. They were raw, young, no better than callow recruits in a sorcer-
ous army, but this was difficult to mistake.

The enemy gathered on the other side of the sky. Gates were stirring.
All too soon they would open. Then this world must be ready; must be
armed and prepared for them.

Seti-re was sitting on a stool that one of his acolytes had brought,
with the waves lapping his bare feet. He started slightly as Daros came
to squat on the sand beside him. To the eye he had changed little in this

year. He was still smooth, plump, slightly sour about the eyes. But the sourness within had turned perceptibly bitter. High priest of Daros' putative cult he might be, and much feted and feasted by kings because of it, but he had had to see the gift of magic given to others—to villagers, even women—but never to him. There was nothing in him from which it could grow.

He was still besotted with Daros' beauty, which he maintained had only grown greater with the passage of time. But for that, Daros might have found this new bitterness disturbing. Bitter men knew no loyalty, in the end, but to themselves.

"My lord priest," Daros said after a while.

"My lord," said Seti-re. For once he was not staring at Daros, but at the restless face of the sea.

"We're going back to Waset, my mages and I," Daros said, "to build walls of light before the enemy comes back."

Seti-re bowed where he sat. "As you wish, my lord."

"I have a thing to ask of you," said Daros, "if you will do it."

"Whatever my lord wishes," said Seti-re.

"No," said Daros, sharply enough that the priest's eyes flicked toward him. He held them with his own stare, willing the man to see what he needed to see. "This must be your free choice. We are not going back to Waset in boats. We are going as I came to this world—by magery. I can take you and any other who will go, but if you choose, there is another thing, a greater thing, that you can do."

Seti-re had brightened in spite of himself. Maybe Daros' smile had something to do with it—he had armed it and aimed it for conquest. "What can I do, my lord?"

"We will be building walls of light in Waset," Daros said, "but if the alliance is to hold and the kingdoms are to sustain their defenses, we need an anchor—a second place of strength. Will you go to Sakhra, and speak for me there?"

Seti-re frowned, in thought rather than in bitterness. Sakhra was the northernmost of the skein of cities, the stem of the lotus before it fanned and flowered into the delta. "Why are you asking me to do this? Shouldn't it be one of your godlings? Perhaps the prince from Gebtu?"

"We need strength," Daros said, "and loyalty, and a talent for speaking to kings. Sakhra's king may come to think that since his city is so far from Waset, he may not be so firmly pressed to observe the terms of alliance—and once the enemy comes, it will be all the more tempting to withdraw within his borders again."

"The same may be said of every king from Sakhra to Esna."

"Yes," said Daros, "but if my high priest is in Sakhra, and I am in Waset, and there are visible proofs of the power that runs from end to end of the river—might he not think twice before he breaks his oath?"

"Visible . . . proof?"

The eagerness in him was almost as strong as magery. "I cannot make you a mage," Daros said, "but I can give you a working that will serve you, when you have need."

"Such as you gave the king of Gebtu?"

"Not quite the same," Daros said.

He stooped and sifted the sand. A pebble came into his hand, smooth and round and silver-grey. A hole had worn itself in the middle. He made a cord of sunlight and shadow and the coolness of spray, plaited it tightly and made it solid and lasting, and set it in the priest's hand.

Seti-re stared at it. Daros saw how he did not quite dare laugh. He was thinking of a moment with Estarion, a promise—a gift given and received, and power bestowed where there was no power to match it.

"When you set your will on this," Daros said, "it will let you summon light. But have a care. If you use it overmuch, or use it against me or mine, it will feed on your spirit as fire feeds on dry tinder."

Seti-re closed his fingers over the stone. A shudder ran through him. It had begun to thrum in harmony with that other one which he kept always about his person, which held within itself the essence of Estarion's spirit.

Daros had given him nothing so powerful, but he need not know that. His bitterness was sweetened somewhat. He was reminded yet again that he had power, real and solid: power over the lives of the gods themselves.

Of all the kings and lords and priests whom Daros had met and wooed and cozened in this long journey, this one remained the most difficult. The power of a name and the promise of divinity had carried him down the river. He had raised the princes of the dead in Abot and called down the sun in Henen. Kings had begun to come to him almost as soon as he began, either in their own person or through noble emissaries. His task had been done for him as often as not by the power of rumor and the terror of the few magics that he had been pressed to perform.

This strange country, many days' journey long and yet hardly wider than its wonder of a river, lay ready and waiting to be brought together. But Seti-re was never as wholly won as even the most doubtful of the kings.

He was a key, of sorts. In Waset he stood highest save only the queen. On the embassy he was second to one whom men called a god. Even without magic, he held power.

Daros had no prescience. That was almost an article of faith. But in giving this man such power, he had done a thing that could not be undone. Whether it was good or ill, he did not know. He only knew that he had had no choice but to do it.

When dawn touched the sky, rising over lush and level green, the fleet gathered to sail upriver. But Daros and his mages did not embark on the boats, nor did Seti-re and the company of his priests. While the boatmen and the guards from a dozen kingdoms watched, Daros opened a Gate.

He had not known until he did it, whether it was wise or even possible. But although the shadow pressed hard upon the borders of the world, the light still ruled within.

He sent the priests first, wrapped in living light. As far as they knew, they simply stepped from shore of reeds to court of the temple in

Sakhra, before the astonished eyes of priests performing the morning rites. Seti-re would be pleased: he had appeared as gods were rumored to do. No doubt they would be calling him a god, too, after this.

Daros brought his mages to Waset with much less fanfare, drawing in the circle of them, binding them with power, and setting them in a dim and quiet hall within the palace of Waset.

Estarion was waiting for them. Daros had sent no word ahead, but he had not expected to need it. Any mage in this world would have known what Daros had done, the moment he opened the Gate.

He stood in the midst of his huddle of startled and speechless magelings, and looked into the eyes of the Lion. Estarion had not changed in the slightest. After so long among the people of the black land, Daros was somewhat taken aback by the emperor's size and strangeness; but then, he thought wryly, if he could have seen himself, he would have been no less disconcerted.

"My lord," he said lightly. "Well met again at last."

"Indeed," said Estarion. Several of the magelings had flung themselves flat. He raised them gently, soothed them as if they had been children, and handed them off to the servants who had come in behind him.

They all went willingly except for Menkare, who would not shift from his place at Daros' back. Estarion smiled at him, which could not have reassured him at all, and said, "Your lord is as safe with me as he can be in this world. If I promise not to eat him, will you go to the place that has been prepared for you?"

Menkare opened his mouth to refuse, but Daros said, "Go, my friend. This I must face alone. I'll come to you after."

"Will there be anything left of you to do it?" Menkare muttered. But he went as he was bidden.

After he was gone, there was a silence that Daros had no intention of being the first to break. He took advantage of it to shut and secure the Gate, and set his magery in order, and brace himself against whatever blast Estarion might level upon him.

There was little he could do against the force of those eyes on him, raking him to the center and taking from him everything he had done since he left Waset. He let it go freely, with neither shame nor guilt. Most if not all of it, Estarion already knew; Daros had spoken with him often. But he had never quite got round to telling Estarion the full extent of the magelings' power.

At length, Estarion let him go. He stiffened his knees before they buckled.

Estarion's voice when he spoke was remarkably mild. "You've grown," he said.

He did not mean in body, though Daros was not quite the child that he had been when he came to this world. "I know of no laws against the making of mages," he said.

"There are none," said Estarion, "because no one knew it was possible."

"No one needed to know," Daros said. "When any village child may be born with magic, and most of the royal and noble houses are thick with mageborn lines, what need for anyone to make mages where there were none?"

"There is a rumor that you've been making gods in order to challenge the powers that exiled you."

"That's true, isn't it?" said Daros. "The enemy exiled us both."

"You think a dozen untrained magelings will be of any use against what we face?"

"I've taught them the art of raising wards," Daros said. "That's useful enough."

Estarion had to grant him that. But he said, "You've taken a great deal on yourself."

"I did what I had to do," said Daros. "As did you, when you gave your soul's key into the hands of a man who could turn traitor in an instant." Estarion stiffened. Daros bit back a small tight smile. "Now I've given him the key to the alliance. He's in Sakhra, no doubt being worshiped as a god, but also, we can hope, holding its king to the oaths he swore."

Estarion raised his hands. Daros steadied himself for the blow, but

Estarion seized him and pulled him into a bone-cracking embrace. "Damn you," said the emperor. "*Damn* you. If my son grows up to be half the man and mage that you are, he'll be the despair of everyone who loves him—and the salvation of a world."

Daros for once had no words to say. Estarion held him at arm's length and shook him until his teeth rattled. "You have done better than I ever dreamed you would—and taken greater risks, at far higher cost to you, than you should ever have done."

"I had to," said Daros. "There wasn't anything else I could do."

"That may be," Estarion said. "The gods know, no one else could have done it. Now come with me. My queen is waiting, and another whom you might like to meet."

Tanit did not waste time in words. She had been sitting with her scribes, going over the accounts, but at their coming, she rose and held out her arms. Daros never paused to think; he swept her up and spun her about and set her down as gently as if she had been made of glass.

She was grinning as widely as he must be. "You look splendid," she said.

"And you," he said. He looked her up and down. She was as slender as she had been when he first met her, lithe and strong. There was a light in her that had not been there before, a deep and singing joy whose cause watched him bright-eyed from the arms of his nurse.

He looked like his mother. He was darker, that was to be expected; in fact he was much the same color as Daros. His hair was black and curling; his eyes were round and dark. He would be tall, Daros thought, and maybe he would have a keener profile than people were wont to have here.

There was no gold in his hand. The *Kasar* had passed down in another line. But that mattered little to a mage's eyes. He was mageborn—splendidly, gloriously so. Daros, meeting his eyes, felt as if he stared direct into the sun.

The child crowed and held out his arms, as imperious as ever Sun-blood could be. Daros was an obedient servant: he took the child from his nurse and cradled him, not too inexpertly.

"Menes," Estarion said, "greet your cousin Indaros."

"'aros!" that half-year's child declared. He grinned at Daros, baring a pair of teeth.

Daros was literally held hostage: this latest heir of the Sun gripped a lock of his hair, as fascinated by its brightness as any other person in this world. Once Menes had examined it from all sides, he gnawed happily on it, and screamed when his nurse ventured to pry him loose.

"Let him be," said Daros. He did not raise his voice, but the lash of magic in it both drove back the nurse and silenced Menes' howls. "And you, sir, may touch but not eat. I am for pretty, not for dinner."

Menes scowled, but Daros was a score of years ahead of him in both power and rebellion; and he had been shepherding magelings for a year of this world. Even a child of the Sun was no match for that.

"Here's another use for mages," Daros said to the child's father. "Surely you didn't think mortals would be strong enough to raise this one."

"I had rather thought to do it myself," Estarion said.

"I hope you may," Daros said.

Estarion looked as if he would have said more, but wisdom forestalled him. Surely he of all people would know how uncertain the worlds could be.

TWENTY-FIVE

DAROS HAD BEEN IN THIS WORLD FOR NIGH ON TWO OF ITS YEARS. How long it had been under his own sun, he did not know, unless he could believe his dreams. That world had barely completed half a year, passing from autumn into winter and from winter into spring.

The first dream of her had been so real, so vivid, that he had been sure for a long while after that it had been no dream at all. Then, just as he began to believe that he had deceived himself in everything— her presence, the love she had given him—he had dreamed of her again. For her it had been a much shorter time, and much less fraught with doubts and desperation. She was Sun-blood. She never doubted herself.

It was comforting, in its way—as the sun's heat could be, even when it flayed flesh from bones. After that he accepted that she would come when the dreams allowed, and tried not to drive himself wild with waiting for her.

On the night after he came back from his embassy into the north, Daros dreamed of Merian again. She had only come to him twice in all of that year, and now a third time she passed through the gate of dreams.

She was unusually distracted; she was as glad as ever to see him, but she had little to say. Her voice kept trailing off.

He tried to charm her. He told her tales that he had heard on his journey, then when those failed to draw her attention, he began to tell her of the journey itself, of the kings, the alliances, the making of mages. But she was not listening. After a while he let himself fall into silence, and simply held her.

She sighed and cradled her head on his shoulder. He stroked the golden extravagance of her hair, and kissed the lids over those beautiful eyes. Her profile was as pure as ivory against the sun-darkened bronze of his skin.

She stayed so all through the night, so close and so vividly real that when he woke in the morning, he could have sworn that her scent still lingered. Of course she was not there, nor had been except in his dream.

The night after that, at last, the shadow came back. It raided a village upriver, where the barley crop had been unusually rich that year, and its harvest had filled the storehouses. The shadow's servants took those stores, all of them, and blasted the storehouses to ash; then they raided the village through wards that had grown lax with time and disbelief, and took all the men and every woman of bearing age, and left the children to drown in their own blood.

Daros had never had a weak stomach. But when he saw that heap of bodies, each rent limb from limb, hacked and mutilated out of all recognition, he choked on bile. Most of his magelings had gone green; one or two were already retching.

Estarion, old warrior that he was, walked expressionless among the carnage. "I've seen worse," he said after Daros nerved himself to follow, "but not by much."

"It's a message," Daros said a little thickly. "Those years of attacks—they were only raids. This is war."

"Maybe so," said Estarion, "but if it really is war, they'll be wanting to end it quickly—sweep over us and destroy us and be gone. They'll be conquering worlds, not simply villages."

"Maybe they are," Daros said. "Maybe they need this world more for its grain and slaves than for its service to oblivion. They left it alone for a while to grow and ripen. Now comes the harvest."

Estarion's glance was almost respectful. "That's an appalling thought, but it's frightfully logical. There's no other reason for this world to have been subjected only to raids for so long. It's been feeding the armies."

"And in letting it be, they told us that there are other such worlds, slave-worlds." Daros stopped. "What if we could raid the raiders?"

"You think we can track them to their stronghold? We can't get past the wall of darkness that surrounds this world."

"We might," said Daros, "if we attached ourselves to the next party of raiders."

"Are you saying we should let ourselves be taken?"

"Why not?"

Estarion cuffed him, and not lightly, either. "Because, puppy, without us this world has no human mages of any skill at all, and the cats, being cats, may not choose to go on protecting every town and village."

"Not if you stay and I go. I'll leave half of my magelings here to bolster you, and take those who are strong enough to stand with me." And, Daros thought, there was another thing he could try, but he was not ready to tell Estarion of that. It would involve too many explanations, and confessions that Merian's kinsman might not be pleased to hear.

"And what then?" Estarion demanded. "You'll go into darkness, you and those children, and very likely die there, blinded and in chains."

"I might," said Daros, "but I've been there. I know what to expect; what to guard against. If the Mage will help—and it well might—I'll be safe enough, considering."

"Yes, considering that that's the most insanely ill-advised plan I've heard in gods know how long."

"I can see that it's mad," Daros said, "but I don't think it's as unwise as that. How long can we hold on here? Shouldn't we try to end it sooner rather than later?"

"Certainly it will end for you," Estarion said.

"Then tell me what else we can do!" Daros said with a flash of heat. "These people are being kept like cattle. Worlds are falling all around them. Theirs will go in the end, when there's nothing else left to conquer. No wards or simple magics can stop it."

"And you can?"

"'Know your enemy.'" Daros recited the words in the singsong of the schoolroom. "That lesson I learned—even I, the despair of my tutors. What do we know of this enemy? Where does he come from? Who leads him? Even what face he wears—has any of these people ever seen it?"

"None who survived," Estarion said.

"None of them was a mage until I came to meddle with them. I went to the dark world once; I came back. I'll come back again."

Estarion stood silent in the sweet stench of death. In those few moments, his face had aged years. "There are worse things than death," he said.

"This world will know them," said Daros, "if I don't do this."

"I'll think on it," Estarion said.

Daros sucked in a breath, but held his tongue. This was as much as he would gain, for now. He clung to what patience he had, and followed Estarion back through the heaps of the dead toward the huddle of guards and mages that had accompanied them from Waset. All of them, save only Menkare the prince, had retreated as far as they could from the horror in front of them.

Estarion's glance was eloquent. Even if Daros could endure the enemy's world, these children could not. They were born to sunlight; the dark was their greatest fear.

Daros turned his back—as great an insolence as he had ever offered this man—and closed his mind. He would do this thing, whether the emperor willed or no.

It was late in the day before Daros was able to speak to the queen. She was closeted with her council, and then with Estarion; and Daros had preoccupations of his own. His mages were in sore need of comfort.

"It's different," Nefret said. She had not wept on the field, nor did she in the palace, in the room in which they had gathered. She looked as if the tears had been burned out of her by the same fire that had consumed the village. "When we were mortal, it was terrible. Now that we have this gift—this curse—it goes beyond that. We can feel—we can see—"

"Shields," Daros said. "Remember what I taught you. You must wall your mind and protect the fire within you."

"And then?" she demanded. "Then it eats us from the inside out?"

"Then it makes you stronger," he said. "I made you for this; I trained you to fight this war. You are strong enough. If you had not been, you could never have endured the gift that I gave you."

"Maybe we don't want it," she said.

Some of the others murmured agreement. He lashed them with a bolt of magic. They gasped. None flinched—that much he was pleased to see. "What I have given," he said to them, "I can take away. But have a care! If I take it, I may take everything that makes you yourself. Seven souls, you believe you have. This power is woven with them all."

"The gods are not kind," said Kaptah the priest from Henen. He was not one of those who had agreed with Nefret. "Lord, did they strike elsewhere? Has that knowledge been given you?"

"They struck villages near Ombos and Hiwa, and Imu in the delta," Daros said. "But they struck no cities, and no villages within sight of cities."

"But they will," Menkare said. "If this is war, these skirmishes will come more often and more strongly, the longer they go on."

"Yes," said Daros. "Tell me, prince of Gebtu. Would you come with me to the enemy's stronghold, and take the war to him there?"

"The enemy is on the other side of the sky," said Menkare.

"So he is," Daros said.

Menkare thought about that. A slow smile bloomed. "Yes," he said. "Yes, that's absolutely mad. I would do it, my lord."

The others glanced at one another. "And I," said Kaptah.

Ramse, the elder of the two priests, shook his head, though not in refusal. "We can't all go. Someone has to stay and defend our cities."

"Half of you will remain," Daros said, "and look for obedience to the Lord Seramon. The rest go with me—but only if you understand, fully and freely, what we will do. We will let ourselves be captured, bound and carried away. It's no failing of courage if you refuse. The defense of this land is a great charge in itself—and if I fail in what I do, it may be the greatest of all."

"We understand," Nefret said. Her eyes were burning. Her husband, her brothers—the enemy had taken them. She had no real hope of seeing them again, no wise woman would, but even the prospect, however remote, struck fire in her spirit.

The queen received Daros between a much lengthened council and a newly fearful sunset. She had her son with her, drowsing in his cradle, and his nurse and the chief of her maids in quiet attendance.

She knew why he had come: it was in her glance. Yet she smiled, because the sight of him made her glad. "I missed you," she said after he had paid her reverence and sat at her feet. "Waset is a much brighter place when you are in it."

"There is no queen like you in all the kingdoms of the river," Daros said.

She laughed a little. "Oh, hush! My husband will never believe it, but any spy would think that we were lovers."

"That we will never be," Daros said, "and that's well—for lovers are common enough, but a friend is a great rarity."

"I should hate to lose you," she said, suddenly somber.

"I don't intend to die," he said. "My lord and I, and my new-made mages—we are going to save your world. We were brought here for that. We will do it."

"My dear friend," she said tenderly. "Don't say that just to comfort me. I know what happened out there. The dark is back, and worse than ever. You'll catch blame for that, you and my lord."

"Not if we can help it," said Daros.

"It was bad. Wasn't it? He wouldn't let me go. I'm still somewhat out of temper with him because of it."

There was no eluding her clear eye. "It was bad," he said. "It won't be as bad again. We've strengthened the wards that had grown lax, and secured the granaries and the cattle-pens. Some of the fields not yet harvested will be lost, but there's no helping that."

"No, there is not." She sighed, but she was neither discouraged nor particularly weary. It was the sigh of one taking up a burden again after a lengthy respite. "So we're at war again."

"I know a way to end it."

She raised a brow. She knew what he would say, but he had to say it.

"If you will give me leave, I'll take six of my magelings and follow the enemy to his own world, and do my best to stop him there."

"You, and six new-hatched magelings." She did not sound too terribly incredulous. "Against—hundreds? In the dark?"

"Light is their most bitter enemy. My magic is born of the light. Let us find their center, the one who leads them, and we'll destroy him.

Then if we can set their Mage free, they lose all their magic; they become no more than mortal. We'll have them—bound to their own world, unable to leave it, to raid or bring war to any beyond them."

"And the dark that they serve? Will it leave us then?"

That, Daros could not answer. Not exactly. "Without their strength to sustain it and the Mage to drive it onward, it will at least stop advancing. Then simple wards should hold it off—maybe forever. Certainly for a very long time."

"Still a death sentence," she said, "after all."

"Maybe not for you or your son, or your son's sons. Maybe not for thousands of years."

"Do you reckon that a risk worth taking?"

"Seven lives, to save a world? There's nothing lost if we fail, but everything to gain if we succeed."

"Seven lives," she said. "Six godlings and a god. He forbade it. And you come to me?"

"He said that he would think on it."

"Ah," she said. She closed her eyes. "Then so will I."

Daros began to rise, but she held him down. Her grip was strong.

"He loves you like a son," she said. "He still grieves for the child of his body who was lost for a foolish and empty cause, long ago. To send you to almost certain death—that will tear at his heart. But if he judges that there is no other hope, he will do it. He will let you go."

Daros said nothing. She did not need to hear his doubts.

No matter; she read them in his face. "Promise me, dear friend. Do nothing until he's done thinking on it."

"There may not be that much time," Daros said.

"Can't you trust him? Can you trust anyone but yourself to do what is necessary?"

Daros flushed. "I am not—"

"You are as arrogant a young pup as was ever whelped in a princely house." Her voice was mild, her tone without censure. "Give him three days. He will have done all his thinking by then—and so will I."

Daros did not like that at all, but she had shamed him into acquiescence. He kissed her hand with rueful respect. "You are as implacable as he is," he said.

"Of course I am," she said. "I'd never be able to stand up to him if I weren't."

He laughed a little painfully, bowed low with no mockery whatever, and left her with her maid and her nurse and the son for whom she had prayed through all the years of her youth.

TWENTY-SIX

YOU MAY GO," ESTARION SAID. HE SPOKE WITH NO PLEASURE AT all, with such a face as he must have worn in grim judgment over the courts of empire.

Daros had never expected to be given leave, or so soon, either. They had passed a brutal night, with raids on half a dozen villages, barely beaten off, and a new and alarming thing: attacks on the wards.

Daros had been standing guard on Waset's walls, holding it with magery while Estarion sustained the web of wards in the greater kingdom. His magelings had known the first test of their new existence, weaving their fledgling powers with either Estarion's or Daros'. Daros had divided them quite deliberately into the half who would go and the half who would stay. He kept Menkare and Kaptah and Nefret, Ay and Huy who were brothers from Sekhem, and Khafre the captain of the

261

king's guard of Ipu. They were all trained in war, all but Nefret, and she, the healer and seer, was perhaps more valuable than the rest.

They had done not too badly that night, but by dawn they were out on their feet. Daros saw them to bed before he turned toward his own too long forsaken chamber.

Estarion was waiting there, seated cross-legged on the bed. He had made the decision that he had no choice but to make.

"We can't take many nights of this," Estarion said. "Gods know, I think you're mad, and I think you'll die, if you're lucky—but without this gamble, there's no hope."

"If it can be done," Daros said, "I'll do it."

"I don't doubt it," Estarion said dryly. "You may have your six magelings. Do your best with them, as fast as you can. You're leaving tomorrow night."

"We can leave sooner. We can—"

"Don't be a fool," Estarion said. "You're out on your feet. Today you'll sleep. Tonight and tomorrow, you'll prepare those children of yours. We'll hold on meanwhile. There is one other thing. A price, if you will."

Daros held his breath. Of course there was a price.

"My cats and my cats' allies," said Estarion. "They're not mages, not as yours are. But give them what you can. Help as you may, for the defense of Waset."

Daros bowed his head. He was willing, even glad to do that. But first he must rest. He was falling asleep where he stood. He needed to sleep long and deep.

And he needed to dream. Dreams might hold the answer. He let himself be put to bed, barely even startled that the servant who tended him had been an emperor in another world, another time. Estarion could be whatever it suited his fancy to be.

Daros had tried before to force the dreams of Merian, and failed. They came when they came. But this was urgency beyond simple desire. He shaped himself into a prayer to whatever god would hear, and offered whatever that divinity would take, even his life, if he could only walk in dream where he needed to walk.

It seemed that one of the gods heard him. He passed through deep water, through darkness that though absolute was not the nothingness that the Mage had wrought. It was a living thing, the breast of Mother Night.

Merian was on the other side of it. She stood atop the tower of a hill-fort, looking down into the crash and roar of a sea. Wind whipped back the golden masses of her hair, and plucked at the folds of the mantle that she had wrapped about her.

He in kilt and bare feet, long accustomed to the heat of a hotter sun than had ever shone in this sea-smitten country, felt the cold like the cut of a knife. The chattering of his teeth brought her about, even in the roar of the gale. Her eyes were wide, her expression flat astonished, but she kept her wits about her. She opened her cloak of wool and fur, drawing him into blessed warmth. Her arms clasped him close; he gasped as she crushed the breath out of him, but he uttered no protest.

She loosed her grip a little and tilted her head back. He had to kiss her; he could not help himself at all. "I'm not dreaming you," she said. "You're real. You *are* here."

"I can't stay long," he said, "or linger for loving, not now. Will you forgive me?"

"Maybe," she said. "What is it? Why are you so somber?"

"The world we've been living in," he said, "is about to fall. I have a plan—the emperor says it's madness, but he's given me leave, because there's no other hope. I think there is a little, if you will help me. Are you terribly beset here?"

"Not quite yet," she said. "We've lured them all to Anshan. This is Ki-Oran—"

"Ki-Oran!" For a moment it seemed to Daros that the tower rocked underfoot. "Gods! You're madder than I am."

She frowned. "You've heard of this place?"

"My father's library," Daros said. "I used to make a game of reading the books he'd forbidden. He has books that tell of the mages in Anshan. They're nonsense mostly, written long years after the fall, but there's a little honest meat on the bones of the stories."

"Your father's library," she said slowly. "We never even thought—"

"He keeps it quiet, mostly," Daros said, "even—sometimes especially—from mages. As useful as the temples are, and as much as he approves of the orders of mages, there are still things, he says, that most of them were better not to know."

"*I* should know."

"And they call me arrogant." He smiled to take the sting out of it and brushed her lips with a kiss.

She was too preoccupied to return the kiss. "I'll send word to him— ask him, command him if I must—"

"Lady," he said firmly, so that she looked up startled. "Whatever the books can tell you, I doubt there's anything you haven't learned already, if you're here, alive, and sane. Are you using the Ring of Fire?"

"Yes," she said. "How did you—"

"It's logical. Lure the enemy in, keep him contained. We've done something like it, though with nothing like the power you can bring to bear. That lack of power is killing us. Therefore, while we're still alive, we've decided to take the war to the enemy."

"With what? Have you armies? Weapons? Magic?"

"A realm half a thousand times as long as it's wide, encompassing the banks of a long river. Reed spears and a copper blade or two. My lord and I, and a dozen fledgling mages, and perhaps twice that many who can make fire if they're pressed to it."

"You're mad."

"So your kinsman said. But he can't think of anything better."

"Tell me," she said, "that you're not planning to let yourself be taken in a raid."

"Is there any other way?"

"You don't know," she said. "You really don't know. When they take slaves—they blind them and take their souls. We saved a handful of men, kept them alive, but they were beyond any power to heal. Some of them are dead now. The rest are eyeless, mindless, stripped of will or under-standing. Nothing that we've done has made the slightest difference."

He stiffened; his breath came suddenly short. But he was not about to turn coward. "We're warned now—I thank you with all my heart. We'll take measures to protect ourselves."

"Even if those are enough," she said, "what do you think you can do in the dark world? Go up like a torch? Take as many of the enemy with you as you can, before the rest overwhelm you?"

"Something like that," he said. "I was thinking—lady, if mages from this world could find us there, we could join together, find and destroy the leader or leaders, and free the Mage from its prison. Then maybe we could bind the darkness, once the powers driving it were taken away."

"My kinsman is right," she said. "You are mad."

"Do you see any other way?"

"No," she said as unwillingly as Estarion had. "Damn you, no."

"Can you help?"

"I would have to ask. This isn't something I'll lay on anyone who isn't as mad as you are."

"Yes, we need good madmen," he said. "But don't take too long, please, lady. Our world hasn't much time left."

"Your—" She broke off. "Come with me."

"I don't think I can," he said. "I'm dreamwalking. I'll wake soon. Can you do it? Will you?"

"You'll trust me?"

"With my soul."

"Don't make light of it," she said sharply.

"That, I would not do," he said. "Lady, will you come to me as soon as you may?"

"I will try," she said.

He kissed her, lingering over it, nor did she try to break free. There was more than desire in it. There was a gift, a pearl of magic that he set in her heart. Hardly had he done that when the dream took him away, reft him out of her arms.

Merian stood alone in the bite of the wind. Her cloak was gone, and he in it. She drew the magic of the place about her, warmer than any wool or fur, and paused to gather courage. Then she said calmly to the air, "Perel. Come. I need you."

He came as soon as he could. It was a long hour, but Merian put it to good use. She had sent word to certain others, lightmages and dark-mages both, and bidden them wait upon word from Ki-Oran.

By the time he arrived, she had prepared everything that could be prepared. He came through the Gate that she had opened, full-armed and on guard, though she had sent him no word that she was in danger.

She wasted no time in preliminaries. "Perel," she said, "if I asked you to be taken by the enemy, would you do it?"

He stood where the Gate had brought him, just inside the door of her workroom, wrapped in Olenyai black, with only his eyes to be seen. They had widened slightly, but he betrayed no other sign of startlement. "You have a plan?"

"The heir of Han-Gilen does."

That did astonish him. "He's here? He's come back?"

"No," she said, "but he dreamwalked here, to ask me this. He's trapped in a world within the shadow, he and the emperor. They're about to fall. He thinks—he hopes—that if he can be taken to the enemy's own world, he can fight from there, and close their Gates, and bind or destroy them at their source."

"That boy has a finely honed deathwish," Perel observed. "Which is all very well for him, but what makes you think that I share it?"

"Don't all the Olenyai?"

"Most of us prefer to stay alive. All of us would rather be unmaimed."

Perel advanced a step or two into the room. Merian rose from the worktable.

Once again she had surprised him profoundly. She was not greatly swollen with the child yet, but in shirt and breeches, she was obviously not her old slender self. She met his stare and said flatly, "I'll thank you not to make a public outcry of this. Nobody else knows, except my loyal people here."

He bent his head to her will. "Only tell me one thing. Please, by all the gods, swear to me that it's not Batan's."

"It is not Batan's," Merian said, "or any other pirate's. Don't fret, cousin. Even Mother won't object to the breeding of this child."

"She might take issue with the timing of it," Perel said.

"Yes—that I didn't do it fifteen years ago." Fifteen years ago, she thought, Daros was a youngling child.

Perel did not press her to name the father; nor had she expected him to. Olenyai were bred like fine animals. Once she had assured him that this child was properly bred, he had ceased to fret over it, except on her behalf.

"I am thinking," Merian said after a pause, "that if lightmages and darkmages went in together under shields, then the slavetakers could be persuaded that they had been duly bound and blinded. Once you were there, you would find Daros and his people, join forces, and do the rest according to his plan."

"That supposes," said Perel, "that they can be found at all, and once found, that all of them are sane and whole. We know nothing of this world, where it is, what it is. We'll be going in, quite literally, blind."

"He knows," she said. "He's been there. He'll set a beacon in the Gate, for only us to find. That will guide you to the enemy's world, and once you've passed the Gate, guide you to him."

"Even so," said Perel, "without knowing what to expect—"

"He gave me this," Merian said, "through the dreamwalking." She held out her hand.

Perel took it warily, braced against the lash of sudden pain or power. She gave him what Daros had given her, the flash of knowledge wrapped in memory: the dark world, the stronghold, the men in it.

Perel let go her hand. He drew a long breath, and let it out slowly.

"No name, no words in their language. No knowledge of what or who leads them, or how, nor very much of why. Their weapons, we know, are stronger than ours. What does he think he can accomplish by invading their stronghold?"

"He believes," she said, "that some force is driving them, and some power ruling them. If that can be removed, the rest won't matter."

"You're asking us to gamble a great deal on a guess and a dream."

"Yes: I'm asking you to gamble your lives on the defense of this world."

He flushed. She had stung him; he was as close to anger as she had ever seen him. "I would die for you, lady of the Sun, and for the empire you'll someday rule. But I want that death to be worth something. If I throw my life away, what good does it do you?"

"Very well," she said, and her voice was as cold as her heart. "Go. I'll find someone else to lead the expedition. For it will go, Perel. It's a vain hope, but it's action beyond simple defense. It might even succeed."

"Did I say I would not go?"

"Weren't you hinting at it?"

"I do not hint," he said stiffly. "I'll go. I'll pick my mages—will you give me a free hand?"

"I've spoken with a number of mages who confess themselves willing. You may choose others, if that's your wish."

"Lightmages as weapons, darkmages to shield them. Masks of illusion for us all." Perel straightened his shoulders. "How many?"

"Enough to be a threat. Not so many that the enemy senses that threat until the knife is at his throat."

"Twice nine," Perel said, "and I. If we're taken like slaves, we'll not be able to bring worldly weapons. That could be a difficulty."

"The enemy has weapons, and probably to spare," she said. "But none of them, in himself, has magic."

"That does give us an advantage," Perel conceded. "Very well. When do we go?"

"Tomorrow night," she said. "You'll be cast like a lure. With luck and the gods' favor, the enemy will seize you."

He bowed. He was not happy with her at all, but he would do what she needed him to do. That was the way of the Olenyai—just as it was the way of imperial blood to use him with ruthless disregard for his life or sanity.

She was not happy with herself, either, but so be it. She gave Perel a gift, because she trusted him, and because in her mind he deserved it. "This child is his—the Gileni's. For her sake, will you serve him as if he had been of the blood royal?"

"How in the worlds—"

"I'm not entirely sure," she said, "but it appears that one can do more than walk in dreams."

Her cheeks were warm. He saw the flush: his lips twitched. "I am glad," he said, "that I don't have your gift for dreaming true."

"I think the gift is his," she said. "He's a mage unlike any other. Will you help him?"

"I will help him," Perel said with a sigh.

"You have your mages," Merian said.

She had tracked him through thickets of dream, past lies and delusions, wishes and fears. He was perched on the prow of a boat, sailing down a broad deep river. Small brown men filled the boat, and one large and very dark one at the steering oar, golden eyes full of the sun.

But she had not come to Estarion, however it gladdened her heart to see him. He looked splendid, strong and young, laughing and trading banter with the men in the boat.

Daros was drowsing, smiling a little, full of sun and empty of fear. She slipped inside the stream of his thought and warmed herself in his sunlight. His smile bloomed all around her.

She hated to darken that brightness, but time was short. "Twice nine mages," she said, "and Perel. Will that be enough?"

"It will be ample," he said with swift joy and a strong surge of relief.

"They'll set themselves in the enemy's path tonight. That will be somewhat after you go, if all goes well. Once they're past the Gate, they'll find your beacon. You'll command them after that. Perel knows; the others understand."

"Are they dismayed to be taking orders from the rakehell of Han-Gilen?"

"Not all of them," she said. "Some allow as how you've earned a little respect through serving the emperor so demonstrably well."

"How very kind of them," he said.

"Most charitable." She could not kiss him, here inside him, but she could envelop him in the sensation. He was warm to the tips of his toes. "Beloved," she said. "Stay alive, and unmaimed if you can. Come back to me."

"I will," he said.

"I'll hold you to that," said Merian.

TWENTY-SEVEN

DAROS WARMED HIS HEART WITH HER MEMORY, AND WITH THE hope that she had given him. Nearly a score of mages, the best and the strongest, and an Olenyas to lead them—he was richer than he had dared to dream.

And yet, like the madman he was, he could not help but think that his magelings had been chosen for this; that they would prove themselves before men and gods. He roused from the last of his dream and turned his eyes toward them where they sat together. They did not cling to one another; none of them wept or trembled. They looked as soldiers should before a battle: a little pale, a little shaken, but strong.

It was a peculiarity of this very peculiar country that if one wished to travel downstream, one rowed; but to travel upstream, one raised a sail, because the river flowed northward and the wind blew from the north.

On this hot bright morning, the wind was like a blast from a furnace, carrying them swiftly upstream toward a village near the border of Esna. The queen had chosen it; she had had kin there before the enemy took them. This would be revenge, after a fashion.

Daros was very calm. He had never fought in a battle, but he had trained long and hard enough, for a layabout. He had lived two years in this country, training fighting men, making and training mages. He was as fit and as ready as he would ever be.

The village was a trap, handsomely baited. Its storehouses were brimming with barley; its cattle-pens were full. The men who appeared to dwell in the houses had the look of soldiers, and their women were sturdy and strong. They greeted the newcomers with respect, and Daros and Estarion with somewhat more than that.

The boat could not linger if it was to return to Waset before sunset. But Estarion did not give the order for it to depart.

Tanit had said that he loved Daros as a son. Daros did not doubt it. He loved this man—as a father? Perhaps. As dear kin certainly, and as his lord, and yes, his emperor. He offered the obeisance of a prince of the Hundred Realms to the Lord of Sun and Lion, and rose into a long and tight embrace.

"Stay alive," Estarion said in his ear, soft as a lion's growl. "Stay as sane as it's possible for you to be. Come back with all your limbs intact."

"Keep this world safe, my lord," Daros said in turn, "for your son if not for me."

"For both of you," said Estarion.

Then he would go. He took his place not on the deck but among the oarsmen as they prepared to row downriver against the wind. As the river bent, bearing them out of sight, he flung up his hand in a last farewell. The flame of gold dazzled Daros even from that distance, as if the sun had come down to rest upon the water.

The boat of the Sun sailed away. Daros' tiny army remained like bait in the trap. They settled as best they could. There was no time to teach them more than they already knew; that would never be enough, but it would have to serve.

They had their shields, and their small workings of illusion, so that when the enemy looked at them, he would see what he wished to see. They could not hope to carry weapons with them, but Daros had a gift from Estarion, a steel knife such as this world knew nothing of, and with it the Mage's feather that he had brought from the place between worlds. He had hung them both on a cord about his neck, and concealed them with a small working.

Apart from those few things, the only weapon any of them carried was his magery. They rested if they might, slept if they could. The seeming villagers went about the daily tasks of tending the cattle and the fields, baking bread, brewing beer. At the time of the daymeal, there was bread, beer, roast goose, a bit of green stuff, and dates from the palms that grew tall around the village.

Daros ate for strength, as did they all. None of them knew when they might eat again. All too soon the sun set; they set wards enough to escape suspicion, but weak and ragged as they had been in other villages when the enemy struck.

Kaptah sang the sun to its rest. He had a pleasant voice; it was comforting, in its way, but there was great sadness in it. Only the gods knew when any of them would see sunlight again.

The magelings drew in a little closer. They were all in the same house near the western edge of the village, as the enemy was wont to come from the west. It was small and the air inside was close, but no one wanted to open the door. That would be done for them soon enough, if their trap was laid as well as they hoped.

Khafre ventured a little magelight as the night closed in, but Nefret damped it with a flick of magery that won murmurs of respect from the rest. "Have you forgotten?" she said sharply in the darkness. "They hate the light. Use the eyes you were given!"

Khafre ducked his head, abashed. She had reminded him, and the rest of them, too, that they had mage-sight.

They did not see Daros swallow a smile—he made sure of that. "Sleep if you can," he said, "but remember to keep your power on guard."

They all nodded. Each was a soldier in his own fashion; they knew the wisdom of hoarding their strength.

The enemy came in the deep night. Daros felt the opening of Gates like the opening of wounds in his own body. They were out in force: they struck up and down the river, not only here. Elsewhere they met stronger wards, though not yet as strong as they would be once the enemy had taken the bait.

All the magelings were awake. Menkare and Khafre had risen, setting themselves shoulder to shoulder nearest the door. Daros was farthest back, cut off from escape save past the others.

When the dark fire struck, their shields were up. The door puffed into ash; the roof of woven reeds vanished, leaving them open to the stars. Daros caught his breath at the force of it, even through shields. Ay, just out of his reach, gasped and crumpled.

Daros reached for him—too late. His shields were broken. Ay convulsed, and began to scream.

Daros seized Ay's brother and dragged him off, caught the next mageling who was near—Nefret, who would have tried to heal a man who was past healing—and swept the rest of them out into the roiling darkness.

Shapes of shadow swarmed upon them. First Nefret, then Huy was ripped from his hands. Bands that felt like iron closed about him and clamped tight.

He sensed the spell in them, strong as a drug, invoking sleep. His shields held, but he went limp as they expected. He could not see through the dark shapes that surrounded him, to discover what had become of the others. Except for Ay—Ay was dead. He had felt the spirit's flight even before he left the broken walls.

He was remarkably calm. It was a terrible thing to be helpless, bound and blinded even to mage-sight. Yet he had wished for this, and planned it, though he had hoped not to be separated quite so swiftly from his magelings.

Slowly he made sense of the darkness. Two robed figures were carrying him, gripping the bands about him as if he had been a bundle of reeds for a boat. They were moving: from the scent of mud and water and reeds, away from the village and toward the river. There were others nearby, moving likewise. Their gait was human, and steady, undismayed by the blind dark. None of them spoke. His captors were on foot, but some of those beyond them were mounted on the strange scaled beasts that he had seen before.

Their Gate lay across the river, and the road to it was not quite in this world. If he strained, he could hear the river running below. His captors' booted feet trod air above the glide of the current.

They passed into the dark world, into perpetual night, and cold that bit deep before his shields closed it out. They did not carry him far. He felt the loom of walls, heard the deep creak of hinges in a gate.

He dared open his eyes to mage-sight. His captors appeared to sense nothing: they paced onward as they had before, through a vaulted corridor and a roofless court, then up a long stair. There were others behind and before them. Not only his magelings had been taken. From the sound of many feet, the captives were numerous. Nor could they all have come from the village outside of Esna.

The stair ended at last in a high wide gate and a cavernous hall. It was not the one in which he had been before. There was nothing royal about this. It had the look and smell of a barracks.

It was vast. Its edges were lost in gloom, even to mage-sight. Broad galleries rose toward the roof, and a webwork of ladders connecting one to another.

The train of slave-takers coiled in a skein round the hall and stopped. Daros' two captors lowered him to a floor of grey stone. The bonds about him snapped free. Hard hands heaved him to his feet. All about him, others did the same. Khafre, Menkare, Nefret—all there, and alive.

Huy, then Kaptah: they were somewhat farther away, among others of their country.

Only they had eyes. All the rest were blind, every one—within as without. They were bound by a slave-spell, their souls lost, all will taken away: row on row of blank and eyeless faces.

There were hundreds of them in this one room, of many in this city, on this world. Thousands all told; thousands of thousands. The sheer magnitude of it went beyond horror. There was no word for what had been done here, to the folk of world after world.

The takers of slaves withdrew. Something in the way they moved made Daros certain: they too were slaves, bound like all the rest. Slaves taking slaves—there was a hideous economy in it.

The soul-lost formed in ranks and stood still. Daros' magelings managed in that surge of movement to set themselves about him. They were pale and shaking, but they were masters of themselves still. Their shields had held, even Huy's, though he was rigid with grief for his brother.

They stood so long, so motionless, that Daros began to fear that they would not move at all for hours, perhaps days. If that was the case, he would have to make his move long before he had intended to, slip away and pray that he could find a hiding place in a world he did not know.

But there was, at last, movement. Figures emerged onto the first gallery.

These were not slaves. Even the guards, great looming figures, walked with volition. Those whom they guarded wore robes that Daros remembered, like darkness cut and sewn into garments.

The robed ones were men. He who led them had let fall his hood. He was white-skinned like a man of Anshan in Daros' own world, but as pale as such a man would be who had never seen the sun. His hair and beard were black; heavy black brows lowered over dark eyes.

He had eyes, though they were all dark, whiteless and strangely blank. It seemed that he could see, though he was not a mage. He looked out over the hall and the ranks of slaves. His face wore no expression.

He was not a mage, but great power was on him. He wore it like a cloak. Perhaps, Daros thought, that was precisely what it was. And if that was so . . .

The man spoke. His words meant nothing. Daros could not shield himself, protect his magelings, sustain the illusion that he was as eyeless and witless as all the slaves about him, and wield his gift of tongues, all at once. Even his power had limits.

The words must have been a spell of command. Daros felt the tug of it. Others near him began to walk, trudging out of the ranks of slaves, toward the far end of the hall. Menkare too was moving, and Khafre, and Nefret, but not Huy or Kaptah.

There was nothing he could do but hope that whatever he went to, he could come back to this place, to the rest of his mages. Those chosen seemed the strongest. They had the look of warriors, or of warriors' women.

He walked where the spell bade him. In so doing, he had to pass beneath the gallery. The man on it was a cold presence, a power that was not magery but was not entirely human, either. It was almost like metal—like a machine.

Daros had that to ponder while he walked slowly out of the hall and down a corridor, then a stair. They went far down, much farther than they had come up. Still he did not sense the weight of earth overhead. They must be descending the steep face of a crag.

They came out into the lightless air, in a reek of smoke and heated metal. There were forges nearby, vast perhaps beyond imagining, but this court showed only the loom of a wall and the waiting presence of the guards. As each of the enslaved approached, he was stripped of whatever garment or ornaments he might possess, swept with cold fire as if to cleanse him, and dressed in a long dark garment rather like that of the men in the gallery. Then he was led, not into another hall, but through a gate and out onto the plain that Daros remembered.

Daros had kept his hidden weapons through stripping and cleansing. The knife was cold against his breast, the feather too light to be called weight, but the presence in it was as strong as the darkness itself.

The place that they had come from was a city behind a high wall. The place that they went to, he remembered all too well: the citadel on the crag, high above the dark plain. The way to it was long and steep, but there was no pause for food or water. Slaves and soul-lost must have no need for such. Daros and his remaining mages were still mortal; they could only grit their teeth and endure.

The citadel swallowed them. As the gates of iron clanged shut, Daros knew a moment of pure and craven terror. To be free, to be away from there, to be in the light, any light—he would have unleashed the lightnings, if a vanishingly small part of him had not kept him sane. This was precisely what he had wished: to be in the heart of this realm, within reach of those who ruled it. The gods were looking after him; this was proof.

It seemed they were to be soldiers in the guard of the dark realm. They were taken to barracks less vast than those in the city; these were like enough to guardhalls in castles of Daros' own world. A hearth in the center radiated heat without light; bed-niches lined the walls. A second hall past that boasted long rows of tables, and benches on which the ranks of slaves all blindly sat.

Here at last was food and drink: harsh dry bread, salt meat, flagons of clear liquid with a distinct, astringent taste. Except for that strangeness, he would have said that it was water.

It restored his strength considerably. Menkare next to him, and Khafre and Nefret beyond, sat somewhat straighter and seemed less grey about the face.

They dared not speak, even mind to mind. Blinded slaves crowded close. Most of those nearby were men and women of Menkare's world, but round about them Daros saw casts of face that he had not seen before. There were perhaps people of half a dozen worlds, all human in some fashion, but none was of his own kind. Nor was any a mage, even to the minute degree that he had found in the country of the river. Magic was a rarity in the worlds, it seemed.

That, even apart from the shadow that had cut off world after world, would explain why Gate-mages did not meet their own kind wandering the worldroads. If there were others, they were vanishingly few. People of the worlds shunned Gates, out of lack of understanding or, if they knew of the dark armies, out of fear.

He fought down the surge of despair. This army of slaves was a single night's harvest. There would be myriads more in this citadel alone, and more to come as each band of raiders returned through Gates. Merian's mages would come. She had promised; he could trust that she would fulfill it.

There was no reckoning night or day in this place. It was always dark, unlit by moon or star. They were fed at what must be regular intervals. They were taken to the barracks and expected to sleep after every second meal. In between, they served as menials in the citadel.

Others like them, who Daros suspected had been there longer, stood guard at doors and gates, or accompanied various of the lords both within and outside of the citadel. Yet others were taught to ride the scaled beasts with their vicious jaws, and to fight with weapons both familiar and alien.

The lords had eyes, all of them. The slave-soldiers did not, but they were not truly blind. Daros, finding occasion to sweep a corridor that led to one of the practice-courts, marked how lethally swift they were, and how faultlessly the best of them struck targets with throwing-spears and darts and, most fascinating of all, the weapons that hurled the dark fire.

Both teachers and overseers were blinded slaves, but they seemed to have more will than the ranks they commanded. The ranks were mute, but the overseers could speak; they gave instruction and issued orders, speaking a language that must be that of the lords; but it addressed itself to each slave in his own tongue. Daros heard it in the tongue of Shurakan, which was rather strange; his mother had spoken it to him when he was small, but once he was grown, he had spoken chiefly the common speech of Keruvarion.

Daros had not yet managed to approach the lords. They kept to themselves in the upper reaches of the citadel; if they had servants, none was of Daros' company. Newcomers were not permitted in the lords' halls; the doors between were heavily guarded.

He wondered what they feared. Their slaves? All of those seemed utterly subjugated, except his tiny band of mages. The Mage was not on this world; it dwelt apart in its prison. If he turned his thought toward the feather on its cord, he could sense that potent presence, and see, if briefly, that strange face with its eyes bent upon him.

The Mage was aware of him. He took a little comfort from that in this darkest of places. What good it would do, what help it could be, he did not know, but any hope was better than none.

TWENTY-EIGHT

DAROS COUNTED DAYS BY THE NUMBER OF TIMES THAT HE LAY down to sleep in that lightless place. His sleep was dark, his dreams unformed. After the second—night, he supposed he could call it, though the night here was perpetual—his magelings had begun to lose their courage. They had managed to stay together through the times of labor, and had claimed bed-niches side by side. They gave each other strength. But night unbroken, even with mage-sight, was a terrible burden on the spirit.

On the third night, Daros woke from a restless half-doze to the sound of weeping. It was silent; it sounded within his mind, with a flavor of the guardsman Khafre. He had seemed the strongest of all, but the soul that opened itself to Daros was deeply horrified by the dark and the eyeless slaves and the strangeness of this bleak world. He, like all his people, was a creature of sunlight. Even in death they sought the light.

"That is your strength," Daros said to him. Daros had brought sunlight into his dream, setting them both in Khafre's own world, standing in a field beside the river, under the pure clean blue of the sky. Menkare was there, and Nefret, and Kaptah looking somewhat shocked. Huy—

"Gone," Kaptah said heavily. "He broke. They killed him."

Daros had not known. He had been shielded too closely. His fault; his folly.

He must not let it crush him. "And you?" he asked Kaptah. "Can you hold on?"

The priest spread his hands. "Have I a choice?"

"Keep this place in your heart," Daros said. "It will strengthen you when nothing else will."

Kaptah bowed.

"Light is strength," Daros said to them all. "The enemy has a horror of it, is even destroyed by it. In light you can take refuge."

"Sometimes I think I'll forget what light even is," Nefret said. "We can't last very long, my lord. This place is too alien to anything we know, except the darkest of dark dreams. If we had a plan—anything to do except wait for the rest of your gods—it would help immensely."

"I had thought of that," Daros said. "You keep the bond with Kaptah—don't lose it. You others, explore as you can; if you can discover the secrets of this place, we may be able to use them."

"And you?" she asked.

"I will penetrate the lords' towers, and learn what I can. There may be a way—did you notice the other slaves? Some are warriors. And some, who are closest to the lords, have will, or something like it. If I can find my way among them, gain their trust, learn their secrets—"

"Alone?"

"Until my brother mages come," Daros said, "yes. It won't be long now."

"And then?"

She was asking all the hard questions. "Then we bring light to the dark land," he answered her.

She did not ask him how. Maybe she had had enough of questions.

Anger made her stronger. Anything that did that, Daros reckoned was worth the price.

The sixth night promised to be no better than the rest. His magelings gathered in the place of brightness as they had done every night. They fed on sunlight and spoke of small things, things that had nothing to do with the dark world.

Daros left them to it. He had tried, the past few nights, to dreamwalk into Merian's presence, but the shadow on this world was too strong. This was the heart of it. It was born in this place, and rolled forth in waves to drown the worlds.

Khafre and Menkare had explored the citadel as best they could. They had found a warren of guardrooms and slaves' quarters, and a maze of deep storerooms under armed guard, and stables for the scaled beasts. They had come across nothing of great use. The armories were heavily guarded. The troops in training either fought with blunted or feigned weapons, or performed their exercises under heavy guard and surrendered those weapons when they were done, to be locked away in the armories.

Daros had yet to penetrate the defenses of the lords' towers. There were wards as well as guards. Both were vigilant. Once he came close to slipping in behind a lord who was coming out, but the lord's guards closed in too quickly. Daros barely escaped into a side passage before he was caught.

That night, the sixth night, he left his magelings to rest in their illusion of light, and went dreamwalking, however futile it might be. The beacon he had set in the Gate was still there; no one had found it, nor had the mages passed it. Time that passed so differently from world to world was not serving him now. Even with the expedients that he had given them, his magelings could not hold for much longer.

The ways of dream were dark and strange. He wandered through dim and twisting corridors, across landscapes of torment, through a chamber of echoes and weird howling. He dared not venture too far: he could lose his waking self in the darkness, and never return to his body.

Just before he would have turned back, the faintest of grey glimmers caught the corner of his eye. He drifted toward it. It grew no brighter, but it grew larger. In a little while he saw the Mage's prison. It was the same as he remembered, round like one of the towers of the dark citadel, and each of its many windows a Gate, but the Mage could pass through none of them.

Daros stepped through one of the windows onto the dark stone floor. The feather on his breast stirred. It drew him toward the shadowed center.

The Mage lay there. Its eyes were open, but perhaps they could not close. Its long strange body seemed to have fallen in on itself. Bonds of shadow confined it; it breathed shallowly, its lipless mouth open.

It was conscious, but that consciousness had retreated far within. Its power raged and surged, bound as it was, compelled by a will outside of its own.

That will led back in direct line from the prison to the citadel in which Daros' body lay. It stretched like a cord across the roads of dream, to one of the towers of the citadel, the highest and grimmest and most heavily guarded of them all.

Because Daros was in dream and not in flesh, he could swim along that cord as if the dark had been water and not lightless air. It undulated a little in the currents of worlds; magic pulsed through it, seeping into him, making him subtly stronger.

It slid through a high slitted window of the tower. Windows, thought Daros, in that place without light: everywhere else in the citadel were shafts to let in air, but no windows. Only here.

He made himself as invisible as he could, mingling his awareness with that of the Mage and letting the cord draw him through the window into . . .

Light?

It was dim. In any world lit by a sun, it would have been the deepest of twilight. But here it was dazzlingly bright. It bathed the body of a man who sat upright in a tall chair. The room about him was full of a myriad things: a great thick-legged table, smaller chairs, stools, boxes and shelves and bins of books in numerous shapes and forms—startling in the dark; proof indeed that these lords could see. Directly in front of the man, on the table, whirred and spun a thing of metal.

The light came from this, and so did the darkness. It spun them both out of the cord that came from the Mage. The light dissipated here. The darkness spread. Some of it streamed back down the cord to bind the Mage ever more tightly. The rest spread like black water through all the worlds.

The man looked like the other lords that Daros had seen. He was older, perhaps; his beard was shot with white. He had an air about him that Daros had seen in men of great power: the surety that when he commanded, men obeyed.

As Daros drifted, insubstantial, in the air, another man entered the room. He shielded his eyes with a dark cloth, which concealed most of his face, but he also was of the kin and kind of the lords of this citadel.

The man in the chair rose. The spinning thing faltered. The other man slid into the chair, and the whirring resumed, spinning darkness, dissipating light.

Daros followed the first man as he made his way slowly, stumbling with weariness, out of that enigmatic place. He recovered a little strength as he went. His steps steadied; his shoulders straightened. He descended a long stair with no nobler purpose, maybe, than to find a bed and fall into it.

But when he reached the landing, a man met him. "Trouble?" said the lord from the tower.

"Yes," said the other.

The first man sighed gustily. "Lead me," he said.

* * *

Daros knew that hall. He had seen it before, where the dark lords gathered. There were only three there now, waiting for the lord from the tower. A small figure knelt before them.

Daros nearly shocked himself out of the dream. It was Kaptah. He had been stripped of the dark robe that all slaves wore. There were bruises on his body, and his eyes were blackened and swollen—he still had them, for what good they would do in the dark.

The lord from the tower circled him slowly. He was tightly bound, his arms drawn cruelly behind his back, and his spine arched just short of breaking. He could not move, but he managed to radiate defiance.

"He was found among the least of the slaves," one of the lords said, "caught wandering apart from his company, spying near the storehouses in the city of the newest slaves."

The lord from the tower brushed a hand over Kaptah's eyes. "He has not been rendered fit to serve us. How is that? Who allowed it?"

"He was found," the other replied. "He came in from one of the worlds that we harvest. The rest who came with him are as fit as any other. It's only this one."

"Make him fit," said the lord from the tower, "and then feed him to the nightwalkers. Unless there is a reason why you trouble me with this?"

"There is a reason," said one of the two who had been silent. He aimed a blow at Kaptah's head.

Kaptah did not mean to respond as he did: Daros could see that. But his shields had been wrought too well. The blow did not strike flesh. There was a flash of sudden light and a sharp scent of lightning. The lords recoiled. Kaptah's captors were less dismayed than the lord from the tower, and swifter to cover their eyes.

The lord from the tower hissed. His eyes had squeezed shut; tears of pain ran down his cheeks. "Another one of *those*? But that world is free of them. We were assured of that."

"It seems the assurances were false," said the man who had struck Kaptah. His face was tight with pain; his hand trembled in spasms.

"Pity," said the lord from the tower. "That world was useful. Now we have no choice but to offer it in sacrifice to the dark, and find another both rich and untainted."

"That . . . is another matter," said the man who had struck Kaptah. "Our advance has halted."

The lord from the tower rounded on him. "It has done what?"

"We are halted," the other said with a goodly degree of courage.

"And how may that be?"

"There is a world," the first of Kaptah's captors said. "All Gates lead there—even those we would divert elsewhere, when we pass through them, we find ourselves there. It's foul with lightmagic; reeks of it. Our warriors need cleansing after every raid."

"Then," said the lord from the tower with a snap of impatience, "why have you not destroyed it?"

"We can't," said the lord who had struck Kaptah. "We have tried. It's walled and guarded. We can pierce it; strip storehouses, take slaves. But no Gate will open beyond it."

"Maybe it's the end," said the first lord: "the last world, the world that the gods will take, and so swallow all that is."

"It is not," the lord from the tower said. "That end is still far away. I have a suspicion . . ." But he did not go on. He bent over Kaptah. Quite without warning, and quite without mercy, he snapped the priest's neck.

Kaptah's shields had risen, but not fast enough. They crackled about the lord's hands. He hissed but held his ground. Kaptah dropped, limp. He was dead before he struck the floor.

"Watch for others like this one," the lord said. "Destroy them when you find them. As for this other trouble, let me rest a little. Then call the conclave."

The other three bowed. Two of them took up Kaptah's body to dispose of it. The third ran the errand that the greater lord had commanded of him.

Daros hung in the air of that hall, with no more substance to him than if he had been air itself. He had had no strength, no capacity to act,

when the third of his magelings died through his fault—because he had
brought them here, and they were not strong enough, and so they broke
and were betrayed. Only three were left, and no sign of the mages from
his own world.

He saw the darkness beneath him, the depths of despair. The light he
had given his magelings was not enough. He was a greater mage than
any of them, and because of that, his weakness as well as his strength
was greater.

He could not be weak now. He could not falter even in the slightest.
These men without magic somehow had mastered a greater working
than any mages of any world had ever ventured.

It was something to do with the thing of metal and glass that spun
light and dark, and the lord who called this conclave. The Mage was a
key, but there was more. He must know more. He must—

"My lord. My lord Re-Horus!"

Daros plummeted into his body. Shapes were stirring about him,
slaves rising, shuffling toward the dining-hall. The guards were watching—more closely than before? He could not tell.

Menkare caught his eye. There were questions there, a myriad of
them, but none of them could escape, not now. Daros looked away—
guiltily, he supposed.

Far above them in the tower, the conclave was coming together.
Daros had to be there. Somehow, if he could find a corner to hide in, he
must dreamwalk again. Or—

He was to labor in the kitchens this lightless day, in the drudgery of
grinding grain and baking bread. As soon as he could, he found occasion
to be sent to the storerooms for another basket of grain. But when he
left the kitchens, he went not down but up.

He risked much—too much, maybe. But he could not stop himself.
He must know what was said in conclave.

The Mage's feather stirred under his robe. It was whispering, speaking words he could almost understand. He closed his hand about it. It tugged, drawing him onward.

He was mad enough, and desperate enough, to do as it bade him. He was less than a shadow, no more than a shifting of air in those silent halls. He passed as he had in dream, but his body was solid about his consciousness. The well of his magery was deep, and brimming full.

It was the Mage leading him, taking him by ways he had not gone before, deep into the citadel. First he went down, into deserted passages and dusty stairs; then he began to ascend. The way was long, the darkness suffocating. Mage-sight showed nothing but blank walls and empty corridors.

There were wards, but the Mage had wrought them. They let him pass unharmed. His thighs were aching, his lungs burning, when he came to the end of that endless stair. The door yielded to his touch, sliding almost soundlessly into the wall.

He was in the highest tower, as he had known he would be. This door opened on a small gallery, hardly more than a niche. The hall of the conclave lay beyond it.

They had gathered but not begun. He counted a score of them in that great empty space, dwarfed by the vaulting. They reminded him somewhat poignantly of the priests of the dark on his own world, in the castle of the secret, which he had destroyed. But those had been the last feeble remnants of a forgotten order. These were commanders of an army that had driven the dark across the worlds.

They were all of the same race and kin, and no doubt the same world—this one, he could suppose. While they waited for the greater lord, they spoke softly among themselves. Daros stretched his ears to hear.

Most of what they spoke of was remarkably ordinary. They spoke of wars, of course; of the management of estates; of rebellious offspring and difficult servants. They did not speak of wives, or of women at all, which was odd. Did they have no women? How then did they get children?

That thought begged him to pursue it, but two men near him were conversing of something that caught his attention. "The captive," one said. "I hear it's weakening. It's not feeding Mother Night as strongly as before."

"And I hear," said the other, "that it's stronger; that it's working its way free. The high ones are working harder to keep it bound."

"It's dying, I heard—freeing itself the only way anything can. The high ones are working harder because there's less power to work with. And there's a rumor—a whisper—that we may have found the End."

"I don't believe that," the first man said. "Something's blocking us. We're going to break that block soon."

"Now that is true," said the second with a gusting sigh. "We should never have given so many worlds to Mother Night—arrogant of us, to think that there would only be more, and the more we destroyed, the more we would find."

"But isn't that the point?"

A third man had come up beside them. He was younger than they; his beard was soft and rather sparse. But perhaps because of that youth, he had a harder, wilder look to him. "Isn't that what we're for? Haven't we sworn ourselves from the first origin of our people, to the service of the Night? Isn't it our dearest ambition to render all that is into darkness and silence?"

The others greeted him with a mingling of wariness and faint contempt. He was young, their tone said, and reckless, and none too wise. "Indeed," the second man said, "that is our purpose before the Mother. But while the flesh constrains us, we must have means to live: air to breathe, food to eat, slaves to serve us. Do you, like a child, believe that this world exists by itself? That it sustains us in blessed darkness without need of intervention?"

"Of course not!" the boy said irritably. "I know that this foul flesh needs the fruits of light to live—that the air of this world would bleed away without certain expedients. But if the End has come, shouldn't we be rejoicing? Why are you conducting yourselves as if this were a disaster?"

"Because," the first man said with conspicuous patience, "the wall we've met is not the End. Something is barring the way. Our source of power is willing itself to death. And our slave-worlds are now too few to feed us all."

"Are they?" said the boy. "Well then, cull the slaves. The fewer we have to feed, the more there is for us."

"We need them," said the second man. "Without them we have no food, no weapons, no armor, and no war. The last culling—of both worlds and bodies—was meant to leave room for new and fresher ones. Instead, we ran headlong into a wall."

"So break the wall," the boy said.

His elders growled to themselves and walked pointedly away from him.

He stood forsaken. For an instant Daros thought he caught a flicker of hesitation. Then the boy bared his teeth. "Aren't we strong enough to break down a simple wall? Are we not the destroyers of worlds?"

They did not pause or respond. He aimed a slap of laughter at their backs. "Cowards! Mother Night has opened her arms, and you're too craven to embrace her."

"Better craven than dead in the light," one of his elders said as he departed.

TWENTY-NINE

THE LORD OF THE TOWER CAME LATE TO HIS OWN CONCLAVE. HE did not look as if he had rested; his face was haggard, his shoulders bowed with the weight of worlds.

Others followed him into the hall. If the lords who waited had the look of warriors, these made Daros think of priests. They carried themselves differently; there was a subtle tension between them and the rest.

The one who led them—for Daros had begun to be certain that he was, if not a king, then something very like one—had somewhat in him of both warrior and priest. He carried a tall staff, which served to support his body as well as his authority. The thunder of it on the stone floor called the conclave to order.

The murmur of voices broke off. The silence was complete. In it, the king ascended what Daros had taken for an altar, but proved to be a small dais or pedestal. It was a contrivance of some sort: when he set foot on it, it was hardly a handspan above the floor, but once he was settled, it rose to set him well above the rest of the gathering.

He looked down upon them, though he could have had no mage-sight. Maybe he perceived them by sound and scent, and by the heat of their bodies. "The rumor is true," he said. "We have come to a wall. We are facing famine. And the source of perpetual Night is willing itself to death."

"Despair is our birthright and oblivion our hope," someone murmured, half in a chant.

"Indeed," the king said, biting off the word. "Still there is the paradox of our existence: that we must feed on what grows in the light to live; that if we are to serve our purpose, we must avoid despair. Oblivion will come for each of us, but if we are to grant its blessing to all that is, we must fight to preserve our strength. We must live so that all else may die."

No one responded to that. Daros sensed the currents in the hall: fear, hostility, a strange exhilaration.

"I have given thought to this," the king said. "Since the days of the first king, the maker of night has been our greatest weapon and our most sacred charge. Now it fails. And yet, this world that halts our war, this nexus, this swallower of Gates, might it not be a power to rival that which we are about to lose?"

"It is filthy with light," said a voice from the conclave. "If it had not trapped us and rendered our Gates useless, we would have made a sacrifice of it and its searing hell of a sun, and mercifully forgotten it."

"Its dark is as strong as its light," the king said. "The slaves of light have polluted it, but once it is cleansed, it will be as potent a weapon as ever the first king found ready to his hand."

"Yet if we are weak," said the other, "where will we find strength to do such a thing?"

"We are strong," the king said. "For a while we were invincible. So shall we be again. Nothing in that pebble of a world can truly stop us, once we discover what it has done to bind our Gates."

"The Gates before it still open on the slave-worlds," said one of the conclave who had not spoken before. "We'll strip them bare—and pray to the Mother that the wall breaks before we starve."

"Strip them," the king said, "but as slowly as you may. No worlds are to be sacrificed until the Gates are free again. See that the lords and commanders are made aware of this. If any disobeys this command, let him be fed to the light."

They bowed to that. None disputed it.

"Go," he said to them. "Harvest the worlds. You, my priests—come to me in the tower at the changing of the guard."

They were all obedient servants. They left to do their duty. He remained, standing still. When the last of them was gone, his head bowed to his breast. He drew a breath that caught like a sob. Then, astonishingly, he laughed. "A war," he said. "An honest war. I will be remembered for it until the last world crumbles into dust."

Daros escaped by the same way he had come in. The kitchens had not noticed his absence; his magelings, the few that were left, were alive and profoundly glad to see him again.

The dark day wound down. Near the end of it, at last, the beacon in the Gate sparked to life. It was brief, hardly more than a tugging at the awareness, but it brought Daros full awake. It was all he could do to move as a slave moved, mute and slow, and to shuffle with the rest out of the kitchens into the dining-hall.

His stomach was an aching knot. He choked down the bread and the hard lump of cheese that had been set in front of him, and drank the oddly astringent water. When the rest of the slaves rose, he rose with them, nigh as mindless as they. He was seeking with his mind for a sign, any sign, that Merian's mages had indeed, at last, passed the Gate.

There was none. When he went walking in dream, he found nothing: not the Mage, not the king in the tower, not twice nine mages of his own world and one Olenyas. He was alone in the dark.

The king's voice echoed in the cavern of his skull, and the voices of the lords in the tower and the conclave. They had found the end of things: a world to which all Gates led. What if . . .

Surely it could not be. His world was no more remarkable than any other. Gates touched it as they touched a myriad worlds—or had done before the dark lords came. All Gates did not lead to his own world, or its mages, either. There had been the Heart of the World, but that was a nexus of powers, like the Mage's prison. It had not been a world in itself.

And yet the lords had seemed most certain. Their advance was halted. They could go no farther. The world that they spoke of, its sun, its moons—it was Daros' world. He was sure of it.

Maybe the war was won after all, or at least frozen in impasse. Maybe—

The power that swallowed stars, that blasted worlds into ash, surely had not been brought to a halt by the simple existence of Daros' world or any other. The raiders only served that power. They were mortal, as he had had occasion to observe. The dark was not.

The raids might end and this human enemy be driven back, but the greater enemy would remain. For a few moments he had indulged in hope, in certainty that a simple war would end it all. But it would not be simple. The great matters never were.

The mages came to the citadel on the third day after they passed the Gate. They came heavily shielded and in battle order, darkmages warding lightmages, and Perel leading them. In his black robes he fit this world rather well.

Daros was aware of them long before they came to the citadel. Khafre and Menkare had found a procession of passages that led to an unguarded postern; he and they and Nefret slipped out together. He almost thought, standing under the sky, that he could sense light beyond the veil of darkness: a sun, stars, moons perhaps.

His magelings drew in closer. They had found a balance in this hideous place; their magery was growing stronger, their spirits less frail, and of that he was proud.

They had steeled themselves to endure the dark world, but the coming of trueborn mages—gods, as they thought—drove them close to panic. Daros found himself in the lead and the others behind him, as the mages came up the steep way to the citadel.

Daros advanced a step or two. Perel quickened his pace as his companions slowed. They embraced as brothers, which in the way of war they were. Perel withdrew first, searching Daros's face with mage-sight. His own face was hidden behind Olenyai veils, but his eyes were keen. "Well and well," he said. "The boy's a man. These are your mages?"

"All that are left of them," Daros said.

Perel bowed to them. "Your sacrifice is great," he said, "and your courage greater still. I'm honored to be in your presence."

He had done a great thing, a thing that put Daros in his debt. The magelings stood straighter, and their hearts were firmer. They had begun to remember their strength.

Truly, it was considerable. More than Daros had thought, more than he had hoped for. They all drew together in the lee of the wall, Perel's mages coming in close, murmuring their names and offering greeting with the courtesy of their order. They eyed Daros askance—even yet his reputation ran before him—but he sensed no hostility, merely curiosity.

He hoped that they were gratified. "We've been exploring the citadel," he said. "Khafre and Menkare have found a number of forgotten or unguarded ways, apart from this one. Nefret has learned the guards' patterns. We could break this place."

"Would it make a difference?" asked Perel.

"Very little," Daros said. "This world is like a hive: it's clustered with cities, tunneled with mines. It reaches through Gates to worlds where the sun still shines, so that its lords and its slaves may eat."

"We had thought," one of the mages said, "that these lords drank blood."

"They're mortal," said Daros. "They worship oblivion; they live in the dark. But they're flesh and blood. They eat bread as we do."

"No blood?" the Mage seemed disappointed.

"Nightwalkers live on blood," Nefret said. Her voice wavered at first, but then grew stronger. "The lords use them like hounds, to hunt through Gates, to find new worlds. Then they reward them with the blood of captives."

"How many Gates?" asked Perel. "How many worlds?"

"Many," said Daros. "But there will be no more, they say, until they break a wall that's risen to bar their Gates. From everything we can discover, it seems to be our world that's stopped them. Did you know you'd done that to them?"

Perel's blank look was answer enough. One of the others said, "You're sure it's our world? Our walls?"

"It can't be any other," Daros said. "Maybe it has something to do with the Ring of Fire. Can you speak to your fellows? Did you keep a binding when you came through the Gate?"

"We tried," Perel said. "It broke once the Gate closed. We're alone here. Unless—maybe you . . . ?"

"Not I, either," said Daros. He stiffened his back and drew a breath. "No matter. You are what I prayed for. You'll be enough. Khafre has found an empty barracks. Better yet, it has a passage to the storerooms. You'll have food, water. No one should find you."

"What will we do, then? Simply hide?"

"For a little while," Daros said, "until you have the lie of the land, and until I'm certain of a thing or two. I think I know what we can do, but it may be more than we're capable of."

"Yes?" said Perel.

"Yes," Daros said. It was almost a sigh. "This world is populated with slaves. If they can be freed and persuaded to turn on their masters . . ."

"Indeed," said Perel. "That would be an intriguing solution. But how does it drive back the darkness?"

"That will take more than this one world. It will take ours, too, and the world in which the emperor is, and one other. That one I can reach. The others . . . if we can't come to them, there may be nothing we can do to end this war."

"I prefer hope to despair," Perel said. "Come, bring us in. We'll settle as we can, then see what we can see."

Daros had been in command too long. He welcomed Perel's air of brisk decision, but it stung a little. He had wavered and wobbled and dithered for a long count of days. This Olenyas stood outside a postern gate, not even having seen the inside of the citadel, and knew at once what to do and how to do it.

The Olenyas had training. Daros had experience, though hardly as much as Perel had, and a degree of headlong folly that could pass, in certain quarters, for courage.

And he had knowledge. He was not sure how much he had yet, or how much of it was truly useful, but he would gather more as he could.

He did not say any of that. He simply said, "Come."

Daros saw the mages settled in the forgotten guardroom, and made certain that they could raid the stores of food and water. He left them eating packets of hard cakes that must be a form of journey-bread, and drinking jars of water. They would have liked him to stay, but he had a thought in his mind, and it was best if he continued among the slaves.

Nefret stayed with them. She would serve as messenger if there was need, and she would teach them all that she knew of this place and its people. The others followed Daros back to captivity.

Sometimes slaves died. Their bodies vanished, and nothing more was said of them. It seemed the overseers reckoned Nefret dead; there was no outcry, no inquiry. Her niche that night was as empty as Daros' dreams.

In the morning, when maybe a sun rose beyond the thick wall of shadow, a lord and his following strode into the dining-hall as the slaves broke their fast. He stood with haughty expression and folded arms while his companions passed up and down the hall, running hands over faces, prodding arms and thighs, singling out this slave and that.

Daros gritted his teeth at the touch of those hard hands, and secured his shields as best he might. The man who had examined him thrust him sharply away from the table, toward the wall. A number of slaves stood there already. Menkare was among them, and after a moment, Khafre.

All of those chosen were larger than their fellows, and stronger. The rest stayed where they were, mute and empty of thought. The chosen formed in a line and marched out of the hall. They turned, not down the corridor to their usual day's labor, but up a stair. It led to more barracks, level upon level, but then to the first of the training courts.

It was empty now of men in training, but the lord waited for them there, and with him one who might be a priest. Neither man had any glimmer of magery, but both had eyes, for whatever use they might be in this place. Daros kept his head down and his body slumped in imitation of the slaves around him.

The priest drew from his robe a thing of metal and glass that looked somewhat like the whirring sphere in the tower. This was smaller; it emitted no light. It did not whirr, but hummed softly as he held it up, balanced on his palm, spinning and spinning.

A faint sigh ran through the slaves. One by one, then all together, they stood straighter. Their faces were still blank, their eyes still gone, but somehow they seemed more awake. Still slaves, thought Daros, but slaves with a glimmer of conscious will.

His heart beat so hard that he feared the lord could hear it. The feather on his breast was still, but there was awareness in it. It might almost have been an eye, looking out upon this place with cold intensity.

The lord hissed softly. His escort sprang from behind him, scattering through the court. Steel rang as they drew swords. They struck without warning.

Not a choosing after all, Daros thought in despair, but a culling. Except that . . .

They were not striking to kill. The ones chosen, freed of binding on their bodily will, whirled into defense. Some fled. Some leaped on their attackers. Some few stood with the passivity of slaves.

Those who fled and those who stood motionless were cut down. Those who fought were let be. Daros understood this in the flash of an instant, even as a long curved blade slashed at him. He darted in under it and caught the wrist of the man who held it. The speed of his attack carried him fully round, and the swordsman with him, sword and all. He braced, twisted.

Hot blood sprang over his hands. The swordsman wheezed and died. Daros recoiled.

He had never killed a man before. But he could not stand in horror, gaping at the thick wetness on his hands. He was a slave—waked to fight but not to think. With all the strength that he had, he lowered his head and his hands, and calmed the swift gasp of his breathing, and stood as the other slaves stood.

The blood dripped from his fingers, dripped and dripped. He felt rather than saw the lord halt in front of him. One of the lord's men knelt and brushed a hand over the body. "Dead," he said.

The lord did not acknowledge the word. It was much too brief to encompass the whole of it: reek of blood and loosed bowels, sprawl of body stiffening in the lightless cold.

He gripped Daros' chin with a gloved hand. Daros struggled not to resist as the lord wrenched his head up. He turned all his furious resentment toward his shields, to conceal the eyes that he had, and the living will.

The lord could see. His eyes fixed on Daros' face. For an instant, altogether without his willing it, Daros saw into and through those eyes. They did not have sight as he knew it: sight that relied on light. This was . . .

He saw heat. Heat of the body, heat of the air about the body. His world was a pattern of shifting shades of darkness, and about them a deep red cast, like the embers of a dying fire.

He saw Daros in red on red on red: a tall and robust man-shape, its heat faintly concealed by the robe it wore. It seemed he did not see eyes. His lip curled at the stink of cooling blood. "Take it," he said to one of his men. "Clean it. Bring it to me."

The man kicked Daros' feet from under him, then heaved him up and carried him out. He made himself as heavy as he could, a limp, life- less weight dragging at the guard's hands. The man cursed him but did not drop him.

In the hall, the culling ended; the dead were carried away. Just before he passed out of earshot, he heard the clang of weapons, and the voice of one whom he had taken to thinking of as a sergeant: "Up weapons! On guard!"

But Daros was not to be trained to fight. He suspected that he would not live much longer, either, for the crime of killing a lord. He bided his time, gathered his power, held fear sternly at bay. Fear was the very breath and life of this place. He would not let it conquer him.

THIRTY

THIS CLEANSING WAS MORE THOROUGH THAN WHEN DAROS HAD first come to this world as a slave. He was stripped of the dark robe—but not of the things he wore about his neck, which were invisible, intangible, imperceptible—and passed through cold fire and cold water and a scalding blast of steam. Then slaves scrubbed him all but raw, and clipped his hair and shaved his beard and scraped every scrap of hair from his body.

When he was as naked as a man could be, they dressed him in a garment as tight as a skin but strangely flexible, binding him from throat to ankle. It covered him, but left nothing to the imagination. He had a brief, thoroughly unworthy thought, of radical fashions and wanton women.

The thought fled as soon as it appeared. In that strange not-

nakedness, he was brought to a room in which stood four others likewise clipped and clad. None was of either world that he knew. They
were all eyeless, but sharply alert. Their stance, their carriage—they
were warriors, honed to a deadly edge: Olenyai of their people.

He did not know what he was doing there. He was quick on his feet
and had some little talent for weapons, but he was not a warrior. If it was
enough to have killed one of the lords, then the lord's kin would be disappointed. That had been blind luck. Daros could hardly expect to
chance upon it again.

Once again they stood in a featureless space and faced attack. This
came in the shape of great looming figures, shapes of darkness that sent
off waves of icy cold, breathing forth the stench of tombs. They
swarmed through more doors than Daros would have imagined such a
room could have. Their claws were long and vicious, their fangs as sharp
as a serpent's.

These were nightwalkers, drinkers of blood. They felled one of the
warriors in that first moment, and stooped over him, rending his throat,
draining the blood from his still twitching body.

Daros fought for his life and soul. Concealment be damned; he freed
Estarion's knife from its cord. It was a poor enough weapon against such
enemies, but it was the best that he had. He set himself with his back to
the wall, though that could trap him beyond hope, and built a second
wall of cold steel.

Those princes of warrior slaves trusted in their skill, but against enemies faster, stronger, and far more hungry than they, one by one they
dropped and died. Only one other withstood the attack. He was quicker
than sight, quicker even than the nightwalkers; he seemed to vanish,
then to reappear in unexpected places.

One of the nightwalkers fell, gutted by Daros' steel. He braced
against the rest, but they drew back. The other surviving warrior had
captured a nightwalker from behind, and snapped its neck.

Those who remained bowed their strange elongated heads and

folded their clawed hands and retreated. Daros sagged against the wall, but kept his dagger up, trusting nothing in this ghastly place.

A lord entered through the one obvious door. As much as they all resembled one another, Daros marked him for the lord who had been in the training court. He was alone, but not unarmed.

He ignored the living men to examine the dead. Each, once he had touched it, shriveled and crumpled in upon itself, then sank into dust. He wiped his gauntleted hand on his thigh and straightened, and turned toward the ones who had done the killing. The warrior stood motionless in the middle of the room. Daros had had the wits to stand straight, but still with his back to the wall. The knife was about his neck again, hidden if never forgotten.

The lord smiled thinly. "You will come," he said.

The warrior obeyed without hesitation. Daros judged it wise to follow suit. Slaves waited outside to dress them in robes of much better quality than they had worn before.

The lord waited with a remarkable degree of patience, but it was not infinite. As soon as they were seen to, he led them brusquely and at speed up through the levels of the citadel.

They passed the walls and wards of the lords' tower. Daros had what he had hoped for, somewhat after he needed it. In truth he would rather have remained a slave below, free to come and go, and therefore to seek out the mages. A fighting slave was taken through Gates; was a soldier in the war. That was the goal he had aimed for—not to be chosen for this, whatever it was to be.

There was no way out but death. He did not want to die yet. He went where he was led, therefore, and observed as much as he might.

They were near the top of the tower before they stopped. Daros thought that he could hear the humming and whirring of the thing that the king guarded so closely. The air had a throb to it; it pulsed just below the level of perception.

A man was waiting for them in a room full of strangeness: dark shapes that, to Daros, meant nothing. The man was a priest; his face was tired, his expression less than delighted as the lord brought the two slaves to him. "Only two? We need more."

"We need soldiers. Those we have in plenty. These—they'll always be rare." The lord jabbed his chin at Daros. "That one gutted a nightwalker with his bare hands."

"And killed one of your own clan before that," the priest said. "Now you own his life. Would that you had brought me a dozen such."

"Often I bring none at all," the lord said. "Do your work, old man, and be content with what you're given. There's no time for foolishness now."

The priest snarled to himself, but when he turned his back pointedly on the lord, it was to gather a selection of what must be ritual objects and spread them on the table between himself and the others. The warrior slave had not moved since he was brought here; therefore Daros did the same. They stood shoulder to shoulder, almost exactly of a height, though Daros was somewhat broader.

While the lord watched with a show of disdain, the priest built a spidery structure of metal and glass, clicking each part into the next. When it was done, it looked somewhat like the visor of a helmet. He performed no incantation, raised no power, but at a flick of a finger, the thing came to life. He laid it over the warrior slave's face.

The man screamed, brief and piercing. Daros came nigh to leaping out of his skin. The priest betrayed neither shock nor surprise. Even as that terrible cry died away, he lifted the visor of metal.

The warrior slave opened narrow dark eyes—in shape like Daros' own, though his face was different, rounder, smoother, and his skin was like old ivory. He seemed neither glad nor frightened to be given back his eyes. Or perhaps he had not, not exactly. There were no whites to them. They were black from edge to edge, but glistening as eyes were wont to do. They were alive; they were unmistakably present. They were like the lords' eyes; exactly like.

The priest approached Daros. Daros' mind gibbered, shrieking at him to flee. But if he moved, he was betrayed, and therefore dead.

His shields were as strong as he could make them. He steadied himself as the visor came near to his face. It was cold, no warmth in it of the man who had made it or the one who had worn it just before him. It clasped him like icy fingers. In the last possible instant, out of pure instinct, he shut down mage-sight, and squeezed his eyes tight shut.

The pain came without warning. It was exquisite—it was agony. It was like needles thrust into his eyes. A scream ripped itself out of him, leaving a taste of blood in his throat.

The cold metal thing retreated. His eyes were open. He still had them. What he saw . . .

A world in shades of red and black. Patterns of heat and cold. Shapes that he could recognize, but altered immeasurably.

Mage-sight was still there. He could see with that as he had seen before. But his own eyes, the eyes of his body, were no longer as they had been.

Many things that he had done were irrevocable. But this one, some-how, seemed more than that. He should have run; should have made himself invisible, and hidden with the mages. He could have freed slaves, fomented revolt. He might even have found another way to win passage through the lords' Gates.

It was all he could do to stand as if it did not matter. When the lord said, "Follow," he followed, because he had left himself no other choice. He must not despair. Despair was death.

The lord led the two of them to yet another barracks, but much smaller than those that Daros had seen before. It could hold perhaps a hundred men, but at the moment he counted barely three dozen standing at attention beside the bed-niches. All were dressed as he was, with eyes that saw the dark as no dark at all. They were all armed: each with a sword and a knife, and a sheath of a shape that would carry the weapon that flung dark fire. Even here, it seemed, those weapons were kept locked away.

These men had volition. They looked on the newcomers as men of any fighting company might, in a mingling of hope and doubt. If their souls were bound, it seemed their minds, to some extent, were not.

The warrior who had passed the test with Daros was coming to himself. He stumbled somewhat as he walked to the end of the ranked fighters. When he took his place there and turned to face the lord with the rest, his face twitched, then twisted in confusion.

Daros fell in beside him, but he had had enough of playing deception. He looked the lord in the face, level and expressionless. The lord seemed somehow amused. When he spoke, the words were addressed to both of them, but his eyes remained on Daros. "Be glad now, both of you. You are the best of the best, the chosen ones, the strongest of all. You serve at our right hands; when you die, the Night will take you as her own."

Daros' fellow recruit bowed his head in submission. Daros refused.

The lord laughed and saluted him. "Good! We need the strong ones. Serve well, and more rewards may yet await you."

He left then, still laughing, as hard and cold as everything else in this world. In his wake, the company of the chosen eased visibly. Their eyes turned toward the newcomers; some of them smiled. There was no warmth in those smiles, and nothing remotely comforting.

"New meat," one of them said, smacking his lips. "Tender and sweet. Tell us, meat—did you taste nightwalker blood?"

Neither answered. The others closed in, smiling and smiling. Daros found himself pressed shoulder to shoulder with the other, and then back to back as the circle eased them away from the wall and out into the free space of the hall.

"Meat," said the one who seemed to speak for the rest. He was tall and lean, a whipcord man. His skin to mage-sight was as white as new milk, his close-cropped hair pallid gold. His eyes, like the eyes of all those here, were black from rim to rim, but Daros had a fugitive thought that when he had lived in the light, they had been the color of a winter sky.

"Meat," he said again. "Fresh meat. How many did you kill, meat? Did you eat any of them?"

"Was it required?" Daros asked. It was certainly folly, but he could not help himself. "I barely had time to work up an appetite."

The pale man moved in close, crowding him, sniffing like a hound. His teeth were small and even, which was rather surprising; Daros would have expected a direwolf's fangs. "Pretty," he said. "Very, very pretty. Have we destroyed your world yet? Are your women as pretty as you?"

"Almost." Daros bared his own teeth. They were much longer and sharper than this man's; much more truly a predator's. "Did your women geld you themselves or did they trust the dark lords to do it for them?"

The pale man's attack was completely silent, not even a growl of warning. But Daros had provoked it; he was waiting for it. Even with that, the other's weight bore him back and down. He twisted in the air. He half succeeded: he came down hard, but the other toppled beside him.

For the third time in that brutal day, he fought for his life. He was tired; the other was fresh. He had a weapon, but he must keep it hidden if he could. He had his hands, and his teeth if he would use them. He had the depth of his anger at all of this, at what had been done to the two worlds he had lived in, at what had been done to him.

The pale man was as strong as a snake and lethally fast. They were all fast, these warriors of the dark. Daros defended himself blindly, striking without thought, beating clawed fingers from his eyes, locked and rolling across the hard stone floor. The pale man jabbed a knee up hard, aiming at his privates. He blocked it and thrust it aside, wrenching with all his force, ripping sinew, cracking bone. The pale man howled and lunged, clawing at his throat.

He snapped at the hands and the arms behind them. He tasted blood—rich and iron-sweet. The great vein of it pulsed in the white throat. He sank his teeth in it, his sharp white teeth. He drank deep.

He recoiled in a sudden shock of horror. His mouth was full of blood and worse. He gagged. The pale man convulsed, locked in death-throes. Daros vomited a bellyful of blood, vomited until nothing came but bile.

Hands drew him up, held him. They were surprisingly gentle. The one closest was the warrior who had passed the testing with him, too new to the freedom of his mind, maybe, to be properly afraid.

Daros could not stop retching. If his stomach would only come up, he could die, and it would be over. But it stubbornly refused to leave its place.

Someone held a cup to his lips. He drank perforce. It was water. He kept it down, somewhat to his amazement. It washed the taste of blood from his mouth. It could never cleanse the stain of what he had done.

He had been so sure, so arrogantly sure, that his spirit was free; that this place had no power to corrupt him. Now two men lay dead by his doing, and the blood of one stained his face and hands. He was as dark as any other man in that room, as deeply tainted by the tide of shadow.

He stood straight. The men about him drew back. There was fear in their eyes. One still held the jar of water. He cleaned himself with it as best he could. They watched him as wolves watch the one who has killed their pack-leader.

"If you are thinking that I will lead you," he said, "stop thinking it now. I have no presence here. I know nothing of what your veterans know."

"The lord who brought you—he leads us," one of the warriors said. "We fight as he bids. Who leads here, that's won by combat. You did win that. Don't tell us you didn't mean it."

Daros bit his tongue. He had meant it—willingly or no. He had known what he did when he locked in combat with the pale man. He must have known in his heart how it must end. How could he not?

"Tell me, then," he said: "what we do here, what we are for. Be sure it is the truth. I will know if you lie."

They blanched—in the strange sight he had been given, their faces darkened as blood, and therefore heat, drained away. One spoke for them all. He marked that one: a warrior from Tanit's world, he would wager, a giant of a man with the full lips and blunt features and the dark gleaming skin of the lands to the south of the black land. He had a deep voice, like stones shifting.

"We are the lords' warriors," he said, "their bodyguards, the commanders of their raiding parties. They give us their eyes, so that we can see as they see, and give us back the great part of our will, so that when we fight in one of the worlds, we may make choices in difficult circumstances, and protect the lesser troops under our command.

"We are not free. You killed a lord in the testing—he was one they could afford to lose, or they would never have given him such duty. You will not be permitted to do such a thing again. If you have dreams of finding your way back to your own world, give them up. You will go back, very likely, if your world exists at all—but you are now of this world and not of that one. Its light will blind you and its sun destroy you. You belong to the dark world now. Never forget that."

"I was exiled from my world," Daros said.

"So were some of us," said the giant. "And some of us were sent to fight the enemy that came out of the night, and were taken into his armies instead. There is no escape from our lords or from the darkness they serve. You are wise not even to dream of it."

"Slave-warriors," Daros said. "My world has had them."

"This world lives by them," the giant said. "Mountains, worlds full of slaves, all bound to the will of the masters. We are the highest of them, the strongest and best. We are the chosen. There is pride in that, if your heart knows any such thing."

"My heart knows the taste of blood," Daros said, "and the lure of oblivion."

"The lords will love you," the giant said, "if you can restrain yourself from killing any more of them. Slaves' blood—you may drink that with fair freedom, if you do it wisely. They'll blame it on the nightwalkers; those will escape and feed, if they can manage it. But lords—never touch those. Lords are our gods. However much you hate them, they hold the cords that bind your soul."

"I shall remember," Daros said.

He turned to face them all. They kept a wary distance. "If I lead you, you do as I bid—barring a lord's command. Yes?"

"Yes," they said in a ragged chorus.

"Good," he said, letting them see the teeth that had ripped the pale man's throat. "Dispose of that carrion. Then come with me. I have weapons to win, and fighting muscles to find again. I was too long below, among the cattle."

They glanced at one another. Oh, yes, he thought as he scanned their faces: he was a bold, bad man, and would be bolder and badder when he was strong again. Which had best be soon.

He could feel the worlds shifting, the tides of darkness turning. It was growing stronger. It was inside him, eating away at his heart. If he was to have any hope at all of vanquishing it, he could not tarry much longer.

"Weapons," he said to the men whose command, by sheer blind luck, he had won. "Now."

They leaped to obey him. He sauntered in their wake, as a prince of slaves should do.

THIRTY-ONE

WITH THE SIGHT HE HAD BEEN GIVEN, DAROS COULD AT LAST distinguish between night and day in this place. Night was cooler, gentler on the eyes. Day was perceptibly brighter. If he turned his eyes toward the sky, he saw the swirling darkness, clouds of heat and cool, and beyond it the furnace of the sun.

On the third day, he was at weapons-practice with the rest of his company. The dark flame was not dark at all; it was red within red within red, a seethe and coil of power that consumed whatever it touched. The weapons that hurled it were simple enough to wield. They needed little precision, only strength to lift them. Swords, bows, spears—those needed art, and of that, he had much to learn.

As he practiced his archery in the largest of the courts, he was aware that one of the lords had come to watch, attended by men like those

about him: slave-warriors with living eyes and bound souls. It was a
great temptation to spin on his heel and aim his arrow into the lord's
heart, but he was stronger than that—barely.

Pity, he thought as he lowered his bow and released the arrow from
the string, and turned slowly to face the lord. It was the king himself.
His dark-on-dark eyes fixed on Daros. "Prepare your men," he said.
"You raid tonight."

Daros bowed. The king's lip curled in what might be a dour smile, or
might be scorn. "Take many slaves," said the king. "Empty all their
storehouses. But leave the fields. We may need them later."

Daros bowed again. The king laid a hand on his shoulder. He tensed,
still bent in obeisance, but held his ground.

"You are not like the others," the king said. "Serve me well and there
may be more to hope for than the command of a simple company."

Daros lifted his head. "Freedom?"

The king laughed. "Are you not free now? The worlds are yours—in
our service. Would you not rather have power? Conquest? Blood in
gleaming rivers?"

Daros set his teeth and was silent. The king patted him like a dog
and left him to seethe in peace.

No one in this world had a name. That was the first sacrifice to the dark:
the sound that embodied a man's spirit. But some of the slave-warriors
remembered who they had been before they were taken away. He who
had passed the test with Daros was Chenyo; the giant was Mukassi.
Others mattered less than those two, but Daros remembered names
when he could.

He was not to take most of the slave-warriors in his company. Three,
he could take; the rest would be true slaves, fighters from the courts
below. He chose Chenyo and Mukassi and a man of his own world, a
Shurakani who had been called Janur. Janur seldom spoke; in weapons-
practice he was single-minded in his quest to be perfect. Daros suspected
that he had kept more of his mind and will than many of the others.

He was not a mage. The lords killed mages wherever they found them, and shattered worlds in which magic was strong. So would they do to Daros' world if they could break the wall that barred the Gates.

It was rather a pity that Janur had no magery, but it mattered little for what Daros had in mind. What mattered more was that there would be no nightwalkers on this raid, and no lords. Those, he had reason to know, were spread dangerously thin. They were mounting a monstrous assault on his world, of which this would be but a testing of the waters.

He knew perfectly well what that made him. He was bait for a trap, he and the dozen other leaders who would raid that same night, some on his own world, others elsewhere. If he came back alive, he would be accorded due honor. If he died, the lords would be rid of him. They could not lose, whichever way the dice fell.

He and his three lieutenants were given armor and mounts. The scaled beasts were not as dangerous as they looked: they were placid in the main, docile and rather sluggish. Still, in armor scaled like the beasts' hides, in tall helms and sweeping cloaks and panoply of weapons, and mounted on the fanged, clawed creatures, they were a vision from a nightmare.

The slave-troops would march afoot, matched in pairs. They shepherded wagons drawn by more of the scaled beasts, and carried the shackles that Daros remembered too well. Those who would fight surrounded them, armed much as Daros was.

Menkare and Khafre were among the fighters. He found them as much by gait and feel as by sight. Their magery was a spark of fierce warmth, burning bright within the ruddy glow of their bodies.

He could not approach them. He was being watched. They must ride out with the rest of the companies, out onto the plain, and there the Gates would open. Their orders were simple: raid, rob, withdraw. They were to fight no more than they must.

They were the third of the companies to ride out. The others were of similar size, with the same orders. They marched in silence broken only by the rattle of cartwheels and the occasional squeal of a beast. No one laughed or spoke or sang. Only the commanders were free to think thoughts that were mostly their own. The rest were altogether enslaved.

They rode down from the citadel and out onto the plain. There where the land rolled to a long level, two pillars stood. They were thrice the height of a tall man, and that same distance apart. The wagons could pass easily between them, or six men abreast with room to spare.

Priests stood on either side, as still as the pillars. They held rods like smaller versions of the flamethrowers. As the first company drew near the gate, the priests raised their rods. Dark fire arced between them and leaped to the top of the pillars. A lintel shaped itself, so that it was a Gate indeed, and a swirling madness of worlds beyond it.

The priests chose the worlds to which the raiding parties would go, speaking a single word as each party came to the gate. The word that Daros heard was *Avaryan*. It was well that he was mounted and not afoot, or he would have stumbled. Did they understand how great was the irony, that they should direct the forces of dark with the name of the god of light?

The Gate hummed and throbbed. Magegates did no such thing. This, like the force or device or spell that the king guarded, had a flavor about it of a thing made by hands. A machine, thought Daros, driven by magic.

They made machines in the Nine Cities, automatons that walked and spoke a tinny word or two, or clocks in which they tried to trap time. None of them had ever, that he knew of, trapped a mage and fed his machines with the mage's power.

That was a potent thought, but he had no time to think the whole of it. The Gate caught him and his following, and drew them in.

They came in under a shield of darkness. Yet with this sight he could see beyond it to the glory of the moons and the myriad of stars. He drew in the air of his own world, his body's home. The earth's power surged up and over him, drowning him in blessed strength.

They rode down a long line of headland, with the roar of the sea on their right hands, and sea-grass hissing as they marched through it. They had not so very far to go. A village huddled in a fold of the coast, ripe with the reek of fish. Nets were spread before the houses; boats were drawn up on the shingle. Even in these days, they were prosperous. They had herds of cattle and woolbeasts, and stores of grain and of salt fish—perhaps they traded the one for the other.

There were walls about the village, raw with newness, and wards on the walls. A mage was in the village. Daros thanked the gods for answering his prayer.

Dark fire broke the walls, crumbled them into dust. Raiders ran for the storehouses and the cattle-pens. People surged out of the houses, strong people, armed and ready. They had fire: torches and magefire. The light of them seared into Daros' brain.

Almost too late, he dropped the visor of his helmet. He could see through it—it was like dark glass. He could ride, raid, fight where he must. He did not strike to kill. The terror of his mount held most of them off; they went for the fighters on foot. Those had orders: to defend the wagons and the herds, once they were taken.

The fighting was fierce, the defenders strong. Daros took little notice. The mage's presence was a beacon before him. It was a woman; she wielded bolts of magefire, blasting attackers who came near. He in his armor, shielded with his own force of magery, struck aside a bolt aimed direct at his head. He overran her, heaved her across his mount's saddle, and turned the beast about. It was remarkably agile for so large and cold-blooded an animal; it wheeled with uncanny speed, whipping its head from side to side, scattering and rending fighters who sprang to their mage's defense.

She was winded, briefly shocked out of her senses. In that brief blankness of mind, he set in her the thing that he had prepared. It was memory and a message, and a compulsion laid on it. Just as she came to herself, he let her slip from his hands.

She leaped to the attack. He had not prepared for that. She surged upward toward his face, armed with lightnings, and struck his helm. It spun away, driven by more than mortal strength.

She hung in midair, eyes as wide as they would go, frozen in shock. He was hardly more in command of his wits. That face—he knew—

Mother?

He never spoke the word. She never dealt the deathblow. His mount leaped away from her, roaring and lashing its tail.

The battle was nearly done. With the mage distracted, the village had been easy prey. They had what they had come for: grain, fish, cattle. There were few slaves; the villagers had fought too hard. They did not linger to destroy the village. Raid only, the king had said. Daros would do exactly as the king had commanded.

The Gate was waiting. He gathered his forces, took swift count of the wounded, gritted his teeth while they were flamed to ash. Death had been swift, and merciful. And none of them was a mageling.

It wrenched at his heart to pass through that Gate again, to abandon his own world for the dark land. But he could not stay, even if he could have abandoned his mages. He could no longer abide the light. He was a creature of darkness now. He could only pray that his spirit would not go the way of his eyes, and give him over altogether to the lords of the night.

THIRTY-TWO

L ADY?"

Merian started awake. She had had no intention of falling asleep on this of all days, but the sun was warm and she was exhausted. The attacks had been growing stronger, the raids more numerous. The enemy had broken out of the bounds of Anshan and begun to raid again in random parts of the world.

Last night had been the worst of all: a dozen raids in a dozen places, towns and cities sacked, but for once no people killed—those who were not taken were left to do as they would. Tonight, she feared, would be even worse. And she dozed in the sun in Ki-Oran, weighed down with the burden of the child. It would be born soon, if there was any world for it to be born to.

"Lady!"

She blinked at the young mage who ran errands for her. He was Asanian, and unusually fair-skinned even for one of those gold-and-ivory people. His face was deathly white now. "Lady," he said, "there is a mage here from the northern coast. She will speak to no one but you."

Merian sighed and heaved herself up. Izarel steadied her; she scowled, but stopped herself before she snapped at him. Gods knew, her condition was not *his* fault. As for whose fault it was . . .

He was in the dark world. More than that she did not know.

She should have had the mage brought to her in the kitchen garden in which she had been sunning herself, but she was too stubborn and the sun too full of sleep that she needed badly but should not indulge in. In the cool of the tower, she roused a little more. She sent Izarel ahead to prepare her receiving-room. The word was rather too grand for that cupboard of a place, but it had a window to let in light and air, a small circle of chairs, and a couch on which she could rest her swollen body.

She turned her steps toward the least comfortable of the chairs. Izarel, ahead of her in mind as well as body, steered her deftly toward the couch. She was settled on it before she could raise an objection. He laid a light robe across her knees, set a cup and a jar—full of clean water very lightly laced with wine—on the table beside her, and arranged a bowl of fruit and a platter of bread and cakes to his fastidious satisfaction. Only then would he yield to her will and go to fetch the mage.

It was a woman of Shurakan, somewhat to her surprise: a strong woman, not beautiful, but her face was difficult to forget. Even so, Merian groped for a name to set to the face. It was never one she would have expected to come to her from a fishing village in the north of Anshan.

"Lady," she said. "My lady of Han-Gilen. What—"

The Lady Varani sat where Izarel directed her. She ignored the wine that he poured and the cakes that he offered. She had the look of a woman at the edge of endurance, a bare hair's breadth from breaking. She was pale under the bronze of her skin; her hands shook, though she clasped them tightly as if to still them.

For a brief, wild moment Merian wondered if the lady had discovered

who had sired Merian's child. It was generally accepted that, like her
mother before her, Merian had bred an heir for herself alone. Easier to
let the world think that and be suitably scandalized, than to try to
explain how the exiled heir of Han-Gilen had begotten a child from the
far side of a Worldgate.

But Varani barely took notice of Merian's bloated body. Her eyes
were fixed on another thing altogether. "Lady," she said, "last night the
dark ones raided us, stole our grain and fish, ran off our cattle; they took
half a score of villagers, but left the rest."

"Yes," Merian said. "It has been reported to me. Your village suffered
lightly in comparison with others."

"Yes," Varani said. Her eyes lowered. "And yes, lady, well you should
wonder why that would require my presence here, away from the people
I was assigned to guard."

"I am wondering," said Merian, "what the Lady of Han-Gilen is
doing in a fishing village and not in one of the cities of the Hundred
Realms."

"I am a Gate-mage," Varani said. "I go where I'm needed. And I
asked . . . I asked for a humble place. I felt that it was necessary."

"Atonement?" asked Merian.

"All of us have sins for which we should do penance."

"You did not raise your son badly."

She flung up her head. The pain in her face, in her eyes, made Merian gasp. "Did I not?" she said.

"Tell me," said Merian. Her heart was cold and still.

Varani seized her hands. It happened so fast, was so strong, that Merian could raise no shields. It flooded her power, overwhelmed and
drowned it. Even shock, even fear—it swept them away. Only one
thought remained, with a glimmer of despair: *I never told him about the
child.*

The child who was close to being born; the child who, doubly mageborn, doubly a mage of Gates, lay wide open and defenseless to that
flood of power and knowledge.

Merian opened her eyes on sunlight, a broad river, a ripple of reeds. He was there as he had been in dream before, in the semblance and fashion of the world in which for a while he had been trapped.

He smiled, but his eyes were somber. "Beloved," he said, "I beg your forgiveness for what I've had to do. As I stand here in this place, the forces are gathering. The Gates are being prepared. The war is truly beginning. Here in this burst of power, I've given you all I know. I would come to you if I could, but I won't endanger you so. I'll find a mage to bear the message; I'll set it in him as best I can, and pray he takes no harm from it. This is not a thing I've tried before—I don't even know if it can be done. But if it can, it must."

All the while he spoke, so clear and yet so remote, his message unfolded itself in all its enormity. She knew, indeed, what he knew. All of it. And yet . . .

"He is alive," she said, a long breath of thanks to the gods. "He is well. The mages are in place, and doing as they had intended to do. Lady, he's done splendidly!"

"Has he?" Varani was still gripping her hands. "He would let us think that. How not?"

Merian's moment of incredulous joy slipped away before she could grasp it. She wondered when she would know it again, if she ever did. "Tell me," she said.

"You never asked how the message came to me," said Varani. "Because I'm his mother? He didn't even know me. See!"

Merian saw night; black darkness. Raiders broke down the walls of the little town by the sea. Varani fought as a mage could fight, with bolts of light. She had reckoned the number of attackers, and taken note that most of them were afoot; only four were riders, massive shapes in fantastical armor, as scaled and clawed and spined as the beasts they rode.

One of them took no apparent notice of the fight, but rode straight toward her, ignoring any who got in his way. She smote him with power, but the bolt flew wide. His beast reared up. He seized her and flung her with bruising force across the pommel of a high saddle.

As she lay winded, he struck her with a bolt of pure power. It pierced her brain; it ripped aside her shields, her protections, even her will to resist. It lodged deep and grew roots. Then at last it set her free.

She rose up in rage. She fought with her body, trusting no longer to her tainted power. She struck off the helm that shielded the gods knew what horrors.

She froze, as Merian froze within the memory. That face—oh, gods, that face. His hair was cut close to the skull as it had been when first Merian saw him. He was leaner, almost gaunt. His eyes . . .

They had taken away his eyes and left darkness in their place. He looked on his mother as if he could see her, but there was no recognition in that lightless stare. The dark was in him, was part of him. The son that she had known was gone.

"No," said Merian—quietly, she thought; calmly enough, all things considered. "No. He can't be. He can't—"

"I think there can be no doubt that he is," said Varani. Her voice was flat, bleak. "It was a risk; we all knew that. We gave him no training, taught him no discipline. Our fault; our failing. Now it has destroyed him."

"No," said Merian again. She knew perfectly well that she might be the worst of fools, but she could not, would not, believe that Daros was lost. "He gave us what we need. We know now what we face. He would never have done that if he had turned traitor."

"He well might," said Varani, "if his masters had in mind to fill us with lies and so overwhelm us."

They are not lies. Merian did not speak the words. She called Izarel to wait on the lady, to see that she was given every comfort. Merian, for her part, called a council of the last resort: the most urgent of all. She summoned one who might have both the knowledge and the power to advise her.

The Prince of Han-Gilen resembled his son little except for the bright copper of his hair. He was a tall man and strongly built, but neither as tall nor as broad as Daros; nor did he have his son's beauty. He had a proud and somber face, a face altogether of the plains, and an air of one whose forefathers had been princes since before there were kings in the world.

Merian did not know him well. His kin had been her kin's oldest allies, but this prince kept for the most part to himself—as, before this war, had she. His lady she had known slightly better, since Varani was a Gate-mage, but they had crossed paths seldom. She had not even been certain that he would answer the summons. He was a very great prince, and more like his son than one might think: neither son nor father took orders well or obeyed them easily.

But he had come, nor had he kept her waiting for much longer than it would have taken him to free himself from his duties in his own city. He had paused to put aside court dress, to clothe himself sensibly in well-worn riding clothes; he came through a Gate of his own making, and presented himself at the gate of the fort.

The guards took him for one of the many messengers who came and went on Merian's business. They passed him easily enough, but without the pomp to which he must be accustomed. She thought he might be offended, but his dark eyes were glinting as Izarel admitted him to her receiving-room. He bowed low, and waved away her apologies for neither rising nor offering him proper respect.

"Lady," he said in a much warmer voice than she had expected, "we need not stand on ceremony. Aren't we kin from long ago?"

Much more so than he knew, she thought. She smiled and held out her hand. He took it and kissed it with gallantry that made her laugh. "May I?" he asked, tilting his head toward the swell of her middle.

It was an uncommon request, but among mages, a considerable courtesy: to pay tribute to the child, and bless it. The child, as far as she could tell, had survived the flood of magic from Varani's mind, and taken no harm from it. She was aware of the prince's presence: Merian sensed curiosity, but no fear.

This was a mage of great power, of whom Merian had never heard an ill word. He was also, and that decided it for her, the child's grandfather. He was kin; it was his right. She nodded.

He laid his hand where the child was, coiled with her thumb in her mouth, dreaming the long dream of the womb. She roused at his touch. Merian felt a thing both familiar and utterly strange: a tendril of magery uncoiling, reaching out, brushing her mother and her grandfather with a flicker of wonder, a gleam of delight.

Merian gasped. The prince's expression was astonished. "But—this is—"

There was no lying to a mage. Merian looked him steadily in the face. "It is."

"But how?"

"Dreamwalking," Merian said.

His eyes widened slightly. "Indeed? There are ancient texts that speak of dreamwalking in the reality of the flesh, but no mage in this age of the world has succeeded."

"He said," she said somewhat delicately, "that you were a great scholar of magic from long ago. He intimated that we might have done well to consult you before we raced blindly ahead."

"As he did?" the prince said. His voice was cold.

"My lord," said Merian, "I need your wisdom badly. I need your understanding as well. Will you allow me to give you the message that he sent to us last night?"

The prince inclined his head. So, she thought: his lady had not told him. Had there been a quarrel, then, that sent the ruling lady of a great realm to be a village mage on the coast of Anshan? Had their son had something to do with it?

She must trust in her instinct, and the urging of her magery. She took his hands and gave him all that Varani had given.

For a long while after it was done, he sat beside the couch, very still, his eyes as blank as his son's had been. Merian slipped her hands free from his unresisting fingers and took the opportunity to rest a little.

When she opened her eyes again, he had just begun to stir. His face had aged years. "I . . . see why you summoned me," he said. "This is far from mere fecklessness. This is treason, high and deadly."

"Is it?" Merian asked him. "Do you believe that, my lord?"

"What am I to believe, lady? What he did to his mother was one of the forbidden arts. It was, in a word, rape. Even if the rest can be true, and he continues to play the game of masks, that is profoundly damning."

"Would he know that it's forbidden? He was never formally a mage."

"My fault," the prince said as his lady had, heavily. "He has so little gift or talent for constraint. I thought that if I left him to find his own way, he would find the right one. His every choice since he became a man has been wrong. Every one."

She rested her hand where the child lay, listening to the echo of their voices within the domed chamber of the womb. "Every choice?" she asked.

"He could have chosen a less difficult time."

"I don't think that was his choice to make," she said gently but with firmness that would remind him, she hoped, of who and what she was. "The gods do as the gods will. I ask you: dare we trust the message that he sent?"

"You ask me, lady? I would have condemned him to death when first he broke the law of Gates. He has done nothing creditable since. Great grief though it costs me, I must face the truth: that my only son is flawed beyond redemption. He was born without the instinct for order that is the mark of a civilized being."

"I ask you to consider," she said, "what you would do if you were in his place. Tell me that, my lord."

She watched him gather his thoughts and turn them away from the bitterness that was his son. "If it were I," he said slowly, "I would play the game of masks to the end. I would do what I could to protect where I was sent to destroy: to slay few or none, and to send word to my people of what I knew."

"That is exactly what he did," she said. "No one died where he raided.

I would wager that the slaves he took will not stay slaves long. There was word among the rest, of the mages' freeing slaves and mounting a revolt. He asks us to be ready, to gather our power, to strike when the time comes."

"If he can be trusted," his father said.

"Can we trust you?"

"To the ends of life," he said.

"I believe that he is your son," she said, "and that whatever darkness may have taken him, in the end he will prove his loyalty to his world and his kin."

"And his daughter?"

"He knows nothing of her," she said.

"And you say that you trust him?"

"I do," she said. "Enough not to put him to such a test."

"Then you need me not at all."

"I need you, my lord," she said. "I need the knowledge that is in you. The Mage who drives the darkness is dying. If we can hasten its death, might not the darkness die?"

"The Mage did not create the darkness," the prince said. "The armies of night may weaken once the Mage is dead, but the dark is like a river. It will hardly fade away because the one who opened the floodgates is dead."

"Even so," she said, "with the Mage gone and the slaves freed, we may be able to destroy the men who serve the darkness. Then maybe— if there is knowledge somewhere, some spell, some working, that can conquer the shadow—"

"I will need my library, lady," he said, "and as many scholars as you can spare. They need not be mages, as long as they can read, and remember what they read."

"I will send you scholars," she said, "and instruct them to read quickly. I think there may not be much time left."

"I, too," he said. "May I have your leave to begin?"

"My lord, you may," she said.

THIRTY-THREE

THE PRINCE OF HAN-GILEN RETURNED TO HIS PRINCEDOM AND his library, to find a dozen keen-witted scholars already exclaiming over the trove of treasure that they had found among the shelves and bins and chests. His lady spoke no word of rebuke for being left to sleep while her lord had come and gone. She asked only that she be allowed to return to her village. "They need me there," she said.

Merian sighed and let her go. If there was to be peace in that family, it would not come tonight.

Already, even before the sun set, she knew that the night would be difficult. It was barely dark before the attacks began. Again they were raids for provisions and slaves; there was little killing and no destruction. Mages and fighters were able to drive back a raid deep in Asanion and another in the north, but the cost of that was high: the enemy

327

would kill if provoked. They swept the defenders with dark fire.

Swords and spears were of no use against that. Arrows had some little effect, and mage-bolts more, but the mages were shackled by their own laws. They could not kill a thinking being with magic. Defend, yes; destroy the dark things that sometimes came with the enemy and fed on blood; but when they faced a raider armed with dark fire, they could strike to wound but not to kill. So were they killed while the enemy escaped.

No word came from Han-Gilen, nor was there another message from the dark world. Mages seeking to pierce through shadow to the world in which Estarion was imprisoned, could not come near him. They could only hold fast, strengthen their armies as they could, and wait.

Greatmoon came to the full five days after Daros raided the village in Anshan. He had not been seen again; if he had been one of the armored and mounted raiders, he had not revealed himself to anyone who fought against him.

Every night Merian dreamed of him. They were honest dreams, not dreamwalking; some were memories, but many were fragments of the message that he had sent. He had left her another key, but it remained as cryptically impenetrable as the bowl that she had bidden Hani bring her from Starios.

She was sitting in her receiving-room that evening, staring fixedly at it by the light of the setting sun. It offered no more answers than it ever had. There was no writing on it, no spell woven in it that she could find. It was only a worn clay bowl with a dark stain inside it.

Water. The thought came from everywhere and nowhere. *Fill it with water.*

They had tried that long before, summoned a mage skilled in scrying and asked that she practice her art on the bowl. She had found nothing. "Worse than nothing," she had said. "This a dead thing. It kills visions."

But the voice in her head was very clear. It was, she realized with a shock, a child's voice. As if to upbraid her for her slowness of wit, the child within rolled and kicked, hard, so that she gasped.

She fetched water from the jar on the table and filled the bowl just to the brim, being very careful to spill none of it. She drew slow breaths to focus, to draw inward to her center. Someone was waiting for her there: a young person with a riot of copper-colored curls, and gold-green eyes with a hint of a tilt to them, and Daros' face carved in dark ivory.

They joined hands and bent over the water. The light of sunset shimmered in it. Then the dark came, much swifter than in the world without.

They looked down into a place Merian had not seen before, yet remembered: it had come to her within Daros' message. The Mage—this was its prison, and the strange angular figure was the Mage itself. It lay bound with cords of metal, yet it also stood upright, wrapped in a shimmer that at first she took for a cloak. After a moment she saw the shimmer of plumes and knew: they were wings.

It was impossibly strange, and weirdly beautiful. It met her stare, gold to gold, and said, "Kill me."

"How?" said Merian.

"Kill me," it said. "Kill me now. Great sorrow comes unless you kill me."

"I see you," said Merian, "but I have no power to come to you."

"Kill me," it said. "Kill me now."

It would say nothing else. She could do nothing. The Worldgates were shut, barred by shadow. The Heart of the World was lost. After a while the Mage's fetch collapsed into its body, withering and vanishing with a long sigh.

She drew back from the water. Both the Mage and the dream-child were gone. She was left with a sense of failure, though what she could have done, or whether she should have done it at all, she could not have said.

Night was falling. Gates were opening, armies advancing. She took up the many threads of duty, the wards, the sendings of mages.

Something thrust a dagger in her belly, and twisted.

She had been sitting at the table, knowing full well that Izarel would object when he came back from running errands and found her. She had a flash of regret for that defiance as she crumpled to the floor.

It was too early. She could not lose this child. She could not—

People were lifting her, carrying her. She saw a blur that might be Izarel's face. There were others: mages, and—Batan?

He did not have the blank, shocked look of many men in the presence of a woman giving birth. The mages twittered, but he waded through them to sit beside her, and took her hand. "You won't be able to claim this one," she said.

He laughed. "But I might claim you after—if this one's father doesn't. Maybe he'll have to fight me for you."

"Do that and I'll feed you both to the sea-drakes," she said.

His grin was broad and insolent and very comforting. "At least then I'll get to see who snatched you out from under my nose."

Pain seized her, rent her asunder, passed. One did not become accustomed to it. She doubted that one forgot it, either, whatever the mothers of many might say. Batan had both her hands in his. The mages had drawn back before the force of his glare. But he smiled at her.

"He'd be jealous if he could see us now," he said.

"Oh, yes," she said, trying to be light, though her breath came in gasps. "He would be furious."

"Good," said Batan.

"Don't you have a holding to defend?"

"Not tonight," he said. "I came here to see you."

She raised her brows.

He did not oblige her with an answer.

There was no midwife in Ki-Oran. She had reckoned it too soon to summon one to a fortress full of warriors. When the baby reached her time, then the chief of the mage-healers in Starios would come, and a small army of midwives and nurses.

The baby was coming. There were mages; Vian was a healer. No one else could come, not at night, not with the enemy infesting every Gate.

They were all more frightened than she. It was too soon—everyone knew that. But the child, for all the shock of the pains that forced her into the world, was unafraid. Her calm flowed into Merian, calming her in turn. This was as it should be, it said. This was the gods' will.

Dream had wrought her. Magic sustained her. She was doubly mage-born, doubly bred of Gates. Was it so astonishing that she should not be born in quite the same way as other children?

She came swiftly, although the pain stretched each moment into endlessness. The mages had raised a wall of light. The child was born in it, wrapped in it as if in sunlight, bearing a Sun in her hand.

Vian the healer laid her on Merian's emptied belly. Merian would not have been surprised at all to see the child of the dream, but this was a newborn infant like any other: tiny, red, bellowing in rage at the shock of the air. Even her supernal calm had been no match for that.

Merian cradled her. Her cries faded to gasps and then to silence. She looked up as her mother looked down, with the clear eyes of a mage in a face so young it hardly had shape yet. She was very small, but perfectly complete: fingers, toes, all tiny but all perfect. The strength of her lungs she had already proved. Her eyes were infant blue, her skin too angry yet from the birth to be sure of its color, but the damp sparse curls that grew on her skull had an unmistakable coppery sheen.

Merian laughed at the splendor of the jest. This was the very image and likeness of her father. Once she began to grow, no one with eyes could fail to know what lineage she had.

Out of that thought, Merian drew her name. "Elian," she said. "Elian Kimerian."

She was too young to smile, but the warmth that came from her was as like to it as made no matter. Yes, that was her name. She was Elian, and Merian-too. Other names would come to her later, but her true-name, the name of her spirit, sealed her to the world.

Morning brought the invasion. The princess regent opened a Gate in Merian's very chamber. Her arrival was like a blast of wind. Merian shielded her daughter from it, but Elian was unperturbed; she was nursing, and that took precedence over any distraction.

Daruya stood over them, fists planted on hips, glaring with a ferocity that Merian had not seen in her since she was as young as this child's father. "You could have died," she said.

"But I didn't." Merian folded back the blanket from Elian's face. "Elian," she said, "greet your grandmother."

"And not before time," Daruya said. She held out her hands. Elian turned her face away from the breast; she deigned to let her grandmother lift her.

Daruya's inspection was swift but thorough. She folded back the fingers from the tiny right hand; a sigh escaped her at the spark of gold there. Of the rest, she saw everything that was to be seen. "The young lord or the old?" she asked.

"Do you need to ask that?"

"No," said Daruya. "Nor will I demand an explanation—yet. You truly believe that I can approve of this?"

"Of course you can," Merian said. "This is a twofold heir; and the father's half of her inheritance is one that our line has never been able to claim."

"He knows?"

"The father, no. The grandfather, yes."

Daruya's brows rose. "You will not explain that, either—yet. So that was how you lured him out of his princedom. No one has been able to do that for time out of mind."

"I summoned him," said Merian. "He came. He never knew how close our kinship was until after he had come."

"Perhaps he suspected." Daruya dismissed the thought, and him, with a toss of the head. "Pack up your belongings. I'm bringing you back to Starios."

"No," Merian said.

Her mother ignored her. Izarel had come in, drawn by the scent of magic. Daruya addressed him peremptorily. "Call the servants. Your lady is going home."

"I am home," said Merian.

Izarel hung on his heel.

"I am not leaving," Merian said to him. "Go now. When I need you again, I'll summon you."

He left with palpable relief. Merian faced her mother. She had been lying down long enough. Rising made her dizzy, but that passed quickly. She held out her arms. Rather blindly, Daruya laid Elian in them. In the manner of very young creatures, Elian was deep asleep.

"Mother," Merian said, "it's touching of you to come roaring in here like the wrath of the gods, but I haven't needed setting in order for some while now."

"This is a fortress on the front of battle," Daruya said. "It is no place for a newborn child."

"Is it not my place to be the judge of that?"

"If you fail to see why she should be taken to safety, then your judgment is even more faulty than I feared."

"Nowhere in this world is safe," Merian said. "It will all be gone before this child is weaned, if we don't find a way to win the war first."

"There is one safe place," said Daruya. "Endros Avaryan."

"What, the old royal city? The Tower of the Sun? Shall we go to sleep beside our firstfather, we three, and hope to wake on the other side of oblivion?"

"Don't mock it," Daruya said sharply. "The well of power there is even stronger than it is here."

"It draws from the same source," Merian said. "When the Ring of Fire falls, so will the Tower. The world itself will be blasted into ash."

"And you speak of it so lightly." Daruya sank into the chair that stood beside the bed. She was as tired as they all were, driven to the edge of exhaustion. "Whatever we do, we should do it quickly. I've called out the armies, and armed the lesser Gates. Wherever the enemy appears, our forces will appear to fight him. They have orders to seize whatever weapons they can. Mages will discover if they can be made by magic or by craft. I have also," she said after a pause, "raised an army of picked fighters to turn the tables on the enemy: to pursue him through his own Gates, and take the war to him in the dark world."

Merian should have been outraged. The mages of Gates were hers; they were not her mother's to command. But whether it was the aftermath of the birth taking the edge off her temper, or the inevitability of the logic that informed all her mother had done, she could muster no more than a spark of irritation. "Your army will be welcome," she said, "to fight beside my army of mages. Those whom we sent are doing as they were bidden. When the enemy's slaves are in revolt, we attack."

"My troops will move in the dark of Brightmoon," Daruya said.

Seven days. Merian set her teeth. Now her temper was rising. "My mages in the dark world will send a summons when the time comes."

"How will they do that? Sacrifice another of their own to the dark army?"

That was cruel. "Some of them are already in it," Merian said sweetly. "They will come with word."

"Seven days," her mother said. "Have your mages ready."

"This is mad!" Merian burst out. "You rush in headlong, you know nothing of where you go—"

"We do know," Daruya said. "Your lover gave us all that we need."

"You trust him?"

"Do you?"

"Yes," Merian said. "Damn you, yes."

"I do not," said Daruya. "But last night we captured another of the dark captains, and put him to the question. It seems your fallen prince told the truth."

"It could be a trap."

"So it could," Daruya said, "but no worse than what we face if we continue to do nothing."

That was manifestly true. Merian hissed but said no further word.

Her mother rose, stiff with exhaustion, and kissed her, and then Elian, on the forehead. "Seven days," she said.

It was an ultimatum. Merian set her lips together and held her peace.

THIRTY-FOUR

SIX DAYS.

The Prince of Han-Gilen arrived much as the princess regent had, but he had had the grace to ask leave before he appeared in her receiving-room. It was much changed since he was last there: rather against Merian's will, it had become the nursery. Elian's cradle stood near the wall. There was never a mage far from her.

The rest of the room was crowded with gifts. Mages had brought them, things that they reckoned an infant could use, or bits of tribute, or garlands of flowers from far quarters of the world. Soldiers had come, too, or sent their captains; villagers who dared venture outside their walls; lords from round about, and lords from farther away with mages, and lesser Gates, in their service. One day had passed, and already this room was full; the stream of booty had begun to overflow the door and trickle down the stair.

It was ungracious to refuse anything that was given. After a suitable interval, Merian would give most of it to the poor; it was the custom. But it must be seen in her possession first, and universally admired.

The prince, like the princess regent, arrived empty-handed. He bowed to Merian and bent over the cradle. The child in it was awake, watching the dance of lights that one of the mages had wrought for her. He wove a net of gold and silver fire and set it to dancing with the rest. She was much too young to laugh, but her pleasure was a warmth in Merian's belly.

When he straightened, he was smiling. He looked much more like his son then, however briefly; he was somber soon enough. "She is an ornament to both our houses," he said.

Merian accepted the tribute as her daughter's due.

"I have a gift for you," he said. "One of your scholars found it. If I may?"

That was mage's courtesy. She lowered her wards to accept the gift.

The book in which the scholar had found it was ancient; the tongue was long vanished from the earth. The scholar had not been perfectly certain of every word, but she had rendered it as best she could.

The text was not long at all. Much of it, if the scholar had known it, was embedded within, in the shape of the words. *Sea of worlds, drifts of foam. Darkness into light.*

A bowl of water. A feather in the wind. Winged splendor bound and forced into servitude.

The seed of knowledge would take root and grow. Merian could only pray that there was time for it to bear fruit before her mother's madness overwhelmed them all.

"I don't think she is mad," the prince said, caught still in her thoughts. "There is another thing that we found, raiding through my library. The message declared this world to be a nexus, a core and center

of Gates. The enemy must break it in order to go on, but in the breaking, might close their own Gates forever. They can do nothing until
they find a way past us. And that did baffle me, lady, because as dearly as
I love this world, I never had reckoned it the heart of all that is. Even
the Heart of the World, despite its name, was only a way-station of
sorts. It, in itself, had no power over Gates.

"We found, buried between household accounts from the reign of the
third prince and a grimoire so black it had to be thrice warded before I
could touch it, a scroll of tales for children. It told of the mages of
Anshan, how they made alliance with a race of gods from the stars.
Falcon-gods, they were called. They flew from world to world and from
sun to sun, and they trailed streamers of light behind them. But where
light is, there must be shadow. As the ages passed, the shadow began to
swallow the light.

"The gods begged the mages for aid in reining in the shadow and
bringing back the light. The mages had sworn oaths of aid and alliance,
and so were bound. Most had no objection; they had gained much from
their allies, had learned great arts and powers.

But a few had always whispered that the gods were no gods at all, but
beasts with the minds and powers of men. They gathered the young and
the foolish and the merely afraid, and convinced them that the false gods
were fair prey; that they should be overcome and their power seized.
Then the mages would rule the worlds, and be as gods themselves.

"There was one among this faction who nursed a great grievance. He
was brother to the ruler of the mages, but his mother had been but a
concubine. He was the elder and the stronger and, he reckoned, by far
the better fit to rule, but the law was against him. He had to see a foolish stripling, a mage of no more than adequate power, preferred forever
above him.

"He was not a darkmage as we would reckon it, but he had long been
a student of the darkness that the falcon-gods had created. In time, he
became enthralled with it. He began to worship it. He became its priest,
and he gathered others of like mind, and founded a cult of oblivion.

"There was a war—one of many, all forgotten now. It ended with the falcon-gods destroyed and the priesthood of the dark vanquished and all their power taken away unto the final generation. Their lord escaped with a number of his followers, after his power was taken but before he could be put to death for the murder of gods. What became of him thereafter, no one knew."

"Not all the gods were destroyed," Merian said. It was enormous, this truth. Too enormous to encompass in these brief moments. "One lived, and was enslaved. The dark enemy—they are our own. Do you think they know?"

"It was a hundred generations ago and more," he said, "and theirs was a cult of forgetfulness. The Forbidden Secrets—I think those might have been theirs, and the order that protected them were their heirs and survivors, escaped to the far side of the world."

"The Gates end here because they began here. The gods found no other world so blessed with magic or so numerous with mages. They built their Gates to pass back and forth." Merian had not known she knew this. It was coming from inside of her, from the place where Daros' message lay, and from the vision in the water. Oh, indeed, she had been given a key, and this was the lock in which it turned. "When they died and the priests' power was taken away, the knowledge of these Gates faded. Their captive would hardly have wished to remind them. Then how—why—"

"Inevitability," he said. "Sooner or later, the dark priests would come back this way, and find the world that they no longer recognized as their own. Their prisoner is weak, and likely dying. It can no longer protect us, if indeed it ever did. Who knows what it remembers? As ancient as it is, and as crazed with confinement, it may not itself know what it knows."

Merian had her doubts of that, but she did not voice them. "Our fault," she said. "In the end, all of this is our fault. We thought we were but one more obstacle on the road to oblivion. Our ancestors—our kin—built that road."

"For myself," said the prince, "I appreciate another irony. The Sun-born devoted his life to battle against the dark. His heir fought against him on behalf of the balance of light and dark. And now, after all, the mad conqueror has been proved right, if not precisely sane. The dark truly was to be feared; truly would come to overwhelm us all."

"Do you think . . ." She could hardly form the words; there was something terrible about them. "Do you think this is the great cause for which he was enchanted into sleep? Is it time for him to wake?"

"No," said the prince, as flat as a door shutting. "You have been in the Tower. Is he sane? Has he dreamed his way out of the rage that would have destroyed this world?"

Merian looked down at her hands, at the golden *Kasar* that had come to her from that first father of her line. It burned perpetually; she was never free of pain. But in the Tower, there had been no pain at all.

She had been very young when her great-grandfather took her there. He had taught her how to use the *Kasar* as a Gate, not quite like the one inside her, but of that kin and kind. He had shown her the chamber in the heart of the black crag above the river of Endros, and brought her before the sleeper on his bed of stone. She had been properly awed, and suitably humbled, by the strength of that son of a god: even enchanted, even in sleep as deep as death.

He had not been sane. Not even slightly. All his being was banked rage. If she woke that, she could only conceive of waking it to do what the dark priests would do: to blast this world to ash.

"We may be as forgotten as the mages of Anshan before that one is ready to wake," the prince said. "No, lady; we have no one to rely on but ourselves. It's fitting, yes? It began with our world. It will end here."

"But," said Merian. "The dark world. I thought it was theirs. How—"

"I would wager," he said, "that it was their refuge after they fled the justice of their kin. They cloaked it in darkness and opened Gates to worlds of light, so that they could be fed and clothed and provided with servants. Women, too, one would suppose, since all the priesthood were men. Their blood may be so far removed from us now that there is little common kinship left."

"They were ours in the beginning," she said. "They remain ours until the end. Ours to burden us with shame; ours to overcome if we can."

He bowed to her. She was the heir of the Sunborn, his expression said. However great a prince he might be, he was and always had been her vassal.

"You have given us a great gift," she said. "We are in your debt."

"You are not, lady," he said. "Are we not kin? Do not kin look after one another? I ask only one thing in payment."

"Ask," she said, "and it is yours."

"Give me leave to visit my granddaughter," he said.

"My lord," said Merian, "that right is yours by blood and bond of kin. You had no need to ask for it in payment."

"I was not done, lady," he said. "Give me leave to do that. And when we both judge that it is time, send her to me. Let me teach her what I know." She would have spoken; his upraised hand silenced her. "Lady, I know I earned no credit in the raising of my son. I would hope to be more proficient in instructing my son's child."

Merian startled herself with the intensity of her resistance. This was her child—*hers*. But she had a little sense left. "When we judge that it is time," she said, "you may foster my daughter."

That time might be never. She left that unspoken. But he was content.

He left her with a great deal to ponder, and little time in which to do it. She had mages to gather, a war to prepare. And there was Elian. Merian had refused a wetnurse: she would nurse her child herself. Yet that day, after the prince had returned to Han-Gilen, she sent for the robust young woman who had been presented to her when Elian was born. She had been polite in her dismissal; she was glad of that now. If she had flung the woman out bodily, she might have had difficulty in persuading her to take the position after all.

Jadis had nursed three of her own, all weaned now, and half a dozen for ladies in Seahold. She was sensible and calm, and she had no fear of mages. Their comings and goings, the opening and shutting of Gates, roused barely a blink after the first hour. She kept quietly to a corner, she tended Elian when there was need, and she intruded not at all on the business of war.

Well before that day was over, Merian's breasts ached abominably. She bound them tight with bands as Jadis instructed, and schooled herself to ignore them. It was harder by far to watch this stranger nursing her child, but that too she endured.

Batan found her late in the day, creaking through the beginnings of the swordsman's dance. He had been in Seahold; she had heard him ride in with a great clatter of armor and hooves, and a shout of laughter that she could never mistake. Batan was not nor had ever been a quiet man.

Except in the birthing of a child. With that in memory, she smiled as he came into the practice-court. "Welcome, my lord," she said. "All's well in Seahold?"

"As well it can be, lady," he said. "And you? I saw the little one—she's grown already. I could swear she smiled at me."

"I wouldn't be surprised if she had," said Merian.

The pause had given her back her breath, or most of it. She returned to her exercises, cursing her weakness but determined to overcome it.

"You're back to it early, lady," he said. "Is it safe for you to do that?"

"I'm not fragile!"

He blinked. She had startled herself; he recovered more quickly than she. "No, lady, you are not fragile. But you're not even two sunsets out of childbed. Should you be pushing yourself so hard?"

"I can rest after all this is over." He frowned at her. She tried to smile—if she remembered how. "Come now, my friend. I'm a mage, and I'm Sun-blood. I'm as strong as I need to be."

"I do hope so, lady," he said.

She lowered the wooden sword and wiped the sweat from her brow. "Batan, will you do something for me?"

"Anything, lady," he said.

"If this goes as I fear it will, look after my daughter. See that she's safe. And when you can, bring her to the Prince in Han-Gilen."

That only slightly surprised him. Word was out, she could see; there were already rumors enough of a redheaded child and the rare gift of the Red Prince's presence. "Not to the princess in Starios?" he asked.

"Take her to the prince," said Merian, "if it's no longer safe here."

"You're riding with the army."

She had been fool enough to hope that he would not come to that conclusion—at least, not until she was safely gone. She should have known better. "Don't tell my mother," she said.

"She probably will come after me, at that," he mused. "How much of an army will I need to defend myself?"

"None," said Merian. "She has a virtue rare in princes: she only blames those who are worthy to be blamed."

"And I won't be, for letting you go?"

"All of that blame is mine," she said. "Will you promise? Take my daughter to the prince; keep silent to the princess until I'm well gone."

"I will promise," he said, "on one condition."

"I will not give you my firstborn," she said swiftly.

He laughed. "Of course you won't. She's already spoken for. A kiss, lady. That's all I ask. Give me a kiss, and I'll be your servant to the death."

That was so preposterous and so utterly presumptuous that she could think of no better response than to give him what he asked for. He was a man of experience; he was thorough, and he much enjoyed the taking of the gift.

She felt nothing. As soon as she courteously could, she withdrew, and resisted the urge to wipe her mouth. He was flushed; it spoke much in his favor that he had not fallen on her in blind passion.

Many men would have deluded themselves with hope, but he looked into her face and saw the truth. His sigh was full of regret, but she sensed no anger in it. "Lady," he said, "whoever has your heart, I envy him with all that's in me. If you aren't the very world to him, then he's the greatest fool there ever was."

She could find no answer for that. What was she to Daros? Did he even remember her? Or had the darkness faded all memory to oblivion?

Batan did not linger long. People were calling him; there was work to do before dark. Merian had her own lengthy tally of duties, but she evaded them for yet a while. This was the last breathing space she would have, maybe, before her mother took the war to the enemy.

Daruya would not ride into the dark world. The regent could not; her place was in the rear, directing the armies. Lords and generals would lead, men Merian knew well enough, and mages of her own order, the strongest and the most skilled. Merian was not expected to have a part in it. She would stand guard over the Ring of Fire, and nurse her child, and let her soldiers and her mages protect her. She was the heart of the empire: the heir to the regent, the empress who would be.

Indeed it was very wise and prudent. Time was when she would have accepted it without a murmur, nor ever dreamed of running off as Daros had, over and over, headlong and heedless and caring only for the whim of the moment. She knew what that had won him: exile and worse, perhaps even his soul's destruction.

She had a sudden, overwhelming need to see her daughter, to hold her, to draw in the sight and scent and feel of her. Elian was asleep when her mother came to her; she roused, but not into the infant's outraged wail. Although her eyes were still newborn blue, Merian fancied she could see the gold-green beneath.

"Please understand," she said, "and if it is in you, forgive—if I don't come back, it was never because I didn't love you. I'm going to find your father and save him, and maybe, if the gods allow, I'll save the world."

Elian did not tax her with the arrogance of that. She was Sun-blood, too; she knew in her bones what they were born for.

Merian sat with her for a long while, marking every moment and sealing it in memory. When she had gone into the dark, this would sustain her. It would, gods willing, give her victory.

THIRTY-FIVE

THE BLACK LAND WAS UNDER SIEGE. NIGHT AFTER NIGHT, raiders burst out of gates, stripped and pillaged, then vanished with their booty. Estarion had strung a cord of magic from Waset to Sakhra, dispersed the magelings along it, and anchored it with the priest Seti-re. It protected the cities and the greater towns, but the villages had only men with spears and arrows to defend them.

With Daros gone, there was no one to make new mages. Estarion tried with the best that he had: the young priest who, with Seti, was as strong as mages could be here. The headache lasted for days. The priest felt nothing whatever, except alarm when Estarion collapsed ignominiously at his feet.

The humiliation passed. The ache of grief did not. He had come to love that maddening and gifted boy as a son, and the boy was gone.

That was the way of the worlds. His task was to defend this one, but it was all too evident that, even with the half-dozen magelings that Daros had left him, he could not do it.

The next dark of the moon after Daros' departure was harrowing. A score of villages were raided, stripped, and abandoned. For a long while after the raiders stormed back through their Gates, the darkness lingered, obscuring the stars.

The sun vanquished it, but it seemed reluctant to submit. Streamers that might have been cloud, but had the depth of darkness, melted away into the morning light.

Estarion had gone up to the roof of the palace to watch the sun rise. Tanit was there when he came. She had his penchant for high places, and a custom of reassuring herself that the sun indeed had risen and the day was come, and for a while the dark was held at bay.

She smiled at his coming and slid in under his arm, resting comfortably against him. Her sigh was weary, but contentment for the moment overrode exhaustion. "A long night," she said.

"And a welcome morning." He bent to kiss the crown of her head. "Tonight you should sleep. The rest of us will stand guard for you."

"When will the rest of you sleep? Do you even remember the last time you saw your bed?"

"Vaguely," he said. "I slept in council yesterday. Was anyone too terribly offended?"

"Most of them were too deep asleep to notice." She looked up into his face. Her eyes were hollowed, her face worn. She was as beautiful as he had ever known her to be. "We can't go on like this. Sometimes I think, if we simply surrender, can slavery be any worse than what we're suffering now?"

"It is worse," Estarion said. "Much worse."

"How so? Slaves have no minds left. They don't even know they're enslaved."

"Their souls do."

She shook her head. "No. No, I shouldn't talk like this. It's the dark; it gets into all of us. Except you. It can't touch the Sun inside you."

"It does try," he said. He ran his finger down her cheek, and coaxed her into a smile. "Are you hungry? I could eat half an ox."

"And I the other half," she said with a flicker of laughter.

They went down hand in hand, to find the nurse waiting with their son and a grand announcement: his first word. "Sun!" he declared. "Sun!"

His father met his mother's glance. It was an omen, that word. It was hope where there had been none, and joy where they had all been sinking into despair.

Estarion swept Menes into his arms and spun him about in the splendor of the morning sun; and sang to him the morning hymn to Avaryan that every priest sang at sunrise of his own world. Menes clapped his hands and crowed, and echoed bits of the hymn, the melody perfect, bright and clear as the song of a bird.

Estarion needed that memory for what he had decided to do. He saw to it that Tanit lay down to rest in the cool of her chamber, tended by maids with fans and watched over by a pair of her own guards. He promised solemnly that he too would sleep, once he had attended to an errand.

She refrained from asking him what it was. Her spies would tell her in any case; Estarion would have found them at fault if they had not.

The temple rested in midmorning quiet. The rites of the morning were over; the priests had dispersed to their daily tasks. There were fewer of them than there had been; some had gone to aid in the defense of towns and villages, some had been killed or taken, and a few had gone home to their kin. Those who remained had much to do to keep the temple in order and to perform all the rites as custom prescribed.

The old priest Seti was sweeping a corridor between the shrine of the god and the priests' houses. He looked like a servant, wizened and frail, but his eyes were as bright as ever.

Estarion deftly extracted the broom from his hands and plied it himself. Seti shook his head. "We're two of a kind, aren't we? Do your keepers fret as much as mine do when you dare set your hand to anything ordinary?"

"Probably more," Estarion said, "though never as much as they did when I was a king of kings. In Asanion especially—in the land of the Lion—it was a great horror to them if I so much as set foot on common earth."

"It is difficult," Seti said, "to be a great lord's servant."

They had reached the end of the passage, and the gate that opened on the court of the priests. Estarion bowed Seti through it and followed with the broom in his hand. Withered and bent though he was, Seti moved briskly enough; Estarion did not have to shorten his stride by much, to keep pace.

The old priest led him to one of the houses, not his own; this one was deserted. It was clean, but a little sand had sifted across the floor; the bed was a bare frame. There was a pair of stools by the wall, and a fan hanging limp from a cord.

It was not so warm yet that the fan was a necessity. Seti drew the stools into the center of the room, sat on one and cocked his head at Estarion.

Estarion sat cross-legged on the floor. Stools here were lower than his long limbs liked, and the floor was comfortable enough, spread with a reed mat over the trodden earth.

"Tell me what you're thinking of," Seti said.

Estarion's lips twitched. "Mischief," he said, "of a particularly dreadful kind. Will you aid and abet me?"

"Need you ask?"

Estarion laughed. "You were a hellion when you were a boy. Weren't you?"

"Not at all," said Seti. "I was disgustingly dutiful and frightfully censorious. Thank the gods, I grew out of it. Tell me, then: what are we going to do?"

"I am going to sit here," Estarion said, "and you are going to watch over me. Don't be alarmed by anything I do, unless I stop breathing. If I do that, rouse me at once. If I vanish, go to my queen and stay with her. Bid her strengthen all the defenses that she can; if it's necessary to abandon the villages, then she must do so. Then pray, because nothing else will save this world."

Seti heard him out calmly. "I understand," he said.

That was Seti: no nonsense about him. Estarion drew long steadying breaths, settling more comfortably, drawing his awareness in toward his center. Seti watched in silence. His presence was a focus, an anchor to this world.

He cast his consciousness outward and upward, into the sun. Without Sun-blood he would never have dared such a thing. Even with it, the roaring blaze of heat and light nigh seared his spirit-self to ash. But the dark could not come near it. He spread wings of flame and flew like a falcon through that living furnace.

It buffeted and battered him. It burned the wits out of him. But he had a purpose, and that purpose was woven into the fabric of his being: to find the other—flesh of his flesh, scion of his blood and bone.

The worldwinds blew him hither and yon. The dark groped for him. But the sun shot him like an arrow from the bow, direct to the target.

He opened his eyes on simple mortal light. His sight was blurred, uncertain. He could not seem to focus. His body yielded to his will, but reluctantly; limbs flailed when he would have stretched out his hand, and a sound escaped him that sounded exactly like an infant's cry.

Dear gods. What—how—

A giant loomed above him. These eyes would not come altogether clear, but the ivory oval of face and the riot of hot-gold curls sparked recognition. Her voice was loud and its timbre strange; he struggled to make sense of the words. "Hush, baby. Hush."

The body only howled the louder. He was as confused as the eyes he wore; only after a long moment did he remember that he did not need a mortal voice to speak.

Merian, he said in his mind. *Merian! Look within.*

She started visibly. "Great-grandfather? Where—"

Here!

Thank the gods, she was not as fuddled as he was. She bent closer, peering; her breath hissed—not in astonishment but in anger. "Get out of there! You madman—she's but a few days old. You'll burn out her mind!"

He would not. The mind he was in was much more elegant and complex a structure than the body it inhabited. Yet for Merian's sake, and out of courtesy to the young mage into whose body his working had cast him, he slipped free of it and stood in more or less his own shape. It wavered; it was transparent. He could not sustain it for as long as if he had had a body to inhabit. He prayed it would be enough.

He looked down at the body that had drawn him to this world, then up at the one who was incontestably her mother. "Great joy to you," he said, "and to this heir of the Sun."

"So there will be," she said sharply, "now that she has slightly more hope of living to inherit. But you didn't know, did you? You were aiming for me."

"Yes," he said. "Would it be possible . . . ?"

He never finished. Her shields had dropped, her power enfolded him. Her body was grown and trained in its magery. It set him in a place of safety, in the outer reaches of awareness. There he could stand as if in the green pasture on the slope of Mount Uveryen, dressed as a shepherd of the north, and she faced him in the mingled grey and violet robes of a mage of Gates.

Her temper had cooled considerably. She embraced him, holding tight for a long moment. He hated to let her go. But time was short.

He took from her, with her consent, the knowledge of the child, her birth and parentage, and all that had happened since he left this world. There was so much of it, so strong and some of it so strange, that he could not absorb it all at once. Yet three things he saw clearly. What Daruya intended, and what Daros had become, and last and least expected, the knowledge that the Red Prince had brought from Han-Gilen.

To take the war into the dark world, that was sense enough in this mad age. Daros . . . His heart mourned, but his head was clear and cold. "That is not well," he said, "for I'd hoped to make use of his presence there. I have a thing in mind, child, but it needs a mage of great power."

"There are over a score of mages there," she said. "Surely one or more of them—"

"Don't be a fool. You know what he is."

"I know what he's been turned into."

"Are you sure of that?" he asked her.

"His own mother saw him. He took her mind by force, and never knew her at all."

"That's grievous," he said, "and in many more ways than one. For what I have in mind, I need mages who can match me, or near enough. One in your world. One in the heart of the dark. And I here, on the other side of the night."

"Why, that's simple," she said. "I'll be the mage in the dark world. My mother will stand here. That's Sun-blood threefold."

"Your mother?" Estarion made no effort to keep the disbelief from his voice. "Even if she would let you do so profoundly irresponsible a thing, what makes you think that she would have anything to do with this?"

"I'll convince her," Merian said.

"How long will it take you? Time is running out, child. We have but days left. Then it will end—one way or another."

"Yes," she said, as intractable as Sun-blood could be. "Tell me what you would do. How mad is it?"

"That depends," he said. "It cost me high to come here, because the dark is so strong between. If we forge a Great Binding, each of us, in the dark and in the light, we may bring light to the dark world. I think, if we do that, we may cleave the darkness itself."

"For that you need Sun-blood," she said: "Sun's fire. Magery alone isn't enough—even as potent as his."

"He knows the dark world," said Estarion, "and the Mage who created it."

"Therefore the darkness is in him," she said.

"But your mother—"

"When did you stop trusting her?" Merian asked him. "Or did you ever trust her at all?"

That stung, though he reckoned himself strong enough to keep his temper. "I gave her my empire."

"Certainly," she said: "when you were tired of it and no longer cared who ruled it. I was too young. Who else could it be?"

"Why, did you want it?"

"No!" He had startled the word out of her. She glared at him—if she had known it, exactly like Daruya in her youth. "What are we quarreling for? Do we have that much time to waste?"

"No," he said. "No, we don't. If you can prevail on your mother, then do so. You have until tomorrow's sunset. If it's only the two of us and what power the mages in the dark world can give us, then so be it. I doubt it will be enough, but better any effort than none at all."

"I will persuade her," she said. From the sound of it, her teeth were clenched.

He brushed her forehead with a kiss, startling her. "Fight well," he said, "but don't take too long."

He let go the bonds that held him to this world. It was like falling through infinite space, spinning weightlessly in a night of stars and darkness. The dark opened below and swallowed him.

He opened his eyes. He was still sitting in the priest's house in the temple. Seti watched him with quiet eyes. The angle of the sun had scarcely changed. Yet within, he was profoundly different. He had learned things that harrowed his heart. It would be a long while before the grief passed.

But what he could use, he would. "Seti," he said. "The war ends soon. If we all die, will you forgive my failure?"

"Do gods need forgiveness?"

"Maybe not," said Estarion, "but mages do."

"Then I forgive you," said Seti, "if forgiveness should be necessary."

His words comforted Estarion immoderately. They were also the last thing he heard for some considerable time. He had felt nothing, no weariness, no weakness, until he toppled bonelessly to the floor. He had no strength left, no power to drive back the dark. So much dark. So little light. For every sun, an infinity of night.

THIRTY-SIX

DAROS HAD LOST HIMSELF IN NIGHT. HE RETURNED TO THE DARK world from the raid in such a state that only the force of habit kept him from dropping every shield and betraying himself. He had done a thing that was as sternly forbidden as the heedless passage of Gates: he had forced a mage's mind. And that mage, by the humor of the dark gods, had proved to be his mother.

He was doomed, he had known that already. He had hoped against hope that he was not damned. Now that hope was gone. He had become what he feigned to be: a slave to the lords of the dark.

After his return from his own lost world, as the sun of this place rose beyond its shields of darkness, he escaped from the lords' tower and went hunting mages. He would not so endanger them as to enter their hiding place, but he sent out a lure, a thread of magic. The one whom it had caught took his time in coming, but after some while, Daros heard his step and saw the blood-red glow that was his body.

Daros drew his hood down over his eyes. When Perel came round the corner in the deserted passage, even to mage-sight Daros would be no more than a shape of shadow.

The Olenyas understood veils and robes. His curiosity had a sting to it, but Daros resisted the temptation to fling off his hood. Perel would learn the truth soon enough. Now, still, he trusted Daros. Daros needed that—the worlds needed it.

"It's done," he said to Perel. "I've sent the message to your lady. Pray your thousand gods that she believes it, and acts on it."

"She will," Perel said. Then after a pause: "My lord, are you well?"

"Well enough," said Daros. "It doesn't matter. You—are you strong? Are you succeeding?"

Perel nodded. "The binding on the slaves is a remarkably simple thing, stamped like a sack of coins from the same mint. Once we free one, the rest of the slaves bound with that one begin to work their way free as well. It's rather wonderful. One working, one man roused to awareness of what was done to him, and twenty more rise up beside him."

"There's no murmur of it above," Daros said. "No one there knows of it."

"Everyone below is sworn to silence," said Perel. "When the time comes, the signal will go out; the slaves will rise. All over this world, they'll raise the revolt."

Daros took a dark pleasure in the news. "Good," he said. "Splendid. The gods must be with us. Who knew that so many people could be so adept at pretending to be enslaved?"

"Well," said Perel with a touch of discomfort. "There is a small binding within the oath, to hold their tongues for them until they're all set free."

Daros' lips stretched in a mirthless smile. "Ah well," he said. "What's virtue in a war such as this? We're none of us innocent, in the end. Only let us win back the light; then we'll remember the laws again."

"My lord," Perel said, drawing closer, peering into the darkness of the hood. "What is it? Have they harmed you?"

Daros wanted to laugh like a mad thing, but he had a little sense left. "They've done nothing that I can't undo." And now he was lying to a friend as he had lied to the dark lords.

It was in a good cause. He lightened his voice as much as he could and said, "I've breathed the air of home again. It's made me remember why I fight."

"Ah," said Perel. "It's been years for you. Why did you even come back?"

"I had to," Daros said.

Footsteps sounded; voices. Daros would not have said that he fled, but he retreated quickly, in what order he could. Maybe Perel tried to call him back; maybe not. He was long gone before the Olenyas might have found words to say.

The mages were safe. The war was proceeding apace. Daros returned to his prison, walking slowly once he had escaped the mage's too-clear perception. His wards were armed; he had not far to go before he walked where slaves of his kind were permitted to walk. His hunger for light was approaching desperation—even knowing that the touch of it would burn out his eyes.

There was no light left inside him. He could remember stars, but when he sought the sun, there was only pain. His fingers clawed, itching to tear out the eyes that had been forced upon him. With an effort that wrenched a gasp from him, he knotted them together within the sleeves of his robe.

They were waiting by the stair that led upward to the lords' tower. The wards that he had set were undisturbed. They had not crossed the line; they stood just behind it: a dozen warrior slaves and the king himself. A priest stood behind the king as if to use him for a shield.

Daros halted. Another dozen men closed in behind. He had not sensed them at all. To magery they were still invisible, warded in a way that he had not seen before.

The priest advanced warily from his hiding place. He had a thing of metal in his hands, round like a ball, made of wire and glass. It looked very like the thing that the king guarded in his tower. Something stirred inside it, something that Daros' eye did not want to fix upon.

The priest trembled as he drew nearer. The warrior slaves closed in behind Daros, barring his retreat. The thing in the priest's hand whirred and hummed. Then, to the priest's manifest astonishment, it began to spin, throwing off sparks of dark light. Completely without conscious will, Daros struck it with a slap of power. It burst asunder.

The priest shrieked and collapsed. But the king was smiling. There was nothing reassuring whatsoever in that curve of thin lips in the black beard. He cocked his head at the warrior slaves who surrounded Daros—none of them from his own barracks; these were all strangers. They got a grip on him; something slipped over his head from behind and snapped tight.

He could breathe, just. It felt like steel cord digging into his windpipe. But worse was the constraint upon his magery. Breath was mere fleshly necessity. Magery was the essence of what he was.

The king's smile widened. He turned and began to climb the stair.

Daros stood alone in a bare cell of a room. They had stripped him of everything but the cord about his neck. Estarion's knife, the Mage's feather, Seti-re's stone—gone. All gone. His arms were drawn up over his head and bound by a rope to a ring in the ceiling. His feet touched the cold stone floor, just.

Warrior slaves had hung him like a newly slaughtered ox and withdrawn. Without magic to warm him, the chill of this sunless place was sinking into his bones. His feet and hands were numb. It would be a great irony if, having survived all this while in the dark world, he died of simple cold.

He had nowhere to go but inside himself. That was not the most pleasant of places, but it was better than the world without. There was light in it after all: sunlight caught in the gold of Merian's hair. She never had been able to tame it; even when she was most severe and queenly, curls of it persisted in escaping any bonds she set on them. He loved to tangle his fingers in it, covering her face with kisses, until she laughed and protested, then retaliated in kind.

In this dream or memory, she was not laughing. She sat in a circle of mages and hard-bitten personages who could only be warriors and generals. Somewhat incongruously, she cradled an infant in her arms. The child was too young to look like anything in particular, but there was no mistaking the color of its hair.

The council was settling the affairs of a great war: matters of armies and weapons, attack and invasion. The child was asleep with its fist in its mouth. He could not focus on the war; his eyes and mind kept returning to those tiny and perfect fingers, and those copper-bright curls.

What he felt, he did not know. Joy. Incredulity. Wistfulness: that such a thing could not be in any world but that of dream.

Something was nagging at him. After a long and reluctant while, he gave it a name: pain. A mailed fist was striking him again and again, with beautifully calculated precision. It broke nothing, but it hurt a very great deal.

He opened eyes on a world altogether alien to that of sunlight and a child's face. Red and black: blood and darkness. One of the lords had the honor of striking him even after he had groaned and come to himself. The king watched, arms folded, dispassionate. After a stretching while, he said, "Enough."

The lord lowered his arm. He was breathing quickly; he flexed the arm as if he were glad of the respite.

The king looked Daros up and down, then walked in a circle, examining him fore and aft. His finger brushed points of particular pain: elbows, knees, back and buttocks, ribs. Daros' breath hissed between his teeth. Perhaps in spite of the lord's care, one rib was cracked.

Last of all, the king laid a hand on his genitals. He held them lightly as they did their best to crawl into Daros' belly. One twist of the fingers would crush them.

With what might have been regret, the king's hand withdrew. "It seems human," he said to the priest who had been hiding behind him. "Can you be sure it has what we need?"

"As sure as I can be, lord," the priest said.

"It seems perfectly powerless now."

"It is bound, lord," said the priest. "Its humanity serves our purpose well: it requires fewer strictures than the other."

"It will be docile? It will serve our purpose?"

"It is bound," the priest said again.

"Do bear in mind," the king said rather too gently, "where we found it, and what it had risen to before we understood that our devices were going mad because of something among the slaves, not some rebellion from the thing in its prison. This slave should have been bound beyond resistance; and yet it was spying in passages forbidden to it."

"This binding will hold," the priest said.

Daros had had enough. "I am not an it," he said. "I am human—at least as human as you. Will you do me the courtesy of killing me quickly, and get it over?"

He more than half expected to be ignored, but the king turned those lightless eyes on him and raised a brow. "But," he said, "we have no intention of killing you. Not at all. You are much more useful alive than dead."

"As what? A hostage? You know or even care who I am?"

"Who," said the king, "no. What you are—yes, that matters. Your kind are an offense before the gods. But my priests assure me that you are more than the usual run of magical vermin. A great deal more, they insist. So much more that we can make actual use of you."

Daros had begun to see where this was leading. "No," he said. "Oh, no. You can't make me—"

"It is fortunate that intelligence is not a requirement of this captivity," the king said. "Only power. And power you have, power like a sun. Light casts shadow, the ancients teach us. The greater the light, the deeper the shadow. Your light will feed our darkness. Your power will make us strong."

"No," said Daros. Desperately he beat against the binding that held his magery. To kill with power was forbidden—not only because it was murder, but because it killed the power itself. Estarion had done it. It had driven him mad.

In the end he had gained back both his magic and his sanity: he was Sun-blood, after all. Daros was mortal. If he killed with power, he killed that power. Then the lords would destroy his body, and it would be over, done with. He would be gone. The Mage would die. And—

Agony rent him to his center. He hung gagging, retching, no strength in him to curl about the focus of the pain.

They had not gutted him, nor gelded him either, though he could almost wish they had. The lord with the iron fist lowered it and stepped back. Very slowly the agony faded.

"I am not to be ignored," the king said mildly. And to the lord: "Cut him down."

The lord looked as if he might protest, but he did as he was bidden. Daros dropped bonelessly to the floor. His hands, his neck, his power were still bound. He lay on his face, trying not to count the number of his hurts. His magic hammered still against the bindings. Were they a little weaker?

A foot hooked beneath him and flung him onto his back. The king stood over him. "If you submit," he said, "and consent to serve us, your servitude will be much lighter and your lot less difficult. But whether you will or no, you will be the most potent of all our slaves."

Daros bit his tongue until it bled. He could cry like a child; he could beg for mercy. He could be defiant or rebellious. It would not matter. There was no escape from this but death.

He lay limp, as if he had been defeated. Warrior slaves heaved him up. He was glad to require three of them; his dead weight was considerable. He only regretted that neither the lord nor the king could be troubled to assist their servants.

They grunted as they hauled him out of the cell and up a narrow stair. They were not above dragging him, catching bruises on every step, until they had come to the top of the tower. A door slid open. Priests waited beyond, and a structure such as Daros had seen before; but those had been small enough to hold in the hand. This was nigh as broad as the room, and as high as a tall man. Set in it was the device that the king had guarded, or its near twin.

They caged him in it. It closed upon him, encasing him like armor, holding him immobile. No fortress between the worlds, this; no prison for an inhuman Mage. He would endure his slavery within this world.

The bond about his neck had let go when the cage enclosed him. It made no difference. Each cold metal band ate a little more of his will, sapped a little more of his strength to resist. It opened him to the whirring, humming thing set in the cage, and tempted his power; it lured it out, into the trap.

So had they captured the Mage long ages ago, and bound him to their will. For all Daros' struggle to shut down his mind and suppress his power, he could not stop the trickle through the cracks in his shields.

This was the thrice ninth hell of the Asanian priests. As before when he was simply taken prisoner, he had no useful choice but to retreat into his own mind. It was a capacious place, crackling with lightnings, most of them dark.

The Mage waited in one of the deep halls. It wore a semblance of life and vigor, but its voice was faint, its shape not quite substantial.

"You," Daros said with no love at all. "You did this."

"The fault is mine," the Mage said, "but this was not my will."

"They know what I am. Who else could have told them?"

"You," said the Mage. "You told them. Your presence in their tower, your hunting and spying—their machines saw you. Be glad, youngling.

If the roar of your magic had not overwhelmed the piping and twittering of theirs, your little mages would have been betrayed."

"Would it have made a difference?" said Daros bitterly. "I'm trapped now as you were. Are. Will be—but not for much longer, no? Now that you have a successor."

"Not much longer, no," the Mage said. "Youngling, listen. The gift I gave you, the feather of my wing—"

"Gone," Daros said. "They took it with the rest."

"No," said the Mage.

It gestured with its chin. Daros looked down. The feather hung as it had for so long, secure on its cord. He closed his hand about it. It felt real—as it would; he was dreaming.

"No dream," the Mage said. "Use the gift. Build with it."

It had been speaking sensibly until then—human sense. For that, Daros had doubted that it was real. But this strange twist of thought, that was indeed the Mage. Did it seem a little more substantial?

"Build," said the Mage. "Hold and guard. Then later, fight."

It melted to mist before Daros could demand that it explain. He could not call it back, even in memory. But its feather remained, solid and real in his hand.

For lack of greater inspiration, he slipped it from its cord and wielded it like a pen. When he drew it through the air, it left behind a glimmering line. He shaped the letters of his name, a little stiffly for it had been a long while since he held a pen. They hung before him, gleaming. With swift strokes he drew walls about it and surmounted them with towers. Then he drew a gate, but locked and barred it.

He paused. He was breathing hard as if he had lifted each stone of a living wall and set it upon another. Yet he moved more freely. The trickle of magic through the wards had stopped.

The Mage's voice whispered through the feather in his hand. "Build strength, youngling. Build resistance. Hold fast."

He fancied that he could hear sadness in that voice, a touch of wistfulness. It had never had that strength, even as great as its power was.

Once trapped, it had had no power to free itself, nor to refuse the use that was made of it. It had lacked even the courage to seek the death that would free it.

Daros had little that the Mage had not given him. It had served him poorly enough. He was as trapped as the Mage had ever been. His magery was protected, yes, but for how long? The dark lords needed it. They would find a way to take it. That was inevitable.

Or he could die. He had thought that he was ready. Yet, enclosed within his wards, he could not find the determination to do the necessary. The mages might succeed; the war might end. Even the darkness—it might yield to light.

Not if the dark lords had his power, enslaved, to do with as they would. He must die. He must not give them even the hope of turning him against all that lived and walked in the light.

THIRTY-SEVEN

NOW. IT MUST BE NOW.

Merian started awake. She had snatched a few moments' rest between the long day's preparations and the night's incessant attacks; but it had not been overly restful. Her dreams were dark, full of madness and pain. And then, sudden and piercingly clear, came that voice like a hawk's cry.

You must move now. There is no time to waste!

It was two days still to the muster. They were nearly ready, but she had yet to speak to her mother of Estarion's message. It was not cowardice, she told herself. The less time she gave Daruya to ponder objections, the easier it might be to win her over.

But the urgency in that voice, the desperation beneath, set her heart to pounding. She knew the voice. It was the Mage, the creature whose power the dark lords had enslaved. She reached to the place where it had been, hoping to catch it, hold it, learn more of it, but it was gone.

Quickly, before she lost courage, she touched her mother's mind, away in Starios. She had good hope of finding Daruya too preoccupied to trouble with her, but Daruya happened to be resting as well. She basked in the sun as all of their blood were wont to do, in the innermost of her chambers, where even her husband must ask leave to enter.

She admitted Merian to her mind with remarkably little testiness. "Trouble?" she asked.

"Maybe," Merian said. "I had a sending. The dark ones' Mage—it summoned us all. Now, it said. We must attack now."

"Did it?" Daruya frowned. "How could it know what we intend?"

"The mages know," Merian said. "It is a mage. Maybe—"

"Maybe we've been betrayed."

Merian's heart constricted. "No. He would never—"

"Is the Mage a he?" Daruya inquired.

"Mother," said Merian, scrambling her wits together. "This is a true sending. Whatever the cause, I believe we should obey it. All is ready, or as ready as it can be. And there is something . . ."

When Merian did not immediately go on, Daruya raised a brow. "Something that rives you with guilt?"

"Something that you may find objectionable, but it comes from the emperor."

"The emperor is lost on the other side of the dark."

"He found his way to me," Merian said: "in strict truth, to Elian; he was hunting the youngest heir of the line. He has a plan that may scatter the darkness."

"A plan," said Daruya, "that you think I may not like."

"I know you will not," Merian said. "It requires one of us in this world, and one of us in his—and one between, in the dark world."

There was a pause. Daruya's understanding was swift. "He was going to rely on the Gileni. Yes?"

"The Gileni is lost," Merian said, though the words knotted her belly with grief, "and in any case it should be Sun-blood. We were born in and of the light; the light is alive in us. It fills us. Who better to break this thing that shatters worlds?"

"Who better to rescue the father of your child?"

"That supposes that he needs rescuing," Merian said with a hint of sharpness. "Mother, we need you to hold this world as he holds the other. I'm the youngest, the mage of Gates. My place is in the dark world."

"Your place is here, as my heir."

"There is a newer heir," Merian said. "If I don't come back, I trust you to see that she lives to inherit."

"You're sending her to me after all?"

"No," said Merian. "She's going to Han-Gilen. But—"

Daruya rose. Merian braced for the blast, but her mind-voice was soft and dangerously mild. "You would send my granddaughter there, and not to me?"

"Elian is the prince's granddaughter, too. And," said Merian, "he, unlike you, is not in the vanguard of the war. He can keep her safe until all of it is over—for good or for ill."

Daruya liked that little, but she had ruled an empire long enough to recognize sense when she heard it. "Were you planning to tell me any of this?"

"I'm telling you now."

"Yes—and telling me to mount the attack without delay. What were you afraid of, that if I had time to think about it, I'd find a way to stop you?"

"Something of the sort," Merian admitted. "But, Mother, there really isn't—"

"I see no other way," said Daruya. The taste of the words must have been bitter. "Tell me what the emperor would have us do."

Merian was almost too startled to reply. "Swear you won't stop me before I pass the Gate."

"I will not stop you," Daruya said. "I will hate every moment that you are gone, and dread every outcome until you come back. But when have I ever stopped you from doing as you pleased?"

That, for her, was tenderness. It tightened Merian's throat. "I will come back. We will win this war."

"You do that," said Daruya.

"You will call the muster tonight?"

"Today," said Daruya.

"Then you trust—"

"I trust you. Now go, or we leave you behind."

Merian went. Even as she retreated into her own body again, the call thrummed through her. It was the Great Summons, that she had not heard in all her years: calling every mage of this world to the muster. Mages passed the summons to mortal lords and commanders. The armies of the Sun began to move.

Almost without willing it, Merian sent the summons winging outward through the darkness, toward Estarion on the far side of the night. She did not know whether it came to him; she could only hope.

Men were stirring in the fortress. Half would stay to guard it; half would go. So too with the mages who had come to her here. Some must ward the world, but some would take the war to the enemy.

She would go in armor, and armed. Her greatest weapon was her magery, but she would fight if she must. Her mail was shimmering steel, the surcoat over it the violet and grey of her order. Gold shimmered through it; Sun-brooches clasped the shoulders. It was rather too splendid for her taste, but the army needed to see that Sun-blood marched with it. It was a price she paid for the rank she had been born to.

Elian's nurse was ready, in a guard of strong mages. She surrendered the child into Merian's arms, for a little while. Merian clasped her close to breasts that still ached in their bindings, and breathed the sweet infant scent of her. It was more than difficult relinquish her into Jadis' care again, to open the lesser Gate, to send them to the prince in Han-Gilen. When they were gone, Merian's heart was as empty as her womb.

She straightened with an effort, and steeled herself. She would come back; she made it a vow, sworn on the searing pain in her hand. She pressed that hand to her heart. "May the gods witness it," she said.

The sun was still high as the last of the armies gathered and waited. Mages linked mind to mind across the face of the world. Merian gathered their power together within the Ring of Fire, in the heart of Ki-Oran. She forged of it a key, and set it to the Gate within her.

Darkness resisted, surging against the Gate like a tide. She set all their conjoined strength against it, to break its power, to open the Gate.

It was too strong. Without the Heart of the World to bolster the rest, all the mages, even with Merian, were not enough. If she had been Estarion—or Daros—

Despair was the darkness' weapon. She countered it with the Sun within her. It shrank away—then roared back like a wave of the sea.

Just before it would have drowned her, it broke. It frayed and shredded and melted into mist. Astonishment froze her in the last act of defense.

Now! cried the Mage's voice. Desperation sharpened it, and yet it sounded faint and growing fainter. *Go now!*

There was no time to waste. Before the dark could come back like the swing of the tide, she thrust open the Gate. The armies of the Sun poured into the dark world.

Estarion sat bolt upright in the queen's council. Her chamberlain told the tally of cattle and fodder, barley and storehouses. Those were vital matters, matters of the people's survival, but they were deadly dull; and the news was all bad. The enemy was stripping them bare.

The Great Summons rang in Estarion's skull. It was so strong, so compelling, that it was all he could do not to leap to his feet and run to a muster on the other side of the sky. Even some of those in the council sensed it, however dimly. Tanit sat as stiff as he, eyes wide, staring into the blank and singing air.

He rose. "It's time," he said.

Lord Bes droned on, but the rest welcomed the distraction. The more warlike rose to face him. He addressed them through the buzz of the chamberlain's voice. "The battle has come. Arm and prepare your men. Tonight, we fight."

Some of them were pale, some flushed with excitement. They were all firm in their courage. They were not a warrior people, but they had learned to fight. Daros had taught them. His legacy in this world, Estarion thought fleetingly. There was no time for sentiment.

He bowed over Tanit's hand and kissed it. It was steady, strong. Only a mage would know how hard her heart was beating. "One stroke," she said to him. "One hard blow. That's all we have in us. Guide it well, my lord."

He should go, but he lingered. He had every intention of surviving this as he had so much else, and yet he could not leave before he had impressed in memory every line of her face. He ran his finger down her cheek, and kissed her softly on the lips. "Until morning," he said.

"Until morning," said Tanit.

The defenses of the city and the string of cities from Waset to Sakhra were as strong as mages and cats, priests and warriors, could make them. Estarion tightened the weaving of the wards and saw that the mortal guards were armed and ready. When that was done, and the land of the river was as well protected as it could be, he turned his steps toward the temple of the sun-god.

Seti was waiting for him. The old priest had summoned a handful of priests whom he trusted, and instructed them in their duties. They had prepared the room for him in the house in which he had met Seti before. The bed was moved to the center and hung with clean linen. Lamps stood at head and foot, ready to be lit when the night came.

There was a light meal waiting, as Estarion had requested: bread, cheese, clean water. He ate and drank carefully. Fasting was no part of this: he needed to be strong. When he had had his fill, he suffered the priests to surround him with their chants and incense. It did nothing for his magic, but it consoled them greatly. It comforted him, too, in its way. He had left his priesthood with his empire, laid it all aside to become a shepherd in the Fells. Yet when all was done and said, he was still what he had been born to be: mage, priest, lord and king.

As the last chant died away, he lay on the bed, which had been made long enough for him. Seti sat in a chair beside him. The others divided: half to retreat to the inner room, to rest; half to take station about him. They would guard him while he journeyed to the heart of his magic.

He settled as comfortably as he might, and steadied himself with long, deep breaths. Each brought him closer to his center, drew him deeper into his power. He was aware of the priests watching over him, of Seti's blind eyes that saw clearly to the soul. The world beyond them, the people, the river flowing forever to the sea, all that had become a part of him since he fell through the Gate, wrapped him about and made him strong. Strongest of all was the queen in her hall of audience, and their son in his nursery, playing contentedly in a patch of sunlight. He gurgled at the touch of his father's mind, and laughed, teasing it with flickers and flashes of power.

Strong young mage. The joy of that rode with him into the heart of this world, and so outward through the memory of Gates. He bore with him the light and power of the sun, and the splendor of stars, and the cold glory of the moon that ruled the night in this world.

The dark had retreated somewhat. It had not faded or died; it hung like a wave about to break. But some strong blow had weakened it.

He sought the Mage in its prison, passing swiftly through the paths of the night. He found the chamber, the many Gates pulsing uncontrolled, and the long strange shape limp and lifeless in its bonds. It was not dead, not quite, but its power had broken, and all the structures of its making had collapsed. The dark world swirled with confusion. Slaves rose up; lords who had never dreamed of such a thing were fighting for their lives.

The Mage's power mustered one last feeble flicker. It touched Estarion's and held, gripping like a soft hand. *Time is short. Be swift. He cannot fight forever.*

"He?"

The Mage slipped free. *Swift,* it said. *Be swift.*

The last of it was no word at all, but a vision as the Mage sank down into death: a shape of shadow caged in steel. Another mage. Another captive. Fighting—resisting.

Estarion did not want to set a face to that shadow. Yet there was no escaping it. No other mage anywhere had that particular strength, that core of bright recklessness.

His long cry of grief and rage echoed through the worlds. Did Daros hear it? There was no telling. He was bound beyond escaping: from without by the dark lords, and from within by the bitter battle to destroy his magic before the dark lords seized it.

There was no time for mourning. Estarion must find the sun in the dark world, and through it bind the sun on the world in which he was born. Threefold power, threefold strength. Sun-blood to Sun-blood.

Merian passed the Gate into the dark world. In the same instant, his power leaped through her to Daruya in the world of his birth. It was remarkably like the skein of mages along the river: each one reaching to the next, and binding all the rest together. They wove and bound and locked. Without pausing to ask leave, he made himself their master. This binding was his. He ruled it as he had ruled empires, with no more effort than it took to draw breath.

THIRTY-EIGHT

MERIAN PASSED THROUGH THE GATE INTO THE DARK WORLD. Armies crossed with her, armed with light. They brought a dawn that this world had not seen in ages beyond reckoning.

Battle raged on the barren plains, in the fortresses and the slave-cities, and across the beds of the dry seas. Slaves had risen against their masters. Mages urged them on. For weapons they had whatever they could find: stolen knives and spears, miners' picks, cooks' knives, even bricks and stones. Anything that could be lifted to strike or hurl, they had. And if that failed, they had their teeth and fists and feet, the power of their bodies, and the sheer weight of numbers.

Merian's forces came through the Gate in the heart of that world, before the king's citadel. The battle was fiercest here, the dark lords most numerous, and not all their slaves had joined the revolt. The warrior slaves fought, many of them, for their lords. Their weapons were strong and their anger terrible. They blasted the lesser slaves with dark fire, mowing them down like grain.

Light alone was not enough against those. Too many wore helms without eyes, shielding them from the searing pain. Freed slaves, who had no such protection, burned and died, but those whom they fought, fought on unharmed.

Merian was aware of Estarion within her, his grip on her power, his enslavement of its will. But she had expected it; she knew him, and she had had the same thought. She had divided herself; her power held its own deep realm, but her body's will kept its freedom. She led the assault on the citadel, mounted on a senel that, being blind, had no fear of the dark.

But she had not come to command these armies. The chief of the Olenyai had that honor here, and at his back the commander of the imperial armies—great lords and generals both, and far better versed than she in the arts of war. Her art was another altogether. She had come for that. The rest, little as the armies might have liked to know it, was diversion.

As the rams rolled through the Gate, driving toward the gate of the citadel, she took a handful of mages and went in search of the postern that Daros' message had promised. She damped the light about them, dimming it to nothing, calling up mage-sight to make her way through the dark. Glimmers of light from the battle cast a fitful glow on the sky, and limned in deeper shadow the curves and corners of the walls.

There was war in heaven. The darkness overhead roiled and surged. The earth rumbled underfoot. The fabric of creation had begun to fray.

Merian thrust down fear. Her companions had enough of their own; she must have courage for all of them. She pressed to the fore. The wall of the citadel stretched endless before her. It was wrought without mortar, stone fitted to stone with no gap between. There seemed to be no gate, either, but that which the armies beset, now far behind her.

The way grew impossibly steep. They had to leave the seneldi; even afoot, they struggled on sheer slopes. Merian began to despair. If there was no way in but the one gate, even an assault of magery might not win them through soon enough. The dark was not yielding to the threefold attack upon it. Something, some force, had risen against them.

She must come to the heart of the citadel. The heart of it all was there—and hope, if any at all was to be had.

She halted on the narrow track, turning to face the rest, taking their measure one by one. If any could not bear the force of dark and fear, she would send him back now.

They were all strong, all firm in resolve. Strongest and firmest of all was one who hung back, almost invisible even to mage-sight. Even as Merian's eye fell on her, she raised power to blur it. Merian struck aside the working with a fierce slap of temper. "My lady!"

The Lady Varani sighed, perhaps in relief, perhaps in resignation, and lowered the hood that had concealed her face. "Lady," she said coolly.

"I never summoned you here," Merian said through set teeth, "nor would I have allowed it if you had asked. What possessed you to—"

"My son is here," Varani said. "Is there time to debate this, lady? If my ears tell me true, the enemy is holding all too well against your armies. His walls are strong and something else rises within. Something that— I fear—"

Merian would not let her go on. "Go back. Now. Urziad, look after her. Don't let her—"

"With all due respect," Varani said, "you need me here. There is a gate ahead. It's well hidden, but I can sense it: there's the dying glimmer of a beacon on it. Let Urziad and the rest go, if you must, but let me lead you. This art is mine, to find what I look for. Would you lose it out of folly?"

"Out of policy," said Merian. "Your rank forbids—"

"As yours does?"

"Lady," Kalyi said before Merian could erupt, "time's passing. The enemy is not growing weaker. If we have to fight our way in, we'd best do it quickly, or we lose all element of surprise."

If indeed there had ever been any, Merian thought grimly. "Very well," she said. "But if your death incites a civil war in the empire, I refuse to accept the blame."

"My lord will cast no blame on you," Varani said. "That will be entirely mine."

"I do hope so," said Merian.

Varani had the grace not to be excessively satisfied with herself. She turned and led the way, surefooted in the dark, on that sheer track. The others, none mountain-born as she was, followed more cautiously. Merian elected to take the rear. Her heart was full of doubt: dangerous in a mage at war, deadly in a commander. If she had erred in giving the lead to Varani, she would lose it all, war and world both.

The postern was indeed well hidden. Merian would have passed it by. But Varani halted, questing like a hound after a scent, and ran her hand along the bend of the wall. It yielded with a sound like a sigh, sank inward and froze.

"Your key," Varani said to Merian. "Here."

"What—"

"You have that which opens all doors. Will you use it?"

A riddle. Merian's wits were thick and slow. Her power was not her own; nor, it seemed, was much of her intelligence. Much too sluggishly, she remembered the thing that burned incessantly in her hand. She set the *Kasar* to the door. The flare of white heat left her blind, dizzy and stunned.

The door slid open. The passage within was black dark. Kalyi kindled a spark of magelight, a dim blue glow to light their feet. Sparks echoed it, a track laid by mages: vast relief to them all, and a glimmer of hope. Perel and his mages had prepared the way for them.

Varani led. The others were there to shield and ward, and to keep watch for the enemy. Merian had nothing to do but follow and keep silent, and try not to stumble.

This she had not foreseen. Nor the length of the hunt, the darkness,

the weight of lightless stone. The diversion had succeeded: these passages were deserted, their defenders drawn off toward the beleaguered
gate.

Urziad went in search of the mages, if any were left here; most or all
of them would be abroad, leading slaves against their masters. Varani
was still on the scent, following the track upward and inward. Merian
knew where she must be going. The compulsion of it reached even
through her own fogs and confusions.

Estarion was weakening. Daruya, with the Sun's power to draw on,
had risen to match him. Merian, trapped in the dark, was no more than
a link in the chain, without strength or volition of her own.

She must break free; must find her will, wield her power. Two alone
could not fight this fight. She was the center, the key. This heaviness of
spirit, this darkness within her, was the enemy—far more so than men
fighting men under the starless sky.

One mage remained in the citadel after all, waiting for them. It was a
darkmage, hardly more than a child, but strong in her power. The track
ended in the passage in which she waited, up against a long stair. There
was a strange scent in that place, somewhat like thunder and somewhat
like blood. It raised Merian's hackles.

The others seemed not to notice it. The darkmage, whose name was
Gaiya, greeted them with rigid composure and a spark of gladness that
she could not quite conceal. She spoke in a whisper. "They have the
prince," she said. "They caught him here. The Mage is dead; they've
bound the prince and will compel him to work their magics for them,
unless he dies first. We didn't know until we'd scattered to wage the war.
If our mages should have come back and tried to free him—"

"No," Merian said. "The war needs them more. Can you guide us to
him?"

"He's in the lords' tower. That's warded. We haven't been able to
break the wards, and he forbade us to force them. Then he was taken,
and there was the war, and—"

As strong as she was determined to be, she was near tears. This had been a cruel duty. That none of the mages had broken was a tribute to their strength and the clarity of their power.

"Go to Perel," Merian said, "and serve him as you may. We'll find our way upward."

"But—" said Gaiya.

"Go," said Merian. "Give him this message for me: 'Fight until it all ends, or until I myself bid you stop.'"

"Until it ends," Gaiya repeated, "or you command it to end."

"Yes," Merian said. And for the third time. "Go."

The child fled with relief that almost cleansed the air of the memory that haunted it. The others would have been glad to follow, but they had a war to fight.

Merian had some of her wits back. It was Varani now who seemed fuddled, who stood slack with despair. "If they have him," she said, "there is no hope for any of us."

"He'll die before he surrenders," Merian said.

No one gave voice to doubt, which was a kindness. Time was running out; but now she had a focus, and knowledge. "Upward," she said. "Those who would come, come. The rest of you, go where Gaiya went. I'll have no deadweight in this."

They all stood watching her. None retreated. She nodded briskly and began to ascend the stair.

There had been wards. They left a memory behind, like the scent of blood and terror below. The Mage's death had broken them. They would rise again if Daros surrendered his will to his captors.

Merian's heart was keening, nor would it desist for any will she set on it. Yet her mind was very clear. She had left confusion down below. The mortal war, the war in heaven, had shrunk to insignificance. It was all coming to this single point, this stair, this tower and its captive.

Varani walked close behind her. The others trailed somewhat, weaving wards as they went. Kaliya, in the rear, climbed with drawn sword.

Merian's weapons remained in their sheaths. This fight would have little to do with steel. The quiet grated on her nerves. No sound of fighting came through the walls. Her legs ached. Her breasts ached. She was weary to the bone.

They were near the top of the stair. Varani's hand gripped her shoulder. She halted. After a moment she heard it: a sound below the threshold of mortal hearing, like the pounding of waves on a distant shore.

Wards, beleaguered by a force such as she had not seen before. It had nothing in it of living spirit. It made her think, somehow, of the automatons that craftsmen made in the Nine Cities to amuse the Syndics' children. Metal and glass; power without soul. Magic trapped and twisted to mortal will.

That was the secret—the key. Stripped of magery, the dark mages of Anshan had found another way. It was darker than dark magic, and cruel beyond conceiving.

If she had harbored any faintest glimmer of pity for those mages so long bereft of their power, it vanished in that moment of understanding. She broke the door at the top of the stair, and blasted the guards beyond it with the Sun's fire.

They went up like torches. Even in her rage, she was taken aback. Altogether without intending it, she had taken all that was in her, Sun-power threefold, and wielded it as if it had been hers to command. Estarion's startlement, her mother's shock, sparked in her awareness.

The light of the working lingered, plain light of day in any mortal world, but unbearably, searingly brilliant here. Those defenders who had not fallen to the blast of fire were felled by the light. They lay writhing, screaming soundlessly. She stepped over them. Behind her, Kaliya did the merciful thing: a swift stroke of the blade to each throat.

Merian was beyond mercy. She followed the path of fallen defenders. The end of it was a door, and a barren room, and a cage of metal about a shape of shadow.

The defenders there wore shielded helms and carried the weapons that spat dark fire. She left them to Kaliya and the other mages. Estarion was broad awake inside her, and Daruya in a rage that nearly matched her own. They confronted the last of the defenders, the tall man who stood in front of the cage. Royal blood knew royal blood.

The dark king had shielded his eyes with a band of metal and black glass. In his pale face with its black beard, Merian saw a distant echo of Batan and his people, the warrior folk of Anshan.

He had no power to see what she was, and perhaps no spirit for it, either. He had courage; that, she could not doubt. His men fell before they could even lift their weapons, but he neither wavered nor flinched. "Whatever becomes of us," he said, "the dark will rule."

"That might be true," she said, "or it might not. Either way, you will be dead. You were condemned long ages ago for crimes beyond the reach of mercy. Your crimes have only grown worse since you fled that sentence. If there could ever have been hope of appeal, that is altogether gone."

"Indeed?" said the dark king. "And who are you to stand in judgment?"

"I am everything you ever feared or fought against. I am the destroyer of darkness, the bringer of light. The Sun begot me. The light reared me. I rule in the Sun's name."

He flung back his head and laughed. "Brave little maidchild! When ours are so puny, we drown them. How were you let live? Pity? Scorn? Weakness of spirit?"

"Only the weak resort to mockery." She raised her hand. The Sun in it roared and flamed.

Just as she gathered power to blast him, a shadow darted past her toward the shape in the cage. The bolt of light flew wide. The king sprang. Merian stumbled aside, warrior skills forgotten, fixed on Varani, who had flung herself at the cage, and at the thing that whirred and spun on top of it.

The king howled and leaped toward Varani. Merian clutched wildly at his arm and spun him about. He slashed at her with a steel claw.

Merian's arm and side burned. She snatched her sword from its sheath, stabbing with all the strength she had. The blade struck armor, turned and snapped. The king spat in contempt. She slashed her second blade, the long sharp dagger, across his throat. The hot spray of blood spattered her face and drenched her armor.

She gagged in disgust, but she had already forgotten him. Varani tore at the cage with bleeding fingers. Merian caught her hands and held them, though she struggled, cursing.

"Lady," Merian said. "Lady, stop."

After a stretching while, Varani yielded. Merian kept a grip on her until she had eased completely, then let her go, but warily. The cage showed no sign of her efforts. The thing of metal spun faster, that was all. The shape within the cage was visible as if through dark glass. The width of the shoulders, the copper brightness of the hair, were unmistakable, though the rest was lost in shadow.

He was alive—just. The king and his guard were dead, the rulers of this world gone away to the war, but the soulless thing that held him cared nothing for that. It ate at his mind and power, sustaining the life in him when he would have let it go, and bleeding away his magery like a slow wound.

The *Kasar* was a white agony in Merian's hand. She raised it to unlock the bonds of the cage, but hesitated. If he was deeply enslaved, wholly bound to the dark, she would unleash a horror that would put the Sunborn's madness to shame.

Varani read it in her eyes. Merian braced for recrimination, but in some deep corner of her spirit, the lady had found both strength and sanity. "If he must be killed," she said steadily, "I beg your leave to do it. I gave him life. Let me take it away."

"Not yet," said Merian. She could barely speak. The tide of the dark was rising. The magery in her, doubled and trebled, strained to hold together. The effort of sustaining it across the worlds, against the force of the dark, had begun to wear on both the powers within.

The dark, like the cage, had neither mind nor soul. It simply and inexorably was. A mage, even a god, one could fight. But how could any fleshly being stand against the universe itself?

"Light," said Estarion within her. "Fight darkness with light."

"Darkness so vast?" she demanded of him. "Oblivion so absolute?"

"Can you see any other way?" asked Daruya.

"No," said Merian. "But—"

"Tides of light," said Estarion. "If all the mages could be gathered— if he could be freed, and persuaded to lend his power—"

"He is dead or corrupted," said Daruya. "The other mages must be enough."

"The other mages are fighting a war across the face of a world," Merian said.

"Call them in," said Estarion.

"There's no time." Merian swayed as she spoke, buffeted by the force of the dark. It smote the bond that joined the three of them, and battered the edges of the light. The war was a bloody confusion; the lords had rallied, and the armies of freed slaves were flagging, their numbers terribly depleted, their makeshift weapons broken or lost. She could feel their despair in her skin, in the outer reaches of her magery.

With no thought at all, she set the *Kasar* to the cage. Its cold metal resisted, but Sun's fire was stronger than any work of hands. The whirring thing spun faster, faster, until it was a blur. It burst asunder in a flash of blinding light. In the sudden and enormous silence, the bars of the cage drew in upon themselves. The shell of glass crumbled into the sand from which it was made.

The captive lay on a bier within, robed in darkness. No breath stirred. His eyes were open, empty of light. His flesh was cold.

His mother breathed warmth upon him. She gave him light; she poured out her own life to feed his. Merian laid her hands over Varani's, not to stop her, but to give her what strength there was to spare.

It might be madness. She could find no light in him. They had taken his eyes, his life, his spirit. There might be nothing left of him at all. But she could not stop herself. She was corrupted, maybe; enspelled. It mattered nothing. There was no hope. The light could not win this war. Not without all the power that they could bring to bear.

THIRTY-NINE

DAROS SWAM UP OUT OF DEEP WATER. HE LEFT THE ARMS OF Mother Night and drifted through stars, drawn inexorably upward.

The thing that he had fled, the ceaseless, whispering temptation, had faded greatly, but it was not gone. It had set in his bones. It murmured through his walls and barriers; it thrummed in the stones of the dark world.

Darkness and corruption. Doom and damnation. He dived back into oblivion, but strong hands held him up. He struggled; he fought. They would not let go. They were too many, too strong.

They wrenched him out of darkness and into searing, agonizing light. He twisted, gasping, biting back the cry. The taste of blood filled his mouth: he had bitten his tongue.

Something hard and cold clasped his face. He lay in blessed dimness. His eyes were shielded. He looked into faces recognizable even to what his sight had become. Mages: Kalyi, Urziad, a stranger or two. Merian. And—

He could flee, but there was nowhere to run. He could not hide. She had seen—she knew—

"Later," his mother said. Her voice was taut with pain. "Help us. The dark—"

The dark was rising. A great hunger was in it, a craving for the blood and bones of living worlds. It beckoned to him, whispering, tempting. He would be its greatest servant, its most dearly beloved. The light was bitter pain. Darkness was sweet; was blessed. It would embrace him and make him its own. He would be the great lord, the emperor of the night. All worlds would bow before him.

"Indaros!"

The light of the Sun's child was bitter beyond endurance. She was made of light; filled with it, brimming over. She touched him with it; he gasped. She, merciless, gripped tighter. "Remember," Merian said fiercely. "Remember what you are!"

Doomed. Damned. Lost to darkness.

"Indaros."

Foolish child. Did she imagine that she could bind him with that name? In the darkness, all names were taken away.

"Indaros!"

It struck like a scorpion whip. It seared him with light and filled his veins with fire. It shot him like an arrow, full into the heart of the dark.

He laughed. Death, had he yearned for? Here was the death of the shooting star: pure glory. He was a conflagration across the firmament, a stream of fire in the face of the night.

The dark fought back, thrusting again and again into his heart. Its whisper rose to a roar. Death, oblivion, annihilation—the surcease of purest nothingness.

* * *

Estarion could not hold. It was too far, the dark too deep. The weight of flesh dragged at him. If he could but cast it off, he would be free. He could fight untrammeled.

There was the answer to every riddle, the key to every door. Cast off the flesh; be pure light. Be magic bare, untainted by mortal substance. Become the light, and so embrace the dark, and swallow it as it had swallowed light.

The flesh disliked that thought intensely. Foolish flesh.

"Great-grandfather." Merian was in his thoughts as he was in hers, interwoven with them. "I'm in the center. Your heir behind me, my heir before me—I'm unnecessary. I stand in the heart of the dark world. If I let go—if I loose the fire—all of it will end."

"And you," he said. "You will end, too."

"I don't matter. I'll be in the light."

"No," said Estarion. The truth unfolded in him, in glory and splendor. What he was; what he was meant for. Why the gods had brought him to the land of the river and set him on the far side of the dark. He understood at last why he had been moved to surrender the key of his life to Seti-re. If he had not so divided his soul, the flesh would have bound him too tightly; he could not have escaped, whole and free. That surrender, that bit of folly, would save them all.

He was not afraid. There was a strange, aching joy in it.

Tanit—Menes—

If he did not do this thing, there would be no world for them to live in, no sun to warm them, no life to live to its fulfillment. The dark would rule. The worlds would crumble into ash.

Merian was still rebelling, still insistent, and Daruya beyond her, for once remembering her headlong youth. "Empress," he said to them, "and empress who will be. Rule well. Remember me."

They babbled in protest. He took no notice. The dark gaped to swallow them all.

Someone stood at the gate of it, a lone still figure, eyes full of darkness but heart blooming suddenly with light. Daros had lit the spark. Estarion fanned it into flame.

The young fool tried to thrust him aside; to take the glory for himself. But Estarion was too strong for that. He eased the boy gently out of the gate. The fire was in him now, consuming him. The pain of it was exquisite. It seared away the flesh; let go the constraints of living existence.

Great blazing wings unfurled. He was a bird of flame, soaring up into the darkness. Song poured out of him: the morning hymn to the Sun that every priest in his empire sang at the coming of every morning; that he had sung to his son in the land of the river, and so consecrated him to the god his forefather.

It was pure adoration; pure light. Pure joy. Freedom beyond imagining—glory, splendor. Beauty unveiled.

Dawn broke over the dark world: true dawn, the rising of the sun above the king's citadel. The last slaves of the darkness burned and died. The armies of the Sun stood blinking in the light, bloodied, battered, but victorious.

FORTY

NO LIGHT CAME THROUGH WINDOWLESS STONE, AND YET MER-
ian felt it like a wash of warmth over her skin. The threefold
power that had been within her was gone. She was herself again,
separate. Her mother blessed her with startling sweetness before slipping away out of this world. Estarion . . .

The name called forth a vision of singing light: a bird of flame soaring up to heaven. In that death was no oblivion. He was gone from all
the worlds—and yet a part of every one, embodied in the suns that
shone upon them, and the stars that brought beauty to the night. There
was no grief, no loss. Only joy.

She laughed, there in that dark place, even though she wept. How
like Estarion to find a way out of the world that none had ever ventured.

She came back to herself to find her mages staring at her, standing half-stunned amid the slain. Only Varani had forgotten her existence. She knelt beside her son. He was conscious, but barely. Flickers of flame ran over his body, tongues of fire born of the power that was in him. It fed on the darkness inside him, burning deep, searing all of it away.

Merian knelt across from Varani. "He did it," she said. "He opened the gate of the light."

Varani's eyes were burning dry. "Yes, he redeemed himself. Now he'll die. May I have your leave to go, to take his body back to Han-Gilen?"

"He won't die," Merian said. "I won't let him."

"Do you have that power? Even you, Sunlady?"

"No," said Merian. "But he does." She laid her hand over his heart. At her touch, the garment that had covered him shredded and frayed, falling away. It was woven of the dark; it could not bear the touch of the Sun.

His skin felt strange: now burning cold, now searing hot. His heart was beating too fast almost to sense, fluttering like a bird's. It could not go on: man's heart was not meant for such a thing. A little longer, and it would burst asunder.

Light was her substance. The Sun was in her blood. Yet she was not purely a lightmage. The dark was in her, soft and deep—not the dark that had devoured the stars, but the softness of a summer night, the sweet coolness of evening after the heat of the day, the blessing of clean water on flesh burned by the sun.

She gave him that blessing. She cooled the fire that consumed him; she softened the dark with light, and made the light gentle, easing the torment of body and spirit. His heart slowed. He drew a long deep breath, and then another.

She slipped the shield from his eyes. They had squeezed tight shut, in horror of the light. She brushed her fingers across them. "Look at me," she said.

With an effort that was almost a convulsion, he opened his eyes. Darkness coiled in them, writhed and melted and was gone. He looked into her face, and saw as a mortal man could see, by the plain light of day.

She looked up herself, in astonishment. The roof of the tower was gone, vanished like the darkness in him. Clear sky arched overhead; a sun shone in it, undimmed by cloud. Her eyes returned to Daros. He lay in the light, bathing in it. With no thought at all, she kissed him, tasting on his cheeks the salt of tears.

"I'm dreaming you," he said. "I must be. The emperor, the dark, this light—it can't be real."

"It's very real," she said.

She helped him to sit up. She would have reckoned that enough, but he insisted on trying to rise, though he did it in a drunken stagger. She braced him with her shoulder. His mother, to both their surprise, bolstered him on the other side.

Little by little he steadied. When he essayed a step, his knees did not buckle too badly.

By the time they reached the door, he was almost supporting his own weight. Merian contemplated the long stair in something like despair. She could not lift him down it: her power was too weak. It would come back, but not soon enough.

But one power was always hers, no matter how weak she was. The Gate inside her was free again, with no darkness to bind it. She could not pass from world to world, not yet; but from citadel to plain, that she could do. The others linked their magery with hers and followed, a skein of Gatemages dropping out of air at Perel's feet.

The battle was over. Mages and soldiers of the Sun moved among the slain. Parties of soldiers and freed slaves had begun to clear the field. Tents were up, and the wounded limping or being carried to them.

Perel stood with the commander of the Olenyai and the general of the armies, looking out from a hilltop over the field. Merian and the rest emerged from the Gate just below them.

Perel was in motion almost before they touched the ground, leaping toward Merian, catching her as she fell. She beat him off with fierce impatience, thrusting him toward Daros. "Forget me! Help him!"

But Daros alone of them all was solid on his feet, oblivious to any of them, staring at the aftermath of battle. He did not seem aware that he was naked, or that the air, though sunlit, was chill. She began to wonder, with sinking heart, if the light had taken more of him than the dark that had lodged in his soul; if his mind was gone, too, burned away by the cleansing fire.

He took no notice of Perel at all. But Merian he did see as she scrambled herself up and came round to face him, gripping his arms, shaking him. It was like shaking a stone pillar: he never shifted.

His eyes were clear. He recognized her, though he frowned slightly, as if even yet he did not believe that she was real.

She wrapped her cloak about them both. That woke memory; he started slightly, and stared harder. "I remember . . ."

"We're not dreamwalking," she said. "Not any longer. This is true. It's over. The dark is gone. The war has ended. We can go home again."

"Home." A gust of laughter escaped him, almost like a gasp of pain. "Where is that, for me?"

"With me," she said. "Wherever I go."

"You don't want me. After what I did—"

"You were the key to the gate," she said. "Every world should honor you."

He shook his head, but he was wiser than to keep protesting. She turned in his arms. Everyone was watching them: the lords and mages on the hilltop, the soldiers and slaves below. "This is my lord," she said to them, "my prince and consort. But for him, this victory would never have been."

There was a long pause. Just before she would have burst out in anger at their discourtesy, first Verani, then Perel and the lord of the Olenyai, and after them the rest, went down in homage. All of them: every living being on that field.

It was no more than his due, though he hardly knew where to look. For a prince, he had precious little sense of his own importance.

"You'll learn," she said.

"Is that a command, my lady?"

"It is, my lord," said Merian.

A smile touched the corner of his mouth. It was a frail shadow of his old insouciant grin, but it would do, for the moment. "I have no gift for obedience."

"But love—you have a great gift for that."

"Ah: I'm an infamous libertine. Are you sure you want that beside you for the rest of your days?"

"How many women have you lain with since you met me?"

He had lost the stain of the sun that had so darkened him in the land of the river: a blush was clear to see, turning his cheeks to ruddy bronze. "None," he said indistinctly; then clearer: "None at all. But, lady, while I dreamed of you, I never—"

"Our daughter is in your father's care," she said.

She felt the shock in his body. "Our—"

"It was real," she said. "Every moment of it. The proof is in Han-Gilen."

"Han-Gilen? Not Starios?"

She nodded.

"Why—" He shook himself. "Questions later. And answers—many of them. But now, the war. There are still dark lords alive. If you would have me find them—"

"You need do nothing but go home and rest," she said.

"Not until it's over," he said. "All of it. My lords, if someone could find clothes for me, and boots—boots would be welcome—I'll begin the hunt."

"You will hunt nothing but sleep," Merian said firmly.

But he was equally firm in resistance. "I belonged to them. They're in my bones. Give me men, mages, a mount—I'll find them all and bring them back to you."

She searched his face, and the mind behind it, which he made no effort to conceal from her. The anger in him was deep and abiding; but he was sane. He was not wild with vengeance.

"Bring them to me," she said, "and I will sentence them. My lords, you will obey him as you would obey me. Whatever he asks for, see that he has it."

There were no objections, spoken or unspoken, save one. "You do insist on this?" his mother asked him.

He would not meet her gaze. He had shrunk, all at once, into a sulky child.

She gripped his arms. One could see, watching them, whence came his height and breadth of shoulder; she was a strong woman, in body as in mind. Her eyes burned on his face. "Do as you must," she said, "and do it well. You are worthy of your lineage. Though perhaps," she said, "your parents are not worthy of you."

That astonished him. He stared at her, his sulkiness forgotten. "How can you say that? I have never been—"

"You have redeemed yourself many times over. Whereas we have acquitted ourselves poorly in every respect. If you can find it in you to pardon us—"

He silenced her with a finger to her lips. "Mother, don't. Don't talk like that. Let's forgive each other; let's forget if we can. There's a long stretch of darkness behind us, and, one hopes, a long stretch of light ahead. Maybe we can learn to be proper kin to one another."

"I can hope for that," she said.

He smiled, bowed and kissed her hands. "Then may I have your blessing?"

"You may have it," she said. Her voice was steady, but her eyes were brimming. She drew his head down and set a kiss on his forehead, then let him go. "You honor us all, my child. You give us great pride."

As long as the fight had been and as weary as they all were, the sheer number of those who came to Daros' muster was astonishing. He had his pick of warriors and of mages; and among them two whom he had thought never to see again.

Neither Menkare nor Nefret had taken physical harm from the battle. Their power was intact, indeed stronger than ever. They had been tempered like steel: forged in fire. They looked long and hard at him, as everyone did now; but like the others, they eased visibly after a while.

"You look," said Nefret, "as if you've been burned clean."

"That is precisely how it feels," said Daros.

She clasped him tight, squeezing the breath out of him, but there were no words left in her. It was Menkare who said, "We mourned you for dead. Thank the greater gods that we grieved too soon."

"I am rather grateful myself," Daros said. "And you? Are you of a mind to go hunting with me?"

"Rats or lions?" Menkare asked.

"Rats in the barley," said Daros.

"I'm in the mood to hunt rats," said Nefret.

"And I," Menkare said. "Pity we have no cats here; they're the best hunters of all."

"You are my cats," Daros said, "my mages of the river. Come, hunt with me."

They grinned at that; Nefret's pointed face and small white teeth were not at all unlike a cat's. With a much lighter heart, Daros turned to the task of choosing the rest of his hunters.

The hunt was not long, as rat-hunts went. Those lords whose slaves had not turned on them and rent them in pieces had gone to ground, away from hunters and the horror of the sun and, come the night, the stars and the dance of a dozen little moons about this barren and stony world.

Daros tracked them by the shudder under his skin. Nefret with her gift of prescience was even better at it than he, and Menkare was blindingly quick in the capture. It grieved them somewhat that they could not kill what they hunted, as it would have grieved the little fierce cats of their own world, but they submitted to the will of the gods—and most especially the goddess of gold, as they called Merian.

They were enthralled with her. It gave them no end of pleasure to discover—and not from Daros—that their lord was her consort; that there was an heir, a child so like her father that no one in the world of the gods could deny her parentage.

That was a thought so strange, so patently impossible, that Daros could hardly think it at all. That Merian loved him, that she wanted him, was shock enough; he doubted it more often than he believed it. But that their dreamwalking had brought forth a child—he could not make himself believe it. He kept his mind on his hunt instead, and left the rest for when the hunt was over.

He hunted through a chain of lesser Gates. Merian and her mages had closed the Worldgates to prevent an escape, but the Gates within this world were open. There were many; most had the soullessness of the dark lords' devices. Those he broke as he found them, scattered them into the elements from which they were made. After the first three or four or five, mages ran ahead of him, seeking out these false Gates and destroying them, while he hunted through Gates that had no need of forged metal or trapped magic.

The lords were barred from both. Their power was broken. The Mage was dead, its prison destroyed in the blaze of light that had overcome the dark. Their devices of metal were only metal now; the lords had no magic with which to bring them to life.

Daros still could not think too much on these matters. The memory of the cage was too strong, the horror of it too close to his spirit. The hunt was his release, the cleansing of his mind and soul.

The last nest was the worst. They had come full circle, back to the citadel and the deep halls beneath, dungeons that descended into the bowels of the earth. There the last of the lords had barricaded themselves with walls of stone and steel. And there, at last, were the women: blind, gravid things locked in cells like the children of bees. Whether they were born or made so, he did not know or care to know. But it made him all the more grimly determined to expunge this race from the worlds.

Daros had to go down into the dark from which he had so barely escaped. The mages and the warriors of the Sun brought light with them, but Menkare and Nefret knew the same horror that he knew: the horror of return to endless night.

They did not flinch from the long descent. He could hardly be less brave than the mages whom he had made. He steadied his mind and firmed his steps and led them all into the darkness.

One weapon he had which he had not been able to use during his long deception: the flame of his power, which was born of the sun. He clothed himself in it, and sent it before him, a wall of light. He struck their wall of stone and steel and shattered it.

They came out fighting. Desperation made them vicious; they laughed at wounds, and courted death. They would take Daros and his hunters with them if they could.

Daros had had enough of fighting. He struck them down with a mighty blow of power, laid them low without ever drawing his sword. It was yet another broken law, he supposed; mages had so many. But he was long past caring. He gathered them up and bound them, and flung them through the Gate within him, on their faces before the princess-heir where she sat in judgment.

FORTY-ONE

MERIAN HAD LONG SINCE LEARNED TO BE SURPRISED BY NOTH-
ing Daros did. Daros was a law unto himself; there would never
be any changing it.

Even so, the arrival of a score of dark lords, beaten unconscious by a
stroke of power, was more than slightly startling. Outrageous, some of
her mother's generals declared. They were not mages, but they were
most careful of mages' laws—both those which they understood and
those which they did not.

It happened that she was judging captives whom Daros had brought
in in the days before. They would not use the citadel; that would come
down, she had decided, and the slave-cities would be razed, and new
cities built for and by the slaves who still wished to live on this world.
Her place of judgment was the plain on which the battle for the citadel

had been fought, just outside the camp that her armies had made. Many
of them were present even so late in the judging, watching and listening
as she heard such defenses as could be offered.

There were not many, but she heard them all, over and over again.
She was putting off the decision, and avoiding the sentence that must be
levied. There truly was no choice. Death for them all, every one. Nothing that they had said had persuaded her to let them live.

And now they were all captured, all brought before her, and Daros
standing above the last of them in borrowed armor. She still was not
accustomed to the changes that this world had wrought in him. He was
thinner but no narrower: he had grown into a man since she first saw him,
an idle drunken princeling in the ridiculous height of fashion. His face
had lost its prettiness but gained in beauty. Time and pain had drawn it
fine; the smile was never so quick as it had been, and the expression into
which it had settled was somber—a prince's face, lordly and stern.

He was distracting her now with his presence. She made herself focus
on the prisoners, all of them, conscious and unconscious. Those who
were awake were sour with scorn, looking with contempt on the beasts
that had conquered them. To them, all not of their blood kin were no
more than animals; slaves, bred for servitude.

She rose from the seat of judgment. "These are all of them?" she
asked Daros.

He nodded. He had a tight-drawn look, as if he had snapped, but
somehow put himself together again. "All but the women," he said, "but
those are no more threat to us than a nest of maggots."

She raised a brow at the thickness of disgust in his voice, but left it
until she had dealt with the men of that nation. "Wake them," she said
to him.

He bared his teeth. It was not a smile. His power lashed out, sharp as
the crack of a whip. Every one of his newest captives snapped erect.

The emotion with which all of them regarded him was not entirely
or even mostly contempt. It was hate. He basked in it; courted it. He
dared them to turn against him.

"I have heard all that I have need to hear," she said through that fog of loathing. "My judgment is made. My sentence is—"

"Lady," said Daros. He did not speak loudly, but his voice carried without effort across the field of the judging. "Lady, may I speak?"

Can I prevent you?

She did not say it aloud, but with him she had no need. The twitch of his smile, though slight, was genuine.

"Lady, you choose death. I can well see why: it would seem to be inevitable. And yet, will you give them what they long for above all else? Will you offer them free passage into oblivion?"

"You would have me keep them alive?" she asked him. "Are you so eager to fight this war again?"

"Not at all," said Daros. "But, lady, death is a reward. Shouldn't your sentence be a punishment?"

"There is no punishment great enough for what they have done."

"Maybe not," Daros said, "but I can think of one that they would find rather painful."

She raised a brow. "And that is?"

"Some of their slaves—born here, or bred of worlds that were destroyed after their capture—have expressed a desire to stay here. Yes? Give the lords to them—men, women, children born and not yet born. Let them be slaves to their own slaves."

"I had thought of that," Merian said. "But if they rise again, if they find a way to restore their rule—who knows what devices might be hidden here, or what powers they might call on? They escaped our world once, and even stripped of magic, still succeeded in destroying a myriad worlds before they could be stopped. I will not risk such a thing. Not again."

"Wise," he said. "Merciful, in its way. Even just. But I am not in a merciful mood. I would rather they live, and live in suffering, than find relief in death. Unless . . ."

She waited. All of them did, even the fallen lords: and that was tribute to the power he had over them.

"Give them to healer-mages," he said. "Let them be made new—the women and children most of all, but the men, too. Set the seeds of light in them, nurture it and let it grow. Teach them to be truly human: to know love as well as hate, awe as well as scorn, humility as well as arrogance. Give them hearts, and let them know the fullness of what they have done. Give them guilt and shame—even redemption, if such is possible."

The silence was absolute. Even the wind had ceased to blow. It was a terrible, a wonderful solution, but there was no mercy in it whatsoever.

"And if they can't be made new?" Merian asked, since no one else seemed to have power to speak.

"Then do as you will," said Daros.

She nodded slowly. "I will grant you this," she said, "as a gift to you. On one condition."

He stiffened ever so slightly, but his voice was as calm as ever. "And that is?"

"That you oversee the healing and dispose of those who have been healed, if any of them can be. Likewise those who cannot—their deaths must be at your command."

He bowed low. It was a prince's bow, and a prince's face that he raised to her. "As you will, my lady."

"You will not leave this world until it is done," she said. "It will be years; it might be a lifetime. Can you bear that?"

"I understand," he said, "and I accept it."

"Then let it be done," she said.

The camp's servants had pitched a tent for Daros among the rest of his hunters, between the edge of the camp and the camp in which the captives remained under guard. He did not indulge in disappointment. He had no right, after all, to expect anything of Merian, still less to be housed in her own tent—especially after he had undercut her judgment. It was generous enough of her to let him lay sentence on the dark lords; he could hardly ask her to admit him to her bed as well. He had the rank and the authority of a consort, and that, as useful as it was, was more than he deserved.

The tent was luxurious, for a tent; it was suited to his newly royal rank. It even had a pair of attendants: Menkare and Nefret, who greeted him with expressions that made him ask, "What did you do to the servants?"

"We let them live," Nefret said, even as Menkare said, "We bribed them to find other masters."

They stopped and glared at each other. Nefret won the silent fight; she said, "We belong with you."

"Your people," said Daros, "the slaves whom you freed—they need you. Whereas I—"

"They've been seen to," Nefret said. "While we were hunting, they were sent home, all of them—they all wanted to go. There's none left here."

"Then you can go home," Daros said. "There's no need to stay with me. These are my people who are here; my kin, my own kind."

Her brows drew together. "Are you telling us that you don't want us any more? That we're not gods, and not worthy to be seen in your presence?"

"No!" He had almost shouted the word. Menkare winced, but she gazed at him steadily.

"Don't you want to go home?" he demanded of her. "Don't you want to see the river again, and go fishing in the reeds, and live among your own people?"

"My people are dead," she said. "Raiders killed them all. You are my people now. My god, if it pleases you better."

"You know I am not a god," he said.

"Close enough," she said.

"Nefret," he said. "You honor me, and greatly. But I won't have you stay just because you have nowhere else to go. Waset would take you, and give you great rank and worship, after what you have done for your world. So would any city along the river, and many a king. You're a god in your own right. You don't need me to give you a place in the worlds."

"I know that," she said. "I want to stay. Your lady, the golden one—she is even more wonderful than you. I want to see the worlds, and walk under strange suns, and know other rivers than the river of the black land."

"We can go back, you know," said Menkare. "Even if we serve you, if you give us leave—we can go home to visit, and if we're needed. There's no dark any longer. The Gates are open. The worlds are free again."

Daros blinked. He honestly had not thought of that. He had been too intent on the fact of their exile; but they did not see it as such at all.

"And your people?" he asked them. "What if they need you to stay?"

"Then we'll stay," said Menkare. "But we got on rather well without magic before the dark came. Now that the dark is gone, I expect the world will go on as it always has. Magic is for gods, my lord. Mortals do well enough without."

"And you? Are you god or mortal?"

"Why, neither, my lord. I'm something between." Menkare smiled suddenly, and patted Daros on the shoulder. "There—don't look so stunned. Do I look as if I'm suffering? It's glorious, this gift you've given—even at the price you laid on it. I've no desire to give it back."

Daros, who had been about to ask that precise question, shut his mouth with a click.

"My lord," said Nefret, reading him as effortlessly as she ever had, "we stay with you because we love you—and because you so clearly need looking after. Would you even know where to find dinner, let alone remember to eat it?"

He bridled at that. "I'm not that helpless! I've fended for myself before. What makes you think I can't do it now?"

"Princes can't," she said with calm conviction. "It's not allowed. You are a prince of princes. You must have attendants—it's required. Wouldn't you rather have us than a flock of strangers?"

"I'm not so sure," he muttered.

She laughed, which was cruel, but bracing, too. "Of course you would. Now stop your nonsense and let us get this armor off you. Has it even *been* off since you put it on?"

"I don't—"

Her nose wrinkled. "Obviously it hasn't. Menkare, find someone who can put together a bath for him."

Menkare was already on his way. Daros sighed and submitted. That was a prince's lot, always: to suffer the tyranny of servants. And these— yes, he would admit it to himself: he was glad that they had stayed. They were more than servants. They were friends.

Still, he said, "If you ever grow homesick, even for a moment, I'm sending you back. Is that understood?"

"Perfectly," Nefret said without a spark of honest submission—and no glimmer of expectation that he would do as he threatened, either.

Daros lay in his soft and princely bed, scrubbed until he stung. The borrowed armor had not fit as well as it might; there were galls and bruises and a boil or two, at which Nefret had been suitably outraged. It was all gone now, and a light warm coverlet over him, sparing his hurts as much as it might.

He should have been dead asleep, but his stubborn mind persisted in keeping him awake. Even closing out all that he had done and would do, he still could not force himself to sleep.

A warm presence fitted itself to his back. Light hands stroked him where it did not hurt overmuch; kisses brushed his nape and shoulders and wandered round to the freshly shaven curve of his jaw. Fingers ran through his cropped hair, ruffling such of it as there was.

"This will not be allowed to endure," Merian's voice said in his ear.

He turned in her arms. She was both smiling and frowning—smiling at him, frowning at what the lords had done to him. "What, I'm not pretty any longer?" he asked her.

"You aren't," she said. "That's all gone. But beauty—you have more of that than ever. Will you promise to grow your hair again?"

"If you'll let me cut it now and then."

"Now and then," she said, "I'll consider it."

"You do mean it, then. What you said. That I'm your consort."

"You doubted it?"

"I don't know what I thought," he said. "This tent—it's not—"

"I need a place to hold councils and be royal. You need a place to rest. As do I. Would you object too strongly if I did my sleeping here with you?"

His heart swelled. He could barely speak. "I would be somewhat . . . dismayed . . . if you did not."

She smiled. The pure golden warmth of that smile nearly reduced him to tears. But those were all burned out of him; he did not know when they would come back.

"This match is approved of," she said. "My mother has no objections. You know that yours does not. The breeding, as they both say, is impeccable."

"My father? *He* approves?" Daros shook his head. "Ah, but he would. Whatever he thinks of me—"

"He loves you," she said. "He grieves for you. He's glad beyond measure that you are alive and well and proving your worth in the worlds."

"And even if he were not, he would still be enormously pleased. Once again at last, Han-Gilen and the Sunborn's line unite in marriage."

"He is not as cold as that," Merian said, "and I am not in the mood for a quarrel. You will have to face him eventually: I gave our daughter into his care until the war was over."

His breath hissed between his teeth. "Our— Tell me. Tell me how it happened. Why you never told me."

"You know how it happened," she said. "You were there, dreamwalking with me. I never told you because there was never time. You were lost to the dark not long after I knew it myself. I didn't believe it, either, not until there was no escaping the truth."

"Is that why?" he asked. "Did you name me your consort because it was the honorable thing? Because a child needs a father?"

"Among other reasons," she said, "yes. But when I chose you, there was no such constraint. I wanted you long before I could admit it to myself. When I understood what our dreamwalking had done, I had already decided that if you came back, if you were alive and still had your wits, I would take you as my lover."

"But not—"

"I'm Sun-blood," she said. "My first lover would inevitably be the father of my heir. You know that, surely."

"Yes, but—"

"If you don't want the rank or the marriage," she said, "I won't force it on you. You will always be Elian's father. I will not—"

"Elian? Her name is Elian?"

"It seemed appropriate," she said.

He did not know whether to bellow at her or kiss her. Elian had been a princess of Han-Gilen long ago; she had loved and in time married the Sunborn, and borne his heir. She was Merian's foremother and his own kinswoman. It was a name of great honor in both their houses.

"Let me see her," he said: peremptorily, he supposed, but he could not help it.

She took no offense. She opened her mind and showed them the child whom he had seen in dream: the child with his face, whose ancestry none could mistake.

"It was true," he said in wonder. "All of it—all true."

"As true as life itself," she said. "Still, if you don't want the marriage, the child is still yours. I'll not forbid you your share in her raising."

"You'd trust *me* to raise a child?"

Her smile grew wicked. "There's no preceptor so strict as a rake reformed, and none so stern as a father who spent his youth in debauching other men's daughters."

"*Ai!*" It was a cry of pure pain, but laughter broke through it. "Lady, you wound me to the heart."

"Good," she said: "you have a heart to wound."

"After all, it seems I do." He paused. She made excellent use of the silence, but he was not ready yet to give himself up to it. "What you've sentenced me to, this task here—it may be long. Are you telling me that when it's done, my exile is ended? I can go home?"

"You can return to the service to which I swore you," she said. "Have you forgotten that? I never have."

"This is all part of—"

She nodded.

"Lady," he said. "You've no need to bind me. I will belong to you if you will it or no, with oaths or without them, wed or unwed, sworn or unsworn, for as long as there is breath in my body."

"That's an oath," she said. "That's a binding."

"Yes," he said. "So it is."

"Forever and ever?"

"Forever," he said, "and ever. Unless—"

She slapped him hard. It struck the breath out of him. "No evasions," she said. "And no grinning at me, either. This is a true binding. Once it's made, you'll not be escaping it."

"Should I want to?"

"Not while I live," she said.

"Even though I am hopelessly disobedient, reckless, feckless, head-strong, and impossibly insolent?"

"Even so," she said.

FORTY-TWO

THE LORD SERAMON WAS DEAD.

Tanit had known in her heart when he bade her farewell, that it was not a simple battle he went to, nor a plain rite of the temple. She had her duties, her people to protect, her armies to muster and send forth; that night was most terrible of all, the worst since the shadow came to the black land. Yet the raids stopped abruptly toward midnight. The darkness lingered, but the enemy turned their backs even where they were winning the battle, left captives and carts of grain from the storehouses, and vanished into the air.

It was not over then. Not for her lord, though the world was almost frighteningly quiet. She endured it as long as she could; saw to the wounded and the merely terrified; set her house in order, and last of all before she left it, lingered in the nursery where Menes lay asleep.

He was breathing—she assured herself of that. He dreamed: his brows knit, his lips pursed, his fists clenched and unclenched. Almost she fancied that she could see a play of delicate flame over his skin, but when she peered closer, there was nothing.

She kissed his brow, smoothed his thick dark curls, and left him with tearing reluctance. He was safe: he had his nurse, his guards, the young godling whom the Lord Re-Horus had made before he vanished into the dark. All prayers and protections were laid on him, and the gods' power, and guardian spells wrought by both of the gods who had come from beyond the horizon to tarry in Waset.

The one who remained lay in the temple. She needed no guide to find him. Her heart knew always where he was.

They had laid him on a bier, surrounded by priests and chanting and the scent of incense. He was alive then, but the spirit in him was far away, lost on the roads of dream.

She knelt beside him. The priests rolled their eyes at her, but none was bold enough to send her away. She made no effort to touch him. It was enough to rest her eyes on the alien beauty of him. Nothing like him was in this world.

How long she knelt there, she did not know. The sun sank slowly toward the western horizon; toward the land of the dead. He never moved, never changed, and yet it seemed to her heart that he sank with the sun: drifted farther and farther away, more and more distant from the flesh that had contained him.

At long last the sun passed out of sight from within the temple. In a little while it would touch the jagged line of cliffs across the river. It was already dark in this room, but a soft glow shone out of the body on the bier, even before the priests lit the lamps at its head and foot.

The glow faded so imperceptibly that she hardly believed it could have existed. But when it was gone, she knew. He was gone. He had flown beyond the horizon, and left his body behind.

She could not find it in her to grieve, not properly, as a wife should when her husband was dead. She laid her hand on his cheek. It was cooling slowly in the heat. She found herself thinking, not of death, but of a nest from which the bird has flown: a bird of light, spreading wings that stretched from horizon to horizon, soaring into the night.

"I told you," she said. "You would leave, and I would be left behind. You never believed me. But I knew."

The priests stared uncomprehending; all but Seti, who though blind had clearer sight than anyone she knew. He was gazing into his private dark, smiling, but as she glanced at him, a slow tear ran down his cheek. "The gods are gone out of the world," he said.

"They live forever beyond the horizon," she said.

"So they do," said Seti, as if he humored a child.

From him she would accept it. She kissed him on the cheek, softly, and said to the priests, "Summon the servants of the dead."

One or two looked as if he would protest, but she was the queen. Under her steady stare, they all bowed and left, all but Seti. He was an untroubling presence; he comforted her with his silence.

She returned to her lord's side. Not even the semblance of life was left in him. She took his hand in hers. It was still supple, but its swift strength was gone. She stroked the long fingers, committing to memory the feel of his skin. It would have to last her for long years, until she saw him again.

She had every intention of doing that. It might be impossible; she did not care. This was the half of her self. She would get it back.

She stayed with him until the servants of the dead came. They wrapped him in white linen, folding it close about his long limbs, and carried him away to their houses on the far side of the river.

Seti left when they left, leaning on the arm of a strong young priest. She sat alone in the flickering lamplight. Slowly it dawned on her: the night was clean. No shadow tainted it. No armies came riding across the river to raid the villages.

There had been respite before, a year and more of it. But this was different. There was no darkness behind the stars; only the night, pure and unsullied. Something about it made her think of her lord: dark beauty with the splendor of a sun in its heart.

She wept then, a little, because she was mortal and she was weak and she yearned for his arms about her and his warm rich voice in her ear. She yearned so strongly that almost—almost—she could have sworn—

"Beloved."

That was his very voice. It lived still inside her. Yet it seemed so real, as if indeed, impossibly, he could be there.

She turned slowly.

He was standing behind her. The light within him was clearly visible. She could not meet his eyes at all, any more than she could stare straight into the sun.

"Dear heart," he said. "What did I promise you?"

"That you would never leave me," she heard herself say. "But—"

"I couldn't keep my body," he said. "There are rules and prices, and that is one of them. But nothing could forbid me to come back to you. That oath I swore, and oaths are sacred. They bind even the gods."

"Even you?"

He seemed bemused. "I suppose I am a god now—truly; not simply a mage from beyond a Gate. I wasn't thinking of that when I did it. There was no other way to kill the dark, except to overwhelm it with light. But to do that, I had to give up whatever mortal substance I had."

His words were profoundly strange, but that was nothing new or remarkable. She reached carefully and touched him.

He was not flesh, no; it felt like holding her hand in sunlight, yet sunlight given shape and form. He moved under her hand. He seemed to breathe, though that might only be habit from his earthly self. She could wrap her arms about him and hold him, and he could complete the embrace. The warmth of it, the sheer white joy, was almost more than she could bear.

A good part of it was his. He had likened his magery once to living with one's skin off. Now his skin was lost altogether.

"I can't stay long," he said. "I can't be with you as I am now, not often; I'm scattered through the worlds, among the chains of Gates. I hold back the dark from all of them. But part of me is always here. It will never leave you. If you need me, or simply want to be with me, look in your heart. You'll find me."

"Always?"

"Always," he said.

"And when I leave this flesh behind? Will I be as you are?"

He ran his finger down her cheek as he had done so often before, a gesture so tender and so familiar that her eyes filled anew with tears. "The greater gods have promised, beloved. When your body has lived out its span, you will come to me. We will never again be parted."

The question that rose in her was inevitable, but far from wise. She did not ask it. The gods knew when she would die. It was not right or proper that she should know. She said instead, "I shall live every day in gladness, and sleep every night in peace, with that before me."

"O marvel among women." He kissed her, long and slow and ineffably sweet. He said no word of farewell, but then he had not left her. Only this semblance was gone. The truth of him, the living essence, lay folded in her heart.

The dawn was coming, bright and free of fear. She wiped away her tears and composed herself. Her son was waking: she felt him within her, close by his father.

She would tarry with him until the day came. Then she would go out, and put on her mask of paint and royal pride, and be queen of her people. They would mourn because the gods had left them, and rejoice because the darkness was gone. She would give them what comfort they needed, and rule them as best she could.

After a while they would forget their grief. Hers was already passing. She must not seem too glad, not yet; none of them would understand. But in her heart, where he was, she could rest in his warmth and be deeply content.